ANN McMAN

THE BIG TOW

AN UNLIKELY ROMANCE

Bywater Books
Ann Arbor
2020

Bywater Books

Print ISBN: 978-1-61294-183-7

Bywater Books First Edition: October 2020

Printed in the United States of America on acid-free paper.
Cover designer: Ann McMan, TreeHouse Studio

Bywater Books
PO Box 3671
Ann Arbor MI 48106-3671
www.bywaterbooks.com

For Michelle Brooks, who delighted and inspired me with wonderfully rich, endearing and hilarious tales from her own childhood.

And for Marilyn Whicker, who taught me to love and appreciate a unique place called K-Vegas.

Books by Ann McMan

Novels

Hoosier Daddy
Festival Nurse
Backcast
Beowulf for Cretins: A Love Story
The Big Tow

The Jericho Series

Jericho
Aftermath
Goldenrod

Evan Reed Mysteries

Dust
Galileo

Story Collections

Sidecar
Three Plus One

THE BIG TOW

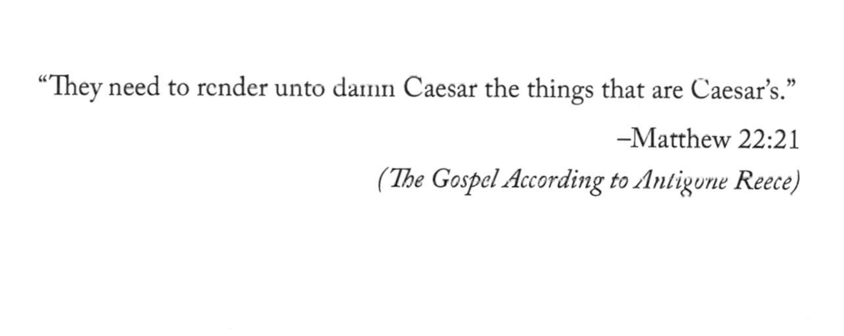

"They need to render unto damn Caesar the things that are Caesar's."

–Matthew 22:21

(The Gospel According to Antigone Reece)

Prologue

Everything's Coming Up Roses

Out on Highway 66 in K-Vegas, there's a local hangout famous for burgers, hand-tossed pizza and bottomless pitchers of sweet tea. Tuesday nights, it's standing room only. That means all-you-can-eat wings, five-dollar pitchers of PBR, and kids eat free. Everybody in Kernersville, aka K-Vegas, knows that the *real* action at the Sixty Six Grill takes place outside—in the parking lot between the restaurant and the paint store, where gleaming icons of the working class face off like gladiators beneath the glare of overhead lights. These days, those rows of quad-cab pickup trucks and big-grilled muscle cars are a lot less impressive. They're more like the people who drive them: beat-up, worn out, and no longer fighting for ascendency in a small town that time has left behind. The starry-eyed people who once went all-in on coveted, high-dollar rides soon lost the means or the inclination to keep up the payments on their EZ credit, no-questions-asked auto loans.

Enter "Fast" Eddie Abrams. His job is to even the score when the balance of power gets shifted too far outta whack. He says his mission is to make adjustments to the natural order. He calls himself an agent of asset recovery.

The locals call him a repo man.

Fast Eddie did most of his business in a back booth at the Sixty

Six Grill, and it was there I went to meet him for the first time when a client of the law practice I worked for engaged me to find someone to recover a car that had gone AWOL from his corporate fleet. It wasn't your run of the mill, beat-to-shit Chevy Impala, either. It was a Mercedes-Maybach S560 twin-turbo 4MATIC. The thing had a solid-gold sticker price of $180,545, and had been used as a limo by the furniture magnate's business. I didn't realize at the time that Mr. Mozelle's "hospitality car" was really a high-priced conveyance that delivered higher-priced evening companions to his out of town customers—a nice little bonus for a select few of the 75,000 buyers who swarmed the streets of High Point twice a year during the International Home Furnishings Market. Mr. Mozelle owned two of the largest showrooms on Eastchester Drive, and his premier clients hailed from the four corners of the earth.

It wasn't clear who'd absconded with the Maybach, but Mr. Mozelle provided me with a list of hired drivers—and escorts—and suggested I start with them.

That figured.

I routinely got saddled with this kind of floor-scraping assignment because, even after six years of eighty-hour weeks and ten times that amount in sweat equity, I was still the lowest hanging fruit on the corporate ladder at Turner, Witherspoon, Anders and Tyler, PA. To be sure, I didn't know jack shit about how to find a stolen car—even though most of the senior partners at the law firm assumed it would be second nature to me.

Yeah. Not hard to figure that one out, either. I was also the only "person of color" working at TWAT, as we lovingly called it, who wasn't on the housekeeping staff. In truth, if I'd still been living in Southwest Philly, I'd have picked up the phone and called my uncle Rio's joint in Chester. He'd probably have a list of the six chop shops that got pieces of the high-dollar ride in my hands by lunchtime. But all connection to those eclectic resources slipped from my grasp as soon as I moved South to attend law school at Wake Forest. Now I didn't have the first idea where to start. Making social calls on a bunch of high-priced

Uber drivers and higher-priced call girls didn't exude all that much appeal, and I was confident it wouldn't yield any useful results.

Although my housemate, Sebastian, promptly suggested I coopt the list of potential companions, and use it to find romance—*for myself.* I told Twinkle Toes he was nuts, but I can't say I didn't think about it—even though that particular promise of romance came packaged with an hourly rate that obliterated what I made at the firm. Little did I know that the hunt for Mozelle's missing car was destined to lead me straight to love—in the *very* last place I'd ever expect to find it.

But right then, only one thing was clear: I was gonna have to go outside for help.

Mr. Mozelle made it clear he wasn't willing to wait around for the thing to turn up in pieces or be found abandoned along an interstate highway in Georgia—and he expressed a clear preference for keeping the police out of the search. He emphasized that the police wouldn't do much except enter the car's VIN into their missing vehicle database, so there was no reason to involve them. For my part, he seemed inordinately more concerned with recovering the *contents* of the vehicle than the vehicle itself. I didn't ask any questions about that part. It was above my pay grade.

So I started researching local businesses that were better positioned than TWAT to recover missing property. Once I had a list, I narrowed it down by visiting Sebastian's brother, Ricky Sprinkle, who ran a body shop up in Rural Hall.

Ricky wiped his nose on his sleeve before pointing a grease-stained index finger at the third name on the list.

"This here's the place I'd call," he said. "They done lots of work for guys who bring shit here." He snickered. "They say the woman that runs that place could shake the rust off a crankshaft."

I fished out my notebook. "What's her name?"

"I dunno." Ricky shrugged. "Some weird-ass kind of name." He thought about it. "Antietam? Anthrax? You know?" He shrugged. "Something old timey."

I sighed and closed my notebook. Yeah. Sebastian was as gay as a two-dollar bill. It was hard to imagine how he and his brother Ricky sprang from the same twisted nest.

"Thanks, man. I'll give them a call."

I drove back to my office in Winston-Salem, and it didn't take me long to figure out what Ricky's customers had been talking about. After I punched in the number for the National Recovery Bureau in Kernersville, the phone on the other end was snapped up partway through the first ring and a voice like a belt sander filled my ear.

"Praise the Lord and thank you for calling the National Recovery Bureau, where your assets are as sacred as God's holy Word."

I was dumbfounded, and quickly hung up.

Ricky must've been on the pipe when he suggested this joint.

Five seconds later, the phone on my desk rang. I stared at the caller I.D. before gingerly picking up the handset.

"Hello?"

"Did you just hang up on me?" A woman's voice demanded.

"Well . . ." I began.

"Don't you hang up on people like that. It's disrespectful."

"I didn't mean—"

She cut me off. "You might be sittin' there in your air-conditioned office at that highbrow law firm, but that don't give you the right to make crank calls that waste the time of decent people who actually work for a living."

I blinked my eyes a few times. "How'd you know where I work?" I asked, stupidly.

"How? Because I'm *good* at my job. That's how. Which is why I suppose you called me in the first place."

"Um . . ." I wasn't sure how to answer her.

"Well?" The bossy woman fired the accusation at me like she'd just unleashed it from a slingshot. "Am I wrong?"

"No." I decided to come clean. "No, ma'am. You're not wrong."

"So, why don't you stop acting like an imbecile and state your business?"

I cleared my throat. "Are you Miss . . .," I paused. "Antietam?"

"Antietam?" The belt sander cranked up again. "Did you just call me *Antietam?*"

"Um. Yes?"

"Where in fire did you come up with a name like Antietam?"

"I guess that's not your name?" I queried.

"*No.* My parents didn't name me after no battlefield."

I thought about telling her it had been a missed opportunity, but thought better of it.

"I'm sorry, Miss . . . um. What *is* your name?"

"Antigone Reece. That's *A-N-T-I-G-O-N-E*. I'm the dispatcher and office manager here at the NRB."

I surmised that her going to the trouble to spell her name for me meant that not many of the NRB's customers read much Sophocles.

"Well, Miss Reece. I'd like to speak with," I consulted my notepad, "a Mr. Abrams about getting some assistance locating a lost asset."

"Mr. Abrams don't waste his time speakin' to *nobody* until I decide their assets are well and truly needing to be recovered."

"Okay." I replied. "How do we establish that?"

"For starters, you state your business to me."

"I'd rather not discuss these particulars over the phone."

Antigone sighed. I could imagine the eye roll that probably accompanied her audible expression of exasperation. "Then I guess you'll just have to come by the office here, and talk with me in person."

That happened the next day.

The Kernersville office of the National Recovery Bureau was housed in a mostly abandoned strip center located off Highway 66. After making two circuits of the parking lot, I finally managed to find a place to park that was more pavement than pothole. The grimy front entrance to the NRB was sandwiched between the "Weevil Vape Shoppe" and a skeevy-looking thrift store.

Inside, there was a narrow reception area with a scuffed-up, red and yellow-checked linoleum floor and a couple of castoff metal kitchen chairs that I guessed came from the thrift store next door. A few dead plants in pots with faded ribbons lined the windowsill under a humming neon sign. "Your Assets, Our Priority," it proclaimed. Scratchy, gospel music played from a radio someplace. A battered counter beneath a glass half-wall limited access to the cluster of mismatched desks and filing cabinets I could see beyond the barrier.

I felt like I was in line at the DMV.

"Can I help you?"

The voice came out of nowhere, and it scared the crap out of me. It sounded eerily like a belt sander.

I suddenly felt guilty.

Yep. Just like the DMV.

"I'm sorry," I stammered, not knowing where to look. "I'm here to meet with Miss Reece?"

The door beside the end of the counter buzzed. I hadn't even noticed the damn door before the buzzer went off. Belatedly, I made my way inside.

Antigone Reece sat, frowning, behind a massive desk piled high with file folders and tiers of wire mesh document racks. A credenza held three telephones, a small transistor radio, and a massive walkie-talkie that looked like some kind of Army surplus relic. On the side wall beside her desk, a pegboard held dozens of keys—each affixed with a big paper tag containing a long sequence of letters and numbers written in bold red ink. Probably vehicle identification numbers.

She'd apparently just taken a drag off her cigarette before I appeared, and an impressive cloud of smoke swirled around her head like a crown.

"Are you Miss Reece?" I asked. I fought the impulse to wave the smoke away.

She nodded and ground her cigarette out in a massive glass ashtray that bore a Roadway Express logo. It looked like it had seen a lot of hard use.

"Sit down." She gestured toward another one of the kitchen chairs. This one had a blaze orange vinyl-covered seat. It was only ripped in two places, so I guessed that accounted for its elevation to the secure side of the barrier.

"I'm Nick Nicholson," I explained. I handed her one of my embossed linen TWAT cards. "We spoke on the phone the other day?"

"I know who you are." She snapped the card out of my hand and looked it over. "It says here your name is Vera." She brought her eyes to bear on mine like the beam of a cop's flashlight. "What's that about?"

"Um, well . . ." *Why was I so flustered?* My real name was none of her damn business. "My parents named me Vera, but I was always called 'Nick' in school. It stuck."

She looked me over. "I'd say it stuck for a reason. You don't look like no Vera."

I wasn't sure what kind of response to make so, for once, I wisely said nothing.

"So, Miss Nick-Not-Vera." Antigone fished a yellow legal pad out of a stack of papers and pulled it closer so she could take notes. "You wanna tell me about your missing property?"

I was impressed that I didn't have to spell the word Maybach for her. That surprised me. Looking around the ramshackle interior of this joint, I didn't get the impression that the NRB dealt with the recovery of many, what you'd call, *refined* motor vehicles.

"One important thing," I began. Antigone tapped the end of her Ticonderoga pencil on the pad while she waited for me to continue. "My client, Mr. Mozelle, appears to be equally concerned with the recovery of the contents of the vehicle, so time is of the essence."

"The *contents*?" she quoted.

I nodded.

She laid her pencil down, sat back against her creaking chair, and folded her beefy arms across her generous bosom. "You wanna be a tad more specific about these contents?"

"I wish I could be. I don't really know what was in the car."

"You don't know? Then how in thunder is 'time of the essence'? Was the trunk full of kishka or something?"

Kishka? I was seriously out of my depth on this one. "I'm sorry . . . I don't know what that is."

Antigone waved a hand. "You spend time around here, you'll find out what it is soon enough."

I perked up. "Does that mean you'll take the case?"

Antigone fired up another smoke. "Don't get too excited, Perry Mason. We still have to do some background checks."

"Background checks? On the firm? I can assure you, Miss Reece . . ." I didn't get to finish. Antigone blew a chest-full of smoke in my face. It was impressive and it hung in the air between us for several seconds.

"Don't be puttin' the cart before the horse, Not-Vera," she drawled. "We need to see some demonstration of the earnestness of your desire to recover this asset. You have already applied a layer of urgency to your petition. Are you, likewise, prepared to bring forth fruits meet for consideration?"

"Um." *Was she asking me for money? Up front?*

Before I could ask for clarification, she opened her desk drawer and withdrew a small, tented plastic sign and slapped it down in front of me. "Cash Only," it read.

I stared at it with disbelief before looking up to meet her brown eyes. "I'm . . . I don't have . . . It's not usual to . . ."

"You wanna dance to *this* music," she tapped the tiny placard, "you pay the piper—up front. Five hundred dollars—*cash*—is our non-refundable retainer."

Her mention of the word "music" seemed to divert her attention to some staccato noise unfurling from her small radio. Like a tidal wave, she whirled away from her desk and snapped up the enormous walkie-talkie.

"Home Base, come back," she barked.

"Home Base, go ahead," a tinny-sounding voice replied.

"Just what in Hades is that unholy mess I'm hearing? This is supposed to be the Power Hour."

Static.

"Lamar? Do not *make* me come back there," Antigone snapped. "I *asked* for an explanation, come back."

More static, followed by a tentative, "We thought something more upbeat might appeal to our younger listeners."

"Younger listeners do *not* pay the advertising budget of this ministry. You get that so-called Christian rock mess *off* my station and queue up them time-honored stalwarts of the Power Hour. This ain't damn Zaxby's. I'm not gonna ask you twice. *Out.*" Antigone slammed the walkie-talkie down on the credenza so hard it caused iced tea to slosh out over the lip of her twenty-ounce Bojangles cup. "Dang millennials." She turned back to face me. "I apologize for that interruption."

"No worries." I held up a hand. "So, you have a radio station?" I don't know what led me to be so brave. Or stupid.

"It's a *ministry*," she clarified. "Global Gospel Radio, 665.9 AM." She jerked her head toward the back wall. "The trailer is out back, behind the building."

I let that last part slide. "Did you say 665.9? Isn't that a little . . . ironic?"

Her eyes narrowed. She took another long drag off her cigarette. One more good pull, and the thing would be burned about down to the filter. I wondered what her record was for dispatching one when she concentrated.

"I see you've had at least *some* kind of churching-up, Miss Not-Vera," she observed.

"Maybe a little." I smiled at her. "A long time ago."

"Well, you're right. Some upstart infidel at the FCC thought it would be *funny* to give my ministry a 666 frequency—thought I wouldn't notice."

"I don't imagine that worked out too well for him?"

She chuckled. "Let's just say that tenth of a megahertz cost him less than the copay to have his family jewels realigned."

I reflexively crossed my legs in solidarity with infidels everywhere—even though I wasn't sporting any family jewels.

"So, um," I continued. "If I'm able to come back later today with the retainer fee, would you take this case?"

Antigone nodded at me through a cloud of smoke. "We might consider your petition."

Why did I feel like I was asking to have my sentence in purgatory cut in half? It wasn't even my damn car.

"Great." I got to my feet. "I'll go back to my office and, hopefully, return with the retainer before close of business today."

Antigone held up a wide hand. "Call me before you head back. I'll see if Fast Eddie can meet up with you today."

Fast Eddie?

"Is that Mr. Abrams?" I asked.

She nodded. "He works out of his satellite office most weekdays."

I looked around the drab space. There was an active leak in the back corner of the large room. Water dripped from a brown-stained ceiling tile into a five-gallon paint bucket. Strange . . . since this was a one-story building and we hadn't had rain in more than a month. Hard to blame "Fast" Eddie for choosing to perch someplace else.

I handed Antigone an envelope containing all the information we had on the Maybach—along with a duplicate set of keys.

She seemed surprised by that. "Kind of making an assumption here, ain't you?"

"I guess I think you're good for it."

She glared at me. "We might can do some business." There was something—unsaid in the way her gaze raked me over. It didn't exactly make me feel uncomfortable—but it was unsettling as hell. I was aware that something in our "relationship" had changed—just not sure what it was. "You call me when you have the cash."

I nodded at her and left.

As soon as I got back to the car, I grabbed my cell phone and looked up *kishka*.

Back at TWAT, Senior Partner Dan Tyler didn't so much as raise a wiry white eyebrow when I told him I needed a $500 cash retainer for the NRB to locate the missing Maybach. He picked up his desk phone and told Belinda in accounting to get up the funds and charge it to Mr. Mozelle's account.

That was easy. This job was beginning to make the hairs on the back of my neck stand up.

I called Antigone to tell her I had the retainer and was on my way back to K-Vegas. Instead of coming to her, she directed me to go straight to the Sixty Six Grill and give the money to Fast Eddie. She said he'd be expecting me.

He wasn't hard to spot when I got there. I wasn't surprised when the hostess pointed him out.

Fast Eddie was holding court in a small booth near the service area at the back. His table was littered with papers, an old-fashioned calculator with about ten miles of coiled paper tape, a red Swingline stapler and a row of five or six cell phones. He noticed me as I made my way toward his table, and waved me over.

Eddie was one of those guys who looked like he'd be the same height standing up as sitting down. He wore big, horn-rimmed glasses with transition lenses that hadn't quite transitioned. They were a smoky blue-gray and made his eyes hard to see. He extended a hand. I was impressed by the pinkie ring he wore. It was studded with chocolate diamonds.

"Vera Nicholson?" he asked. "I'm Eddie." He squeezed my fingers tightly before waving his stubby hand at the booth. "Sit. Sit."

"Thanks. And please call me Nick." I slid in behind the table. "I appreciate your taking time to meet with me today."

"Hey, it's not even a thing. Antigone filled me in on your problem."

Of course she did. "What do you think?"

"What can I say?" He waved a hand. "My parents saddled me with a shitty first name, too. Cloyd. Who the fuck names their kid *Cloyd?* I'll tell you who—schmucks who want to see you get your ass kicked every day at school because they think it builds character. Am I wrong?"

Wait . . . was he talking about my nickname?

"No," I tried to explain. "That isn't what I . . ."

Fast Eddie cut me off. "No worries, kid. We don't care what you wanna call yourself. So tell me about this missing car and how you happen to know Mozelle."

My head was already reeling. "Well . . ."

"Hold up." He beckoned a passing server over. "Carla? Bring my friend here some wings. Nuclear. And some fries, too." He looked me over. "You want a beer?"

"Um . . . I . . ."

"Bring a pitcher," he told Carla.

"You want two glasses with that?" she asked.

"Nah. If I have anything else I'm gonna plotz."

"I'll have it right out." Carla continued along her way.

"So," Eddie pushed his calculator aside and opened a manila file folder, "Antigone ran the VIN. It's been two days since the car disappeared. You got any leads?"

"No. Mr. Mozelle seems to think maybe one of the drivers made off with it."

"Yeah. Wishful thinking on his part."

I was intrigued by Eddie's confidence. "Why do you say that?"

"Let's just say I know Mozelle. We've crossed paths before. That car might be a nice ride, but trust me: what's in it ain't something his drivers will wanna fuck with. None of them wanna get crossways with Mozelle. He runs with the big dogs."

"You think so, too?" I was surprised Fast Eddie shared my suspicion that Mr. Mozelle's interest was more tied to recovering the cargo than the car.

"Hell. I *know* so. My guess? Some clueless schlemiel made off with it thinking he could fence it for some quick cash."

"Do you have any way to check local body shops or junkyards?"

"Already have. No dice. A high-dollar ride like this one won't get chopped up locally. They'll unload it someplace out of state where it'll get cloned and probably end up on a boat headed for some Middle Eastern country where they don't give two fucks about where it came from." Fast Eddie pulled another sheet of paper from the folder. "This is the best guy I know to find it."

I took the paper and examined it.

Hugh Don Rockett, Jr. Age 76. Last known employer: Old World Meats, Lexington, NC.

"A butcher?" I was confused.

Eddie snickered. "Pig entrails ain't the only thing Hugh Don's got experience chopping up, if you catch my drift. He used to do wet work back in the day. He can find it, all right. And fast. But there's one catch."

Of course there is. I knew this wasn't going to be good. "What's that?"

"His eyesight is for shit and his knees aren't worth bubkes," Eddie explained. "He can't drive anymore. You'll have to ride with him."

"*Me?*" I was dumbfounded. "Are you *crazy*? I can't do that. I don't know anything about this . . ." I searched for the right word. "*Business.* Can't one of your other employees go with him?"

"All of my people are already booked for the holidays." I must've looked as confused as I felt because Eddie clarified. "Passover."

Passover? *Was there actually a spike in car repossessions during Jewish holidays?*

"I need to get out more," I muttered.

Carla appeared with the food and the biggest pitcher of beer I'd ever seen. She plopped it all down on our table with a flourish. "Need anything else, give me a holler." She pulled a bottle of ketchup from the front pocket of her apron and slapped it down in front of Eddie before gliding off.

Eddie took up the fat Heinz bottle and began liberally squirting the ketchup all over the mound of French fries.

"It's a piece of cake," he said. "All you have to do is drive and follow orders."

"Orders? What kind of orders?"

"*Orders.*" Eddie shrugged and snagged a fry covered with ketchup. "Whatever he asks you to do."

"I'm not sure . . ." I stopped myself. Who was I kidding? The firm wouldn't give a shit about what Eddie asked me to do as long as Mozelle got his precious car back. "Nothing illegal," I said instead. At least I could be clear about that part. TWAT might not care about my future prospects, but I didn't want to risk getting disbarred before I even had a chance to pay off my damn school loans.

Eddie looked offended. "I run a legitimate business," he began. He was interrupted when one of the phones in his battery of devices started ringing. It took him another two rings to figure out which one he needed to answer. "Yeah?" he growled into it. "Whattaya got for me, Weasel?"

Weasel? I began to rethink my decision.

Eddie listened to the call for a minute. "Hey, that shit's not *my* problem," he barked. "What do I care if his paint got scratched by the fucking winch? Tell that ungrateful ass-wipe I said he can take it to Earl Scheib." Eddie hung up, but checked the readout on the phone before tossing it aside. "Eighteen more minutes left on that one." He looked at me. At least I *think* he looked at me. Those smoky lenses made it hard to tell. He could just as easily have been staring at the ass of the waitress taking orders at the booth behind us. She'd already walked past our table. Twice. To be fair, she did have a rather nice ... back porch. "As I was saying," Eddie continued, "everything we do is by the book. All you have to do is drive and follow orders. If you do, I can guarantee you'll have Mozelle's ride back in twenty-four hours—thirty-six, tops." He flashed me a big, toothy grin. Fluorescent light flashed off a gold incisor. "Bet there'd be a nice little bonus in store for you if you could wrap this job up *that* fast."

Why did I suddenly feel like I was sharing a platter of hot wings with Mephistopheles?

"Okay." The word was barely out of my mouth before I began to regret it.

"Great." Eddie fluttered his fingers at me. It took me a second to realize he was asking for the cash. I passed the envelope across the table to him. He stuffed it into his briefcase before snatching up a phone—different from the one Weasel had called him on. "Antigone? Get Hugh Don spooled up. Yeah. The Maybach. I know, I know. I got that covered. Vera's gonna ride with him." He held the phone away from his ear and proceeded to eat half of the remaining French fries while Antigone reacted to his announcement. I couldn't make out everything she said, but the words *insane, certifiable, uninsured* and the phrase *not on my damn watch* came through loud and clear. "You finished?" Eddie asked when Antigone's tirade showed signs of winding down. "Now tell Hugh Don Vera's gonna call him tonight. Oy gevalt. *Stop* with this already! I know what I'm doing." He hung up. "That woman is gonna put me in an early grave. She's pushier than my ex-wife on the loose in Borough Park with a new credit card."

I couldn't disagree with Eddie's description of the bossy woman. "She's . . . a force of nature, all right."

"That's one way of putting it. Her voice gives me the yips." Eddie's watch alarm beeped. He checked it, then reached for another phone—one he hadn't used yet. "I gotta make a quick call. One second."

While Eddie waited on his call to connect, I decided to live dangerously and try one of the wings. *Why not?* I didn't see how this day could get any weirder.

Wrong. My first bite was like swallowing a blowtorch. I reached for the pitcher of beer in a desperate move to put the fire out. My eyes were watering and I knew my face was probably turning purple.

"Yeah," Eddie was saying. "Gimme a nickel on Keopka. Yeah, yeah. It's all good." He sighed. "Look. I told you I'll take care of it. Yes—*this* damn week." He disconnected. "My accountant," he explained. "How're those wings? Hot enough?" He grabbed for one.

I still couldn't speak. My tongue felt like it had swollen to five times its normal size.

"Stick with me, kid." Eddie pulled a flask from his shiny coat pocket and dumped a generous glug of whatever it contained into my glass before filling his empty coffee cup and raising it in a toast. "The house, the car, the kids," he chanted. "Everything's coming up roses."

I had no idea what he was talking about, but the fire raging in my gut told me I'd soon find out.

Eddie was right. Hugh Don Rockett Jr. managed to track down Mozelle's car practically overnight.

The day after my meeting with Eddie, he caught a ride up to Winston-Salem on one of Old World's delivery trucks and I picked him up at 5:45 a.m. at a gas station near Baptist Hospital. Eddie hadn't been kidding when he said Hugh Don would need somebody to ride along with him. The wizened old man with a snow-white 'fro was bent over like Quasimodo, and only managed to stand halfway upright because he had one of those tricked-out, wheeled walkers.

He smoked like a freight train, too, and had what looked like permanent nicotine stains on his fingertips. He also smelled slightly coppery . . . I decided it was probably best not to think too much about that.

Hugh Don wasn't much for small talk. In short order, he explained, in his colorful way, that finding Mozelle's car had been simple: one of his contacts just slipped the concierge at the O'Henry Hotel a couple of C-notes and got access to their closed-circuit videos of the concierge and valet stations from the night the car disappeared. Sure enough, it wasn't the driver who'd made off with the Maybach.

Hugh Don passed me some grainy still photos of a skinny twenty-something wearing tennis shoes and a windbreaker, climbing into the unattended car while it was idling beneath the portico of the hotel. We sat in a booth at Cagney's Diner on Miller Street. Hugh Don wanted to get some breakfast while we reviewed what he'd found out about the car. I'd already eaten that morning—for once, Sebastian had cooked something mostly edible before he took off to attend a real estate sales conference in Cary.

"The driver dropped off some asshole's evening entertainment," Hugh Don explained, "then ducked inside to take a piss. That's when this Grub Hub delivery jockey came out of the hotel and saw the car just sitting there—and the fucker was running. Dumbass walked past it twice before taking a shot and climbing inside. Nobody paid any attention to him when he gunned it and took off. His piece of shit Yaris is still parked there by the damn curb." Hugh Don pointed out the small car, visible in the background of one of the stills. The Grub Hub magnetic sign was plainly readable. "Fucking cops still haven't towed it. Typical. I had the concierge write down the tag number and got Antigone to run it." He handed me a slip of paper. "Belongs to some dude named Cockerham, up in Yadkin County. Family runs a hog farm."

A hog farm? "Why would a hog farmer want to steal a high-class car like this?"

Hugh Don stared at me like I'd just asked my question in French. "I don't think he had a clue what kind of car he was making off with. The fact the damn thing was running and not sunk up to its axle in hog shit was incentive enough. Stupid jerk probably thought he could lower it, trick it out and race it on some dirt track—probably at Friendship up in Elkin. That place is a redneck mecca. Mark my words, that car is holed up in his daddy's barn right now. We just need to go and get it before him and a bunch of his pals have a chance to pull the goddamn engine."

Pull the engine?

Any hope I had of getting that big bonus Eddie predicted was evaporating as fast as the lake of sausage gravy on Hugh Don's plate.

"Okay," I said. "When do we go and get it?"

Eddie sopped up his last glob of tan-colored goo with a fat biscuit. "No time like the present."

"Right now?"

"Why not? You got something better to do?"

"Well . . ."

Hugh Don fished a set of keys out of his pocket and tossed them down on the table. "These are the duplicates you gave Antigone." I must've look confused when I picked them up. "Eddie gave them to me yesterday," he explained. "Since these came from Mozelle, I'm guessing they'll also open the trunk. Probably, Mozelle's driver only had a valet key the night the car got stolen. With luck, that means maybe dumbass hasn't jimmied the trunk lock yet, and Mozelle's cargo is still safe."

That sounded hopeful. "You think so?"

"Like I said, this asshole probably thinks the only thing in the trunk is a spare tire. We just need to get the damn thing back before he gets curious." Hugh Don was busy fishing his cigarettes and lighter out of another pocket.

"And you think right now is a good time to do that?"

"Hell to the yes. This early in the morning, he's probably still pounding his ear." He slid toward the outside of the booth. "Let's get outta here. I need a smoke."

Twenty minutes later, I had Hugh Don and his walker loaded into my Outback, and we were rolling up US 421, heading for Yadkinville and the Cockerham hog farm. I wasn't too sure how any of this was going to go down once we got up there, and I said as much to Hugh Don.

"What do we do when we get there? Have the sheriff meet us so we can get the car?"

"The sheriff?" Hugh Don flicked ash from his lighted cigarette out the half-open passenger-side window of my car. Normally, I'd have asked him not to smoke—but I knew in this case, it'd be a lost cause. "Hell, no, we don't call the damn sheriff. And in case you forgot, Mozelle was pretty clear about not wantin' the cops involved."

That much was true. "So what do we do when we get there?"

"We park your car someplace safe near the entrance to the farm, and you hike up in there to find the car."

"*Me?*" I was dumbfounded. "I can't . . . I don't know how to . . ."

Hugh Don flashed me a palm. "Don't get your panties in a wad, Vera. It ain't rocket science. You find the barn, you start the damn car and you drive it out. Piece of cake."

Piece of cake? Yeah . . . right then, I had visions of *all kinds* of cake—like the ones baked with files inside them that people brought you when you were locked up in the joint.

"Where will you be while I'm doing this?" I asked, stupidly.

"Sittin' in your car, waitin' for you to call me when you're on your way out. Eddie is already on standby, and will meet up with us to take the car back to K-Vegas."

Another thought occurred to me. "What if they have dogs? *Or weapons?*"

"Relax. They're hog farmers, not members of the Bundy clan. Ol' man Cockerham probably doesn't even know his idiot son made off with the car. We'll be doing him a favor by taking the problem off his property—without landing his kid in the county lockup on a GTA."

I still wasn't convinced. The turnoff for Hoots Road was just ahead. We were getting close to ground zero.

"How do I know where to look for it?" I was grasping at straws now.

"I got some satellite images of the layout on Google Maps. I'll show you how to find the buildings that ain't part of where they keep the sows. There's only two or three, tops, that you need to check out. Don't think nobody'll be around at this hour, but if you get stopped, just hand 'em one of these cards and say you're there to meet with the boss man about a contract, and he told you it was okay to have a look around at the operation." He handed me one of his Old World Meats cards. "They won't think nothin' about it, and you go on about your business."

I took the card from him. "This says my name is Hugh Don."

He shrugged. "Tell 'em it's a family name." His gaze took in my androgynous ensemble. "I think you might can pull it off."

It was beginning to worry me that Hugh Don's plan was sounding . . . plausible.

"One more thing," he added. All the alarms in my head started going off. "Watch out for them guineas."

Guineas? I looked at him in shock.

"Them bitches can be fierce," he clarified. "You don't want to get crossways with any of 'em."

I was too stunned by his tone-deafness to reply. Did this dude seriously not notice I was a woman? And as a Black man, how could he be so cavalier about tossing out such an offensive racial slur?

"Yeah." I said. "I'll be careful."

Hugh Don didn't seem to pick up on my sarcasm. "See that you do," he warned.

We'd reached the entrance to the Cockerham farm. "Drive past and turn around," Hugh Don ordered. "Then come back and pull into that church lot across the road."

I did as he directed and shut off the car. It was now just after 7:30 a.m. Hugh Don pulled another grainy photo out of his folder. "Here's the driveway," he pointed out. "Up here, on the back side of the lagoons, is a barn and two outbuildings. That car is probably in one of them. Once you get up the lane, hike off to the right around the lagoons, then cut back toward them buildings. That'll be the best way to make sure nobody sees you coming."

"Okay." I steeled my nerves and got out of the car. "Here goes nothing."

"Call me when you find it, and I'll be waiting over there." He pointed to the opposite side of the road. "You can stop and pick me up. Then we'll go on and meet up with Eddie."

I thought about suggesting to Hugh Don that at the snail's pace he moved on his walker, he should think about heading across the road right now.

"What about my car?" I asked.

"He'll have somebody bring us back to pick it up."

I nodded at him and made my way across the road to the farm entrance. It was lucky that I'd dressed casually that morning. Normally, I'd be wearing slacks, a blazer and "girl" shoes. Since I was meeting Hugh Don so early, I had figured I'd have time to run home and change before heading into the office. I had no idea I'd end up hiking across a hog farm in Yadkin County. Good thing I'd opted for my Blundstones.

Sebastian called them my *vagitarian disco boots.*

Hugh Don's map was pretty accurate. The one thing it didn't prepare me for was how fetid the air got once I drew closer to the hog lagoons. I caught my first whiff of it when the lane curved around and dipped below a man-made rise. The smell was overpowering. It reminded me of the time some joker left raw chicken breasts in his dorm room fridge over Christmas break. I had been stuck on campus finishing a twelve-month internship, and the stench was so overwhelming they had to evacuate the entire residence hall. As I drew closer to the hog lagoons I realized that this smell was like *that*—times a hundred.

I clapped a hand over my mouth and nose and tried not to upchuck.

How could anyone work around this?

Hugh Don had been right about one thing: the place looked deserted. I didn't see any signs that workers were on site yet—although there were a couple of battered pickup trucks parked near a long, low building that I surmised was the hog house. And none of Hugh Don's bitchy "guineas" were in view, either. That much was good. If I lucked out and found the Maybach, it should be easy enough to drive it out without getting busted.

That thought stopped me dead in my tracks.

What the hell was I even *doing* out here? This whole errand was surreal. I had no more reason to be up here wandering around a damn hog farm and getting ready to heist Mozelle's car than I had gowning up and performing laparoscopic surgery on one of these damn sows.

TWAT is gonna owe my ass big time if we pull this one off.

I'd managed to make the circuit of the two lagoons and approached the first of the three outbuildings. I hauled an obliging crate over and used it to hoist myself high enough to peer inside a grimy window on the back side of the building. *Score!* There it was. The Maybach sat on a straw-covered floor in blissful repose. The only worrisome signs were an oil-stained tarp spread across its hood and a couple of nearby sawhorses covered with warped boards and an assortment of tools. I prayed that our intrepid Grub Hub driver hadn't done anything to the engine . . . *yet*. The last thing I needed was to get stuck out here inside a hot car with an engine that wouldn't turn over.

I had a damn law degree, and even I couldn't parse all the statutes that surely applied to the act of stealing an already stolen car.

When I crept around to the front of the building, its big rolling door was cracked open, so it was easy to duck inside. It was notable that the smell in here wasn't much better than outside. I guessed Mozelle would have his hands full getting the car detailed to be rid of that. I didn't think even a dozen of those piña colada-scented air fresheners hanging from its rearview mirror would be equal to the task of cloaking this particular odor.

The car windows were down so I didn't have to unlock it. I removed the tarp from the hood before rolling back the shed door.

I climbed inside the Maybach as quietly as I could and pulled the door closed behind me with a gentle click. Even as laced as I was into a state of abject panic about the situation, it was impossible not to notice how incredibly plush and soft the seats in the car were. *God* . . . under other circumstances, I could've closed my eyes, sunk into that hand-rubbed leather, and slept like the dead. It occurred to me then that many of the luxury cars' interior appointments were eerily . . . *funereal.* Even the dashboard was inlaid with embossed leather. The damn thing was opulent enough to double as a pharaoh's sarcophagus. I wondered if high-priced rides came with optional, gold-plated burial vaults.

I patted the pocket of my jacket to check for the key fob, snapped my seat belt into place, and gingerly pushed the auto start button. The interior of the car promptly illuminated with a soft, blue glow and I felt more than heard the faint hum of an engine as the big machine came to life.

I didn't bother to try and adjust the mirrors—I was sure that simple act would have required a couple of graduate-level seminars to figure out. I slid the gearshift into drive and slowly started rolling forward toward the exit.

Then I heard it . . .

It started as a low-pitched kind of keening. But it quickly gained in intensity—and decibels.

What the fuck?

Something began to scramble and flutter in the seat behind me. I saw flashes of it in the rearview mirror as it flopped around. It looked like some kind of . . . *chicken?* No. It was too *big* to be a chicken. Too big and too *angry*. Its head shot up and glared at me in the mirror. It was ugly as sin, too. Whatever in the hell it was, it was pissed and not at all happy its roost was moving. The thing began squawking and shrieking and slamming itself against the back of my seat in some kind of frenzy. I didn't know what the hell to do so I just floored the accelerator and hauled ass out of there. I was racing down the curving lane when the giant thing heaved itself into the front seat and attacked me. Its wings and beak were everywhere. I felt like I was being lacerated by a hundred tiny razors. I wildly waved my arms at it and spat feathers out of my mouth while I fought to keep the car on the road.

"What the serious *fuck* are you?" I shouted. The bird's fat body blocked my view of the road now. In desperation, I grabbed it by its sinewy neck and thrust it away from my face.

"*Oh, good lord!*" I jerked the wheel of the Maybach so hard the back end fishtailed and spun us precariously close to the edge of one of the lagoons. I felt the back wheels begin to sink into the soft ground and the car began to slide backwards. "*No, no, no, noooo . . .*"

The giant, ugly-as-fuck bird took a protracted, disdain-filled parting look at me before hurling its fat ass across the seat and leaping out the passenger-side window to safety. Its mouth was still streaming abuse as it clambered up the bank away from the filth that would soon envelop me.

Damn rats always leave a sinking ship . . .

In desperation, I slammed the car into its lowest gear and straightened the wheel, closed my eyes and prayed to every god I could summon up in every language I knew as I depressed the accelerator. Slowly, all twelve of the Maybach's glorious cylinders began pulling the massive machine back up the embankment.

"Praisegodpraisegodpraisegod . . ."

I didn't care that the ruckus had probably roused rednecks from ten counties. I gunned the engine and hauled ass off the Cockerham hog farm, spraying gravel and muck in my wake.

I didn't bother trying to call Hugh Don, either. He was still sitting in my car, placidly smoking, when I shot out the lane and onto the main road like I'd been fired from a cannon. Somehow, I navigated the turn into the church lot on two wheels and screeched to a stop scant inches from the side of my car.

Hugh Don took a long drag on his cigarette and gave me a slow nod.

"Real subtle, Vera. You appear to have an aptitude for this work."

"Just fucking get in," I hissed. "I want out of here before that thing comes back."

Hugh Don took in the cuts and abrasions on my face and hands. "I see you found the guineas?"

Good god . . . the guineas? That's what that feathered demon was? *A fucking attack chicken?*

"Yeah," I said. "I *found* them all right." My face felt like it had a thousand tiny cuts on it. "Let's just get this thing back to Eddie and be done with this bullshit."

"I dunno." Hugh Don chuckled. "I think you got a great future in asset recovery, Vera."

"Fuck you."

Five minutes later, we were headed for the Waffle House in Shacktown to meet Fast Eddie for the handoff.

Eddie was already deep into a short stack of pancakes by the time we parked the Maybach and met him inside.

"What the hell happened to your face?" he asked me as we approached his booth.

"Guineas," Hugh Don volunteered.

Eddie speared another forkful of pancake. "Those bitches are a menace."

"That's what I told her." Hugh Don leaned his walker against the table and slid inside the booth. "She's got feathers in her hair, too."

"What?" I compulsively ran my hands over my head. "*Where?*

Why didn't you tell me?" I plucked a couple of downy-looking, spotted feathers from the short hair above my right ear and dropped them to the floor. "Geez, Hugh Don . . ."

"Relax, Vera." Eddie handed me a menu. "Get something to eat."

I wasn't really hungry, but his pancakes *were* looking pretty appetizing. The hash browns looked good, too. "Don't you have to get the car back to Kernersville?" I asked Eddie.

"Not until Weasel gets up here with the tow bar."

Tow bar? "What's that for?"

"*Your* car," he explained. "You and Hugh Don are gonna drive mine back."

"Oh." I hadn't thought about Eddie's car.

In the end, I broke down and ordered a hash brown bowl—and Hugh Don got a side of cheese grits. After we ate, Eddie paid the check and we went outside to pile into the cars for the ride back to K-Vegas.

Eddie handed me the keys to his Escalade and jerked a thumb toward Hugh Don. "Don't let his sorry ass smoke in my ride."

I glanced at Hugh Don. "You heard that, right?"

"Nothin' wrong with my ears." He growled at me. "They're just about the only part of me that still works right."

Eddie chuckled. "You mean that Viagra didn't put any lead back in your pencil?"

"Fuck you, you old geezer. My pencil is none of your goddamn business."

"Guys . . ." I held up a palm. "Can we just get this show on the road? Come on, Hugh Don." I approached the back door on Eddie's gold Escalade. "Let's get you loaded up."

"Hold up, you two." Eddie said. "Don't you want to open this thing up and see what's inside Mozelle's trunk?"

That stopped us both in our tracks.

"Hell, yeah," Hugh Don said.

I had to admit that I was more than mildly curious about whatever it was that Mozelle was so intent on recovering—besides the damn car, which by itself was worth about three times my annual salary.

We walked over to stand behind the Maybach. Eddie pressed the button on the key fob, and the trunk lid opened in slow motion to reveal . . . *nothing*.

The trunk was empty.

"That ain't good," Hugh Don muttered.

"Hold up a second." Eddie reached into the cavernous space and lifted a carpeted panel that concealed a deep well beneath the floor of the trunk. "Bingo."

The well contained a dozen or so zippered black bags. They were about the size of gym bags and most of them were bulging from whatever they contained. Eddie picked one up, unzipped it and looked inside. Then he started laughing. "That fucking perv."

"What is it?" I asked.

Eddie passed the bag over to Hugh Don. His eyes bulged when he looked inside. "Well I'll be damned." Hugh Don held it open so I could see what it contained.

It took me a few seconds to take in what I was seeing. The bag was filled to the gills with . . . *dildos. Big* dildos. True, I was a woman lacking in heterosexual experience, but they seemed impressive by just about any standard one could apply. "Are these . . . um . . .?" I didn't know how to finish my question.

"Oh, yeah," Hugh Don said. "They ain't no training models, neither. These look like your advanced line of pleasure aids."

Eddie lifted one of the *objets* out of the bag and turned it over. "Let's just see *how* advanced they are."

Dear god . . . I couldn't believe he was messing around with one of those things in broad daylight in the middle of a Waffle House parking lot.

"I thought so." Eddie found a tiny tab that opened an access panel hidden just behind the . . . scrotum area. "That smart fucker. This is ingenious." He showed us the plastic bag stuffed inside the appendage.

Hugh Don started singing, "Let it snow, let it snow, let it snow . . ."

I was still clueless. "What is it?"

"Unless I miss my guess," Eddie explained, "if these fake dicks are all packing, I'd say it's about a million bucks worth of blow."

Blow? My jaw dropped. "You mean *cocaine?*"

"Jesus, Vera. Let's not advertise it, okay?" Eddie returned the pleasure aid to the bag and stowed it back beneath the floor panel. He closed the trunk.

I was still in shock. "What are you going to do with it?"

"Well for starters," Eddie tossed the key fob in the air and caught it with a flourish. "I think you might need to tell your associates that Mozelle's recovery fee just went up."

Chapter One

Blow Gabriel, Blow

I wish I could tell you that Mozelle was so overcome with gratitude about getting his car *and* contraband returned that he showed his appreciation to the firm in material ways. By that, I mean material ways designed to work like the best examples of trickle-down economics.

Not so much.

When I got my next paycheck after the recovery heist, I expected to see a fat little bonus tucked inside the envelope. Imagine my surprise when all I got was a hastily scrawled "atta girl" note from Tyler and $250 in Kohl's Cash.

Seriously? This was my reward for risking life, limb, reputation and facial integrity to get his damn car back?

My loyalty to the firm wasn't helped by the competing bonus I got from Fast Eddie. A week after the transfer of rightful assets was concluded, I met Eddie for lunch at the Sixty Six Grill, and he passed me a sealed envelope that contained ten thousand dollars. *In cash.*

I was overwhelmed. "What's this for?" I asked with bewilderment.

"It's profit sharing. I treat my recovery agents right, Vera."

"But I'm not . . ." I let my protest die unexpressed. *What was I?* I sure as hell wasn't a valued member of the TWAT team. And ten large from Eddie would go a long way toward defraying some of the law school debt crushing me.

Ten large? Dear god . . . one job for the NRB and I was turning into Joe Pesci.

"Think it over," Eddie was saying. "Hugh Don was right. You've got a knack for this kind of work."

Was Eddie offering me a job? A job repossessing cars?

"But, I don't know *anything* about asset recovery," I said, lamely.

Eddie seemed to notice that I hadn't immediately dismissed his suggestion out of hand. "You already understand the important parts: follow orders and keep your mouth shut. The rest is just technique."

Technique? Like how to stay out of the slammer?

"I'm not sure . . ."

Eddie cut me off. "Mark my words, Vera: six months with me, you'll be out of debt and on your way to financial independence."

I demurred. Did Eddie somehow know about the humiliating bonus I'd received from the partners at TWAT? An even more mortifying thought occurred to me. *Was I actually considering his absurd offer?*

I was.

It was nuts. *Me?* Quitting my job to become a repo man . . . *woman?*

I squeezed the envelope full of hundred dollar bills. It was a tidy little package of pragmatic incentive.

"Fate, she show up in mysterious ways," my abuela always said. Of course, she was usually referring to the time my uncle Rio won a million bucks in a grocery store Monopoly game. He went in to pick up some cigarettes and a six-pack of Schmidt's, and went home with a winning scratch-off card in his pocket. He and aunt Estela promptly bought matching Yukon Denalis, a time-share on a condo in Belize, and a ridiculously overwrought McMansion in Radnor.

My mother just clucked her tongue and called her brother-in-law *un imbécil.*

Mamá didn't suffer fools.

If I quit my job to go to work for Eddie, what the hell would I tell my parents?

Papa would be easy. He was a criminal defense attorney who could summon up about twelve zillion legitimate explanations for just about any kind of mess a person could get into. He was also the first African American to make partner at Fleischman, Metzger and Mehta, LLC. But Mamá always said the best thing about him was that none of his people had ended up in prison . . . yet. Papa knew better than to argue with her when she was on a roll about something. He'd just wink at me and announce that he was heading out to play fifty-four holes of golf.

Papa? Papa was very forgiving . . . The entirety of his lifetime advice to me was easily summarized: keep your ass clean and save receipts.

He was a man of few words.

But Mamá? Not so much. *She'd kill me.*

I looked at Eddie. "Six months?"

"Hell yes," he said. "Maybe less. Hugh Don says you've got real chutzpah."

"Chutzpah" didn't sound like a word Hugh Don would use to describe anything, unless he was talking about liver mush. Still, I knew enough to understand that this was pretty high praise from an industry stalwart.

"Tell you what." Eddie leaned toward me. "Go by the office and talk it over with Antigone. She'll give you the scoop and set you up with an internship. That way, you can test the waters. Do a couple of jobs and see if it's a fit."

"An internship?" I was tempted to ask if I could get CEU credits, too.

Eddie nodded. "We do 'em all the time. Got one working with us right now. Sweet little thing." He chuckled. "Nobody'll see *her* coming, that's for sure. She's been riding with Weasel on the weekends. He says she's ready to fly solo. Maybe you can hitch up with her? We could start you off easy . . . give you a couple of SmartTrack jobs. They're no-brainers."

"'SmartTrack'?"

"Yeah. We call 'em 'No Fuss Repossessions.' A lot of your nickel-and-dime roach motel lots install these GPS devices under the dashboards of their cars. Some schmuck defaults on the loan and, *blammo*—we know exactly where it is. All we gotta do is go and grab it. It's usually back on the lot and on its way to a new loser the next day. Hell, we've hauled in the same damn cars a couple dozen times."

Maybe Eddie was right. Why not give it a try? Commit to a weekend or two and see if it clicked. I was going no place at TWAT. If I paid off my law school loans, I could think about relocating. Start fresh. Go someplace with better prospects and a climate that didn't imitate the sun. Maybe even be able to buy a bottle of wine without having to show six forms of identification. Hell . . . I worked so many damn hours a week that I didn't even have friends—unless you counted Sebastian and Carol Jenkins.

Yeah. I deserved a chance to have a life and a chance to meet somebody. I hadn't had a date in . . . I couldn't even *remember* the last time.

Wrong. I could totally remember. It had been a year ago at the firm's annual summer picnic at Tanglewood. I took Deloris Tyson from the Clerk of Court's office. Sebastian met her when he had jury duty and she set off his gaydar. But *that* wasn't unusual. Any woman with less than collar-length hair and lace-up shoes set off *his* gaydar. He managed to talk me up to Deloris and more or less pushed me into calling her. Understand that I don't have the best track record when it comes to women. I'm kind of a one-hit wonder. Deloris was no exception. To this day, I have *no* idea what lies Sebastian told her, but Deloris seemed wholly underwhelmed when I presented myself at her door the day of the picnic. She actually looked over my shoulder and scanned the street, obviously hoping there'd been some mistake and Halle Berry was still out there, waiting in the car. To give her credit, she hung in with me for most of an hour. When I went to get us each another glass of profoundly cheap wine, she disappeared. Jason from group management later told me he saw her getting into an Uber.

Yeah. I could remember, all right . . .

A fresh start in a new place was just what I needed.

Thirty minutes later, I was seated across the desk from Antigone Reece.

She eyed me with suspicion. "This ain't no patty-cake enterprise, Not-Vera. You dip your pampered toe into this pool, it's likely to get bit off."

"Well," I began. "I wouldn't say my toes are exactly 'pampered.' And Eddie said I could start with some simple jobs."

"Simple jobs?" Antigone fired up a smoke. "They ain't no 'simple' jobs here. Understand something, Missy: the NRB specializes in premier recovery assignments. We're professionals, not day traders."

"Okay. But, Eddie said you have another intern working here right now. Someone I potentially could partner with to learn the ropes?"

"*Intern?*" Antigone blew an impressive plume of smoke toward the yellowed ceiling—which was still leaking. It looked like there were two five-gallon paint buckets in use now. "We don't do none of that affirmative action hiring here. So, if by 'intern,' you mean *her*," Antigone tilted her head toward a smallish woman who was busy decorating something at the back of the room, "she ain't no intern. She's a damn pox eating away at my last nerve."

A pox? The woman looked harmless enough. Kind of cute, too. She was standing on a stepstool, stapling light blue construction paper to a bulletin board. She was wearing a print dress and she had nice legs . . .

Antigone cleared her throat.

I looked back at her guiltily. "Sorry."

"I was saying . . . we don't have no interns. Or trainees. You want to work here, you make a commitment."

"What kind of commitment?" I don't know why I was still sitting there. Clearly, Eddie had sold me a bill of goods. *Big shocker there.*

"A commitment to keep your nose clean and follow orders. You do that, and top-tier assignments will come your way."

I hesitated. "How long would it take to get the more lucrative assignments?"

"Cut right to the chase, don't you Not-Vera?"

"I'm . . . I have another job," I explained.

"Divided loyalties won't serve you well in this profession. No man can serve two masters." Antigone tapped her yellow pencil. She seemed to be deliberating about something. "Maybe I can kill two birds with one stone and buy myself some serenity in the process." She swiveled around on her chair. "Stohler! Get up here."

The pert woman who'd finished covering the bulletin board with blue squares of paper was now stapling puffy-looking clouds along the perimeter. She turned around when Antigone bellowed and beamed at us before scampering down off the stepladder. "On my way, Chief."

Antigone rolled her eyes. "Try and cheer your ass down, okay? This ain't Romper Room."

I watched the woman approach. She reminded me of somebody, but I couldn't quite place it. I got to my feet. Antigone noticed and slowly shook her head. "Oh, this is gonna work out just *fine*."

The woman smiled at me as she joined us.

"Stohler?" Antigone aimed her cigarette at me. "Meet Vera—your new partner."

"Really?" The woman beamed at me. "Hi. I'm Frankie." She extended a small hand. "It's so great to meet you."

"Um." I nervously shook hands with her. "I'm Nick. But I'm not really . . ."

Antigone interrupted me. "Nick-Not-Vera here is Eddie's idea of a trainee," she explained. "Weasel says he thinks you're ready to solo—so Eddie wants you to show her the ropes."

"Of course. How exciting." Frankie smiled at me. "I'd love to. Mr. Weasel is a great teacher."

"Uh huh." Antigone finished her cigarette and ground it out in the Roadway ashtray, which didn't look like it had been emptied since my last visit to the NRB. "Weasel is a regular Mr. Rogers." She opened a desk drawer and pulled out a sheet of paper. "Eddie says he's picked out a job for you two—real easy. Here are the details." She handed the paper to Frankie.

Frankie took the sheet of paper and scanned it. I saw her eyes widen.

"A school bus?" she asked Antigone.

"Why not?" Antigone shrugged her wide shoulders. "They get

behind on their obligations same as everybody else."

"But it says here this belongs to a Baptist Church."

"Damn Skippy. Biggest bus ministry in two states. Looks to me like they bit off a bit more'n they could chew with this latest luxury acquisition." Antigone pointed at some highlighted text. "Six months in arrears on payments."

"But, a *church?*" Frankie was beside herself. "How do we take a bus away from a *church?*"

"Same way you take it away from anybody else. These people ain't no angels. They need to render unto damn Caesar the things that are Caesar's. And this bus right here still belongs to Mr. Caesar—for at least another fifty-four months. So until they cough up the cash—plus our recovery fee—this chariot of God's fire is gonna cool its sanctified jets in our impound lot. Now . . ." She cut her eyes back and forth between the two of us. "You want this assignment, or not? No matter what Eddie says, I ain't gonna ask you twice."

"We'll take it," I blurted. Frankie looked at me with surprise. "How hard could it be?" I was pretty sure there wouldn't be any phantom guineas lurking around at the Mt. Zion Full Gospel Baptist Tabernacle in China Grove.

At least, I hoped not.

"Okay," Frankie said. "I guess we'll give it a go."

"Wise decision." Antigone flipped Frankie an enormous key. I was impressed that Frankie seamlessly snatched it out of the air with one hand. "We got this from Thomas Built. It's a universal key that should start it. *Should.* If it doesn't, you'll have to hot-wire it. You checked out on that?"

Frankie nodded. "We practiced on Linda's car."

Antigone scoffed. "Don't tell her that."

"Oh, it's okay. Weasel says that's how she starts it, too." Frankie met my eyes. "Linda drives a primered '68 Road Runner. I'm told it's a pretty nice ride. Weasel says it has something called a 426 Hemi."

I suddenly felt out of my depth. "Um. That's . . . cool."

"I suppose it is." Frankie's tone was noncommittal. "There's a lot I need to learn about the particulars of the vehicles."

"Hello?" Antigone snapped her long fingers. "Earth to Debbie Reynolds? You wanna get crackin' on this before I change my mind? Eddie asked for you two, especially—and I got nothin' to say about that."

Debbie Reynolds? That seemed like a stretch. *But she did look like somebody . . .*

Well. Maybe Debbie Reynolds with a few decades lopped off?

I stole another look at her. *Jennifer Aniston! That was it.* She could've just walked off the set of *Friends*. Although the tiny cornflower pattern on her dress didn't quite mesh with that image.

Shit. She had to be straight. Terminally straight. I stole another glance at her prim little print dress. *And square, too.* In my experience, all women who looked like Jennifer Aniston—or Debbie Reynolds—were straight. Straight and square—not necessarily in that order.

What difference did it make? I wasn't here to find female companionship. I was here to get myself out of debt and on the road to a better life—a life someplace light-years away from towns like K-fucking-Vegas.

"Why'd Eddie ask for us?" Frankie asked.

"Fortunately, he don't involve me in the intricacies of his thought processes. If he did, I can assure you that damn leak in the corner wouldn't be like a fountain, flowing deep and wide."

"We'll do it." Frankie sighed.

"Well, praise Him. Miracles still happen." Antigone shooed us away. "Now get outta my hair and go take care of business. I got better things to do." She turned away from us and snapped up her walkie-talkie. I surmised that meant Lamar's day at Global Gospel Radio was about to get worse.

"Come on, Vera." Frankie touched my arm. "Let's go to my desk and get organized."

"Nick," I muttered, as we made our way toward the back of the big, bleak room.

"Pardon?" Frankie turned back and looked at me. She had nice eyes. Friendly and appealing. Golden retriever eyes—except they were hazel. They contrasted nicely with her sandy-colored hair.

Straight eyes, I reminded myself.

"My name," I explained. "It's Nick. Not Vera."

"Nick-Not-Vera?" she repeated.

"No. Nick. *Just* Nick. *Not* Vera." This was going nowhere. "Vera is my birth name, but I go by Nick."

"Oh." She seemed to catch on. "Why does Antigone call you 'Not-Vera'?"

"I thought it was better not to ask her."

"Good instinct." She smiled. "Mine's Frances. But everyone just calls me Frankie."

Nick and Frankie, I mused. We sounded just like characters in a Dashiell Hammett novel.

Perfect names for a couple of car thieves.

At least, I was sure that's what Mamá would say when it all blew up in my face.

"You're doing *what?*"

This wasn't a good sign. I'd just told Sebastian, in fairly direct language, about my decision to give a temp job with the NRB a try. We were in the kitchen because he was cooking . . . *something*. It smelled eerily like one of those hog lagoons in Yadkin County. I knew better than to ask. Sebastian's other passion in life, apart from selling real estate, was to become a contestant on *Chopped*. That meant he was always experimenting with horrifying combinations of ingredients—and I was his self-appointed taste tester.

"I said I'm going to do a little contract work for the recovery place that found Mozelle's car. Just to make some extra cash and help me get ahead on my law school loans."

Sebastian glared at me through the miasma rising from a big skillet on the range.

“The joint in K-Vegas with the AM radio station out back?”

I nodded.

“Are you insane?” He held up a manicured hand. “Never mind. I already know the answer to that.”

“It’s just temporary. One or two jobs, max.”

“Yeah.” Sebastian slammed a lid into place on the skillet. “Don’t kid a kidder. I saw *Goodfellas*. I know how this works.”

“The NRB is *not* the mob.”

“And you know this how?”

“Now you sound like my mother.”

“As if.” Sebastian poured us each another glass of wine. At least that part of the meal was always guaranteed to be good. He didn’t compromise when it came to swill—thank god. It didn’t hurt that he was in a three-year relationship with Feliz Vargas, twenty years his senior and a sales associate at Total Wine. Sebastian called him *Feliz Navidad*. “Ro-Ro called today, by the way,” he added.

My mother’s given name is María Manuela Álvarez de las Asturias, but Sebastian, in some bizarre homage to *Will & Grace,* has always insisted on calling her “Ro-Ro.” Surprisingly, Mamá, who under the best of circumstances has the sense of humor of a can opener, just rolls with it and reciprocates by calling him “Karen.”

They have an understanding.

“Mamá called you?” I was intrigued—and nervous. Mamá had a nose for trouble . . .

“Uh huh. She said she’d left you, like, nine voice mail messages. She wanted to be sure you weren’t in jail or off on a bender someplace.” He stirred a simmering pot of something beige and gelatinous. “Good thing she doesn’t know about this harebrained scheme . . .”

The word *yet* seemed implied by the way his sentence trailed off. “If you tell her about this, I’ll kill you.”

“Hey. I won’t *have* to tell her about it. She’ll sniff it out on her own.”

Great. Something new to digest my organs worrying about. Maybe if I just did a couple of jobs for Fast Eddie, I could make enough cash to wash my hands of the NRB *and* the dead-end job at TWAT. *Yeah. Right.* That would happen about as fast as the vat of toxic waste now reducing on our stove would land Sebastian a slot on *Chopped,* and a dream date with Ted Allen.

I waved a hand back and forth in front of my face to try and clear the air. "What the hell is *in* that pot, anyway? It smells like liquid plague."

"Pork bung," he explained.

Pork . . . *bung?* "Oh, dear god . . . are you kidding me?"

"Of course not." He held up the recipe. "It's a delicacy."

"Where? *Gansu?*"

"Stop being so judgmental. This is gonna be delicious, so just slap the hogs and add it to the recipe book."

Sebastian's mention of hogs prompted a painful surge of memories that didn't make me feel much better. "What else is in it?"

"It's jackfruit-stuffed pork bung, finished with a flash mole sauce and agar-agar noodles."

My stomach turned over. "Where's the phone?"

Sebastian retrieved his phone from the counter. "Why?"

"I'm calling Door Dash."

Sebastian yanked his phone back. "How *dare* you order out when I'm slaving over a meal this rich in *soigne*?"

"What the hell is *soigne*? It sounds like some kind of grill baste."

"Very funny." He wasn't ready to forgive me yet.

"And I'm not calling to order food," I explained. "I'm calling to ask them to come get this and deep-six it in Salem Lake."

"So, why are you avoiding Ro-Ro?" Sebastian had moved on. He was prone to making sudden conversational lane changes without signaling.

"I'm *not* avoiding her."

"What about the nine voice mail messages?"

"Dude. She calls me a minimum of nine times *every* day."

"She's just worried about you. With good reason, I might add." Sebastian was now basting his bung.

Even the simple, cognitive act of stringing together the words to describe that action made my stomach roll . . . I had to work hard to clear my mind's eye.

"The only thing Mamá worries about is the looming certainty of not getting grandbabies."

He huffed. "Fortunately, your complete lack of competency when it comes to women is no longer an impediment."

That confused me. "Why?"

"Because." He waved the turkey baster around like a magic wand. "*Science!*"

"Yeah. *That's* not gonna happen."

"I agree that in your case, it's becoming a time-value proposition. Your eggs are about parboiled by now."

"Hey . . ."

"Am I lying? How old are you?"

I didn't answer him.

"Thirty-seven. *That's* how old you are."

"Hey, you're no spring chicken either."

"Unlike you, I have no biological restrictions on my ability to procreate. Every night, I worship the god of sexual prowess."

"Viagra?"

"No," he glowered at me. "Mickey Rooney."

"My mistake." I started rummaging in the pantry for something edible. It was pretty slim pickings. Almond butter. Matzo crackers. Soba noodles. Bits O' Brickle. I did a double-take. *Yep* . . . Bits O' Brickle. I pulled it out. "What's this for?"

"I'm going to crust some brisket with it," Sebastian explained. "I found a great recipe. You throw it in the Instant Pot with rainbow chard and Heering Cherry liqueur."

"That sounds perfectly disgusting."

"Not in Denmark," he insisted.

"Remarkably, a place not distinguished for its cuisine."

"Says you."

"Yeah." I grabbed for his phone. "Where did you stash that

Carrabba's home delivery menu?"

"Cut me to the quick."

I was already dialing. "You want anything?"

He sighed and stared down at his creation. "I suppose I could give this to Ricky's crew. They'll eat it—especially if I dump a quart of Texas Pete on it."

"Is that a yes?" I asked.

He thought about it. "Fettucine Weesie—and a side of sautéed broccoli."

While we waited on the food to arrive, Sebastian opened more wine, and we sat down at the kitchen table.

"So when are you starting this insanity?" he asked.

"Tomorrow. We've got an easy job. Just a quick trip to China Grove to recover a school bus."

"Did you say 'we'?"

I nodded.

"Color me intrigued."

"It's not a big deal. I'm riding with someone. She's new, too."

"*She's* new?"

"Yeah. She's a part-timer, too."

"How old is she?"

"I don't know . . . my age maybe? A year or two on either side? I'm not sure."

"I see." He tented his fingers. "She married?"

Dear god. This was like talking with Mamá. "How should I know?"

"Easy. Did she look browbeaten? Worn down? Did she have any pronounced facial tics? Was she wearing a wedding ring?"

"No, no, no and no." I took a sip of my wine. "Why the third degree about Frankie?"

"Frankie? Her name is *Frankie?*" He narrowed his eyes. "That's a lesbyterian name if ever I've heard one . . . *Nick.*"

"You're delusional."

"*I'm* delusional? Let's do the math, shall we? A middle-aged woman with a guy name, moonlighting for a repo agency. Not exactly a candidate for the cotillion circuit, is she?"

"Since when am I middle-aged? And she's *not* gay."

"You know this because?"

I was losing patience with this inquisition. "Sebastian . . . she's a total sororitette. A girlie girl."

"A girlie girl who repossesses cars to get her jollies? I doubt it."

"Well, that's hardly breaking news. You also doubt the existence of gravity."

Sebastian dramatically selected an overripe pear from a dish on the table, extended his arm, and casually dropped it to the floor. It hit with a loud splat. We both stared down at the impressive debris field its impact had generated.

"And yet, not so much," he said.

"I am so not cleaning that up."

"No worries. Carol Jenkins will eat it."

For the record, Carol Jenkins is Sebastian's traditionally built cat, who has never missed a meal or an opportunity to editorialize. I call her Sebastian's cat, but in actuality she came with the house. When we moved in and discovered her, lounging on a Buick-sized bed in the back bedroom, we called the previous tenants to report that they'd left their cat behind.

Not so much.

"You try moving her fat ass," the man said. "I couldn't dislodge her with a Hoyer lift."

So we ended up with a twenty-four-month lease and a bad-tempered cat with an appetite like Jabba the Hutt. But it was true that we never had to worry about how to dispose of leftovers—not even the more creative ones that should've been destined for Yucca Mountain. Carol Jenkins took care of everything.

"So, I want to meet her."

I looked at Sebastian with confusion. "Meet who?"

"Your new partner. The not-gay sororitette—Frankie Whoosis."

"What? Why? I barely know her myself."

"That's why I want to meet her. So I can get the lay of the land before you have a chance to muck it up."

My knee-jerk response was to ask why he assumed I'd muck it up—but giving in to that impulse meant I'd dignify his ridiculous supposition.

I was on to his reindeer games.

"Okay, wise guy. She's picking me up here tomorrow. If you're around, you can meet her."

"Interesting." Sebastian considered the new information. "Why is she coming here?"

"Because she lives in Winston, too—and there's no reason for both of us to drive to K-Vegas just to turn around and head back toward China Grove."

"What time is she getting here?"

"Around nine."

A flash of car headlights lit up the kitchen window. Our food had arrived.

"Whose turn is it to pay?" I asked.

"Yours." Sebastian pushed back his chair and headed for the front door, being careful to dodge the pear-slick on the floor. "But I'll buy anyway since you'll soon need all of your money to post bond."

"I appreciate the vote of confidence."

"What are friends for?"

I had a sinking feeling I'd learn the answer to that question at nine tomorrow morning . . . .

Frankie arrived right on time. Fortunately, I'd left the exhaust fan over the range going full-blast all night, and the worst of the lingering bung odor had dissipated.

And Sebastian had been right: Carol Jenkins had made short work of the pile of pear chutney on the kitchen floor. All that remained was the stem and a smattering of seeds, which were distributed in a pattern bearing an unmistakable resemblance to Stonehenge.

Carol Jenkins watched a lot of *Nat Geo*.

I wasn't sure how to dress for The Great School Bus Caper, so I had opted for something innocuous: jeans, a rugby shirt and some high-top sneakers. Sebastian offered to disguise my features with grease paint, but I declined. I had no desire to look like Bill Bojangles' demented little sister.

When Frankie rang the bell, Sebastian laid a patch getting to the door ahead of me. He opened it with a flourish.

"*You* must be *she*," he said, in his best Michael Jeter impression. "*S'il vous plait venez.*" He held the door open for her.

Frankie didn't seem to miss a beat—nor did she seem very surprised by his greeting.

"*Merci Monsieur.*" She stepped inside and extended a hand. "I'm Frankie."

"Yes, you certainly are." Sebastian was giving her a good once-over. Frankie was more casually dressed than she'd been yesterday: a print blouse, slacks and low-heeled shoes. "I *love* that bag," he gushed. "Ann Taylor?"

"Nope." Frankie held it up so he could examine it more closely. "Knockoff. Stein Mart. Fifteen ninety-nine."

"No way!" Sebastian was impressed. "How'd you find it?"

"Persistence. I go through there about twice a week. You have to, if you're interested in finding anything other than last year's Nine West closeouts. I really hoped to score on a Louis Vuitton Neverfull knockoff, but that idea was a total fantasy."

"Honey, can we talk? I've seen a couple of those on eBay. One numbskull even called them 'Louis Futon' Neverfull bags. That's just fine by me. I live for a good bargain."

"Me, too," Frankie agreed. "I have to on my teacher's salary."

"You're a teacher?" He cut his eyes at me. "Nick didn't mention that."

I cleared my throat. "That's because Nick didn't *know* that." I approached the two of them. "Hi Frankie. I see you've already met my housemate, Sebastian?"

She smiled at me. It was another one of those full-on Jennifer Aniston smiles. I was aware that Sebastian was watching me watch her. His scrutiny made me feel itchy beneath my clothes. Guilty, too. Like I'd been caught having impure thoughts about the Blessed Virgin.

Probably not too far off the mark, actually.

"So." I clapped my hands together. "Ready to get this show on the road?"

"What's the rush?" Sebastian took hold of Frankie's arm and led her toward the kitchen. "I made coffee."

"Well," I said to their retreating backs. "I think we ought to get an early start."

"Why?" Sebastian called over his shoulder. "It's Saturday. Does that bus have a hot brunch date?"

I heard Frankie chuckle. "Some coffee would be wonderful."

Okay. This little drama was going off the rails at warp speed—even for Sebastian.

On the other hand—what had I been thinking? Stein Mart? Why *wouldn't* these two get along? They were both total valley girls.

I hated my life sometimes. I should've listened to Mamá and stayed in Philadelphia. By now, Aunt Estela would have me married off to her third cousin, Juana, from Trenton. Juana was a Teamster—and a USBC three-time bowling champion.

Yeah. Life could've been so much less complicated if I'd just listened to Mamá.

The three of us sat around the kitchen table and drank cups of Sebastian's ridiculously strong coffee. I had to cut mine with two packs of Splenda and about four ounces of Half-n-Half. Unhappily, I noticed that the creamer just floated on top of the coffee like a beige oil slick. Not a good sign.

Frankie, however, seemed to have no issues with the hot sludge Sebastian called "coffee."

"This is delicious," she remarked. "Is it a local roast?"

Sebastian nodded energetically. "It's Krankies. I try to support the local economy."

"Me, too," Frankie agreed. "Although, in my case, it's kind of required—since both of my parents run businesses."

Sebastian's eyebrows lifted. "Do tell?"

"Heard of Stohler's Funeral Home?"

"No way!" Sebastian was practically vibrating on his chair. "You're a Stohler?"

"Through and through." Frankie looked at me. "Surprised?"

I wasn't sure what to say. I fought hard to keep any hints of reaction off my face.

"It's okay," Frankie said. "I'm used to people being creeped out by the information."

"I'm not creeped out," I lied.

Frankie laughed. "Of course, you aren't."

Sebastian had been slowly tapping a finger against his chin. "*Stohler*," he pondered. His eyes widened. "Does your mama own Shear Elegance?"

Frankie seemed surprised by his question. "Guilty, Your Honor. Both counts."

"Well butter my ass and call me a biscuit. I *love* that place." His voice grew reverential. "Nobody does Balayage hair painting better than your mama. She's a *legend*."

"I'll agree with you that it beats the hell out of wrangling perm rods." Frankie sighed. "Sadly, not a skill I've inherited."

Sebastian giggled. "Knowing your other options, I'd say you need to try harder."

"I don't know about that. It took five years of independent living to shed the combined odors of embalming fluid and activator. I'm very happy now just to be dealing with chalk dust and finger paint."

"So you teach little kids?" I asked.

"Uh huh. Third grade. South Fork Elementary."

"Not exactly the high-rent district," Sebastian noted. "Why isn't a Stohler breathing the rarified air at Forsyth Country Day?"

"Because Forsyth Country Day doesn't *need* any more good teachers . . . they've already bought enough talent to succeed."

"You talk about them like they're the Yankees."

Frankie batted her eyes at him. "And your point would be?"

Sebastian was enthralled by Frankie. I could see it in his eyes. He had that same dreamy expression he got whenever he binge-watched *Project Runway*. "Screw my Pilates class. Can I ride along with you two today?"

"*No.*" I stood up. "Come on, Frankie. Time is money."

Frankie got to her feet, too. "May I use the restroom before we head out?"

"Sure." I pointed down the hall that led toward the bedrooms. "First door on the left. And make sure you don't miss it and take the *second* door." Frankie looked confused. "It's complicated," I explained. "You don't want to wake Carol Jenkins."

"Okaaayyy . . ."

"My cat," Sebastian added. "She's not a morning person."

"Right." Frankie looked at me. "You'll explain later?"

"Count on it." I said.

After Frankie disappeared behind the correct door, Sebastian leaned across the table. "*Ohdeargod* . . . you absolutely *have* to marry her," he whispered.

"Are you *insane?* Stop with that shit. She'll hear you."

"I'm just saying . . . a hot-looking Stohler and a lifetime of *truly* exceptional haircuts—or Aunt Estela's cousin, Juana. You do the math."

Frankie drove us to Spencer, an old Southern Railroad town on the Yadkin River, and parked her car in the big public lot across from The NC Transportation Museum.

"I thought we'd leave my car here," she explained, "and Uber over to China Grove. Once we have the bus, we can come back and pick it up."

That sounded like a good plan—with one exception. "Who's going to drive the bus?"

I didn't know much about this business, but even I knew you had to have a multi-axle license to drive a ninety-passenger bus.

"Oh, I will." Frankie shut off her car. "I do it all the time on field trips."

Right. *Of course she did.* It seemed the Stohlers were regular Renaissance women.

"Okay." I unfastened my seat belt. "Hey . . . I apologize if Sebastian was a little too . . ."

Frankie looked at me. The close quarters in the car made it possible for me to see the little green flecks in her eyes. I felt myself shrink back against the passenger door.

Damn Sebastian and his infernal meddling . . .

"Too what?" Frankie asked. "Charming?"

"Well, that wasn't exactly the word that occurred to me."

"Relax." She patted my knee. "He's wonderful. I adore him."

"I have to ask you something."

"What?" She looked amused.

"How'd you get into this business?"

"Repossessing cars?" she asked.

I nodded.

"I agree it does seem like a stretch. And my parents would die a thousand deaths if they ever found out. But teaching—especially in the public schools—barely pays a living wage. I refuse to ask my parents for help, and it takes half of my take-home pay to keep the kids in supplies. So I need part-time work to fill in the gaps."

"But the NRB?" I let the rest of my question remain unasked.

"You mean, why aren't I working at Stein Mart so I can reap the benefits of the employee discount?"

I shrugged. "Something like that."

"Let me ask *you* a question. How much of a bonus did Eddie give you for getting that Maybach off the hog farm?"

I was surprised. "You know about that?"

"*Everybody* knows about that. Weasel laughed for a solid twenty minutes when Antigone told us about you and the chickens. And trust me—Weasel doesn't laugh. Ever."

"Those guineas are real bitches," I muttered.

"So I've heard." Frankie laughed. "Now, about that bonus?"

I sighed. "You're right. I'm cheap. He bought me."

"Same here."

"The money?"

"Pure and simple. I make more doing weekend work for the NRB than I could ever make in the classroom. It's simple math even I can do. So when a friend at the elementary school floated the idea, I decided to take a chance and look into it. It seems to have paid off. Weasel says I'm good at it because nobody would ever see me coming."

"I think he's right about that. You don't exactly fit the mold."

"Trust me." She chuckled. "I never much have—at anything. It's all window dressing."

I was tempted to follow up on that, but it seemed too personal. "I, on the other hand, seem ideally suited for the work."

Frankie looked perplexed. "I don't follow you."

"Really? The senior partners at my law firm had *no* difficulty discerning how perfectly disposed for 'asset recovery' work my genetic makeup rendered me."

"That's a ridiculous supposition. And offensive. I hope you're joking."

"Not really. But you're right about one thing: Eddie's approach to profit-sharing does provide powerful incentive to try something new."

"I rest my case." Frankie plucked her iPhone out of the center console and ordered our Uber. "It says they'll be here in eight minutes."

"Okay." Something occurred to me. "Hey, do we always have to use our own cars on these jobs?"

"Oh, that." Frankie shook her head. "No. Once Antigone thinks we're solid and not a total insurance risk, we'll get to use one of the special stealth trucks. Of course, Linda will have to teach us how to use the stinger."

"Stinger?"

Frankie nodded enthusiastically. "It's a hydraulic tow bar that folds up and retracts beneath the bed of the truck so it looks just like a normal trailer hitch. Eddie has two of them, installed on F-150s. They're very specialized."

"Who is Linda?"

"You haven't met her yet?" Frankie seemed amused.

I shook my head. "I haven't really met anybody but you."

"Linda is an old-timer. Used to be the finance director for a score of used car lots all over the state. Antigone says she's got experience with most of our skips."

"Skips?"

"Sorry. *Delinquent clientele*. Weasel says it's best not to fuck with her."

I blinked. Frankie's casual use of the word *fuck* surprised me. She must've noticed because she laughed. It was a merry sound that filled the small space.

"Sorry. Did I offend you?"

"I'm not offended. Just . . ."

"Surprised?"

"Well. Maybe a little."

"Don't be. I went to college at St. Mary's, so I can knot a sweater with the best of them—but I also swear like a sailor. My father loves to point out how this shortcoming made me a bad fit for the family business."

"Lucky you."

"You don't know the half of it. Fortunately, I have an older sister who's made for it. She gives the whole goth vibe new meaning." She pointed at the white Honda Accord pulling in beside us. "Our Uber is here. Ready to go recover an asset?"

I opened my door. "Right behind you."

"That's the biggest damn bus I've ever seen."

Frankie and I were crouching behind a large recycling dumpster at the back of the Mt. Zion Full Gospel Baptist Tabernacle and School.

"No kidding," Frankie whispered. "It must be one of those high-dollar coaches with the wheelchair lifts."

"I guess the salvation business is good in Rowan County?"

"I suppose we should be thankful that God is ADA compliant."

I bumped her shoulder. "Don't make me laugh . . . I don't want us to get busted."

"Me either. I've heard the food in the Rowan County J sucks out loud."

"I mean it . . . don't make me laugh."

"Okay, okay." She pulled the big bus key out of her oversized Stein Mart bag. "It looks like the coast is clear. Ready to go?"

I took a deep breath. "I guess."

We left the safety of the dumpster and walked as casually as we could toward the row of buses. Our target was easy to spot. It was plainly the newest member of the fleet, and the VIN was clearly visible on the windshield in front of the driver's seat.

Nobody was around the church school this early on a Saturday. That was the *good* news. Maybe with luck, we'd be able to drive this behemoth out with no ceremony—and, I prayed, *no guineas.*

The doors stood slightly ajar on all of the buses, which made getting inside easy.

"This thing is fucking *plush.*" I was dumbfounded. It even had leather seats. "School buses sure weren't like this in Philly."

"Is that where you grew up?"

"Yeah. Our buses were more like the ones you see hauling inmates around—only with bigger cages and more bullet holes."

Frankie strapped herself into the driver's seat. "Here goes nothing." She tried the key. It fit, but wouldn't turn. "*Son of a bitch.*"

"What's wrong?" I fought a surge of panic.

"This so-called 'universal' key doesn't work."

"What? Are you *kidding* me?"

Frankie tried the key a few more times. "Nope."

"What do we do now? Call Weasel for the tow truck?"

I was grasping at straws.

Frankie looked at me with incredulity. "Not if we want to be *paid* for this job. We'll have to improvise."

Improvise? That didn't sound good. "Do I want to know what that means?"

"Watch and learn."

Frankie extended her arm and felt around beneath the dashboard. I could hear her fumbling with something, and then she jerked her arm down sharply. Her hand reappeared, clutching a wiring harness with a bunch of cables attached to it. "*Et voila,*" she said, proudly.

"What the hell are you doing?" I was sure we were going to get arrested now.

Frankie calmly detached two wires and proceeded to spark them against each other until there was a low rumble and the bus engine turned over.

"Holy shit!" I was dumbfounded. "You mean that really works?"

"Of *course* it does." She released the brake and shifted the bus into gear. "Now sit down. We've got *other* problems."

"What do you mean?"

"Company! *Over there.* Coming right at us."

I looked out the window toward the school building. Two rather rotund men wearing white shirtsleeves and sporting what Sebastian called, Republican hair, were charging toward us. They did not look very forgiving . . .

"Hey!" The larger of the two hollered as they closed in on us. "Stop! What do you think you're doing? That's private property!"

Frankie started pulling out of the parking space—after first closing and securing the door.

"Can you go any faster?" I asked with urgency. The men had caught up with us and were pounding their fists on the side of the bus. "They might have guns."

"Will you relax?" Frankie was busy working her way through the lower gears. "They don't have guns."

"What makes you so sure?"

"Because state law forbids carrying weapons on school campuses."

"Are you crazy? Did you get a look at these dudes?" I ran to the back door, and watched as the men peeled off and made their way toward the row of buses. "I think they're getting into one of the buses," I hollered. I watched their progress with horror before running back toward the front. "They are! They're going to follow us. Besides, aren't we supposed to stand down if the owners raise objections?"

"These guys aren't the owners. They don't know we're repossessing this thing. They think we're *stealing* it." Frankie watched me in the giant rearview mirror. "Will you *please* sit down and stop running up and down the aisle? It's dangerous."

"Didn't you hear me? They're chasing us!" I ran toward the back again.

"Yes," she replied calmly. "I think the entire county heard you. Now *please* take a seat."

"Frankie! They're coming after us in another bus."

"Seriously?" Frankie met my eyes in the mirror. "In another *bus?*"

"Yes, yes . . . *in another bus*. Can you *please* go faster?" Frankie made the turn onto the main road at about the rate molasses flowed in January.

There were two loud reports. Something dinged off a nearby metal signpost.

"Sweet mother of pearl!" I screamed. "They're shooting at us! They have guns! Step on it, Frankie—*now!*"

"I am driving as fast as permitted." Frankie stole another look in the mirror. "Besides, they'll never catch us. It looks like they're in a short bus."

Short bus? I let that one go. I stared at her. "Permitted? Permitted by *what?*"

"The law. This is a *school bus*, remember?"

"Frankie—did you not hear those bangs? They fucking *shot* at us."

"I am *not* breaking the law, Nick." Frankie ground the gears. "Not for you. Not for the NRB. Not for *anyone*. I'd lose my license."

I anxiously looked out the rear window. The beefy Republicans were gaining on us. I sank down onto a seat and looked back and forth between them and Frankie.

I just know I'm gonna start having black and yellow nightmares . . . .

It was worth one more try. I got to my feet and unsteadily made my way back up the long aisle, crushing an open bag of Cheez-Its that had slid into my path. I stopped just behind Frankie's seat, being careful not to cross the white line, and held onto the shiny metal support pole.

"Frankie?" I was desperate to come up with an argument she'd buy. "Those two Bible-beating goons behind us are having *no* problem breaking the law. They've already fired a gun at us. If they catch us, god knows what they'll do." She looked at me in the mirror. That was a good sign. "I need to make extra money as much as you do—but I'll be *damned* if I'll risk ending up on a slab in your daddy's basement because you don't have the guts to exceed a fucking speed limit."

That seemed to work. Frankie narrowed her eyes briefly, then floored it. The bus shot forward and I about lost my footing.

"Will you *please* sit down?" Frankie ordered.

"Yes, ma'am." I took the seat behind her and twisted around so I could watch the road behind us.

The shorter bus began to recede into the distance, and mercifully there were no more gunshots. I slowly began to relax. We were only about a mile from the intersection with I-85. Then it would be clear sailing back to Spencer. My heart rate slowed and my breathing returned to its normal state of only half-panicked.

Then Frankie abruptly slammed on the brakes and the bus screeched to a stop. I lurched forward against the metal bar. *Damn! That shit's going to leave a mark.* Frankie flicked a switch on the dashboard and the bus's hazard lights began to blink.

"What the fuck are you *doing?*" I shrieked.

She shrugged. "Railroad crossing."

My head was about to explode.

We sat there for a full ten seconds before she turned off the lights and started rolling forward again. It was only ten seconds, but it felt like ten lifetimes. It gave me a chance to rethink all the ways I needed to revise my will . . . .

"You're *killing* me here," I grumbled.

Seconds after we'd cleared the double set of tracks, the earsplitting alarm signaling an advancing train sounded, and a big set of striped crossing gates dropped down across the road.

That meant the assholes chasing us would be held up while the train passed . . . .

I prayed it would be one of those long-ass trains, too—the kind that always rolled through during rush hour when you were desperate to get home—pulling about five thousand freight containers from China.

I stared at the back of Frankie's head. "One of us leads a charmed life."

Frankie was still shifting gears, getting us up to speed for the interstate. "I'm guessing it's *you*," she quipped. "It took some balls to play the funeral home card."

I felt irrationally proud. "That was pretty good, wasn't it?"

She nodded. "They teach you those tactics in law school?"

"Yes. Absolutely. Just like I'm sure they taught you how to hot-wire a bus at St. Mary's."

"It was an elective." She smiled at me.

If I hadn't known better, I'd have sworn the look she shot me was downright flirty. Fortunately for me, I *did* know better.

"I guess we understand each other." I said.

"Oh, I think we're beginning to."

I didn't reply because I was sure I'd say something profoundly stupid, and then I'd have to spend the rest of the night reliving the horror of my bad instincts.

Frankie navigated the turn onto the highway and we roared back toward Spencer, never exceeding fifty-five miles per hour, to pick up her car. I spent the rest of the ride marveling that I'd actually survived my second heist for the NRB. With luck, we'd drop the bus off in K-Vegas and find ourselves one step closer to earning Antigone's coveted stamp of approval.

And confronting my desire to gain *that* bizarre approbation was the most horrifying revelation of them all.

It was Frankie who suggested we stop for a bite to eat when we got back to Winston-Salem. I was surprised by the suggestion, but not unwilling. I hadn't eaten much for breakfast and a cocktail—*or five*—was sounding pretty damn good.

"Sure," I agreed. "Got any place in mind?"

"Someplace with alcohol?"

"You'll get no arguments from me. How about Sweet Potatoes?" The arts district restaurant featured Southern-inspired uptown and down-home cuisine, and was famous for its innovative menu and superior cocktails. And for me, it was a warm reminder of my paternal grandmother's cooking. Sunday suppers at her house were always special for me. I still had her old cast-iron skillet and used it to make cornbread whenever I could commandeer the oven between bouts of Sebastian's test kitchen antics.

Frankie looked over at me. "You like Sweet Potatoes?"

"Yeah. But if you'd rather go someplace else, that's totally okay."

"Are you kidding? I *love* that place. I've already decided to name my firstborn Fred—regardless of gender."

I laughed. "Fred is a damn fine bartender." I knew firsthand how Fred's particular brand of TLC could make any lingering effects of my worst days at TWAT disappear.

We lucked out and got a parking space on Trade Street, about a block from the restaurant. I wasn't positive, but I saw a man who was a dead ringer for Eddie going into Single Brothers bar. He was walking with another man who was very oddly proportioned. The guy topped Eddie by at least a foot, had an unusually long neck, short torso, and gangly arms that flopped against his sides as he walked.

I nudged Frankie. "Is that Eddie?"

"Where?" she asked.

"Up the street, going into Single Brothers with some strange-looking dude."

She squinted. "I don't see him."

The two men had already disappeared behind the door. "Never mind. It probably wasn't him."

"Probably not. I think the only time he ever leaves the Sixty Six Grill is to meet with his bookie."

"Bookie?"

"Oh, yeah." Frankie nodded. "Weasel says Eddie bets on *everything* . . . NASCAR, horse races, boxing—even golf."

"Golf? People actually bet on golf?"

"Of course. People will bet on anything with a spread or a score."

"Yeah . . . but *golf?* I mean . . . my father is addicted to it, but I always assumed that was because it got him out of the house for nine hours at a clip."

"Not *my* father." Frankie laughed. "He says if he's going to chase something around all day, he's either going to eat it or have sex with it."

I looked at her with surprise.

"What? Being a mortician doesn't make him a man of refinement."

I was beginning to get a sense that the still waters of the Stohler clan ran deeper than expected.

When we entered the restaurant, we were seated at a great table near the windows. Fred recognized us as soon as we walked in, and we both had cocktails within ten seconds of taking our seats.

Frankie all but purred when she picked up her drink—an Uptown Cosmo. "Did I mention how much I love this man?"

"Only about five times." My Classic Manhattan tasted pretty divine, too. Memories of my recent near-death hell ride on a Thomas Built bus began to recede. I took another sip of the perfect cocktail. "I don't even care about food anymore."

"That's why God put me here—to make you care."

While it's true I was beginning to have my own questions about why God put Frankie in the chair across from mine, coercing me to eat wasn't among the roster of possible explanations.

"Okay," I said. "How about an appetizer?"

Frankie nodded with enthusiasm. "Fried green tomatoes and okra?"

I thought about it. "Why the hell not? But you have to eat the okra—I don't really care for it."

When the server came by to take our order, Frankie took the liberty of adding a side of the 3-Cheese Macaroni and Country Ham Soufflé and, of course, a skillet of sweet potato cornbread.

Oh, yeah . . . we were gonna need a shit-ton more drinks . . .

"Antigone seemed pretty pleased with our progress," Frankie observed.

"What tipped you off? Rapid eye movements?"

Frankie laughed. "Once you've spent more time around her, you'll catch on to her tells."

"She's got tells?"

"Of course she does. Everyone does."

"Not me."

Frankie had been taking a drink of water and nearly sprayed a mouthful across the table.

"What?" I feigned innocence. "You're saying I have tells?"

"Yes." She set her water glass down. "You might say that."

"Such as?"

"Nick." Frankie leaned toward me. I caught a scent of her . . . *something*. Hair? Cologne? Body wash? Whatever it was, it was sweet and slightly intoxicating. Or it could've just been the way it combined with the bourbon now coursing through my veins, nicely warming up every part of me. *Every* part. "You're practically the poster child for tells."

"Am not," I declared.

"Are, too," she insisted.

I folded my arms. "How?"

"How? Let's see." She began to tally up the tells on her fingers. It took both hands. "Facial tics. Hyperventilation. Sweaty palms. Dilated pupils. Spastic gestures. Stertorous respiration. An increase in profane language." She batted her eyes at me. "Shall I go on?"

"You mean there are *more?*"

"At least five or six more, yes."

I slumped in my chair. "You make me sound like an inpatient at Butner."

"If the wraparound blazer fits . . ."

I tossed my swizzle stick at her. "So kill me if I don't have your level of advanced field training for this work."

"You mean teaching third graders?"

"Something like that."

Frankie patted the back of my hand. "Relax. It'll come to you."

"That's what I'm afraid of." I shook my head morosely. "Maybe I *should* go back to Philly and marry cousin Juana . . ."

Frankie looked perplexed. "Who is cousin Juana?"

"It's a long story."

Our appetizers arrived. Frankie loaded my plate with a couple of perfectly crusted fried green tomatoes. "It appears we have plenty of time. I'm all ears."

I looked at her. She was a lot of things, but "all ears" didn't come close to describing the overall picture she presented.

"Maybe another time," I said, lamely. "Tales of my abortive love life will just succeed in giving us both heartburn."

"Really? I bet I can one-up you in that particular relay race."

"Wanna bet?"

We looked at each other. Did I *want* to bet her? Bet her on *anything?*

I was a total coward and I knew it. Unfortunately, I could see by the way Frankie's expression changed that she knew it, too.

"Don't worry," she said in a more level tone. "Let's order another round."

We were halfway through the appetizers when Frankie seemed to recall something. She picked her bag up off an empty chair and rummaged inside it. She withdrew a sealed envelope.

"I almost forgot. Antigone slipped this to me as we were leaving."

I was suspicious. "What is it?"

"I have no idea." Frankie opened the envelope. It contained a single key and a folded sheet of paper. Frankie scanned the document. She met my eyes. "Well, I'll be damned. It's another job."

She passed the paper across to me.

I read the details. *Twice.* "Are you kidding me?"

Frankie shrugged.

"A *hearse?*"

"Why not?" she said. "They default on loans, too."

"Wait a minute . . . are you seriously entertaining this . . . heist?"

Frankie sighed and snapped the paper out of my hand. "It's not a 'heist,' Nick. It's a recovery. And trust me—I *know* this place. They're a fly-by-night operation with a terrible reputation in the industry. We'll be doing the community a service if we take their cold-cut wagon offline."

Cold-cut wagon? Dear heaven. . .

I raised a hand to rub my forehead. "Frankie . . ."

Fred delivered our next round of drinks. "Here you go, beautiful ladies."

Frankie beamed at him. "Keep 'em coming, handsome."

"You know I will." He squeezed her shoulder before returning to the bar.

Frankie pushed my drink toward me.

"Drink up, sidekick." She raised her own martini glass. "Gabriel's blowing his horn, and we're gonna answer his call."

Chapter Two

(If I Knew You Were Comin') I'd Have Baked a Cake

Despondent didn't begin to describe my mood the next morning.

Well. Maybe despondency tinged with hangover.

I'd lost count after my first three cocktails. Of course, Frankie had better sense, and the constitution of an ox—yet another of the contradictions seeming to define the total mishmash of her character.

Tells. There was something about tells . . .

And a hearse.

I looked into the bathroom mirror and stared at my reflection with bleary eyes.

What the fuck have you gotten yourself into?

Don't answer that, my subconscious replied.

It was worth noting that my subconscious always sounded a whole lot like Mamá.

I sat down on the edge of the bathtub. Who could I ask for clarity? There was no one. Sebastian would be *no* help. I'd already exposed myself to his wild assumptions and smug insinuations when Frankie handed what was left of me off to him last night. That event alone was enough to make me consider enrolling in a witness relocation program.

More jumbled thoughts flashed through my hazy mind.

Cold-cut wagons.

Good lord. I shook my aching head to try and clear it. Was *this* who I was becoming?

Wait a minute . . . *cold cuts*. That was it!

Hugh Don.

I stumbled back to my bedroom to look for the paper with his phone number. It was ridiculously early—and it was Sunday. But I didn't care. I grabbed my phone and punched in his number. He answered on the third ring.

"Old World Meats."

"Hey, Hugh Don. It's Nick."

"Who?" he barked.

I sighed. "Vera. It's Vera."

"Oh. Hey kid." He chuckled. "How's the hair?"

"It's *fine*—and wonderfully free of feathers."

He was still chuckling. "Whattaya need? We're running a special this week on brisket."

I made a mental note to conceal this information from Sebastian. "No. I don't need any meat. I need advice."

"Advice? What kind of advice?"

"About a job."

"A job? You doin' another recovery for Eddie?" Hugh Don sounded impressed.

"Yeah. Something like that. It's just that . . . I don't know. Something about this one feels not right."

"Believe me, kid. Them jitters is normal. They go away after the first three or four times—just like wedding nights."

Three or four wedding nights? "No . . . it's not jitters. Not that kind of jitters, anyway. It's something else. Something bigger. How do I know if I'm right for this work? What if I'm just making a big mistake?"

"What if you are? I'm guessin' it won't be the first time. And trust me, it won't be the last time, neither."

"Yeah, but . . ."

"Listen to me. You gotta revise your thinking. You approach this like a job, and I'll guarantee it'll bite you on the ass. You approach it like a calling, it'll give you serenity like you've never known. The best and freest I ever felt was when I was hauling one of them assets back to its rightful owner—setting things straight . . . evening the score. It's all about balance. Balance and order. That's what makes the world go round. Recovery agents are the keepers of the natural order."

I stared at my phone. Had I fucked up and called Wayne Dyer's hotline by mistake?

"Did Antigone call you?" I asked.

Hugh Don laughed. I could hear him lighting up a smoke. "That woman don't make calls on Sundays. You should know that by now." He paused. "Not unless it's to God—or maybe that poor Lamar fella at the radio station."

"Yeah. Okay. I'm just feeling . . . a little lost."

"Lost is fine. You can't get found if you ain't lost first."

"So you're saying I'll find myself repossessing cars?"

"I'm saying everybody's gotta do something. Just do whatever it is the best you can. It don't much matter what it ends up being because sooner or later, The Big Tow's gonna claim us all—no matter how we spent our time."

"You mean death?"

"That's another way to say it."

I pondered what Hugh Don suggested. "I guess that makes sense."

I heard a bell ring in the background. "That's the loading dock. I gotta go. You let me know about that brisket."

"Okay. Thanks for talking to me, Hugh Don. I . . . appreciate it."

"No sweat, Vera. You're a good kid. Lemme know how things work out."

He disconnected.

I sat down on my bed. *Shit. Now what am I gonna do?*

"What are you going to do?" It was Mamá's voice again. "You're going to clean yourself up and go jack a hearse . . ."

Frankie and I agreed to meet up in the parking lot of someplace she called "boots-mobile" on Akron Drive. She said it was a good location because it was only a dozen blocks away from our target, and it had easy access to Highway 52 and a straight shot to K-Vegas.

I drove up and down the 200 block of Akron Drive four times looking for the elusive rendezvous site. Nothing. It was when I was idling at the Patterson Drive stoplight near the entrance to Northside Shopping Center that I saw the sign: *Boost Mobile.*

What the hell?

I felt like an idiot. I never questioned Frankie's obvious malaprop because I was in the part of town where a joint with a name like "boots-mobile" easily could've been a titty bar.

I parked my car behind the store and waited for her to arrive. It was a few minutes after 3 p.m., and the Bojangles next door was jamming. The air wafting toward me was thick with the enticing scent of fried food.

It was making me hungry. A sure sign I was on the road to recovery from last night.

In line with our recent MO, we were taking an Uber to the Blessed Slumber Funeral Home on Ogburn Avenue. When Frankie called me to arrange our rendezvous, she said she'd driven by the place twice already, and our target hearse was parked in the lot behind the "loading dock." She also reported that two men had been out back detailing the cars, so it was a safe assumption that they'd be there for a while.

"I checked their website," she said. "The only funeral scheduled for today is at eleven, so we should be fine to grab it early this afternoon."

"What if they get a . . . *you know* . . . today?"

"A pickup?" she asked. "They normally use one of the transit vans for hospital or home runs."

Clearly, there was a lot I didn't know about this business.

"Okay," I said. "Should I wear dark clothes?"

"Dark clothes? You mean like all black?"

"Well. Yeah."

"Nick? We're picking up a Cadillac—not doing a reenactment of *To Catch A Thief.*"

"I thought it would be respectful . . ." I murmured.

Frankie laughed. "You're so damn cute. Wear whatever you want."

I gave in to my predispositions and chose dark slacks and a striped gray shirt. Frankie smiled when she pulled into the Boost Mobile lot and saw me leaning against the back of my car.

I waved at her as she got out of her car and walked toward me. She was much more casually dressed than me: cropped cotton pants and a lightweight blue pullover with "Dolphins" stenciled across the chest. She had her hair pulled up into a messy knot on top of her head. I thought she looked terrific . . . just like the enticing—*and unobtainable*—daughter of the guy next door. Or in her case, the *mortician* next door.

"Ready to rumble?" she asked.

"Don't use the word 'rumble,' okay? I'm still kind of queasy from last night."

"I'm sorry about that." Her tone seemed genuine. "I tried to get you to eat more."

"It's not your fault. I've always been a lightweight."

"Yeah. This week has kind of been a baptism by fire for you, hasn't it?"

"Sort of. I'm still having a hard time getting my head around all of this."

"Don't worry," Frankie said with a note of encouragement. "It gets easier the more you do it."

"You mean like self-flagellation?"

"Yes. *Just* like that. Only the paycheck is better."

"I guess that's something."

"Nick? It's *everything*. Do you think I do this to get my jollies? No, I don't."

I thought about following up to ask how she *did* get her jollies, but given that we were about to go hijack a hearse, the prospect of doing so seemed anything but *de rigueur*.

"Okay." I took a deep breath. "Showtime."

Frankie nodded and ordered our Uber.

We lucked out, and there was an available car less than a block away. In five minutes, we were on our way to Blessed Slumber on Ogburn Avenue.

Frankie had the driver drop us off several doors down from the target. We walked past the mortuary twice to be sure there was no sign of anyone out back near the bank of parked funeral coaches. It looked like the coast was clear.

"Okay," Frankie said. "Let's do this."

We casually made our way up the service entrance driveway and approached the queue of wagons. We had to dodge a few puddles of standing water—evidence of the recent detailing the cars had undergone earlier. We crouched low as we crept up next to the shiny new Cadillac. Frankie fumbled inside her inevitable quilted bag and withdrew a retractable, slender-looking rod with an S-hook-shaped tip.

"What the hell is that?" I whispered.

"It's a Slim Jim. I'm going to unlock the door."

"Why not just try the key Antigone gave us?"

"Because Antigone's keys *never* work."

"Wait a minute." I reached out to stop her. I took hold of the door handle and lifted it up. The hearse was unlocked.

"Smart ass," Frankie hissed.

I crawled inside. "The keys are in the ignition." I was having a hard time concealing my excitement. Maybe I wasn't a total write-off at this?

"They are?" Frankie sounded like that wasn't the good news I thought it was.

"Yes, yes. Just sneak around and get in."

I didn't have to ask her twice. Thirty seconds later we were rolling out of the lot and cruising down Ogburn Avenue.

I was feeling cocky and slightly self-confident. It was a brand-new experience. I decided I liked it. "That went great!" I gushed.

"Yeah? I think we got lucky."

I cut my eyes at her. "What do you mean?"

"The keys were in the ignition for a reason, Nick. Somebody was probably coming out to use the car."

"Really?" That thought hadn't occurred to me. *Oh, lord . . .*

When I made the turn onto Akron Drive, I swerved to avoid a monster-sized pothole, but didn't quite succeed. The big wagon bounced in and out of it wildly. Something in the bay behind us shifted and resettled in sync with the car.

We looked at each other.

"What the hell was that?" I asked.

"You keep your eyes on the road," Frankie twisted around on the seat. "I'll check it out."

I tried not to panic while Frankie stole a peek behind the white curtains separating the driver compartment from the . . . *cargo* area.

"Uh oh." She straightened in her seat and shot me an anxious look.

"What is it?"

"Don't look now, but we've got a plus one."

"*A what?*"

The hearse swerved wildly, and we roared dangerously close to a public bus kiosk.

"Hey!" Frankie grabbed the steering wheel and quickly righted our trajectory. "Will you *please* watch the road?"

"Okay, okay." I gripped the wheel with both hands so tightly, my knuckles grew pale. "What do you mean by a 'plus one'?"

"What do you *think* I mean?"

Sweet mother of pearl . . .

I risked a look in the rearview mirror. Frankie had left the curtains parted enough to allow me to see the top of a longish, brown box, secured with straps to double rows of bier hooks.

"*Oh, mother of pearl. . .*" The landscape in front of me began to pitch and roll, in a seamless *pas de deux* with my stomach. "I think I'm gonna hurl."

Frankie looked at me with alarm. "Pull over someplace!"

I was fighting hard to keep the big wagon centered in our lane—and the contents of my stomach stowed inside. "Where?"

"*Anywhere!* Just *do* it."

I jerked the wheel hard to the right and jumped a curb into the nearest parking lot, barely managing to stop before slamming into the back of a Hyundai minivan. Car horns blared and I heard another set of tires screech behind us.

"Oh, nice move," Frankie said. Her sarcasm was unmistakable.

"Hey," I was sweating profusely. "You said *anyplace*."

"Yeah." Frankie swirled her hand in a wide circle to encompass the crush of cars that now had us hemmed in on all sides. "You chose well. We're now stuck in the drive-through lane at Mountain Fried Chicken."

"*What?*" I looked around us. "Well, fuck."

"You can't blame me for this one." Frankie sounded downright smug.

"Blame? Who gives a *shit* about blame. Think of something."

Frankie sighed and relaxed against the seat. "Might as well make hay while the sun shines."

"What's that supposed to mean?"

"I'm kind of peckish. I think something greasy would be good for your stomach, too."

"You *cannot* be serious. You want to order *food?*"

"Why not?" she suggested. "We get a per diem."

Someone behind us tapped a car horn. The line had inched up. I eased my foot off the brake and rolled forward. "This is a goddamn nightmare. I'm in a nightmare."

"Did you actually say 'mother of pearl' back there?" Frankie asked.

I shrugged. "We weren't allowed to take the Blessed Virgin's name in vain."

"Riiiight." Frankie scanned the menu board. "Let's get a Moose and couple of Cheerwines."

"What the hell is a 'Moose'?"

"Wings, Nick. A moose is fifteen chicken wings."

"*Only* fifteen?" I jerked a thumb toward our dark passenger. "Think that's enough?"

I had no idea where my bravado was coming from because I was plainly on the verge of a total mental breakdown.

Frankie laughed. "If you mean Ice T back there, I don't think he's got much of an appetite."

My near-hysteria had now settled into a comfortable kind of quasi-euphoria. "What makes you think it's a he?"

"Simple," she said. "That box is a six-footer. Not many women require those."

"I guess that makes sense."

We crept forward another car length.

"What are we gonna *do* with . . . Ice T?" I asked.

Frankie met my eyes. "That one's above our pay grade."

"You mean we let Antigone figure it out?"

"Roger dodger." Frankie picked up her cell phone and proceeded to text Antigone with the news that we were incoming with the asset.

The Hyundai ahead of us had finally placed its order and rolled ahead to the payment window.

I sighed and looked over at Frankie, who was now watching me with an amused expression.

In for a penny, in for a pound.

"Want fries?" I asked.

Antigone failed to express much sympathy for our predicament.

We stopped back at Boost Mobile so I could retrieve my car and follow Frankie to K-Vegas. When we arrived with the hearse, Frankie ducked inside to ask Antigone to come out to the NRB parking lot. The big woman stood scowling at the car—and at us, in turn—for a full thirty seconds before asking why we needed her to meet us outside.

"Um," I began. "We encountered an . . . unexpected . . . and somewhat . . . difficult . . . complication."

"*Complication?*" Her tone made it clear she didn't much care for the word. "What kind of complication?"

"The dead kind." Frankie walked to the back of the hearse and opened its big bay door.

Antigone's eyes rapidly grew to the size of dinner plates. "What on God's good earth is *that?*"

"A personal effect?" Frankie meekly suggested.

"*Personal effect?*" Antigone shot Frankie a murderous look. "That ain't no personal effect. That's an *unholy abomination.* Close that damn door," she bellowed at me. "And *you,*" she faced Frankie. "Gimme your copy of that work order!"

Frankie meekly retrieved the paperwork from her ubiquitous bag. Antigone yanked it from her hand and unfolded it.

"Do you see this box on line 24?" Antigone pointed it out. "Where it says 'and personal effects'? Is that box checked?"

Frankie looked at the form. "Well . . ."

"*No,*" Antigone continued. "No, that box on line 24 is *not* checked. You were sent to recover the asset *only* . . . no clothing, no jewelry, no loose change, no CDs and no damn *stowaways.*"

I leapt to Frankie's defense. "Hey . . . this isn't our fault."

"*Stow it,* Not-Vera. You're already hangin' by a thread. I told Eddie when he asked for you that you were too green for a job like this. But *you.*" She focused the full force of her righteous indignation on Frankie. "You're an undertaker's daughter. You should know better than to go joyriding with a damn corpse. That ain't conduct becoming of a lady, and it sure as hell ain't respectful. And this work order explicitly states that you were to recover the vehicle *after* 6 p.m., so Eddie could be here to pick it up. So I'll ask you: is it after 6 p.m.?" Neither of us replied. "Then allow me to clarify the time for you. No, it is *not* after 6 p.m. That means I'm stuck having to deal with this thing until Eddie shows up. Now you two get that poor soul off this property and take it back where it belongs before them people show up here lookin' for it. *Now.*"

I was confused. "You want us to take the car back?"

Antigone glared at me. "*No,* not the damn car." She pushed past me and retrieved the keys from the hearse's ignition. "*That.*" She pointed at Ice T. "You take that poor soul back to where it belongs. I ain't gonna be responsible if the police show up here lookin' for that lost property."

Back? *She wanted us to take the body back?*

"Just how are we supposed to do that?" I was flabbergasted. "Tie it to the roof of my car?"

"I do not give one rat's ass how you do it. Just *do* it."

I looked at Frankie for help, but she was busy scanning the length of my Outback.

Antigone must've noticed what Frankie was doing, too, because she raised her giant walkie-talkie to her ear and pressed its talk button. I didn't even realize she'd carried it outside with her until she fired it up. "Lamar?" she barked. "You and your brother-in-law-Roger-Coble get your asses up here right now. I need you to redistribute some inventory. *Out.*" She shot us a final, disgusted look before storming off, leaving us stranded there with our contraband.

Frankie had wandered over to my car and was opening the back door.

"Wait a minute." I faced her with desperation. "You are not seriously thinking about putting that thing in my car, are you?"

"You got a better plan?" she asked.

"It won't fit."

"We'll put the back seats down."

"I carry *groceries* in there." I was getting desperate.

"Just consider this a giant vegetable."

"Frankie . . ."

"Nick?"

I was growing frantic. "I cannot be a part of this."

"We'll deliver it in a couple of hours . . . after dark," Frankie countered. "And you're *already* a part of this."

"Not *this.*" I waved my hands around to encompass the NRB and environs. "*This.*" I pointed at the hearse.

"I'm trying, Nick. But I'm not following your logic, here."

"*No?* Well, lemme make it real simple for you. I'm a Brown

woman in a redneck state, about to go cruising around the *wrong* side of town—after dark, with a *stolen* dead body hanging out the back of my Subaru. How do *you* think that's gonna work out for me, *Becky?*"

I saw the way her features stiffened when I called her "Becky," and I regretted it right away. But it didn't change the fact that I was right, and that she knew it as well as I did. She took a moment to process our dilemma as she stood beside my car, tapping her index finger against the rear passenger door.

"Okay," she said finally. "*I'll* do it. If I get caught, I'll say I stole your car."

I slouched against the Cadillac in defeat. This day had gone from bad to worse to ridiculous at light speed.

When Lamar and his brother-in-law-Roger-Coble showed up, I watched in dumb silence as Frankie directed them to remove the box containing Ice T from the hearse and stow it in the back of my car. I marveled that they did so quickly, and without asking a single question.

Antigone ran a tight ship at Global Gospel Radio.

There was only one hitch: the box didn't quite clear the inside of the hatch door. It was about five inches too long.

"We'll have to tie it down," Frankie was saying.

Tie it down? I jerked upright. "There is no fucking way . . ."

Frankie pulled a silver Leatherman tool and a roll of synthetic twine out of her bag. "This should do it." She looked at me. "Got any rags in your car? Preferably red or orange?"

I stared back at her with my mouth gaping open.

"Never mind," she said. "We'll improvise."

She disappeared inside the NRB and emerged a couple of minutes later with some lengths of faded ribbon that she'd obviously pulled off a couple of the dead plants in the reception area. Even in my distress I admired her industry: one of the ribbons had "In Deepest Sympathy" stenciled across it in a glittery, cursive font.

Five minutes later, Ice T was safely stowed, the Outback hatch was tied down, the safety ribbons were ready to stream, and Lamar and his brother-in-law-Roger-Coble had retreated to the sanctity of their broadcast trailer behind the shopping center.

Frankie faced me. "Ready to roll?"

"What kind of people *are* we?" I asked, knowing the question was rhetorical.

I already knew the answer.

It was well after sundown before we felt it was safe enough to make the drop.

Once we were on our way back to Winston-Salem and I'd had a few minutes to adjust to the absurdity of the situation, I apologized to Frankie and told her there was no way I'd let her do the "errand" by herself. We'd gotten into this mess together, and it wasn't fair for me to leave her holding the bag—so to speak.

"Are you sure?" she asked.

"Frankly, I don't know what I am anymore," I said. "But, yes. I'm sure about this."

"I'll still drive," she offered.

"Okay. That'll help." At this point, I was thankful for any small mercy.

We agreed that waiting until just after dark to make our return visit to Blessed Slumber would ensure there'd be less chance of getting busted. Frankie suggested we drive my car straight to her house and hang out there until night fell and we knew the coast would be clear. I jumped on her idea at once. The last thing I needed was for Sebastian to get curious about our cargo. I imagined with horror the content of his first conversation with "Ro-Ro" following my hijinks. We also decided we'd pick her car up at "boots-mobile" after the drop.

Frankie also noted that not delaying our delivery for very long would be beneficial to us in *other* material ways.

"What ways?" I asked.

"Nick?" she said patiently. "It's probably 70 degrees outside. We're not going to want to leave our friend hanging around at nature's room temperature any longer than necessary."

Okay, that certain complication had not yet occurred to me.

I was duly creeped out, but I had another burning question for her. "Apropos of that, why is . . . *he* . . . in a cardboard box instead of a . . . you know?"

"A casket?"

I nodded.

"Because," Frankie explained, "he was likely on his way to a crematory."

A crematory? Dear lord . . . "How do you know that?"

"Because there's a little label on the back of the box with lots of numbers and bar codes on it. Chain of custody stuff."

"Right." I looked at my watch. We had about three more hours to wait.

I'd already decided to trade in my car.

Since I'd been in no condition to operate a motor vehicle when we left K-Vegas, Frankie drove the Outback to her place. It turned out she lived in a hundred-year-old bungalow located outside of town on Shattalon Drive. Truth be told, I was more than slightly interested in this chance to visit her house.

I did, however, insist she stop at Walgreen's on our way into town, because there were a couple of things I needed to pick up . . . right away.

"Emetrol?" she asked, when I told her I needed to make the stop.

"Very funny. I don't need any anti-nausea pills—yet. Just stop, please."

I was in the store for a bit longer than anticipated because an assistant manager decided to follow me around and hover close by while I tried to make my product selection. Why not? I mean, at any moment I might decide to shoplift a couple dozen packs of eyelash extensions or toenail fungus pads.

Whenever this happened, I intentionally took my time—regardless of how much of a rush I was in. And although I was now accustomed to this drill, it still chapped my ass.

When I got back to the car, I had to explain to Frankie why it took so long.

"Why'd he follow you around?" She seemed genuinely baffled.

"Seriously?" I waved a hand to encompass my visage.

Frankie's eyes blazed. "That's *contemptible*. What is this—1956?"

I thought about her question. "When it comes to advancements in retail policy? Pretty much."

It took the rest of the drive to her house to convince her it wasn't worth going back to the store to complain to the manager. If it hadn't been for our dark passenger, I think she would've won the argument.

A few minutes later, we pulled into the long driveway leading to her house. It was suddenly clear to me why Frankie had suggested her place as a good spot to kill the few hours until we could venture back out. The old farmhouse was located in a pretty remote area. There was little chance anyone would see our strange cargo out here.

Frankie parked in front of her detached garage—in the shade—and turned off the car. "Are you going to show me what you were so desperate to buy?"

"Only if you promise not to make fun of me."

"Why would I do that?"

About a thousand reasons occurred to me, but I kept them to myself. "You have to promise," I insisted.

"Okay." She raised her fingers in a Girl Scout salute. "Cross my heart."

I passed the small bag over to her.

I have to hand it to her: she didn't laugh—even though I could tell how much she wanted to.

She held up the sappy condolence card with "Sorry for Your Loss" written across the front in a flowery script. "What do you plan to do with this? Tape it to the box?"

"Something like that." I snatched the card back from her. "I'm Catholic, okay? Give me a break."

"I'm not judging you," Frankie insisted. "I think it's kind of sweet."

Sweet? That wasn't usually an adjective people used to describe me. "Thanks . . . I think."

"But about this other purchase . . ." Frankie held up the tube containing a boscia charcoal facial mask. "You felt an urgent need to luminize?"

"Very funny." I retrieved the mask. "It's not for *me;* it's for the license plate."

"The . . ." Now Frankie did burst into peals of merry laughter. "You're going to smear your license plate with a thirty-five dollar facial mask?"

"You got a better idea, Einstein? We haven't had rain in, like, a year—so it's not as if there's a ready supply of mud lying around."

"That is true." Frankie was still chortling. "Come on. Let's go inside. I need a drink."

"Me, too."

Frankie looked surprised. "You sure you want to risk it after last night?"

"Yeah." I opened the car door. "That Moose really took the edge off."

Frankie gave me a quick tour of her house. It was a great space. Someone had done a masterful job updating the place, but allowing it to retain most of its original farmhouse charm. It was small, but tastefully and comfortably furnished, accented everywhere with primitive antiques, colorful artwork and a lot of hand-thrown North Carolina pottery. I liked it a lot.

We went into her kitchen, and she opened a nice bottle of Portuguese wine. I was amused by the crayon drawings attached to the doors of her fridge with magnets. Several of them showed a woman with yellow hair, holding hands with a row of little people. They were surrounded by mini-trees with rounded tops, jagged rocks, and wide banners of blue sky.

"Are these pictures of you?" I asked.

"And my kids," she explained. "Those are from a field trip we took to the nature center."

"They must really like you," I commented. "They all look pretty happy."

"In fact, they mostly like field trips. But we get along okay . . . mostly." She smiled and handed me a glass of the wine. "Let's go relax. We've got some time to kill."

We spent the next couple of hours hanging out on her wide back porch, playing several cutthroat games of Scrabble.

"That is *so* not a real word." Frankie huffed and took a sip of her Tinto Alentejo.

I'd drawn the *X* tile several plays earlier, and had leapt at the first chance to offload it.

"Yes it is," I insisted.

"*X-Y-S-T-I*?" she quoted. "No way. You totally made that up."

"Is that a formal challenge?" I drummed my fingers atop her battered compact edition of the *Oxford English Dictionary*.

Frankie sat back and did her best to try and stare me down. I had news for her . . . she was gonna *lose* this contest. Perfecting an imperious stare was the first thing they taught us in litigation class.

"You suck," she said at last. "I yield. How many points is that?"

"Let's see." I rubbed my palms together. "One, plus one, plus eight, plus four, equals fourteen—times triple word score, equals forty-two. Plus one, plus four, plus one, equals six. Six plus forty-two equals forty-eight." I beamed at her. "That's forty-eight points, ma'am." I lifted my own wineglass. "Your play."

"Fuck you." Frankie added the total to my column. Her handwriting was very tidy and uniform, like a teacher's.

I smiled and looked out across her large backyard. It was surprisingly well maintained. There were numerous Asian pear trees and a small vegetable garden. She also had a bevy of bird feeders that were seeing a lot of robust business. I hadn't seen that many downy woodpeckers in eons.

"It's really nice out here. How'd you find this place?"

"It belonged to my husband's family," Frankie said. "I lucked out."

Husband? *Shit . . . it never occurred to me that Frankie was married.*

"Oh?" I tried to mask my rush of surprise tinged with disappointment. I felt like an idiot. "What's he do?"

It was a lame-ass question, but the best one I could come up with under the circumstances.

"Right now, you mean?" Frankie sounded amused. "I honestly have no idea. But if I had to guess, I'd say probably anything in a skirt. Fidelity was never his strong suit." I must've looked as perplexed as I felt. Frankie took pity on me. "We're divorced," she explained. "About six years now. He got his freedom, I got the house."

"I'm . . . sorry."

"Why? I'm not. The whole thing was a disaster. But I grew up a lot, and I figured some things out. And we're both much happier."

"At least you got this place. It's wonderful."

"I won't argue with you about that. I was shocked when his parents offered it up in the settlement. Turns out they were used to making accommodations to fix his indiscretions."

"How'd your parents handle it?" I asked.

"The divorce, you mean? They were unhappy about it, of course. But they're used to being made unhappy by my choices, so it wasn't very surprising for them."

"You mentioned you have a sister?"

"Oh, yeah. *Lilah*." Frankie pushed her chair back and crossed her legs. I made a concerted effort not to stare at the toned expanse of calf the simple action revealed. It wasn't easy. "Lilah is *not* a disappointment—apart from her penchant for dyeing her hair black and a questionable fondness for Egyptian eye makeup. She's four years older than me, an enterprising funeral director, and the heir apparent to the Stohler family business."

'She's a mortician?"

Frankie nodded. "An enthusiastic one, too. Even as a teenager, Lilah begged Dad to let her tag along to trade shows. Imagine . . . a kid her age getting off on prevailing trends in green burial. It was bizarre. For my part, I couldn't get away from that mess fast enough."

I was curious about one thing. "Did you live over the . . . you know?"

"The funeral home?"

I nodded.

"No, thank god. Mom was always adamant about that. In truth, I think the business weirds her out, too. We're alike that way. Dad used to try and coerce her to do hair at the mortuary occasionally, when things were busy. She'd always look at him like he'd just fallen off a turnip truck. 'Abel Stohler,' she'd say. 'I am *not* coming down there to backcomb hair on a corpse.' Poor Dad would just look wounded and bewildered." Frankie smiled at her recollection. "They're supremely odd, but somehow they make their relationship work."

"That's a rarity, I'll agree."

"What about your family?" Frankie asked. "Any siblings?"

"Nope. Just me. I feel bad for Mamá, too. She really wanted to have a girl—five or six of them, actually. But, alas. Her failure to pop out a legion of little Catholics became my cross to bear."

"Your father didn't want more kids?"

"Oh, no. He was fine with the idea. Strength in numbers and all of that. But Mamá said that because Papa was an infidel, she'd been cursed by St. Maximón, the trickster. He's an anomaly in Guatemalan culture—a saint who can bless you or fuck you up, according to his whim." I sighed. "So poor Mamá was deprived of having many children, and never got her precious girl."

Frankie squinted her eyes as she regarded me. "Am I missing something here?"

"You know . . . *a girl*. Foundation garments. Makeup. Birth control pills." I hesitated. "Guys."

"You don't like foundation garments?" Frankie feigned distress. "Fetch the smelling salts . . ."

"Asshole." I threw a Scrabble tile at her. To my surprise, she caught it easily—with her left hand, even.

"Hey!" she exclaimed. "This is the *Q*. It figures you'd have this one, too. Got any more bogus words up your sleeve?"

"*Xysti* is *not* a bogus word. I told you."

"So what is it, then, wise guy?"

"It's a kind of covered shelter. A place where Greek athletes trained."

"For real?" Frankie sounded impressed.

"So they tell me." I shrugged. "We played a lot of Scrabble at my house. Mamá said it was a great way to learn how to spell. She's a stickler for that since English is her second language."

"Really? Great concept. Is her first language Spanish?"

"Yes. She was born in Guatemala."

"Okay," Frankie said. "My turn to ask. What does Mamá do?"

"She's a pediatric oncologist. And a clairvoyant—at least when it comes to premonitions about anything I manage to get tangled up in."

"Good of you to keep her paranormal skills sharp."

"It's a holy calling."

Frankie smiled. "What about your dad?"

"He's a criminal defense attorney. See how complementary their skill sets are? It provided them each with an exceptional parenting experience."

"I'm going to go out on a limb here and assume they know nothing about your new job with the NRB?"

"That would be correct."

"Are you going to tell them?" she asked.

"You mean before Mamá sees it in a vision or Sebastian *accidentally* rats me out?"

"Uh huh."

"Doubtful. Besides, after today, I doubt Antigone will be offering me any more jobs."

"I wouldn't be too sure about that. Contrary to what she projects, she's terribly forgiving. And it's obvious that Eddie wants to keep us working."

"Oh, come on, Frankie. I practically had a meltdown in the damn parking lot."

"Nick? Believe me when I tell you that happens on a daily basis at the NRB."

I thought about her pronouncement. "Tell me something . . . is that place as fucked up as it seems to be? I mean . . . it's like it exists in some alternate space-time continuum where, for some inexplicable reason, people still covet overpriced muscle cars and take out bad loans to acquire them. I mean . . . Antigone and Fast Eddie? Weasel and Hugh Don? That browbeaten gospel radio guy, Lamar—*and* his cohort, Roger Coble? They're not *real* people—they're like central-casting extras who escaped from the set of a Fellini movie."

"Haven't spent a lot of time in K-Vegas, have you?"

"Apparently not. And here I thought Southwest Philly was surreal." I slowly shook my head. "This place makes my old neighborhood look like Newport with the Vanderbilts in residence."

"You're so damn adorable." Frankie patted me on the knee. "It's not surreal—it's just *real*. You've spent too much time in that ivory tower and aren't used to rubbing elbows with people who actually *work* for a living. Come on. The sun's going down. We've got about another hour to kill, so I'll make us a little something to eat. And I'll try to shed some light on your new profession."

"Okay." I got up dejectedly and followed her back inside the house. A terrifying thought crossed my mind. "You don't have any Bits O' Brickle, do you?"

Frankie was as good as her word about not teasing me for applying the charcoal facial mask to my license plate—or for the sympathy card. She even gave me a piece of duct tape to adhere the card to the top of Ice T's box. I knew it was irrational, but the simple attempt at respect made me feel better.

The other good news was that Ice T seemed to be keeping his cool . . . literally.

But that fact didn't change my resolve to offload the Subaru as soon as possible. From this day forward, the word *Outback* would always be synonymous with "cold-cut wagon."

Frankie drove us across town, wisely avoiding highways and sticking to back roads and side streets. We stopped about a block from Blessed Slumber and watched the building for about fifteen minutes, just to be sure there was no sign of activity. It seemed to be deserted. Frankie rolled forward with the lights off and slowly pulled beneath the big portico at the side of the structure, near the chapel entrance.

We kept the car running as we carefully shimmied Ice T out and lowered his box to rest atop a low wall that bordered the brick steps. There was no way we'd be able to wrangle the thing up the steps, closer to the chapel's double doors, so this was the best we could do.

"Ready?" Frankie asked me, after we had him safely situated.

"As I'll ever be," I whispered.

She darted up the steps and pushed the after-hours call button a couple of times before racing back down. We hauled ass back into the car and sped away as quickly as possible—keeping the headlights off until we cleared the next intersection. Then she hightailed it for Akron Drive and the parking lot behind Boost Mobile so she could retrieve her own car. I noticed that she managed to miss the pothole that had been my undoing earlier in the day. Once we were safely parked beside Frankie's Nissan, we sat for a couple of minutes without talking.

Frankie was first to break the silence. "So, I guess that all just happened?"

"Yeah." I felt strangely sad that our evening was at an end. For a moment, I wondered if she felt the same way. I was too chicken to ask. "What are you gonna do now?"

"Go home, I guess. Try to unwind before school tomorrow." She gazed at me through the dim light inside the car. "What about you?"

"Probably the same. I mean . . . not the school part."

"I guess going back to your day job will be a nice break from the crazy of late?"

"I suppose."

"You don't sound very sure."

"That's because I'm *not* very sure." I struggled with how much to say. "My job at TWAT is going nowhere."

"*Twat?*" Frankie repeated the word like it had nine syllables.

"Oh, god." I reached across the seat and touched her arm. "Sorry. That's the unfortunate acronym for the firm: Turner, Witherspoon,

Anders and Tyler. But, believe me," I added, "in this case, the shoe totally fits."

"Dear lord. And here I was completely mortified about 'bootsmobile.'"

I laughed. "Yeah. I don't intend to let you forget that one any time soon."

"Oh, I hope not."

I was unprepared for that response and had no idea how to reply.

I was very grateful for the dim light inside the car, and hoped it hid how flustered I felt. It wasn't the first time Frankie had said something that could be construed as flirtatious. And as much as I was beginning to understand that I wanted her to flirt with me, I knew hoping for that would only spell disaster and disappointment on an apocalyptic scale.

Just like it always did.

Frankie had been right last night: I *did* have a tell. A big damn cosmic tic that was hardwired to the pile of knee-jerk insecurity that cluttered up my core. I was hopeless.

Frankie broke our awkward silence. "Guess I'd better get going," she said. "We both have early starts tomorrow."

"Yeah. I guess."

She unfastened her seat belt and got out of my car. I got out, too, so I could reclaim the driver's seat.

"So I guess we'll see what happens next with Antigone?" I asked.

"I have no doubt we'll hear from her soon."

I paused behind my car. "Do me a favor—and don't ask why?"

She smiled. "You want me to help you peel the charcoal mask off your license plate?"

"No . . ." That problem hadn't yet occurred to me. "But I guess I should take care of that before driving home."

"Might be a good idea. I predict the tag numbers will be much more vibrant."

"They should be for thirty-five bucks."

Frankie bent down to examine the plate more closely. "I'd say let's try some of those napkins left over from lunch, but I don't think they'll do much good."

"Why not?"

"It's a mask, Nick. We're going to have to peel it off."

"*Peel?*"

"Of course. How did you think they worked?"

"I didn't think about how they worked at all." I tapped my chest. "Not a real girl, remember?"

"What-*ever*." Frankie started picking at a corner of the mask.

"Is it coming off?"

"Not easily. I think this is gonna be more complicated than you imagined."

"That figures."

Frankie looked up at me. "Maybe take it inside when you get home and try steaming it off?"

I sighed. "Sure. I can just hold it over whatever viscous vat of putrid matter Sebastian is cooking up. I'm certain it will recoil and peel away on its own."

"Let me know if that works out." Frankie's tone was droll. She stood up. "Was there something else you wanted to ask me?"

"Um. Yeah." I hesitated. "Will you shoot me a text to let me know you got home safely? I mean," I added quickly, "now that I know you live out on the edge of civilization."

Frankie could see through my flimsy explanation, and I knew it. But she was a good sport about it, anyway.

"I'd be happy to."

She was as good as her word, too. I'd only been home about fifteen minutes when I got her text.

FS: The eagle has landed.

NN: Great! Just getting ready to steam the tag.

FS: Sebastian got something cooking?

NN: Nope. I'm doing a solo. He must've had a date.

FS: On a school night?

NN: There are no school nights for gay men. Don't you know this?

FS: Apparently not.

NN: I figured I'd go ahead and take care of it. Especially since I can't go in my room right now.

FS: Why not?

NN: Carol Jenkins is in there, sprawled across my pillow.

FS: The cat???

NN: Yes, the cat.

FS: That's . . . interesting. Why not just move her?

NN: Move Carol Jenkins? You mean without full body armor or a forklift?

FS: Don't be so dramatic.

NN: I'm not being dramatic. You don't know this cat.

FS: No. But I DO know cats.

NN: Meaning?

FS: Let me talk to her.

NN: What?

FS: Let me talk to her. Call me and put her on the phone.

NN: That's crazy.

FS: It isn't crazy. I have a way with cats. It's documented.

NN: Then why don't you have any?

FS: Allergies. Bad ones. Without them, I'd have a dozen.

NN: Cats?

FS: No. Gay roommates.

NN: Smart ass.

FS: I'm not kidding, Nick. Now call me, and put her on the phone.

I was torn between giving it a try and giving in to my cascading fear that Frankie had finally gone around the bend. After all, that was destined to happen with *any* woman who piqued my . . . interest.

I was still deliberating when my cell phone rang. *Frankie.* I answered.

"Hi," I said, lamely.

"Will you stop worrying that I've turned into Bertha Rochester, and take the phone to Carol Jenkins?"

I was irrationally thrilled by her *Jane Eyre* reference probably because I felt like my prospects were about as bright as Jane's had been for most of *her* life. I tried to affect a more upbeat tone. "What makes you think I was worrying?"

"Nick . . ."

"Okay, okay. Let me try to rig something."

"Rig something? For the license plate?"

"No," I clarified. "For the phone. I'm not going to get that close to her. It isn't safe."

"Oh, please."

"I'm not kidding. The last time I tried to chase her off my bed, she shredded my comforter and I nearly lost two fingers off my right hand."

"Nick . . ."

"Just give me a minute. I'm going to attach this thing to one of Sebastian's twenty-five selfie sticks."

"Oh, good god."

"Hey." I defended myself. "It's not *that* strange an idea."

"Not that," Frankie clarified. "Sebastian really has 25 selfie sticks?"

"Welcome to my world."

Once I had the phone attached, I walked back down the hall to my bedroom and carefully stepped inside. I could see Carol Jenkins' tail begin a cautionary thump, thump, thump as she watched me.

Not a good sign . . .

"Okay. I'm now in the room," I whispered. "I'm going to approach the bed and deposit the phone next to her head. You can start talking in about five seconds."

"Roger."

After I carefully positioned the phone on the pillow beside Carol Jenkins, who was now growling, I retreated back toward the door so I could observe the progress of their "conversation" from a place of safety. I couldn't hear anything Frankie said to the obese feline, but I did notice changes in Carol Jenkins' . . . *demeanor*. There was no doubt she was listening to whatever Frankie was saying. Her eyes narrowed at first, as she shot homicidal looks at me. And her ears changed position about four times. Flat against her head, then at full alert, then flat again before ultimately relaxing into a more natural posture. She still watched me with suspicion as I hovered near the door. Finally, she stood up, stretched, yawned, and licked her front paws a few times before padding her way toward the foot of the bed. It was clear she was intending to depart the pattern, so I wisely backed out of her way. As expected, she stopped at the doorway before exiting and turned around to hiss at me.

I was pretty dumbfounded when I retrieved the phone.

"What'd you say to her?"

"I take it she left?"

"Well, yeah."

"Good. My work here is through."

"You're not gonna tell me what you said to her, are you?"

"Nope."

I was confused. "Why not?"

"Embrace the mystery, Nick. Magic is real."

"Okay, this is getting more fucked up than K-Vegas."

I could hear Frankie laugh. "There are more things in heaven and earth than are dreamt of in your philosophy."

"Right. Thanks a lot, Svengali."

"My pleasure, Trilby. You have sweet dreams now."

She disconnected.

I sat down on my bed, still holding the phone attached to the damn selfie stick.

Sweet dreams?

Not very likely.

I'd probably never know what Frankie said to Sebastian's demon cat. But I was sure about one thing: I was headed for another sleepless night.

Chapter Three

You Can't Get a Man with a Gun

Mondays at TWAT were never much fun. That was especially true if you hadn't logged twelve or twenty hours on the weekend days preceding Monday. As was the case for me when I showed up bearing two dozen Krispy Kreme doughnuts.

Belinda was in the firm's canteen getting a cup of coffee when I came in with the big, flat boxes of happiness.

"Steer clear of Tyler," she said, nabbing a doughnut before I even had a chance to deposit the boxes on the break table. "He's in a mood."

"When isn't he in a mood?"

"Today is different. The partners are all locked up in a meeting. Been in there two hours now. Jason's already got an office pool going about who's going to get canned." She took a generous bite of her doughnut. "God, I love these things when they're hot." She nodded at me. "You keep your head down, girl."

She headed back to her office in accounting.

Canned? Great. I picked exactly the right weekend to stay away from the damn office.

We were all on pins and needles until word spread that the partners' meeting had broken up. Sure enough, at ten-thirty, I got an intranet message from Tyler's admin, stating that several of the firm's senior associates should report to the conference room at eleven sharp.

Jason was in my office in less than one minute. He closed the door.

"You know what this is, right?"

"No," I answered, "but I'm sure you're going to tell me."

He was pacing back and forth in front of my desk. He was a squirrelly little guy. Frenetic, actually. He was several years younger than me, and had joined the firm six years ago, when I came on. He had a wife, three kids in private school, and a ridiculous home in Bermuda Run—an enclosed golf community located in the rarified air of western Forsyth county. It was obvious that he cared more about the zip code than the green fees. As far as I knew, Jason had never swung a golf club in his life. And it wasn't like he'd ever get the chance to play a few rounds with the senior partners.

"Dude." I raised my hands in a placating gesture. "You need to calm down."

"I *can't* calm down." His pacing had accelerated to striding. "Brittney will lose her shit."

"Sit down, man." I got up and pushed a chair toward him. "Lose her shit about what?"

He collapsed into the chair. "Does your spinal cord not touch your brain? They're going to *can* us."

"Oh, come on. *That's ridiculous*. Why would they do that?"

"History, man. It's what they *always* do." His foot was tapping faster than a Goldwyn Girl in a Busby Berkeley production. "Cocksucking bottom feeders . . ." he muttered.

To be clear, it wasn't like I'd never heard the apocryphal stories about how firms like TWAT routinely shed half of their junior associates every six or seven years, and took on a new crop of freshly minted law school grads. It was a reviled business model and unethical as hell. But "unethical" conduct for a law firm was a floating decimal point, at best. Still, I chose to eschew those conspiracy theories and believe that hard work and industry would be rewarded.

Cue the soaring refrain from "America The Beautiful."

"What the fuck am I gonna do?" Jason was now talking aloud to himself. "I'm gonna end up as a capper for some ambulance chaser. I just *know* it." He dropped his head into his hands. I was shocked when the overhead light revealed how much his hair had thinned out. "I'm so screwed."

"Come on, man." I was desperately trying to come up with something encouraging to say to him, even though his distress was becoming infectious. "We're *bigger* than this. If it happens, we'll figure something out."

"Easy for *you* to say," he looked up at me. "You'll be the last one they let go."

His implication was impossible to miss. My reaction to his comment must've been apparent by the look on my face.

"Hey . . . I'm sorry, Nick. That was outta line. I didn't mean that . . . I'm just . . ."

As pissed and disappointed as I was, I let him off the hook. "Don't worry about it. It's fine."

I could hear Uncle Rio's voice in my head, telling me I should knee him in the balls.

It was sad and depressing, but it was always the same. When push came to shove, it didn't matter how well you thought you knew somebody. When people got scared or threatened, they retreated to their safest and most reflexive spaces—no matter how base or foundationless they were. It left me with a strange predicament. If Jason's fears proved accurate, would my mixed race ensure that I'd be the one associate left standing?

Did I even want that outcome? I'd been miserable at TWAT for years. The only thing that kept me hanging on was the vague belief that I'd eventually make partner. And even if that came to pass, which was looking increasingly unlikely, what would I have to look forward to? Thirty more years of kowtowing to other upstanding pillars of the community like Mozelle?

For once, I actually wanted to talk something through—with Mamá . . .

Jason was back on his feet. "I need a drink. I've still got that bottle of Dalwhinnie I lifted at Witherspoon's retirement party. You want some?"

I shook my head. "No. Go knock yourself out."

"I wish I could, man." He looked at his watch before heading to the door. "T-minus twenty minutes. Guess I'll see you in there."

I sat down and stared at my phone.

Who could I call? There really wasn't anyone who could talk me off this ledge.

My cell phone began to vibrate. I fumbled beneath a stack of papers and picked it up to silence it. The caller ID read, "Antigone Reece." I held it in my palm for a few seconds, debating whether or not to answer it.

What the hell? I pushed the talk button.

"Hello?"

"Not-Vera?" Her greeting was like an accusation. I felt my ambient sense of guilt wake up and roll over. "I got one more recovery job for you and Debbie Reynolds. You get this one right—with no damn surprises—you can start training with Linda on one of the stealth trucks. You interested?"

Was I?

"Um . . . you talked with Frankie yet?"

"That wasn't my question, was it? You interested? Yes or no? I ain't got time to waste while you figure things out."

Through my office window, I could see some of the other beleaguered associates making their fateful way toward the conference room.

I closed my eyes.

"Yeah," I said. "I'm interested."

I was a mess at home that night.

They gave us each twenty minutes to collect our personal belongings before escorting us out like a chain gang of convicted felons. I sat in my car with a cardboard box filled with the detritus of my tenure at TWAT on the front seat beside me. It was pathetic, really. Six years at that place and all I had to show for it was a chipped Camel City coffee mug, a tiny "Gatti di Roma" desk calendar Mamá had sent me from their vacation in Italy last summer (a tribute to Carol Jenkins), my prized Aurora fountain pen, a dented tin of cinnamon Altoids, an ancient gray cardigan of Papa's, and my framed JD degree from Wake Forest.

That was it.

I called Sebastian on the ride home and filled him in on what had happened.

"Those assholes," he said. "Good riddance to bad fucking news."

"You did hear me, right? I just got fired."

"*Au contraire.* You didn't get *fired*, you got laid off. It's not the same thing."

"When it comes to our household finances, it's a semantic difference without meaning."

"Pish, posh. It's not like you're a profligate spender or anything. You'll be *fine*. We'll be fine," he added.

"I wish I shared your optimism."

"Do us both a huge favor and don't get how you get? They're scum and you're better off rid of that place."

"Sebastian?" I was dangerously close to losing it. "Will you give me permission to feel like shit for at least an hour or two? I worked my ass off at that place and they just tossed me out like yesterday's trash. I'm feeling kind of fragile right now."

"Hey." He relented and relaxed his tone. "No worries, all right? You go home, fix a drink and take a long, hot bath. I'll pick us up something great for dinner. We'll figure things out, I promise. And after we do, we'll binge-watch *Killing Eve*."

My level of distraction made it impossible for me to argue with him—or to worry about what he might choose to make for dinner.

I was still in the bath when I heard him enter the house.

"Nick?" He hollered from the kitchen.

"I'm in the bathroom," I called back.

"Well, get dressed and come out here."

What's his damn rush? I thought, as I dried myself off. *Dare I hope he got takeout?*

No . . . the universe was never that kind.

I was rolling up the sleeves on my denim shirt when I joined him in the kitchen. He was busy setting the table . . . for three.

"What's going on?" I asked with more than a trace of panic.

"Frankie's coming over."

"*What?*" I was incredulous. "You *called* her?"

He shrugged. "She said she needed to talk with you about another heist. So I thought, why not kill two birds with one stone?"

"*What* two birds?" I was torn between wanting to murder him, or running back to the bathroom to try and do something with my hair.

"Bird one: making you some money until you figure out your next move. Bird two: planting your flag on Planet Stohler."

"You're completely off your rocker. I cannot believe you'd do this . . . tonight, of all nights."

"Why *not* tonight?" He walked to the wall oven and set the temperature. "You're more malleable when you're demoralized."

"I don't want her to see me like this . . ."

Sebastian turned around and looked me over. "While it's true that your current presentation leaves a lot to be desired, Frankie has *no* problems with how you look. You're gorgeous—in that clumsy, accidental, exotic-blend-of-genes way."

"'Exotic blend of genes'?" I quoted.

He waved a hand at me. "You know what I mean . . . that whole Guatemala-meets-Wakanda thing you've got going on. Even *your* total lack of fashion sense can't completely disguise it."

I looked at him in wonder. "Who says shit like this?"

"Just go open some wine." He waved me off. "Something decent that'll go with spicy food." He was unloading aluminum containers from a big shopping bag. "I got takeout from The Porch."

The Porch was our favorite Tex-Mex restaurant.

I actually perked up for a moment. "Did you get me Texas Pete Chicken Flautas?"

"Yes."

"And a side of tots and queso?"

"*Yes.*" He hauled an enormous receptacle from the bag. "Enough to make your preteen palate sing snappy Old Testament songs."

I smiled. Sebastian was a total pain in my ass, but he was also my best friend, and I loved him dearly.

"Thanks for doing this, man," I said with sincerity. "I mean it."

"Try not to worry, okay?" For once, his big brown eyes lacked their customary tinge of mirth. "It'll all work out. I promise."

For a minute, I almost believed him.

I threw caution to the wind and opened our last two bottles of the Spier 21 Gables South African Sauvignon Blanc we'd bought on sale at Thanksgiving. I filled a large bucket with ice and stuck them both into it. They'd be perfect with the spicy food.

I debated about whether I should go and try to make myself more presentable, but decided against it. This wasn't a *date,* no matter how Sebastian chose to characterize it. My biggest concern was how to avoid appearing as miserably inadequate as I felt. Luckily, I knew that pulling that off would take more than a change of clothes. It would require another twenty-four months of therapy—probably twice a week.

When Frankie arrived, she didn't seem the least bit concerned about decorum. She walked straight toward me and drew me into a bear hug. It didn't last long, but it was warm and genuine, and it felt . . . *nice*. I hugged her back belatedly and was quickly confronted with one of those awkward situations where you didn't want to hang on too long, but you didn't want to be the first one to let go, either.

As usual, Sebastian took care of the situation for me.

"Okay you two," he blustered, "we came to see a fight, not a dance."

Frankie and I stepped apart.

"I'm so sorry that happened, Nick," she said. "You certainly didn't deserve it."

"It's okay," I replied, trying to project that it wasn't as cataclysmic as it actually was. "I can't say it wasn't unexpected. The firm has a reputation for behavior like this."

"Yeah. Real princes at that joint." Sebastian ushered us both toward the kitchen. "Let's go get some wine and sort this mess out. I think a lot better with a ninety-plus-point vintage coursing through my veins."

"That's debatable," I muttered.

"Sounds inviting." Frankie elbowed me as we made our way to the kitchen. "What are we having?"

"I opened a South African Sauvignon Blanc," I explained. "Two of them, actually."

Frankie beamed at Sebastian. "That should go perfectly with Tex-Mex."

"Honey, they go together like Roberta Flack and Donny Hathaway." Sebastian snatched one of the bottles from the ice bucket and poured us each a generous glass. "Sit down while the food hots up. I'm gonna put on some music." He retrieved his iPhone from the kitchen counter.

"Not that dance crap," I begged. "I'm already hanging by a thread here."

"Will you please show a little *R-E-S-P-E-C-T*?" The unmistakable, honey-infused cry of Nina Simone snaked around us.

At least somebody was "Feeling Good."

"I love this song," Frankie cooed.

"Outrage and genius, baby. They go hand in hand." Sebastian wielded his wineglass with a flourish before glaring at me. "You got the outrage part down. It's time to jump-start some genius."

"Meaning?" I asked.

"Meaning we need to turn this liability into an asset . . . the *recoverable* kind. Right Frankie?"

Frankie nodded with enthusiasm. "We got another assignment offer from Eddie. And Antigone says that this one, if we can pull it off, promises a big payout."

Big? Big could encompass a lot of real estate. "What neighborhood of 'big' are we discussing?" I asked.

"The four-figure kind." Frankie withdrew the work order from her inevitable quilted bag. It occurred to me that the seemingly bottomless accessory accompanied her everywhere.

"What is it with you and that purse?" I asked. "It's like the Queen and her Kelly bag."

Frankie gave me a blank look. "What's a Kelly bag?"

Sebastian's sharp intake of breath was momentous. He regarded Frankie with a pained expression. "I thought I *knew* you."

I waved him off. "Don't listen to him. He's already around the bend. It's her *purse* . . . the little black bag QE2 carries everywhere—even inside the palace. Nobody can figure it out. I mean, what could the Queen possibly need to keep at arm's length at all times?"

"Her lipstick?" Sebastian suggested. "A compact? Hankie? Cab fare? Her Match 6 winning Lotto ticket?" He thought about it. "A prehistoric IUD she keeps for sentimental reasons?"

Frankie stifled a laugh. "Maybe Britain's nuclear launch codes?"

"Doubtful," I offered. "If she had access to those, she'd probably have solved the Prince Andrew problem by now."

"Well, whatever she carries around," Frankie explained, "I doubt it includes three dozen generic car keys, a collapsible Slim Jim, a roll of synthetic twine, mace, and the phone numbers of four bail bondsmen."

"Dang, girl." Sebastian was visibly impressed. "I've clearly underestimated you."

"Oh, I also have lipstick in here," she added. "Just no IUD. At least, not anymore."

Sebastian regarded me with one of his *I told you so* looks. I did my best to ignore him.

"So what about this potential job?" I asked her. "Why's it offer such a big payoff promise?"

"It's a car repo," Frankie explained. "Nothing exotic about that part. It's some kind of hopped-up muscle car. A vintage Mustang Shelby GT500. The guy—his name is Larry Cecil—is apparently some kind of repeat offender, so he's got history with Eddie. But the pickup is tricky this time because Eddie says Cecil is wise to us, and never leaves the car parked anyplace accessible, or out of his sight. I gather they've already tried to jack it a couple of times without success. And he cautions that Cecil is usually packing."

"*Packing?*" I wasn't sure I'd heard her correctly. "You mean he's always carrying a *gun*?"

She nodded. "Something like that."

"Are you *nuts?* We're not doing this."

"Don't be so hasty." Sebastian held up a restraining hand. "Let the woman share the rest of the pertinent details."

"Sebastian," I faced him. "There is only *one* pertinent detail related to this job: the one that involves *guns*." I looked back at Frankie. "We are not doing this."

"It might not be that complicated." She addressed Sebastian. "He's in construction. I looked up the site where's he's working right now. It's in a residential neighborhood, and all the guys have to park their cars on the street near the building site, so that presents the best opportunity for recovery. At night, he keeps it locked up in a garage behind his house."

Something piqued Sebastian's curiosity. "What are they building?"

"A house. A couple of them, in fact. It's part of a new subdivision over off South Peace Haven Road."

Sebastian reached for his laptop. "Know the address?" The oven timer dinged. "Get that food out, will you Nick?"

While I retrieved the containers of hot flautas, enchiladas and tots, Sebastian looked up the subdivision project on his MLS software. "Yeah. It looks like they're adding three more units backing up to Deep Ravine Court, with plans for a butt-load more. We have a few listings over there."

"That matches with what Antigone said in her notes. I gather the site is pretty wide open and doesn't offer much cover."

"I don't doubt that." Sebastian refilled our wineglasses. "They pretty much clear-cut and bulldoze everything before throwing up these shitty slab houses. You'll need a monster-sized distraction."

I stood regarding the two of them with amazement. "You're both certifiable. Are you choosing to ignore the whole 'he's usually packing' caveat?" I waved my hands around in circles to get their attention. I was still wearing a pair of big, padded oven mitts that looked like great white sharks, so I'm sure I looked more than half crazed.

In fact, I *was* more than half crazed.

"*R-E-L-A-X.*" Sebastian addressed me with exaggerated calm. "I have a plan that might level the playing field for you."

"Would you *please* quit spelling shit? You're giving me hives." I dropped into my chair.

"What kind of plan?" Frankie was leaning toward Sebastian in rapt attention.

"The units they're building back up to a cul-de-sac." Sebastian began heaping our plates with generous portions of everything. I noticed that he gave me most of the tots, but even that was cold comfort. "It just so happens that we're managing one of those houses as a rental. And unless I miss my guess, it's still vacant."

"Okay," Frankie said in a way that invited him to continue with his idea.

"So, he's a bubba, right?" Frankie nodded. He looked her over critically and waved his fork around to encompass her . . . *distractibles.* "Honey, I think you're packing everything you'll need to keep him occupied long enough for Eeyore over there to jack his ride and drive it straight into financial stability."

Frankie and I exchanged glances. Although I couldn't argue with Sebastian's summary of her "distractions," I knew enough to be wary of his plan. "Please," I entreated her. "Remember Lot's wife. Leave this evil place, and don't look back."

She swatted at me playfully.

"As I was saying," Sebastian continued. "Imagine a scenario where one fine, *hot* sunny day, Miss Thing here gets a hankering to hand-wash her car . . . out behind her new lovely cul-de-sac home—in full view of the construction site, wearing her Daisy Dukes and a flimsy tank top . . . a *white* tank top. I'll even provide some ZZ Top CDs for the boom box."

He clapped his hands together to suggest this was all a no-brainer.

I jumped to my feet so fast I nearly knocked my chair over.

"Absolutely not!"

Frankie laid a restraining hand on my arm. "Wait a minute. I think it could work."

"Are you *crazy?*"

"Honey," Sebastian observed, "it's not healthy to always be flying around as torn up as a wind-blown newspaper. You gotta quit saying that every blessed thing is *crazy*. It's time to update your toolbox of snappy comebacks."

"Fuck. You." I growled. "There is no *way* we're doing this."

"Nick," Frankie said patiently. "This can *work*. If it does, you'll be looking at a payoff that might take some of the sting out of what happened today. It can buy you time to figure out your next move."

My next move? I wondered if COBRA would cover gunshot wounds . . .

I rubbed a hand across my forehead. I was getting a migraine. It was true that I'd never *had* a migraine before, but I was pretty sure the absurdity and hopelessness of the situation would be enough to spark one.

"Can we just eat and think about this later?" I pleaded. "I don't feel so good."

"Sure we can, love chunks." Sebastian ladled about a pint of molten queso atop my mound of tots. "Everything goes better with carbs."

Miraculously, Sebastian's plan seemed more reasonable after we ate—and had finished the second bottle of wine and were well into a third. Well . . . *I* was well into a third.

Frankie and I agreed to do a drive-by the next evening and scope out the site—and the rental house.

"You'll have to hot-wire the car," Frankie explained. "There is no extra key."

I was alarmed. "How do I learn how to do that?"

"Same way I did," she said. "We'll go by the NRB and practice a few times on Linda's car."

"She won't mind?"

"Nah. She views it as a public service."

"Nice of her," I muttered.

"If everything checks out, maybe we can shoot for grabbing the car on Saturday?"

I was surprised by that. "You think they'll be working on Saturday?"

Frankie looked at Sebastian.

"Oh, yeah." He nodded. "They'll be working. They're already running six weeks behind schedule. They want these matchstick houses ready to flip ASAP. They're already missing the first wave of new residents flocking to Baptist Hospital. They gobble up available housing like locusts."

I knew better than to question Sebastian's authority when it related to any discussion of the current real estate market. When it came to housing trends—and cosmetics—he knew his business.

Truthfully, I was running out of arguments to short-circuit the ridiculous plan. If these guys were human—and I had no doubt they were—there'd be next to no way they'd be able to resist the spectacle Frankie would present, washing her car in such skimpy clothing. I wasn't even sure about my own ability to stay focused on the goal of her performance.

It was mortifying to admit that this latter concern formed my profoundest objection to Sebastian's absurd enterprise.

"Okay." I reached for the wine bottle. "Will one of you promise to pour me into bed later?"

Frankie gave me another one of those *this might be flirty* looks, but I was too morose and too persuaded that the universe was teetering on the brink of imminent incineration to allow myself to wonder.

Thankfully, Sebastian was always prepared to step into any obliging void.

He raised a perfectly tweezed eyebrow. "I'd say sweet snoozles are definitely in your future."

I picked Frankie up after school the next afternoon and we drove out South Peace Haven to cruise the construction site.

Sebastian's hunch about the rental house on the cul-de-sac proved accurate. It was empty, as were the houses on both sides of it, and readily available as a staging ground for the recovery plan. We parked in the driveway, and Frankie and I got out of the car and walked around to the back of the rental house. It had a large, concrete slab patio in lieu of a deck, and a conveniently located hose bib. The lot was woefully bereft of trees or any other kind of landscaping, so there was an unobstructed view of the construction site. One or two workers were still there finishing up, but most of the crew had left by the time we arrived. The high-dollar Shelby was nowhere in sight—although we could see the makeshift dirt road at the front of the site, where the crew parked their vehicles.

Places like this depressed the shit out of me. Empty little cookie-cutter houses that were bleak, characterless and perfectly situated to host the little floor show Sebastian and Frankie had cooked up.

"Are you really sure about this?" I asked Frankie for about the zillionth time.

"Yes. Will you please relax? If anyone should be worried, it's me. About you."

"Me?" I was surprised by her comment. "Why on earth would you be worried about me?"

"Because, nimrod—you'll have *one* shot at getting that car out of there. If I don't manage to fully distract Mr. Always-Packing, this entire enterprise could go south in a hurry."

As much as I'd worried about this scheme, that prospect had never occurred to me. Probably because I found it impossible to imagine that anyone would fail to be distracted by Frankie, draped across the massive hood of a ridiculous car, soaking wet. It wasn't exactly a counter argument I felt comfortable making right then . . .

"I'll get it out," I said, instead. "And as soon as I'm outta there, you invent a reason to hightail your scantily clad butt out, too."

She laughed. "I might need time to rinse the soap off first."

"This isn't funny, Frankie. I mean it . . . you get out of there. I don't want you hanging around when Bubba discovers we've jacked his ride."

She laid a hand on my arm. "I'm just teasing you. Of course I'll take off as soon as you're clear."

"Just see that you do."

"I guess Sebastian's told you that his brother is lending us a hopped-up ride to use as a decoy?"

"He mentioned something about it."

"We can already have it parked out back, along with all the washing paraphernalia, so I can leave my car at the street for a quicker getaway. Sebastian said we could retrieve Ricky's car and the rest of the gear later that night. He's even getting us a key so I can exit through the house."

I was impressed. "Maybe Antigone needs to put *him* on the payroll, too?"

"Don't think the thought hasn't occurred to me."

I stood there for a few moments lost in thought. Frankie noticed.

"What are you going to do the rest of the night?"

I shrugged. "Probably sit at home and grow tumors."

"I don't think so." Frankie took hold of my arm. "Come on. Let's go get something to eat."

I followed her with reluctance. "Not too expensive, okay? I'm now on a fixed income."

"I think you can afford the place I have in mind."

Fifteen minutes later, we were seated on plastic chairs at one of the six or seven tables located inside Slappy's Chicken on Acadia Avenue. To say the place looked . . . *sketchy* . . . was an understatement. The interior was spartan and eclectic—but it looked clean. Frankie described their fried chicken as somewhere between Nashville hot and Southern barbecue, but different—both spicy and sweet in perfect harmony.

We each ordered leg quarters with sides of collard greens and Slappy's signature mac-n-cheese, topped with toasted Cheez-It crackers. The food wasn't just good, it was mind-blowingly good. Not even the plastic flatware or paper iced tea cups dulled the sheer epicurean pleasure of the dining experience.

"What is it with you and all the fried chicken?" I asked her between mouthfuls of food.

"You're kidding me, right? I grew up in this town. There are two things a Stohler can always tell you: how much your grandaddy's eternal sendoff is gonna cost, and where to get the best fried chicken. In Winston-Salem, that pretty much means this place, Miss Ora's, or Mountain Fried Chicken."

"Oh, god." I held up a palm. "Please don't ever say the "M" word again."

"Oh, come on. Once you got over the creep factor of eating fried food in a hearse, you loved it."

"Do not remind me, okay? I still have nightmares about that."

"Still? Nick it's only been two days."

"Whatever. It's a trauma that'll take me years to recover from."

Frankie laughed. "How about some banana pudding?"

"How can you possibly still be hungry?"

"I have an active metabolism. Always have. Fortunately, I don't seem to gain weight . . . yet. My mother loves to tell me that one day I'll wake up and look like Totie Fields."

"Totie Fields?"

"Legendary performer before our time." Frankie waved a hand. "Imagine Carol Jenkins onstage at the Copacabana."

"Oh." I was tempted to thank her for a new mental image that was worse than my memories of Mountain Fried Chicken. "Well, I guess we have that in common."

"Active metabolisms?"

"No. Mothers who love to warn us about certain doom or, in my case, failure." I sighed. "Nice of me to hand her a fresh supply of raw material to prove the veracity of her prognostications."

Frankie reached across the small metal table and took hold of my hand. "Will you please try to go a bit easier on yourself? What happened at the firm was not your fault."

I met her eyes. "Tell that to Mamá."

"I hope I get the chance."

I wasn't sure how to reply to that. More than anything, I wanted to be brave enough to throw caution to the wind and simply ask, "What *is* your damn story, anyway?" But I wasn't brave enough. And right now, I needed her friendship too much to risk losing it over a mistaken supposition.

I decided to play it safe and retreat to higher ground. It was getting too dangerous down here in the trenches.

"So, when are we going to K-Vegas to practice on Linda's car?"

Frankie's expression changed. It was subtle—just the slightest hint of some shift in her gaze.

She slowly withdrew her hand. "I thought maybe tomorrow, if you're free? You can pick me up after school again—or I can meet you over there, if that's easier."

Easier? Why would driving to K-Vegas separately be easier?

Because you're an idiot, Mamá's voice reminded me.

"No," I replied quickly. Probably too quickly, because Frankie looked startled. "I'll pick you up. Same time as today?"

"Sure. That should work." She started collecting our plastic plates and flatware.

"Aren't you getting dessert?"

"Nah. I'm not really hungry after all."

I felt like a lout and I didn't know why. "What are you going to do the rest of the night?" I asked lamely.

"I dunno. Probably some schoolwork and watch reruns of *The Great British Baking Show*."

"For real?" I hadn't expected that response. "You watch that?"

"Yeah." She nodded. "Why are you surprised?"

"Probably because Sebastian makes me watch cooking shows all the time, and this is the *only* one I can get through without becoming completely homicidal."

"It has a calming effect on me, too. It's amazing how mesmerizing it can be to watch people be completely absorbed with nothing more than baking the perfect sponge. It's better than Xanax, actually."

"I guess so. Some of the other shows aren't that bad, either." I was still thinking about Sebastian and his addiction to *Chopped*. "At least Amanda Freitag is pretty hot."

It was Frankie's turn to express confusion. "I guess so . . ."

"You kind of look like her," I added—plainly without considering the implication of my comment.

Frankie seemed genuinely flummoxed now.

I didn't blame her.

What the hell was I doing back in the trenches?

"I'm sorry," I blurted. "I shouldn't have said that."

"It's okay. I'm . . . flattered."

"You are?"

"Sure."

Okay. That was a relief. *Maybe I hadn't gone too far . . .*

"I think she's kind of hot, too." Frankie added.

Suddenly, "too far" became a moving target—one that was shifting around so quickly I could no longer track it. I needed a distraction. *Fast.*

"Do you wanna go cruise car lots?" I asked.

By now, I think Frankie had given up trying to make sense of anything I said. She didn't even bother to ask me why I was still thinking about trading in my Outback when I'd just lost my job—which would've been the first words out of Mamá's mouth.

"Why not?" She stood up and carried our dishes to the waste bin. "It beats the hell out of lesson plans."

As relieved as I was that she agreed to go with me, I wasn't sure I agreed with her summation.

After all, I suspected that lesson plans were precisely what *I* needed—especially if they could teach me how to avoid sinking into the gargantuan pit of quicksand that suddenly stretched out all around me.

But the advent of a roadmap to save me wasn't very likely.

Soy un imbécil.

I didn't even need Mamá's help figuring this one out.

The rest of the week was kind of a blur for me. I was like a fish out of water. Not having to go into the office was just . . . *weird.* I wasn't used to not working. Even throughout high school and as an undergrad at Haverford, I had part-time jobs. My parents pretty much required it. Neither of their families had the financial wherewithal to help them, and they both believed paying my share of the freight would build character and eliminate any stray sense of entitlement I might fall heir to by virtue of our upwardly mobile circumstances.

Fat chance.

I don't think any lingering traces of "entitlement" would've come my way even if my parents had popped for the full tuition tab. My moribund spirit was pretty much established early in life. According to Aunt Estela, I'd been born "dragging the chain of El Cadejo." Since Guatemalan folklore taught that there were both good and bad incarnations of the dog-like spirit, I had a lot of latitude to interpret her prophesy as either a blessing or a curse. These days, it was pretty much even money.

Of course, Papa just shrugged and said Aunt Estela was nuts, like most of Mamá's people. It's worth noting that Mamá didn't usually disagree with his assessment of her kin.

I puttered around the house the first full day, cleaning out closets and drawers—the kinds of things you always swear to do but never quite get around to. While engaged in this busywork, I also had the misfortune to answer seven landline calls from someone identified as "Potential Spam."

For my money, "Potential Spam" deserved some credit for their great industry in trying repeatedly to sell me, in no particular order, a subscription to Dish TV, an extended warranty on my Outback, Visa fraud protection, and a shiny new set of French Leaf Guard gutters. Oh. And some Medicare supplements that offered first-rate vision care, which sounded interesting, but were a bit premature.

Maybe they were trying to reach Carol Jenkins?

I was actually tempted to bite on the gutters. Sebastian wasn't much for manual labor, and yard work normally fell to me. Of course, I'd have more time for it now . . .

As much as I tried to push Sebastian's absurd erotic car-washing scheme out of my mind, I couldn't quite shake it. It wasn't clear to me whether my frustration about the plan was tied more to the certainty that we'd get busted and I'd end up with a bullet in my ass—or the even greater certainty that I'd be so distracted by Frankie's performance that I'd screw up the entire enterprise myself.

Either way, I was pretty sure I was going to end up with a bullet in my ass . . .

That prognostication wasn't helped when I went outside to dump a load of shredded paper into the recycle bin and saw that a hopped-up, vintage white Trans Am had been parked commando-style in our driveway.

What the hell?

The thing had a massive black-and-gold screaming chicken decal on the hood.

Screaming chicken . . . *sweet mother of pearl.*

If Mamá'd been there, she'd have clucked her tongue and told me the omens were bad. *Very* bad.

There was no driver in sight.

I got a sinking feeling. *Ricky.* I had nearly forgotten that Sebastian was going to ask his brother if we could borrow one of his doped-out rides for Saturday's escapade. "Leave the details to me," he'd said at dinner the other night. Unless I missed my guess, one of those 'details' was now cooling its jets in our driveway.

Dear lord . . . even parked the thing looked like it was going 150 miles per hour.

Yeah. My ass was grass all right. I decided I should just go ahead and tattoo a target on my butt and make it easier for Heathcliff, the pistol-packing construction worker. We'd *never* pull this caper off.

The rest of the week didn't get much better for me. I ran out of drawers and closets to clean by Wednesday, and I was getting bored and desperate enough to think about tackling Carol Jenkins' room—if I could come up with a way to smoke her out of there first. Fortunately, sanity prevailed and I ended up spending most of the day watching back-to-back reruns of *Airplane Repo* on Hulu.

I considered this research for my new career path.

On Thursday, Frankie and I went to K-Vegas, as arranged, to meet Weasel at the NRB so I could practice hot-wiring Linda's car.

Mamá would be so proud of her baby girl . . .

I was intrigued about finally getting to meet someone I'd heard so much about. I didn't really know what to expect, but the man who met us in the lot out behind the NRB, beside the single-wide trailer that housed the broadcast studios for Global Gospel Radio, was unlike anything I could've imagined. For one thing, he was a lot taller—uncommonly tall, in fact. And he was rail thin, too. His skin was dark and leathery, like he'd spent a couple of lifetimes working outside in direct sun. It was impossible to guess how old he was—he could've as easily been fifty as seventy. He wore a grease-stained and faded navy blue jumpsuit with a tattered pocket patch that read *Kyle*. One look into his humorless, dark brown eyes persuaded me that *not* asking about the name would be the better part of valor.

When Weasel set about teaching me the nuances of starting a car without keys, he exhibited a kind of timeless ease and patience, which I hadn't experienced since I was a kid and my grandma spent an entire Saturday teaching me how to make old-fashioned thumbprint cookies. Weasel was that kind of teacher: almost genteel, in his quiet, abbreviated way. Every time I got it wrong, he'd just patiently demonstrate the right sequence all over again.

Just like Grandma . . .

It was clear he had a soft spot for Frankie, too. He called her "little sister," and seemed to take an almost paternal interest in teaching her the right ways to do things.

Hot-wiring a car was a tedious process with about six steps. And it was important to be able to work your way through them all quickly and efficiently—without electrocuting yourself in the process. I was nervous as hell at first, but after my fourth or fifth try, I grew less tentative and seemed to get the hang of it. Weasel grunted to show his approval and suggested we try an alternative maneuver on another obliging vehicle parked out back.

"This un'll work." He walked toward a beat-up, pea green Plymouth Reliant and motioned for us to follow him.

I shot a nervous glance at Frankie. "Whose car is that?" I whispered nervously.

She smiled. "I think it's Lamar's—or maybe his brother-in-law, Roger Coble's."

Lamar's? *Dear lord.* "Doesn't that poor man suffer enough already?" I asked.

"Hey, Weasel?" Frankie called out to the beanpole of a man. "Will Lamar be okay if we practice on his car?"

"Hell if I know," he said. "If we bust the starter I can put another one in for him. Got about twenty of 'em in the shop."

I wasn't sure if I agreed that ripping a wiring harness loose from the steering column of someone's car counted as not breaking anything . . . but I guessed Weasel knew as much about putting things back together as taking them apart. Which, in retrospect, seemed like an enviable life skill.

"Now this here is a technique that works real well on your older cars. A lot less fuss, and all you need is a flathead screwdriver and a hammer." He waved the aforementioned tools at me.

"What kind of older cars?" I asked.

"Just about anything built before about 1990."

I looked at Frankie and she flashed me a thumbs-up sign. I didn't know any of the details about the car we were going after on Saturday—just that it was expensive, and that Heathcliff never let it out of his sight.

Weasel had me sit down on the driver's seat of Lamar's car and handed me the screwdriver and a hammer. "Stick the screwdriver into the starter with the flat part straight up, like a key." I did as he directed. "Now take the hammer and tap it on in."

"How far?" I asked.

"Couple of taps. Just until you feel it break past the starter pins. You'll be able to tell."

I did as he directed. After about three good taps, the screwdriver slid in past the first barrier and seemed to seat.

"Now turn the screwdriver like a key," Weasel directed.

I did, and the car started right up.

Weasel nodded his head. "On these older cars, you don't have to worry about bypassing the steering wheel lock. So once it fires up, you're good to go."

"Hot damn." I felt irrationally pleased. Part of me wanted to call uncle Rio and let him know I wasn't a complete failure as a dyke. Proficiency like this was the kind of thing that would give me serious street cred in Southwest Philly.

After I climbed out of the battered K car, Weasel promised he'd repair Lamar's starter cylinder, and gave us his blessing to go forward with our plan to jack the elusive muscle car on Saturday.

"Don't you two take no shit—and don't go gettin' into a situation that might get you shot up, neither. Ain't no damn car worth that." He looked at Frankie. "You hear me, little sister?"

"I hear you. I promise . . . if it looks bad, we'll bail on it."

"See that you do. You two get on with the rest of your night." He waved us off. "I'll fix this starter and tell Antigone y'all are checked out."

Frankie and I got into her car for the short ride back to Winston. We hadn't driven very far when I asked her about what Antigone had said about this job.

"Why do you think Eddie asked for us to jack this car?"

"Beats me. Maybe he thinks it's the best way to get Antigone to give us some work. I don't think she'd do it on her own."

"Me either." I thought about what Frankie suggested. "But why would he *care* about giving us work? I mean, us in particular?"

"I have no idea. Why? Are you concerned about it?"

"Maybe. I don't know. We aren't exactly the most experienced people on the payroll at the NRB."

"True. But maybe it's because we *are* inexperienced he thinks we'll take on these trickier repos—because we don't know enough to know better."

That seemed to make sense. "Probably," I agreed. "But something about it still seems odd."

"Hey, we've got a pretty good record so far."

"Unless you want to count that minor kerfuffle with Ice T."

Frankie laughed merrily. "I wouldn't call that a 'kerfuffle.' I'd call it a first-class goat fuck."

"That's one way to put it."

"Besides, Antigone seemed to deal with it pretty well."

"If you call that 'well,' I'd sure hate to see what *badly* looks like for her."

Frankie didn't say anything and we rode along in silence for a bit. It started to drizzle. Part of me hoped it would intensify and settle in for a few days—long enough for us to have to cancel the car-washing scheme on Saturday.

"This wasn't predicted." Frankie turned on the windshield wipers.

"Almost nothing in life is—except death and taxes."

"You're always so damn cheerful."

"This from the woman who grew up with an undertaker?"

Frankie shrugged. "And a hairdresser. Don't discount that. I like to think I had hope and despair doled out in even measure."

That made me smile. "I forgot to tell you that Ricky dropped off a car for us to use on Saturday. It's now holding court in our driveway."

"Really?" Frankie sounded excited. "What'd he bring?"

"Brace yourself. It's a turbo-charged white Trans Am. Complete with smoked windows and a big-ass bird decal on the hood."

"Oh, dear god." Frankie chuckled. "That should get the job done."

"You think? You'll look like a refugee from *The Dukes of Hazard.*"

"Isn't that the idea?"

I turned in my seat to face her. "How come you're not rattled by this?"

"By what?"

"By intentionally parading your girl stuff around to lure a bunch of drooling construction workers to ogle you?" I waved my hand around in circles to encompass her attributes.

"'*Girl stuff'?* Nick? At my age, getting *anyone* to ogle me is kind of a tall order."

"That's nuts. Anybody with a pulse would ogle you—especially soaking wet."

Oh, sweet mother of pearl . . . what had I just said? I looked out the window in mortification.

"Oh?" Frankie batted her eyes at me. "You think so?"

"Um. Well . . ." *Me and my big mouth.* "Yeah. I mean . . . *sure.*"

Frankie laughed. "You're so full of shit."

I blinked. "Why do you say that?"

"Why is it so hard for you to admit that you *might* find me attractive—I mean under certain circumstances?"

Certain circumstances? *How about any circumstances?* "Because I don't want to offend you?"

"Offend me? Why on earth would that offend me?"

"Well. I guess because I'm . . . you know . . ."

"Because you're . . . *what?* Left-handed? Republican? A Trekkie? Someone who only eats root vegetables?"

"I'm not a Republican," I muttered.

She glared at me.

"Okay, okay." I gave up. "Because I'm queer."

"And I repeat," she said. "Why would that offend me? This isn't 1965."

"Maybe because you're *not* queer?"

"I'm not? And you know this, how exactly?"

My head was swimming. *How the hell had this conversation gone off the rails so fast?*

"Well. I mean . . . you're kind of a poster child for straightness. And you said you were married—to a man."

"That's true. I *was* married to a man. But . . ." she didn't finish.

"But what?"

"But now I'm not married. To anyone."

"So, what are you saying?"

Frankie sighed dramatically. "You have an advanced degree, right?"

I nodded.

"What do you *think* I'm saying?"

I was out of my depth on this one. It seemed like any response I made was too significant—and too self-revealing. In a moment of fear and weakness, I decided to tell the truth.

"I'm afraid to speculate."

"Afraid?" Frankie looked at me. We were nearing the outskirts of Winston-Salem. The hazy outlines of the Wells Fargo tower and the iconic R.J. Reynolds building were barely visible beyond the rows of old brick tobacco warehouses that now housed upscale restaurants and luxury apartments. "What on earth are you afraid of?"

I stared at the raindrops rolling up the windshield. "Could we maybe not talk about this in a moving vehicle?" I remembered that line from an old Kate Clinton comedy CD. It seemed to apply to the current situation.

"Okay," Frankie agreed. "How about we get something to eat and continue the conversation?"

Great. Continuing the conversation was not what I had in mind. But it was also hard to say no to an opportunity to spend more time with her. And that was becoming another quandary for me. Frankie was rapidly becoming my new best friend. *How did I become so pathetic this fast?*

"What do you feel like?" I hedged my bet.

"Pizza." She didn't hesitate.

"Geez. You didn't even have to think about that."

"Does anyone ever have to think about eating pizza? Do *you* have to think about eating pizza?"

"Well . . . not usually."

"I rest my case." Frankie turned on the blinker and moved over a lane. "So. Burke Street delivery or homemade?"

"Homemade?"

"Oh, yeah. I make *great* pizza. It will change your life."

That made me smile. "You make it kind of hard to resist a promise like that."

"I know. It's all part of my master plan."

I took the bait. "You have a master plan?"

Frankie sighed. "If you have to ask me that question, it's plainly not working very well."

Any reply I might make to that statement seemed too loaded, so I changed the subject. "Have you ever noticed how much the old Reynolds Building looks like a mini version of the Empire State Building?" We were rolling past the downtown exits now. I pointed the smaller building out as it nested behind the massive and profoundly ugly Wells Fargo tower. "I noticed that the first time I came down here with Papa to visit Wake Forest. It's almost like a little model of it."

Frankie followed my gaze. "You're half right. The RJR building was built first, and it was the original inspiration for the Empire State Building."

"No kidding?"

"No kidding. Did you know that every year, the Empire State Building sends a Father's Day card to the RJR Building?"

"That's hilarious."

"Stick with me, kid . . . you'll learn things."

"That's one thing I have no doubts about." I looked at her. The spontaneous rain shower was drying up, and the early evening sky visible through the window beyond her profile was alive with bright oranges and ragged slashes of blue-violet. "If anyone had told me six weeks ago that I'd be a certified car-jacker, I'd have spit in their eye."

"Really?" She smiled. "If anyone had told *me* six weeks ago that I'd meet somebody like you, I would've sent them a tower of cheese."

Cheese? "Is that a good thing?" I asked.

Frankie shrugged. "It's what informed shoppers choose now in lieu of flowers or Candy-grams."

"Makes sense." I thought about it. "Pears."

"Pardon?"

"I'd send pears. I mean . . . to the person who said I'd meet somebody like you."

Frankie actually blushed. That surprised me. Probably because I was more accustomed to her having the upper hand in these double-entendre-laced conversations. "Don't you like pears?" I teased.

"On the contrary. I love pears."

"It's said they go pretty well with cheese."

Frankie met my gaze. "Between the two of us, we have half of a great appetizer."

"I know." I nodded morosely. "It's the *other* half that worries me."

"You worry too much." Frankie slowed her car and moved over to exit the highway. "One thing at a time."

"Is that like a twelve-step kind of thing?" I asked.

"No," she explained, "it's like a pizza kind of thing."

Frankie hadn't been kidding about her skills when it came to making pizza. It was magical. And it was a gooey, melty, savory, salty and sweet combination of flavors I'd never encountered before.

Gorgonzola cheese and pear.

It was finished off with fresh thyme and toasted walnuts, and it was heavenly. We also drank a very good bottle of Côtes du Rhône because she'd had it for a while, and said its window for drinking was about to slam shut. I was impressed by that. Nothing ever stayed around our house long enough to advance even close to the sill of its window of drinkability.

After my second glass of wine, I decided to give up on my favorite pastime of chastising myself for my weakness when it came to jumping at opportunities to spend time with her.

Well. Maybe not give up on it *entirely* . . . more like send it on hiatus for the rest of one evening.

And why not? I was tired of living like a Trappist monk. Not going in to TWAT seven days out of seven was growing on me. I was beginning to realize how much I missed not having a life—not having friends. Not having female companionship that, in all defiance of reason and good taste, seemed to *like* spending time with me.

And as difficult as it was for me to comprehend, Frankie seemed to like spending time with me—even when we weren't jacking cars for Fast Eddie.

That thought caused a few mental eye rolls. *Jacking cars?* What the hell had I gotten myself into?

Who cares? Maybe I *could* try to relax a little and see what might develop if I didn't keep getting in my own way.

"You're being awfully quiet."

I jumped at the sound of Frankie's voice. I hadn't realized that I'd descended into silence.

"Sorry," I said. "I was just thinking."

"About?"

Okay. Here it was—my chance to put up or shut up. *Was I brave enough to tell the truth?*

I gave her a half smile. "About us, actually."

Frankie seemed surprised, but she didn't appear distressed by my admission.

"It took you long enough."

I hadn't expected that response. "What makes you say that?"

"Sebastian said you moved at a glacial pace."

"Okay." I sat back and folded my arms. We were still sitting at the small pub table in her kitchen. "So I don't know if I'm more offended by that description of my caution—or the fact that Sebastian has seen fit to suggest *anything* to you about my . . . *pace*."

"Oh, come on." Frankie waved off my pretense at umbrage and topped off my wineglass. "Don't get your panties in a wad. You know he only wants the best for you."

"That's what he said?"

Frankie shrugged. "Words to that effect."

"I bet."

"You don't think that's true?"

"Oh no," I replied. "I'm sure it's true. I just doubt those were the words he used to describe my predicament."

"You have a predicament?" Frankie asked with a tinge of irony.

"You know what I mean—and don't change the subject."

"Okay. So maybe he didn't use those exact words."

"Yeah. I thought so. So, what'd he actually say?"

Frankie shook her head. "Why does it matter?"

"I'm just curious about what my best friend has to say to my . . ." I stopped myself—too late.

"Your . . . *what?*" Frankie was all ears now.

Great.

"My . . . approach to . . . *relationships.*" It was a flimsy response, but given the direction our conversation was taking, I thought it was best to retreat to higher ground.

I have to hand it to Frankie. She didn't miss a trick. "Is that what we have?"

Damn. She could've been a trial lawyer. Papa would've been impressed by her ability to hone in on the underlying kernel of truth in a statement.

"I dunno. Sort of?" I paused for a moment and focused on continuing to twist the stem of my wineglass between my fingers. I'd been putting so much effort into it, I was surprised the thing hadn't managed to screw itself into the oak tabletop. "Maybe?"

"Maybe?" Frankie lowered her voice. "What might it take to convince you?"

Right then about twenty profane acts that I was pretty sure were still outlawed in at least thirteen U.S. states flashed through my mind, but I was confident those weren't the kinds of actions Frankie was offering up. When I finally felt brave enough to raise my eyes and look at her, I wasn't so sure.

"Um . . . I don't know?"

"You don't know?" she asked. "Would it clarify things for you if I told you I'm a lesbian?"

To say I was unprepared for that admission was an understatement. I stopped twisting my glass and clutched it so tightly the stem snapped in half.

"Shit!" I pushed my chair back, sloshing wine all over my pants. I felt it running down my hand, too, and quickly realized it was mingling with something else—something warm and sticky. My hand began to throb in tandem with the pulse pounding in my head. "*Oh, fuck.* I cut myself."

"What?" Frankie leapt to her feet and snagged a towel off the sideboard. She took the bowl of the wineglass out of my hand and nested it on top of hers. "Let me see it," she demanded. I held it out for her. The pair of gashes across the insides of two of my fingers were small, but they were bleeding dramatically, like hand wounds were prone to do. Frankie wrapped them up tightly with the towel. "Let's wash this off." She tugged me to my feet.

"I'm really sorry," I kept muttering as we made the short journey to her kitchen sink. "I made a mess."

"Oh, shut up," Frankie said. "I don't give a crap about that. I just want to be sure you don't need a stitch."

"I don't need any stitches. They're not deep. I was just stupid."

"It was my fault. I shouldn't have just come out to you in that way. This might sting a little bit." She held my hand beneath a stream of warm water. It burned like fire. "I don't see any bits of glass. These cuts look clean."

"I told you they weren't serious."

She rewrapped my hand with the towel. "Hold this in place. I'm going to go get some antiseptic and a couple of Band-Aids."

"You really don't need to fuss."

"I'm getting you a clean pair of pants, too."

Okay . . . there was no way I was taking my pants off.

"Please don't bother with that. Sebastian's a whiz at getting bloodstains out of clothes." Frankie looked perplexed. "He tends to cut himself a lot while attempting to cook," I explained. "He thinks that doing his own butchering makes the culinary experience more authentic."

"I think I was a lot happier not knowing that."

"Welcome to my world."

"Stay put," she ordered. "I'll be right back."

Frankie disappeared to get the bandages, and I stood stupidly in the middle of her kitchen, holding the towel around my throbbing hand. My head was spinning. I kept going over Frankie's disjointed comments: "I shouldn't have just come out to you in that way" and "This might sting a little bit."

Yeah. *Sting* was precisely the right word for everything I was feeling. You'd think that recent events would've given me better skills to adjust to shifting realities. I mean . . . I'd even learned how to bypass a car's starter using only a flathead screwdriver. *This?* This should've been a cakewalk.

Not so much.

By the time Frankie returned with the bandaging paraphernalia, I had determined to be less introspective and more . . . reactive. She uncapped a brown bottle of something and poured a small stream of liquid over the two cuts. Watching the stuff foam and fizz as it ran over my fingers was hypnotic. It didn't exactly sting, but it tingled—along with the rest of my parts. Standing this close to Frankie was wrapping me up in a different kind of spell.

She dried my fingers gently before wrapping them snugly with Band-Aids.

"Hopefully, you won't hurt too badly." She moved to step back, but I kept hold of her hand.

"I don't want either of us to hurt," I said.

I knew I probably wasn't making much sense, but Frankie seemed to understand what I was saying.

"Do you think we might?" she asked.

I nodded.

"Why?" Her voice was like a whisper.

"I don't have the best track record with women." It was a tired but true refrain. One I repeated to myself often—especially lately.

"Maybe it's time to change that?"

Frankie's face veered closer. I wasn't sure if that was because of her or because I was pulling her forward. At that moment, I didn't really care.

"I think I want to kiss you." I muttered. *Okay . . . news flash from Planet Obvious.*

Frankie blinked. "When will you be sure?"

Mamá always insisted that actions spoke louder than words, so I decided to test her hypothesis.

I don't know what ideas I had about what kissing Frankie would be like, but the actual experience exceeded anything I could've imagined. The only parallel my fractured mind could cobble together was a vague notion that this must've been a lot like an astronaut's first bout of weightlessness. I was floating all right—not just above the Earth, but also beyond the boundaries of anything I'd ever known. It was a dizzying, exciting, alluring and altogether terrifying journey. Terrifying because the intoxication I felt seeping into every pore was warning me that if I kept on, I might not have the wherewithal to find my way back if Frankie let go.

But Frankie showed no signs of letting go. We held onto each other and swayed in place like two awkward dancers in search of an elusive rhythm. The heat of Frankie's embrace was melting something inside me. Something basic. *Something primal.* Something I'd spent years hiding from exposure. In one simple, explosive moment, I knew that all of my emotional levees were giving way. Somewhere just beyond the boundary of reason, I could hear the creaking and groaning of those once impenetrable walls, straining against the insistent crash of wave after wave of sensation. A lifetime of pent-up resolve was breaking apart like a fragile vessel made of clay—all of its tiny shards swirling madly around an expanding eddy of longing.

I yanked my head back to breathe.

"We," I began. "We need . . ."

"*This,*" Frankie replied. "We need this."

Yes. Had I spoken the word aloud? "Yes," I repeated, loud enough to be heard above the rushing din that thrummed between my temples.

"*Yes,*" Frankie repeated, tugging me forward again.

The waves kept coming—faster, higher. Overtaking everything. I felt myself surrendering. Sinking into them. Beneath them. The roar in my head slowly began to abate. I could make out other sounds: our frenzied breathing; a dog barking someplace; the chirp of a car horn; and, after a few moments, the unmistakable sound of someone knocking on Frankie's door.

We lurched apart.

"Frankie? Are you home?" A woman's gravelly voice demanded from the porch.

"Dear god." Frankie closed her eyes and dropped her head to my shoulder. "It's Lilah."

Lilah? *Oh. Lilah,* I remembered. *Her sister . . . the goth mortician.*

"What do we do?" I asked, stupidly.

The knock sounded again. It was more insistent this time.

Frankie sighed and pushed away from me. "We answer it. My car is out there. She knows I'm home."

"Um . . ." I wasn't sure what to do or how to comport myself.

"Relax." Frankie gave me a roguish smile. "I won't forget where we were." She kissed me quickly and headed for her front door, smoothing her hair as she left the room.

I tried to steady my breathing and clear my head—neither of which was going very smoothly. It took me a moment to realize that my shirt had somehow become untucked. I set about trying to fix it with my one good hand, and realized I still had gaping stains of red wine and blood splattered across my pant leg.

Great time to meet the family, I thought morosely. *I probably look like somebody's idiot cousin.*

My thoughts swung to Aunt Estela and her limitless supply of card-carrying idiot cousins. Oh, yeah. *Mamá would be proud of me today.* I was ready to represent the fabled Álvarez de las Asturias clan with true panache.

I could hear Frankie and Lilah talking as they made their way to the kitchen.

"Dad insisted that I bring this over to you," Lilah said. Her voice was like a cross between Lorraine Bracco and Froggy, from the Little Rascals.

"I don't see why," Frankie replied. "It's not like I need these—especially not four thousand of them."

"You know how he is," Lilah said. "He hasn't seen you in a month, so he worries."

They entered the kitchen. Lilah's appearance was startling. And not just because she had pale skin, jet black hair, and was dressed like a stylish Grim Reaper. She was like a photographer's negative image of Frankie. It was hard not to stare at the perfect picture of yin and yang presented by the two Stohler girls.

"Lilah, meet Nick." Frankie gestured toward me with her head. She was carrying an oversized plastic bin full of . . . something. "Nick, meet my sister, Lilah."

I gave Lilah a wave with my Band-Aid-clad hand. "Hi. Nice to meet you."

Lilah was giving me a good once-over. I couldn't tell what kind of assessment she was making. It felt like she was sizing me up for a correct fit on a casket.

"Nice to meet you, too," she said. "I'd say you're exactly the way Frankie described you, but since she hasn't mentioned you before, I can't."

"Nice try, Lilah." Frankie set the large bin down on the kitchen counter. "Nick and I have been working together for nearly a month now, and since I haven't spoken with you since Mom's birthday in February, there's been no opportunity for me to tell you about her."

"That's okay," I offered. "I usually excel at failing to exceed expectations, anyway."

Lilah looked me over again. This time, her dark eyes showed a trace of amusement. "Where are you from?" she croaked. "That's not a local accent."

"Philadelphia," I replied. "I came down here for law school."

"Wake?"

"Good guess." I was impressed. "What tipped you off?"

Lilah waved a hand. "You dress like a Deacon—bloodstains, notwithstanding."

"You always were a quick study, Li. Nick broke her wineglass," Frankie explained. "I just finished bandaging a couple of cuts on her fingers."

"Soak your pants in hydrogen peroxide," Lilah suggested. "Works like a charm." She winked at me. "Trade secret."

"Yeah, TMI, sister." Frankie retrieved two more wineglasses from the sideboard. "Want a glass?"

"Why the hell not?" Lilah sat down at the table. I followed suit belatedly. "So, are you working for a local firm?" Lilah asked me.

"Me? No. I'm . . . between opportunities right now."

"Curious." Lilah eyed Frankie. "Didn't you say you were working together?"

"That's right." Frankie opened another bottle of wine. "We're both doing some temp work right now."

"Temp work? That's kind of vague. What *kind* of temp work? Like Kelly Girls or something?"

"Not exactly," Frankie explained. She shot me a quick, cautionary look. "We're providing support services for an asset recovery agency."

Lilah narrowed her eyes. "Asset recovery?"

Frankie nodded.

"For an insurance company?" It was clear that Lilah wasn't ready to suspend her query.

"No." Frankie chose not to elaborate.

Lilah looked over at me. I felt a nerve begin to twitch in my face. "Exactly what type of asset recovery are you both supporting . . . temporarily?"

"Um. Cars?" I saw Frankie raise a hand to her forehead. "I mean, mostly," I added belatedly.

"*Cars?*" Lilah looked back and forth between us. "You're working for a *repo* agency?"

Frankie nodded with obvious resignation.

Lilah's jaw dropped. "Are you insane?"

"It's not like that, Li." Frankie filled her sister's wineglass. "It's totally legit and by the book."

"Oh, I am *so* sure it is." Lilah swept up her glass and took a healthy swig. "Just like I can tell people that I manage a 'Chapel of Rest' or specialize in 'Aftercare.' But that doesn't change the reality that my day job involves pumping antifreeze into dead people."

"Li . . ."

Lilah faced her sister. "Putting lipstick on a pig still gets you lipstick on a pig."

"Yeah." Frankie took hold of the plastic bin and lowered it to her lap. "Apropos of that. Why did Dad think I needed my weight in cheap lipsticks?"

Lilah shrugged. "He ordered them on some eBay site—for the mortuary. But Mom said they were horrible colors for corpses." She looked at me. "She explained to him that not many dead people have 'summer' complexions. Poor Dad was bereft. Turns out certain eBay vendors have pretty unforgiving return policies."

Frankie sifted through the dozens of little tubes. "So he thought *I* could use them? There are enough here to last about twenty lifetimes." She held up a sample. "And 'Cool Chiffon' is really not very practical—except for those late afternoon gatherings on the Cape."

"It could happen, I suppose." Lilah cleared her throat. It didn't do much to improve the raspy quality of her voice. She really did sound like Lorraine Bracco. And right now, she was going full Dr. Melfi on Frankie's ass. "So, say more about this temp job. Are you actually jacking cars? I need *details*." She rested her chin on her hand. "I may have underestimated you, Pippi Longstocking."

Frankie sighed.

I decided to try and help her out. "It's not really jacking cars. It's restoring assets to their rightful owners after sustained periods of gross delinquency."

Lilah chuckled. "Almost thou persuadest me." She shook her dark head. "Mom is gonna have a shit fit when she finds out about this."

Frankie leaned toward her sister. "But she's not *going* to find out about this . . . is she Li?"

"Oh, she'll find out, all right. That salon of hers has a better newswire than TMZ. You know we could never keep secrets from her when we were kids."

"That's because *you* lacked discretion."

Lilah sat back against her chair. "I'm sure I have no idea what you're talking about."

"Li . . . you did embalming experiments on road kill—*in our bedroom*."

"Well . . ."

"Never mind." Frankie flashed a palm. "I haven't told her about this for a reason, and I'd appreciate it if you keep it on the DL. The money's good, and it's only temporary."

Lilah eyed me. "What about you?"

"Same here," I replied in solidarity.

Lilah laughed. "Too bad I'm not more of a homebody. I won't be any good at baking you two cupcakes once you're inmates at the Crowbar Hotel."

"Store-bought will do just fine," Frankie replied.

Lilah noticed the leftover remains of our dinner. "Sorry I interrupted your evening. Was this a social event, or were you plotting your next heist?"

"Nice try." Frankie didn't take her bait. "And they're *not* heists."

"Right. And I'm a stealth debutante, too." Lilah tossed her head. "By the way, did you hear that somebody made off with Blessed Slumber's new wagon? It was in broad daylight, too—while the Caddy was locked and loaded for a trip to the Franklin stove."

"Stolen?" I could tell Frankie was making an effort to keep her tone neutral. "Are they sure it was stolen?"

"Hell yes, it was stolen. I know because we were in a bidding war with them for it. Old man Russell pulled a fast one at the eleventh hour and paid cash for the damn thing—seventy-five thousand bucks on the barrelhead."

Frankie and I exchanged nervous glances.

"That isn't the best part of the story," Lilah continued. "The clowns who jacked the car apparently didn't realize they were getting an accessory not disclosed on the window sticker. They actually had the decency to bring the stiff back—in the middle of the night." She chuckled. "Even left a damn condolence card. Honor among thieves, I guess." She looked at me. "I swear . . . you can't make this shit up."

"No," I agreed. "You really can't."

"Couldn't happen to a better candidate, in my opinion. That joint has been hustling people for years."

"Hustling?" I asked.

"Hell, yeah. Let's just say they don't have the best quality control protocols in place for their contracted services. About eighteen months ago, a family returned to pick up the cremains of a loved one and got quite a shock when they got home and unpacked their treasure."

I knew I'd regret asking, but I went for it anyway.

"Why? What happened?"

"Well . . ." Lilah leaned toward me. The simple act was unsettling. Her dark eyes were like obsidian coffin nails. "The abject solemnity of the event was entirely lost when they opened the box and discovered it contained a pecan-crusted cheese ball."

I nearly swallowed my tongue.

Lilah cackled gleefully. "Those stupid charlatans."

I was still too horrified to speak.

"Nice one, Li." Frankie ran a soothing hand across my back.

"Hey, not my circus, not my monkeys." Lilah drained her wineglass. "You'd think they would've been tipped off by the big Hickory Farms logo emblazoned across the front of the damn container." She looked at me. "This is why we handle our barbecues in-house."

Frankie growled at her sister. "Not helping, Li."

"Whatever." Lilah got to her feet. "You two just be careful. If you're really this desperate for extra cash, I can always find something for you to do. Between the mortuary and the beauty shop, there's enough extra work to go around. It's nice to meet you, Nick." She shot an inquisitive glance at Frankie. "I daresay our paths will cross again?"

"I hope so?" I offered.

"I *know* so," Frankie clarified.

Lilah smiled. "Until then, I suppose."

Frankie got up, too. "Lemme walk you out."

"No need. I know the way." She gave Frankie an impish grin. "You two can get on with whatever you were doing." She waved a hand over her head as she headed for the front door. "Later."

We both waited until we heard the front door open and close, followed by the sound of her car starting.

Then we looked at each other.

"Fuuuuuccckkkk," we said in tandem.

Chapter Four

My Mother Would Love You

To say the mood of our evening had been spoiled by Lilah's revelation about the hearse would be understating the obvious. Frankie drove me home shortly after Lilah left. Neither of us had much to say—not about Lilah's insistence that the Blessed Slumber hearse had been stolen, and not about our close encounter in her kitchen, either. Both topics seemed too loaded. We each needed time to sort through the competing sets of revelations. Or, at least, I did.

I had a fitful night. My mind, along with various other parts, kept fixating on how intoxicating it had been to hold Frankie . . . to kiss her. I was like a horny teenager wrapped up in the hot daze of a first crush. When I finally woke up on Saturday morning, the sun was shining and the sky cloudless. That meant our dastardly plan to crank up the mobile exotic car wash was definitely on. I felt my anxiety about the risky enterprise increase with each passing hour. Thankfully, Sebastian's garrulous mother was joining us for brunch, and Doreen was always a great distraction. What I didn't realize, but should have expected, was that he'd also invited Frankie. She arrived promptly at ten, carrying her ubiquitous oversized handbag, a large jug of pulp-free orange juice, and a brilliant bouquet of fresh-cut Asiatic lilies.

I was surprised when I answered the front door and saw her standing there, but I shouldn't have been. Frankie beamed when she saw me, but she was careful to do a quick sweep of the living room before she leaned up to give me a quick kiss.

"How'd you sleep?" she asked with a shy smile.

"How do you think I slept?" I replied.

"I'm hoping not very well."

"Then you'll be very happy. I slept like crap."

"That *does* make me happy. Isn't it great?"

I had to laugh at that. After all, it *was* kind of great. "How'd *you* sleep?"

"Oh, I didn't. I'm thinking about having that wineglass bronzed."

"Bronzed? Why?"

It was her turn to laugh. "Because without it, you'd probably still be lost in some moribund reverie about the hopelessness of entertaining any kind of relationship with me."

"You seem pretty smug," I teased. "What makes you think I'd never come around on my own?"

"You're kidding me, right?"

"No . . ."

"Nick? You're like a walking Thomas Hardy novel. You know . . . *Tess of the Lower Schuylkill.*"

"Tess would never live in the lower Schuylkill," I responded in as droll a tone as I could muster.

Frankie slapped the bouquet of lilies against my chest. "You get my point."

"Is that Frankie?" Sebastian bellowed from the kitchen. "Hurry up and get in here with that juice, woman. Doreen is about to drink up the rest of the champagne."

"Maybe we can continue this conversation later?" I asked.

"Oh, I think you can count on that." Frankie led the way to the kitchen.

Sebastian's mother Doreen all but purred when Frankie entered the room. She knew better than to believe that Frankie was some hopeful answer to prayer, come down from heaven to shock her flamboyant son into rabid heterosexuality. That meant she correctly intuited that Sebastian was matchmaking . . . again.

"Aren't *you* simply an adorable little thing," she cooed. "Come on over here and sit down next to me, sweet pea." Doreen slapped the seat of an empty chair. "Are you Abel Stohler's little girl? The teacher? I swanny . . . you're just like a miniature version of your mama. She did my hair for Ricky's wedding—the second one—to that Nixon girl from Birmingham. The one who sold Chevys? Best backcomb I ever had." Her eyes were dreamy. She looked up at her son. "Doesn't she look just like her mama, Dwayne?"

"Yes, Mama." Sebastian uncapped the orange juice and topped off his mother's champagne flute. "They're like split-aparts."

Frankie looked confused. "Dwayne?" she asked Sebastian.

"It's a long story," he explained. "Don't ask."

"And your daddy is a saint in our family, too." Doreen was still talking to Frankie. Before she could elaborate, the oven timer dinged.

Sebastian took up his oven mitts with a flourish. "Saved by the bell."

He retrieved a savory-smelling egg concoction from the oven and deposited it on a wooden trivet in the center of the kitchen table. I was impressed. It was rare for Sebastian to create something that wasn't noxious.

I claimed a chair next to Frankie, and picked up a blue pottery bowl that contained a brightly colored mixture of cut-up seasonal fruits.

"Would you care for some fruit, Doreen?" I asked.

Sebastian's rotund mother nodded with enthusiasm. "My doctor says I need to eat more fresh fruits and vegetables. I do love my grapes and potatoes."

"Mama, I don't think he meant wine and vodka."

"Oh, Dwayne . . . stop your silliness. You worry too much—just like your sweet daddy always did . . . God rest his soul."

"You lost your husband?" Frankie asked with concern.

"Lord, yes, honey. Nearly ten years ago. And let me tell you, your daddy and your sister at that sainted mortuary were absolute godsends. It wasn't easy to clean up his remains, but they worked miracles." Doreen's expression was wistful. "Randy looked as good as the day I met him, forty-two years ago at Clark's Barbecue. Not a line on his face."

I could tell by her rapt expression that Frankie was dying to ask for details, but decorum was holding her back.

Sebastian stepped into the void.

Voids always seemed to follow Doreen around . . .

"He fell out of a fourth-story window," Sebastian explained. "It wasn't pretty."

"That's *terrible.*" Frankie laid a sympathetic hand on Doreen's plump forearm.

"Lord, yes it was." Doreen shook her head. "Randy managed a Window World store up in Mt. Airy. They were replacing the windows in some condo units on the top floor of a building on Main Street. Randy always stood behind his products, and he loved to demonstrate how unbreakable the glass was." Doreen sighed. "He was showing off for some new customers who were there to look at his work, so he went charging across the room and threw himself at one of the big plate-glass windows that overlooked the street."

Frankie's eyes grew wide. "Oh, no."

"Oh, yes." Sebastian dumped more champagne into his flute. "Not one of the brightest bulbs in the Sprinkle family chandelier."

"Now, Dwayne . . . you be *respectful.* Your daddy was a good man."

"Yes, Mama."

Doreen faced Frankie. "I don't know what we woulda done without your daddy and your sister. Randy was cut up all to pieces. They stitched him back together so good you couldn't see a single mark. It was like magic."

Frankie turned to me with a look of sheer bewilderment. "Lilah failed Home Ec," she whispered in a voice so low, only I could hear her.

Doreen was still lost in her reverie. "It's just so sad that Randy's last big sale fell through like that."

"No pun intended," Sebastian added.

Doreen glared at her son.

I cleared my throat. "So, Doreen? What do you think of that casserole?"

Doreen took a big forkful and chewed it thoughtfully. Then she gave a mournful sigh.

"Dwaaaayyynnnne?" She drew the name out like it had nine syllables. "Mama can't taste the bourbon."

"Mama . . . that's because it's *quiche*."

Doreen looked so crestfallen that I got up and went to our booze cupboard to retrieve the Maker's Mark. I held it aloft so Doreen could see it. "Want ice with this?" I asked.

Doreen nodded with enthusiasm. "But no water." She nudged Frankie. "I like things pure, the way God intended them."

"Speaking of things appearing the way God intended them," Sebastian said, "do you have your outfit all picked out for today's Washapalooza, Miss Stohler?"

"*Outfit?*" Frankie flashed Sebastian a trademark, legally blond look. "You mean I'm supposed to *wear* something?"

I nearly dropped Doreen's tumbler of bourbon. "I sure as hell hope so."

"Oh, will you just quit with the righteous expressions of Puritan umbrage?" Sebastian waved me off. "She's *totally* joking."

I handed Doreen her bourbon. She took a grateful sip. "What am I missing here?" she asked.

"Frankie is gonna wash the Trans Am today, Mama—in her Daisy Dukes."

"Well I *hope* she's not washin' it in a ball gown. But I did wonder why you needed to borrow Ricky's car."

"It's like this," Sebastian leaned over his plate. "The girls here are doing a spot of asset recovery to make ends meet, and today's target works on a construction crew out on Peace Haven. Nick needs a distraction so she can sneak up and grab the guy's car, so Frankie is gonna oblige by giving the guys a show guaranteed to distract them from their nail guns. On the other hand," he considered, "they just might get distracted enough to discharge some other kinds of rounds, if you get my drift."

"*Dwayne!* You stop with that crude talk." Doreen shook her head full of platinum waves. "I swanny. You get more like your daddy every day."

"Well, Mama. You always said the apple doesn't fall far from the tree. I mean . . . except for that one time in Mt. Airy."

Doreen had moved on. "Just what in thunder are you two girls gettin' involved in? This don't sound to me like it's safe."

"Hold on, Mama. You said you and Aunt Poutine did the *same* thing back in high school—and that your car-washing scheme was exactly how you hooked Daddy and Uncle Skeeter."

"That was *different*, and you know it." Doreen leveled her gaze on Frankie and me. "It was for our Keyettes chapter. We were raising money for Kiwanis scholarships. It was hotter'n Hades that day, and Poutine and I wore our bathing suits—but they were decent, one-piece suits that only hinted at untapped treasures." She smiled at the recollection. "Randy and Skeeter had us wash that AMC Rebel five times. It was magic."

Frankie looked at Sebastian for help. "*Aunt Poutine?*"

"Oh, yeah," he explained. "Meemaw wanted to give her baby girls names that rhymed. Aunt Pou-Pou's name was a good fit, too. She actually won a 4-H poetry contest with a sonnet about ham gravy."

Frankie raised a tentative hand. "Could I please have some of that bourbon?"

Once brunch had ended, I was forced to embrace the reality that there was no forestalling D-Day—or "Double-D Day," as Sebastian irreverently dubbed it.

I failed to see the humor in his bawdy double entendre. But Frankie laughed merrily, and thanked him for his "preposterous overestimation" of her endowments.

"That reminds me," he said. "I got you something special for the occasion."

"This cannot be good news," I remarked. But Frankie was dying to see what it was.

Sebastian passed her a slick-looking black box. "Open it," he drawled.

She did. Once she unwrapped what seemed like an entire ream of fuchsia-colored tissue paper, she withdrew the skimpiest, sluttiest-looking black bra I'd ever seen.

Frankie held it up.

"Oh, my god," she gushed. "Is this really a Bluebella bra?"

"In the glorious flesh . . . so to speak. I guessed at the size," he added.

"You're a genius! I've always wanted one of these."

I sat staring at the skimpy thing that could only loosely be called a bra. It looked more like a bunch of black strings, connected in some kind of spiderweb pattern.

"You cannot *seriously* be thinking about wearing that," I blurted.

"Of course I am," Frankie replied. "It's perfect."

"For what? The second show at *Bada Bing!*?"

"*Relax.*" Sebastian waved me off. "Go take a Xanax, will you?"

I didn't want to tell Sebastian, or Frankie, for that matter, that seeing her in that . . . *gizmo* . . . would make doing my part of our assignment next to impossible. How was I supposed to stay focused on jacking a damn muscle car when I'd be even more preoccupied than the very crew of drooling, Neanderthal construction workers we were there to distract?

It was all shaping up to be a five-star recipe for disaster.

"Well," Frankie stashed the Bluebella creation inside her omnipresent bag of tricks and beamed at me. "I think it's show time."

"Just one more thing." Sebastian handed her a jewel case. "I made you a special mix CD for the boom box I left in Ricky's car. Make sure you crank the volume up nice and high."

I knew enough to be suspicious. "Lemme see that, please." Frankie handed it to me and I read over his hand-lettered list of tracks. I gave Sebastian a withering look. "Seriously?"

"What's on it?" Frankie sounded excited.

"Oh, trust me. It's chock-full of top hits from the bona fide hoochie-mama soundtrack. Let's see . . . we've got 'Legs' by ZZ Top. 'Cherry Pie' by Warrant. 'I Touch Myself' by Divinyls. 'Bang A Gong' by T. Rex. 'Pour Some Sugar On Me' by Def Leppard. 'Closer' by Nine Inch Nails. 'Wild Thing' by Tone Loc. 'Rocket Queen' by Guns N' Roses. 'Sex On Fire' by Kings of Leon. And last, but never least, 'Glory Box' by Portishead." I handed the disc back to Frankie. "I dunno, Sebastian. I think you're holding back. Do you think it's possible these tracks contain a tad too much . . . *nuance?*"

"*Va te faire foutre*," he said. "And that includes the lame-ass horse you rode in on." He took hold of Frankie's arm. "Now if you'll excuse us, Miss Thing here needs to get busy and saddle up all 310 of *her* horses."

That had been just under an hour ago. Now I was cooling my heels about half a block from the construction site, waiting for Frankie to show up behind the house on the facing cul de sac. We'd left my car at home and Frankie had dropped me off at the entrance to the subdivision. I made my way as casually as I could to a cleared but mostly vacant site, where several stacks of clay drainage pipes and sump pits created enough of a barrier for me hide from view. I had a clear line of sight from here, and would have no problem seeing Frankie—and Ricky's ridiculous car—as soon as she drove it around the back of the empty house to begin her floor show.

I was nervous. Our target was plainly visible: a bronze metallic Mustang Shelby with bold, black accents. It was situated in front of the site, with pickups parked tightly at either end. Linda or Weasel could've nabbed it easily enough with the stinger, but not without being spotted—especially out here, where there was nothing to hide behind.

Nothing except these damn culvert pipes.

Come on, Frankie. Let's get this damn show on the road . . .

It looked like a full contingent working on the house today. Sebastian had been right about that. I counted seven vehicles, in addition to Larry Cecil's high-dollar ride. I could hear tinny-sounding music coming from a radio, the high-pitched grind of a power saw, and the unmistakable bang and whoosh of a couple of compressor-driven nail guns.

I wondered how far would one of those projectiles fly if someone fired it at my fleeing ass?

I turned a flathead screwdriver over and over in my hand like some kind of worry stone. What would I do if the damn thing didn't work? Weasel said it was pretty much a foolproof method on any car built before 1990, and this one certainly qualified. I still had my doubts. I remembered our school bus caper, and how Frankie ended up having to rip the wiring harness out to get the damn thing started.

I also had Frankie's compact Slim Jim with me, but I was terrified about using it—even though she'd made me try it out about fifty times on her car.

I checked my watch. It had only been ten minutes, but it felt like two hours.

It was hot as hell. The sun was beating down on me and I was sweating profusely. The heat radiating off the tower of clay pipes wasn't helping. I knew my shirt was going be soaked by the time I got out of there. That, of course, made me think about Frankie being soaked . . .

It was a ridiculous and inconvenient time to indulge in my newest, profane distraction. I just needed this madness to *end*—hopefully without acquiring a load of buckshot in my derriere.

Then I heard it—the unmistakable rumble of a car engine . . . a big, full-throated rumble. I peeked around the drainage pipes in time to see Ricky's blinding white Trans Am roll into position behind the empty spec house on the cul-de-sac.

Showtime.

I stashed the screwdriver inside the backpack containing the Slim Jim and hammer, and prepared to watch the show.

Sebastian had already dropped off a hose, stepladder, bucket, detergent, squeegee and a stack of oversized washcloths last night, so everything Frankie needed was already in place. I held my breath when the big car door swung open and Frankie climbed out.

Sweet mother of pearl . . . I don't know what I'd been expecting, but Miss Bliss ended up being built like the legendary brick shithouse. The tight denim cutoffs hugged her pert behind like . . . like . . . I had no words. All I knew is that I had never longed to be reborn as a swath of faded fabric so badly in my entire life. And her legs? Bless Babel . . . her legs had to be five miles long. That cropped white t-shirt wasn't leaving much to the imagination, either. Whatever that Bluebella creation had added to Frankie's natural landscape made me want to cash in my 401(k) and buy stock in the company.

And she wasn't even wet yet.

I had to close my eyes, clutch my knees together and force myself to concentrate on why I was there, instead of behaving like some pervert at a peep show.

Think about something else. Otters. Baseball. Old Yeller. Dear lord . . . think about Trump's hair.

In my desperation, I imagined another voice. *Get a damn grip on yourself, Not-Vera.*

Okay. *Channeling Antigone*. That was working. It was impossible to experience erotic stimulation with a belt sander grinding in your ear. I opened my eyes and took another look. Frankie was bent over, filling her wash bucket.

I sagged against the drainage pipes.

And yet, not so much . . .

I took a minute to steady my breathing and realized that I wasn't the only one having a hard time concentrating on the task at hand. The bang and whoosh of the nail guns had stopped. So had the power saw. It was apparent that Frankie's sudden debut had borne fruit for our enterprise.

It made sense for me to wait another minute or two, until Salomé had all seven of her veils flying at full mast in a mesmerizing reenactment of a working man's ultimate fantasy.

My wait wasn't long. Frankie used the hose to fill her wash bucket with soapy water. She'd already retrieved Sebastian's boom box from the back seat and positioned it on the brick steps leading to the house. She'd made sure to push the play button before approaching the Trans Am with the hose. Sebastian's custom mix CD began blasting out at ear-splitting volume. I was pretty sure that everyone living in the occupied houses in the new subdivision would soon be grooving to the beat of ZZ Top. Sun glinted off the spray of water jetting from Frankie's hose, bathing the entire scene in a wild swirl of rainbows. The music was pounding and driving.

Oh yeah . . . she had legs all right. And she definitely knew how to use them.

Above the din of the music, I could detect sounds of stomping and clapping. Frankie had amassed an appreciative audience in record time.

She dropped the hose and pulled an oversized, soap-laden sea sponge out of the bucket and began pushing it back and forth across the hood of the car in rhythm with the music. Wide swaths of white foam spread out over the screaming chicken decal. Frankie's torso stretched and undulated with each thrust as she moved the sponge over the surface of the massive hood.

Dear god. . . this woman taught third-graders?

The men were now whooping and hollering and shouting words of encouragement.

"Wash it baby!"

"I think you missed a spot over here, sweet thing . . . it's *real* dirty, too!"

"Show us that grille, girl!"

¡Papá también quiere bañarse!

Lord, I thought as I wiped actual drool from the corner of my mouth, *men are such pigs.*

Frankie had finished soaping the hood and stood back to admire her work. That's when the real fireworks started.

Her cropped T-shirt was completely soaked and the outlines of the

Bluebella bra were plainly visible. I swallowed hard and thought maybe the addition of that—*garment*—had been a bridge too far because the men were now growing nearly apoplectic in their expressions of admiration. Frankie even had the brazen temerity to flash them a smile and a happy little wave, as if she were rolling down Main Street atop a damn float instead of standing in the sun, soaking wet and showing off most of what God—and some perverted lingerie designer—gave her.

I was having a hard time remembering why we were even staging this ridiculous show-and-tell. But *one* thing was clear: I had to get my ass in gear and go for the Shelby now, so Frankie could get off the stage before any members of her audience decided they wanted to get a closer look.

I cinched up my hold on the backpack and began walking toward the row of parked vehicles. I tried to advance casually, like I had every right to be there—just in case anyone noticed me. But that wasn't going to happen. Not with Frankie's little bump-and-grind floor show in full swing. The music had changed again, and the not so subtle lyrics of the classic, "I Touch Myself" were unreeling.

I resolved that the first thing I was going to do, if I lived long enough, was punch Sebastian in the middle of his pert little Roman nose. What the hell had he been thinking with this damn "come hither" music? We'd be lucky if Frankie got out of here without becoming a hood ornament.

Fate must've decided to take pity on me because it was hot enough that Cecil had left the Shelby's windows lowered, allowing me to reach inside and unlatch the door. As unobtrusively as I could, I slid into the driver's seat. The black leather upholstery felt like the surface of the sun. Good thing I'd decided to wear jeans and not shorts. I placed my backpack on the passenger seat and quickly withdrew the flathead screwdriver. That's when I saw it.

An ignition interlock device.

There it was, big as life, attached to the dashboard right beside the steering column.

Sonofabitch. Cecil had a damn breathalyzer wired to his ignition.

Just our stupid luck. That meant this delinquent asshole had racked up god knew how many DWIs. How was it possible that neither Eddie nor Antigone knew about *this* little complication?

Oh. Yeah. My bad. *Antigone didn't do complications . . .*

Now what?

I shot an anxious look at the construction site. Frankie's music was still blasting and the men were now clapping and whistling to, "Bang A Gong." That meant I had to think of something—and fast. Frankie and I had timed the music tracks out for exactly long enough to give me time to grab the car and lay a patch out of there. "Bang A Gong" ran for seven minutes, eleven seconds. I had to be free and clear before Def Leppard's, "Pour Some Sugar On Me" queued up and ended Frankie's set. We'd agreed that win, lose or draw, this little charade would last no longer than twenty-five minutes.

My dilemma continued. There was no screwdriver on the planet that would start this absurd car—not with that Guardian Interlock attached. Any attempt to subvert it would permanently lock the driver out. The device would automatically alert law enforcement, and I'd be using my one phone call to beg Papa to come bail my ass out of the county lockup.

Think, Nick. Think.

Okay . . . okay. Two years ago, I'd been saddled with defending Turner's idiot nephew when he got busted for trying to disconnect one of these units on his Porsche. I'd been lucky enough to discover that the monitoring company was getting all kinds of false reports due to some glitch in a recent software upgrade. Even though that wasn't the case with Turner's nephew, we successfully got the report recanted by threatening to sue the interlock manufacturer for carelessly transmitting a slew of bogus reports of malfeasance. In the process of litigating the case, I'd had to watch about fifty damn videos about how these things worked. Now it was time to see how good my memory was.

First, I took the screwdriver and hammer and tapped the flathead into the ignition until I felt it slide past the starter pins.

Interlock units only worked when the cars were turned off, so I was careful not to move the screwdriver once it was seated. I picked up the handset of the breathalyzer and pressed its power switch. The LED readout cycled through its startup screens.

Come on. Come on. Hurry the fuck up.

Finally, the readout displayed the word "BLOW" in big red letters.

I hesitated. Was I really going to put my lips around this mouthpiece used by this Cecil guy?

Did I have any choice?

Not really.

I took a deep breath and blew into the thing, thanking every god known to man that I hadn't had any champagne with brunch.

When I lowered the handset, the tiny screen read, "ANALYZING," followed by, "49 DAYS UNTIL SERVICE." *Yeah. Whatever. Come on. Come on. Come the fuck ON.* Finally, the word "PASSED" displayed.

Eureka!

I dropped the handset like a hot potato, grasped the handle of the screwdriver, and slowly rotated it forward—just like Weasel taught me. The big 355 horsepower V8 engine roared to life. The damn thing was so loud I jumped in my seat and banged my head on the roof. I was terrified that Cecil would hear it over Frankie's music.

Fat chance. A Stealth bomber could've dropped its entire payload on this building site and those guys wouldn't have cared—not as long as Frankie was still shaking her waterlogged bootie at them.

I slid the gearshift into reverse and began the slow process of inching my way out of the tight parking space. I was impressed that it only took me five short cycles of turns to gain enough clearance to pull out. Once I was free, I rolled the big machine away from the site as quietly as I could, not hitting the throttle and hightailing it out of there until I made the turn onto Peace Haven Road. Just before I pulled out of the building site, I heard the head-banging intro to the Def Leppard song.

Sweet mother of pearl, that was too fucking close . . .

I waited until I had a couple of miles under my belt before I dared to breathe again.

Now I just had to pray that Frankie would wrap things up and be out of there before Cecil recovered enough faculties to realize his precious ride had gone missing.

Frankie and I had agreed to meet up in the parking lot behind Boost Mobile on Akron Drive.

Why not? The place had sentimental meaning for us. Besides, it was halfway to K-Vegas. I'd been parked there for nearly twenty minutes, cooling my heels and checking my cell phone about every five seconds to see if she'd texted yet to tell me she was clear. I grew more anxious with each passing minute.

What if something had happened? What if Cecil saw that his car was gone and put two and two together? What if he went after Frankie?

I knew I couldn't risk driving back over there. That would be suicide. I had just about decided to call Sebastian and ask him to ride over and see if Frankie had gotten out safely when my phone chirped. It was a text from Frankie.

> *FS: All clear. Headed your way.*
>
> *NN: Thank god! You scared the crap out of me.*
>
> *FS: I couldn't just roar out of there on a wave of soapsuds! I had to rinse the car off.*
>
> *NN: You're making me old before my time.*
>
> *FS: Relax, sweetie. It's over and we DID it. Be there in about 12 minutes.*

Relax? Was she kidding me? I didn't think I'd ever be able to relax again.

Wait a minute . . . *did she just call me sweetie?*

I had to stifle a goofy smile. *Frankie called me sweetie.* No one had called me that since Sister Anjelica in the second grade. It wasn't that

Mamá didn't use endearments when I was little. She did. But they were nearly always in Spanish, and I had next to no idea what they actually meant. Besides . . . with Mamá, endearments were usually tied to directives about doing something—like a quid pro quo. "If you hang up your clothes like a good *doncella*, Mamá might allow you to watch the television."

Frankie's casual use of the endearment felt . . . special—like a present. It was something unexpected that I wanted to treasure . . . press it between sheets of waxed paper and sleep with it beneath my pillow for safekeeping.

I leaned against the side of the Shelby and felt the beginning of a breeze. It slowly gained in intensity the longer I stood there. The cooler air it brought felt wonderful. It had rained someplace nearby. I could sense it. The air was thick with that sweet, evocative scent of earth and new grass that always lingered after a late-spring storm. There were dark clouds building toward the south. It seemed that we had timed our little bait and switch exactly right. Any later, and the weather would've washed us out.

The nearby Bojangles was doing a lively business. The aroma of French fries made my stomach growl.

I checked my watch. It had been nearly three hours since brunch. A big plate of Smothered Yard Bird at Sweet Potatoes was sounding pretty good. Chicken gravy always managed to calm my nerves.

Maybe I had that in common with Aunt Poutine.

I wondered if Frankie would be up for getting some dinner after we met Eddie to hand off the Shelby.

Eddie. It was strange. This was the second time Eddie had asked us to deliver a car directly to him, instead of dropping it off at the NRB impound lot. No. *Third time.* Because this alternative procedure had originally been intended for the hearse, too. Antigone had been irritated with us because we'd dropped the car off early—well before Eddie said he'd be there to take the handoff.

My curiosity grew.

Lilah. Last night she'd said that Blessed Slumber's hearse had been "stolen." Maybe that was just a euphemism? After all, if your car suddenly disappears, it doesn't matter if it's been picked up by thieves or by a repo agent. It's just *gone*.

Still . . . Lilah was adamant that Blessed Slumber had paid cash for the Cadillac—had beaten the Stohlers out for it in a bidding war. If that were true, how could they be in default on loan payments?

And what about Mozelle's Maybach, with its impressive, high-dollar cargo? Eddie had taken direct responsibility for the disposition of that vehicle, too.

No. I was making a mountain out of a molehill. This was just nuts. Another example of my free-floating angst. Every time I heard hoofbeats, I thought it meant zebras, not horses. The truth was that I knew next to nothing about the ins and outs of this strange business. I just needed to relax, like Frankie said.

Frankie . . .

I was a goner. It was clear to me now. I knew it was more than being date-deprived or operating under the influence of hormones run amok. I was enthralled with Frankie. I wanted to *be* with her. To know her in ways that transcended the biblical meaning of the word.

Although, in a pinch, I'd take that one, too.

But my life was a mess right now. I had nothing to offer her—or anyone. No job. No direction. And no clear idea about where I even wanted my life to go once I figured out how to get it restarted. Frankie was perfect. She deserved better than me. And, of course I'd meet her *now*—now when my career and my prospects were in the proverbial shitter.

I'd never felt more pathetic. And that was saying a lot for me. I needed someone to talk sense to me. To snap me out of this haze of inertia and self-loathing. To help me regain focus and realign my internal compass. I'd sunk low enough. It was time for desperate measures.

It was time to call Mamá.

There was a low rumble and I thought I felt the ground tremble beneath my feet. Was it an earthquake? A roll of thunder signaling an advancing storm?

My heart began to race.

Or was it a sign? One of Mamá's visions, come to show me the way.

Close . . .

It was Ricky's Trans Am, rounding the corner of Boost Mobile and rolling into the parking space beside me. Frankie cut the engine and flashed me a rakish smile. I could tell she was still soaking wet. The Bluebella creation was still gloriously on display beneath the thin fabric of her T-shirt.

"Howdy, stranger. Come here often?" she asked.

"Not really," I replied. "But I'm thinking maybe I need to change that."

"You'll get no arguments from me."

"Are you cold?" I asked. "I have another shirt with me."

"That's nice of you. In fact, I am kind of chilly."

I didn't bother telling her that I could see pretty clear evidence of that on my own. Covering it up was more a matter of self-preservation at this point. I retrieved the shirt from my backpack and passed it over to her. "Do you have any wet wipes or hand sanitizer in that mystical bag of yours?"

"I think so." Frankie looked perplexed. "Why?"

I jerked a thumb toward the Shelby. "That asshole Cecil has an ignition lock system on this thing."

Frankie was busy pulling my shirt on. "A what?"

"A breathalyzer attached to the starter. I had to blow into it before I could crank the damn thing."

"Oh, dear god. You're kidding?"

I shook my head. "Nope. Good thing I wasn't keeping pace with Doreen at brunch."

"How on earth did you know what to do with it?"

"Because I've done my time getting the underachieving spawn of my former bosses out of hot water with the legal system. I think their number of DWIs increases in direct proportion to the advanced degrees of their parents."

Frankie laughed. "Well, thank god it worked. I'm proud of you."

"Me? You're the one who did the heavy lifting on this one, Daisy Duke."

"That's crazy. All I did was wash a car."

"Um . . . Frankie?"

"Yes, Nick?"

"You did a helluva lot more than wash a car. I doubt any of those guys will be able to walk straight for at least a week."

"Oh?" she asked coyly. "You think so?"

"Oh, yeah. Take it to the bank. Who knew you had so many unsung talents?"

"Well, maybe if you're nice to me, I'll wash *your* car sometime."

It took me a moment to think of a reply. "I might need to update some paperwork first."

"Such as?"

"I'll need to revise my DNR."

Frankie threw her head back and laughed. It's a good thing she was wearing my shirt because I doubt that flimsy bra would've prevented . . . *things* . . . from jiggling in sync with her waves of laughter.

"I'm glad you think that's funny," I said.

"Of course I do. Do you wanna get in and sit for few minutes before we head to K-Vegas? I'd love to hear your ringside report."

Oh, no you wouldn't . . .

"Sure." I opened the door and climbed in beside her. *Colossal mistake.* For such a big-ass ride, Ricky's Trans Am was actually pretty cramped inside. I realized too late that the passenger seats were awfully close together.

In truth . . . there wasn't anything *awful* about the proximity, at all.

"You smell good." *Oh, good one Nick—really smooth.*

"I do?"

"Uh huh. Like . . . clean sheets."

Frankie smiled. "It's laundry soap. Sebastian left a jug of Gain to wash the car with."

"Oh. That's nice. Judging by the amount of foam you created, I'm guessing it wasn't the high-efficiency, low-suds variety."

Why was I suddenly talking like Ward Cleaver? *How was your day today, June? Did you finish all of that ironing?*

Frankie just nodded and seemed to roll with it. I guess by now she was used to my nervous quirks.

"Did you call Sebastian to let him know we pulled it off?" she asked.

"No. I wanted to wait until you showed up. In fact, I was just about to ask him to ride out there and check on you when you texted."

"That's sweet." Frankie seemed touched. "You were worried about me?"

"Hell, yes, I was worried. Weren't you? Those construction workers were getting pretty ramped up. That damn music of Sebastian's wasn't helping."

"They're just men." Frankie's tone was dismissive. "That's how they *all* act—especially in groups."

"You mean like a pack of salivating dogs at a pig picking?"

"More or less." Frankie laid a hand on my knee. "I'm glad I gave them up."

"Pig pickings?" I teased.

She rested her arm on the center console. "And men."

"Um." I swallowed. "Me, too."

She leaned toward me. "Are you?"

It was truth or dare time. I had to choose fast. Opportunities like this one could vanish just as quickly as they showed up.

I'd like to say my answer was delivered gently, with all appropriate attention to circumstance. But that would be a lie. I pretty much launched myself at her and effectively pinned her against the seat back. The damn console made it difficult for me to do my best work, but I tried to show sufficient evidence of sincere intent. I hadn't kissed anybody like that since ... well, the truth was that I'd *never* kissed anybody like that. We were grabbing at each other and fumbling around like two teenagers at their first drive-in movie. Only there was no drive-in, and no movie. Nor was it dark. It was broad daylight, and we were climbing all over each other inside a ridiculous muscle car while parked in a public lot behind a cell phone store.

I was just about to suspend chewing on Frankie's ear long enough to ask if her seat reclined when someone tapped on the roof of the car, and I heard a wispy, female voice say, "Excuse me?"

I jerked back from Frankie so hard and fast I landed on the car horn, which, unfortunately, was one of those aftermarket Wolo Bad Boy creations that are so loud, they make your fillings hurt.

A sprite-like young woman stood there straight as a ramrod, staring into the car at us. She looked like she was about twelve years old, but she was smartly dressed and wore a Boost Mobile name badge that proclaimed "MANAGER" in inch-high letters.

"I'm sorry to disturb you," she said in her childlike timbre, "but these spaces are reserved for store customers. Unless you're interested in . . . faster connectivity without . . . roaming charges . . . we'll have to ask you to move your . . . base of operations . . . to another . . . coverage area."

Beneath me, I felt Frankie begin to chuckle. It was infectious. Soon, I was laughing, too. And not just a little bit, either. It was uncontrollable. We couldn't stop. We began pitching and shaking with loud and boisterous guffaws.

The wispy young retail professional stood there gaping at us for a moment longer. Then she quickly raised a pale hand in a wave of dismissal and said, "Have a nice day," before turning on her heel to head back toward the store.

Frankie followed me to K-Vegas in Ricky's car. We were meeting Eddie for the handoff at the Sixty Six Grill. Yet again, I thought it was strange that he didn't want us to drop the car off at the NRB so he could put it into the impound lot. But Eddie was the boss, and I didn't think he'd appreciate us not following orders. According to Antigone, he'd been pretty pissed that we screwed up with the delivery of the hearse, so neither of us wanted to risk not getting any more assignments.

We parked the Shelby where he told us to—behind the restaurant, near the dumpster—and went inside to meet him.

He sat in his usual booth, and the table was arrayed with a new stash of burn phones. I could tell they were new because the colors were all different from the last time I'd met him here. When he saw us come in, he stood up and waved us over. I noticed how he adjusted his glasses as Frankie approached. It was pretty clear he wasn't used to seeing her dressed this . . . *informally.*

"Here they are—my prodigies!" he announced. "Sit, sit." He gestured at the booth. "Do you want some food? Working outside in this heat is for shit. It's like a schvitz out there today."

We both slid into the booth opposite him.

"Nothing to eat, thanks," I said. "We parked the Shelby out back, where you told us to." I lowered my voice. "The flathead is still in the ignition, so you might not want to leave the car out there unattended for very long."

"No worries, doll face. That's not a problem." He held up one of his phones. "I got a guy on his way over to pick it up."

"Yeah, well, the thing also has an ignition interlock on it. That wasn't a very happy surprise, lemme tell you."

"It does?" Eddie chuckled. "That rat bastard." He shook his head. "I'm proud of you, Vera. It took some chutzpah to start that thing, what with all the shit diseases floating around these days."

"Please don't remind me, okay?" I was already having visions of having to explain to Mamá how I managed to contract a virulent case of HSV-1. I was certain this new possibility was slated to roar to the top of my late-night list of *bête noire.*

"So how'd you two make the grab?" Eddie asked Frankie. His tinted lenses made it difficult to see where he was looking, but I didn't have to wonder. "I'm guessing you played a pivotal role," he added. "Am I wrong?"

"No, sir," Frankie replied. "You're not wrong at all. We decided it was a good day to wash a car. And we found the perfect place to do it: right behind the construction site where Mr. Cecil was working."

Eddie threw back his head and laughed. "You mean that stupid schlemiel got a free boner in the bargain? What a putz. He should pay extra for that."

I was about to take umbrage at Eddie's crude characterization of Frankie's performance, but she laid a restraining hand on my thigh.

"It's true," she agreed. "It's never a mistake to count on the lowest common denominator when you're dealing with men."

Eddie stared at her for a moment. Then he smiled broad enough for me to see his gold tooth. "You're a smart cookie. Antigone said you had good instincts."

"I hope I never disappoint her," Frankie replied.

"You haven't so far," Eddie assured her.

"I'm not sure about that," I said. "She wasn't very happy with us when we showed up four hours early with the hearse."

"Oh, *that*." Eddie waved it off. "She overreacts. That's why I try not to involve her in things that have a higher risk factor."

"Like the Shelby?" I asked.

"Exactly. Antigone runs a tight ship, but she won't take chances. I learned the hard way that her beliefs interfere with her judgment when it comes to business. That's why I like to deal directly with my agents on some of our more sensitive assignments. Which reminds me," he withdrew a manila envelope from a stack of papers in front of him, "I got another job for you two—and this one's a plum. Look it over later and let me know if you want to take it on. I have to warn you: it's a fast turn. You'll need to make the grab soon—no later'n next Friday. I'll hook you up with a truck and trailer. But this has to be on the DL—so no blabbing about it to Antigone. The woman's a total yenta. You tell her about this, and it'll be all over five counties before anybody can get close to the target. You get my drift? The asset is tied up in a messy divorce, and we can't risk tipping off the parties." Eddie passed the envelope across to us. "You know how reckless people can get. Time is money and there's a big payoff on this one, girls. You bring it in clean, and you're looking at a bonus of 5 Gs—each."

Frankie and I exchanged glances. *Five thousand dollars?*

Frankie took hold of the envelope. "We'll call you tonight."

I waited until we were outside and seated back in Ricky's Trans Am before I asked her if she'd lost her mind.

"What are you talking about, Nick?" Frankie was merging onto US 421, so we could make the trip to Mt. Airy to return Ricky's car. Sebastian had dropped my car off up there yesterday, and had ridden back with Doreen this morning. "This is five thousand dollars. I thought the point of this was for you to make enough money to pay off your school loans?"

"It is. But these jobs are starting to give me the yips."

"Now you sound like Eddie."

"*Exactly.* That's my point. I'm starting to *think* like Eddie, too. And that scares the crap outta me."

"Why?"

"I don't know." I drummed my fingers on the center console. "Maybe because these jobs are too easy."

Frankie looked at me like I had two heads. "What do you mean 'too easy'? You thought today was *too easy?*"

I shrugged.

"Nothing about shakin' my groove thing out there in front of a herd of Cro-Magnon construction workers felt 'too easy' to me."

"Excuse *me*—I thought you said 'boys will be boys,' or something equally dismissive?"

"It wasn't dismissive: It was *descriptive.* And it didn't change the fact that I felt like a harlot in cheap, borrowed robes."

"Why didn't you tell me that?" I was frustrated by her confession. "We could've figured something else out."

"Like what? It was a good plan. And P.S.—it worked."

"Yeah. Too well." I sighed. "Eddie is a pig, too."

"Pretty much." Frankie agreed.

"I really liked watching you," I blurted before I could stop myself. "Does that also make me a pig?"

Frankie thought about it. "No."

"Why not?"

"Because whenever I got freaked out about what I was doing, I thought about you watching me. Then I didn't feel cheap or tawdry."

I felt intrigued and mildly excited by this revelation. "You didn't?"

"No. I felt . . . desirable."

"That has to be the understatement of the century."

Frankie smiled. "Thank god."

We rode along in silence for a while. The storm clouds that had been gathering when we left Winston-Salem had finally rolled in. It was raining by the time we made the turn onto US 52.

"Are you going to open the envelope and see what this new job is?" Frankie asked.

I'd tossed the thing onto the floorboard when we climbed into the car. I didn't want to open it. I feared it contained something radioactive—or worse. These assignments were turning into some kind of Pandora's box. It was just a matter of time before we blundered into something we couldn't get out of.

I retrieved it unwillingly. "Are you sure you want to know what's in here?"

"It's five thousand dollars, Nick. Yes, I'm sure."

"Okay. Don't say I didn't warn you." I took a deep breath, opened the envelope, and scanned the work order inside.

Holy mackerel . . . he cannot be serious? There's no damn way . . .

"Well?" Frankie nudged my arm. "What's the job?"

"Impossible. The job is impossible."

"Could you be a tad more specific?"

"Okay. What do the words 'drowning' and 'maritime disaster' suggest to you?"

Frankie squinted at me. "A boat?"

"Ding, ding, ding, ding, ding. Wanna go for the daily double?"

"Um. A *big* boat?" Frankie suggested.

"You're half right." I showed her the photograph attached to the work order. "Try a damn aquatic *Ferrari*. This thing is a thirty-eight-foot Donzi speedboat equipped with Mercury twin staggered 860 engines. And is it sitting quietly on a trailer at some storage facility up in Catawba County? Oh, *hell* to the no. It's tied up in the marina at the damn Peninsula Yacht Club on Lake Norman."

"Is that a bad thing?" Frankie asked with perfect innocence.

I dropped the papers to my lap. "Bad? No. Not bad. More like im-*fucking*-possible."

Frankie took a moment to consider the information I'd just shared with her.

"You seem to know a lot about boats."

I looked at her with incredulity. "*This* is your only response?"

"Well . . . do you?"

"What difference does it make? We are *not* taking this assignment."

"Come on," Frankie entreated. "Where'd you learn about boats?"

I gave in to her entreaties. "My parents always sent me to summer camp at a place called Promised Land. It was up in the northern part of the state, near Lake Wallenpaupack. We took boating lessons there."

"That sounds sweet."

"Trust me . . . it wasn't sweet and it was far from a 'Promised Land.' I lost my virginity up there with a nineteen-year-old camp counselor named Serena, who thought introducing me to the joys of sex in the shallow hull of an aluminum Kingfisher was the height of romantic experience."

"You mean it wasn't?"

"Hardly. I emerged from the encounter with rope burns and a Texas rig embedded in my ass. I got five stitches and a spirited reenactment of the Spanish Inquisition from Mamá."

Frankie laughed at my recollection. "That's right up there with my timid introduction to the realm of erotic possibilities."

I was intrigued. "It is?"

"Oh, yeah," Frankie explained. "When I was fourteen, I walked in on Lilah and a salesman having sex inside a Titan Orion, steel Atlas XL Oversized casket. I guess he was demonstrating how commodious it was. To be fair, the thing was a real beauty. It was tricked out with sculpted hardware and reinforced stationary handles with classic, square-corner design, and finished with a high-gloss exterior. As I recall, I ran screaming from the showroom. Lilah later explained to me that this was the perfect way for her to honor such a seminal experience in her life." Frankie shook her head slowly. "I don't know why I didn't become a lesbian on the spot. I wasted a lot of years, figuring that crap out, let me tell you."

Frankie's story left me in a daze. *Lilah'd had sex in a casket—with a salesman?*

There was clearly a lot I still didn't understand about the funeral business . . .

But I was still sure about one thing: we were *not* going after this Donzi.

I grabbed my cell phone from the center console.

"What are you doing?" Frankie asked.

"I'm calling Eddie to tell him thanks, but no thanks."

Frankie laid a hand on my arm. "Wait."

I paused. "For what?"

"I just think we should talk about this a little before we dismiss it out of hand."

"We have talked about it."

"No we haven't. You issued an edict. That's not a discussion."

I lowered the phone. "Come on, Frankie. We'd never be able to pull this off."

"Why not? You know how to drive a boat, don't you?"

"Yeah—a nineteen-foot bass boat with a one-lung outboard engine. That's hardly comparable to one of these Donzi water rockets."

"I don't see why not. Don't they all work pretty much the same way?"

"Frankie," I said with frustration, "that's like comparing a Lamborghini to a Ford Pinto. And even if I could manage to operate it, we'd never get into that place. The Peninsula Club is too exclusive. It's gated. We'd never make it past the security checkpoint."

"On, come on. We could concoct some reasonable story."

"*Sure we could.* I mean . . . we could always just explain that I had an accident and fell asleep in the tanning bed at the clubhouse. *Are you nuts*?"

"Don't be so dramatic. We can come up with a perfectly legitimate reason to be there. You're an *attorney*, remember? Don't you still have tons of business cards from *other* attorneys?"

"Yes . . ."

We were nearing the turnoff for Ricky's garage.

"So," Frankie continued, "let's table this discussion until after we drop this beast off and go get something to eat. I'm starving."

It was hard to argue with that suggestion. And I had to admit that it made me happy Frankie assumed I'd want to get some dinner with her.

We were becoming what Aunt Estela would wink and call "*un articulo*"—an item.

I was totally okay with that. I shot Frankie a hopeful look.

"Do you like chicken gravy?"

Once again, Fred saw us coming and our cocktails appeared moments after we'd taken our seats at Sweet Potatoes. It was a Saturday night, and the place was hopping. But being on good terms with the accommodating bartender meant that even if the place was crowded, you could usually be squeezed into a space at the end of their large community table. That was okay by me. I liked the vantage point of looking out over most of the restaurant. And this spot gave us an unobstructed view of the kitchen, too.

"I can't believe I agreed to come in here dressed like this," Frankie complained.

"Will you relax? We probably got a table so fast precisely because you *are* dressed like that."

"That's nuts. They wouldn't give us preferential treatment because

I'm dressed like a hooker."

"No. But they'd probably do it to prevent a riot. Did you see how every man and half the women in this place started drooling as soon as we came in?"

"I reiterate: you're nuts."

"It's a moot point. Your gams are safely under wraps now."

Frankie scowled and picked up her menu.

I watched a couple of steaming entrees pass by.

"Chef must be in a good mood tonight," I remarked. "Looks like there might be some specials."

"What makes you say that?" Frankie was scanning the list of appetizers.

I pointed behind her. "I just saw a rib eye go that-a-way."

"I thought you said you wanted slathered lawn chicken, or something?"

"Slathered *lawn* chicken?"

She blinked up at me. "Isn't that what it's called?"

"No. It's *Yard Bird.*" I pointed it out on the menu. "Smothered Yard Bird."

Frankie rolled her eyes. "A rose by any other name . . ."

I picked up her drink and sniffed it. "Just how many shots of vodka did Fred put in this thing?"

Frankie took the glass away from me. "In your dreams, Matlock."

"You got that part right."

"So, since you mentioned it . . . maybe now is a good time for us to talk about things?"

"*Things?*"

"You know what I mean."

I did know what she meant. And I'd been thinking the same thing; only I was too much of a . . . *a slathered lawn chicken* . . . to bring it up first.

"You're right." I said. "You start." Frankie gave me a deadpan look.

"Nuh uh." I demurred. Frankie socked me on the arm. "Hey! I never said I was brave."

"Yeah. About that . . . how come *you* didn't volunteer to do the car washing and let *me* be the one to grab the Shelby?"

"*What?* If you'll recall, I didn't want *anyone* to do the car washing. This whole enterprise originated in Sebastian's twisted little brain. Besides—I don't think I could've commanded quite the same reaction from those Syndics of the Builder's Guild."

"That's a load of hooey. You're drop-dead gorgeous."

I know I must've sat there like a cipher with my mouth gaping open for some time, because Frankie finally reached over and gently pushed it shut.

"You're letting the flies out," she said, retracting her hand.

"I'm sorry," I apologized. "I wasn't expecting that."

"Apparently. Why are you so stubbornly unaware of how attractive you are?"

I was at a loss for words. "How does a person answer a question like that without sounding like either an idiot or an asshole?"

"I dunno. Maybe truthfully?"

"Okay." I thought about it. "Truthfully . . . it's not something I ever think about."

"Why?"

"I don't know. I just don't. You know, I don't have the best—"

"Track record with women?" Frankie cut me off and finished the declaration for me. "So I've heard. Methinks you might protest too much."

"Why would I do that?" I knew I was doing a crappy job concealing how busted I felt by her suggestion.

"Maybe to protect yourself? Maybe to avoid becoming vulnerable? Maybe because you think it's easier to not take chances on something that might not work out—again?"

I was close to pouting. If I could've gotten away with it, I'd have started kicking the table leg.

"That's quite a list. Sounds like maybe you've been giving my shortcomings some thought for a while."

"On the contrary," Frankie said. "I didn't have to think about it much at all."

"No?" That answer surprised and irritated me. "Am I really that transparent?"

"You? Not at all. Me? *Entirely.*" My face must've conveyed the confusion I felt. "I was talking about myself, Nick. These are all the reasons why *I'm* not in an any kind of relationship right now."

"Oh." I was unprepared for that revelation. It was a lot to take in, and I had no ready response.

The seconds ticked by while I thought about everything she'd just said. Thunder rolled outside. A swirling cacophony of glasses and silverware clinked and clattered, mixing together with the happy sounds of diners laughing and sharing bites of food. Servers came and went. And all the while, the sonorous voice of Carmen McRae wound itself around us, crooning that the only wise and sensible thing left to do was, "Come In From the Rain."

I had to hand it to Frankie: she knew when saying nothing was saying everything.

"I wish I had your courage," I said.

"What do you mean?"

"It would've taken me years to get where you just took us."

"Well, neither of us is getting any younger. Maybe it's worth another gamble?"

I smiled at her. "Maybe it is."

Our server arrived. "Have you ladies decided on what you'd like tonight?"

I was about to say, "Bring us two of everything," but Frankie piped up first and ordered for us.

"Yes, indeed. She'll have the rib eye, medium rare. And I'll have the Smothered Yard Bird. And could you bring us two extra plates?" She added, "We've decided to share."

After we ate, I drove Frankie back to her place and she asked if I wanted to come inside for a nightcap. Since tomorrow was Sunday, I knew

Frankie didn't have to be up early to go to school. But even with that, I didn't detect any hints of an ulterior motive in her suggestion. I wasn't sure if that made me happy or sad. But I wasn't ready to say goodnight to her just yet, so I agreed right away. Besides, we still hadn't discussed Eddie's latest ridiculous job offer.

Once we were inside, Frankie made a beeline for her bedroom, saying she wanted to change clothes.

"These damn shorts are about to cut off the circulation to my brain."

"Maybe that's why they call them cutoffs?"

"Very funny."

"Hey. Fair is fair. After all, they've been doing the same thing to my brain all day."

"Poor baby . . ."

"Go ahead and yuck it up. You don't know how powerful those things are."

"My shorts?"

I nodded. "And your other . . . parts."

She smiled. "Well, why don't you go into the kitchen and fix us something to drink? And when I get back, you can tell me all about it."

I followed orders and wandered into her kitchen in search of refreshment. In addition to several bottles of wine, Frankie had some cognac, a couple of good single malt scotches, and a bottle of port. I picked up the port and gave it a closer look.

Nice. It was a Quinta das Carvalhas 2012, Late Bottle Vintage. It had been opened, but was nearly full. I looked around for some small glasses. No luck. I wasn't comfortable ransacking all of her cupboards, so I stood back and gave her a holler.

"Hey, Frankie? Do you have any sherry glasses?"

"In the lower cupboard, right in front of you," she answered from very close range. I started and nearly dropped the bottle.

"Sweet mother of pearl! When did you get back in here?"

"About two seconds ago." She scooted around in front of me and retrieved the glasses. She had changed into a less provocative pair of shorts and had ditched the white T-shirt. I was irrationally pleased to see that she was still wearing my shirt, however, and had to fight an impulse to ask if she'd shed the Bluebella. Holding my peace on that query seemed like the better part of valor.

"Wanna go out on the porch and listen to the rain?" she asked.

In fact, I wanted to do that very much. But I had to admit that if Frankie had instead suggested we sit on the floor and set our hair on fire, I'd have jumped at that idea, too.

I was such a goner.

It was actually nice on her porch. I sat down on the swing, and Frankie joined me. We sipped our *porto* in companionable silence. It was lovely—a perfect blend of black cherry, dark chocolate and trailing hints of vanilla. The rain was falling more softly now. There were still rolls and rumbles of thunder and the occasional distant flash of lightning, but it was moving away from us. I guessed the entire system was now settling in over K-Vegas.

I wondered if Eddie's guy had had any problems starting the Shelby. I shuddered and reflexively wiped my mouth on my sleeve. I was due a big damn bonus for that one.

Maybe Frankie was right, and I was being too hasty in rejecting the Donzi job. After all, if we could finagle a way to get past the gatekeeper at the entrance to the club, we could probably gain easy access to the boat. The biggest problem would be where to take the damn thing to haul it out of the water.

"You're lost in thought."

"Not really." I shifted on the swing to face her. "I was thinking about the job."

"You mean the marine disaster?" Frankie quoted.

"Yeah. That one."

"I won't coerce you into doing it if you really have strong reservations, Nick."

"I know. But you're right: it is a big payout if we're successful."

"True."

"And maybe we *can* figure out a way to get in there that's at least a tiny bit plausible."

"Also true. Did the paperwork give any details about the owner of the boat?"

"Just his name. Ransom Jackson." I sighed. "Sounds like some small-penis, old-money kind of name to me."

"I suppose they can default on loans, just like the rest of us."

"Are you kidding? Their ilk wrote the book on how to dodge paying their bills. The only incredible thing about this circumstance is that he's about to get caught."

"Oh?" Frankie sounded intrigued. "Does that mean you think we should do this?"

"Don't get hasty. I'm not saying that. I'm just pointing out that whether it's us or some other collector, Mr. Jackson is about to meet his fiduciary maker."

"So how much is that boat of his worth?"

I thought about it. "A thirty-eight-foot Donzi with an engine rig like that? Probably three or four hundred thousand bucks. Maybe more, depending on how it's tricked out."

Frankie's eyes grew wide. "*A boat?*"

"Oh, it's not just a boat. It's a status symbol. You'd happily pay the absurd membership fee at a place like the Peninsula Club just for the privilege of mooring your boat there—whether you ever took it out on the water or not. I mean, it could just sit there and shimmer like an aquatic paperweight, as long as it inspired envy from the other, lesser club members."

"I so do not understand that."

"Trust me," I explained. "I just spent nearly seven years of my life helping people like Mr. Jackson shelter and protect their exaggerated assets. Remember Mr. Mozelle's Maybach?"

Frankie smiled at me in the half-light. "Of course I do. It's the reason we met."

"Yeah." I reached across the swing and gave her hand a quick squeeze. "Who knew a trunk-load of dildos packing cocaine could lead to something so nice?"

"Sometimes, you just get lucky."

"I know I sure as hell did. And I think I'm finally getting smart enough to realize it."

"You *think?*" Frankie's tone was teasing. "When will you be sure?"

"That's an answer with multiple parts."

"Meaning?"

"Meaning the part of me that lately seems to have no problem jumping your bones at every opportunity is already pretty sure."

"Okay." Frankie reflected on that. "So, what about the other parts?"

"Ah. That's where it gets complicated. The other parts are the ones that rear their ugly heads in the midst of my night terrors."

"You have night terrors?"

"Doesn't everyone?"

"Um. I hope not."

"Chalk it up to another happy area where I'm an overachiever." I finished my *porto* with a flourish and set the tiny glass down on a side table. "So, can I tell you a story—a true story—without scaring you off or making you think I'm a total looney tune?"

Frankie nodded. "I certainly hope so."

"Believe me when I tell you that this uncertainty of mine has nothing to do with you. Far from it. It might seem silly, but folklore and traditions in Guatemalan culture aren't just quaint superstitions. They're real, living things. Things with *teeth* . . . teeth that can fly up and bite you on your unbelieving ass. And that's true even for a person like my Mamá, who is a scholar and a woman of science. So when my Aunt Estela told me I was born with the curse of El Cadejo—a dark spirit who seeks you out at night—I *believed* her. The catch with my particular affliction is that El Cadejo is also a trickster, who can either help or hurt you according to the intentions of your heart. The anxiety of growing up with that contradiction, along with the self-doubt that sprang from it, became my particular curse. And it's what has kept me, until now, walking a very lonely road without any hope that I'd ever find real happiness." I looked at her mournfully. "I know this makes me sound like a loser, but I promise it's the truth. I am my own worst enemy when it comes to relationships. I've always been so tentative and certain of failure that I've front-loaded every one of them with the seeds of their own demise. Now? With you?" I hesitated. "I'm terrified of making the same mistakes all over again."

It was a lot for Frankie to take in, and I knew it. Part of me expected her to thank me very politely, before looking at her watch and inventing an excuse for why we needed to cut the evening short.

But she didn't do either of those things. She reached over and took hold of my hand—the one I'd been using to fidget with a loose button on my shirt.

"Tell me what I need to do?" Her voice was low and soft. "I'm not going to collude with your fear or do anything to make it easy for you to run away from us."

"I don't want to run away. That's the one thing I'm certain of."

Frankie leaned over and kissed me softly, then retreated to her side of the swing. "That seems like a good start," she said, hopefully.

"It's a great start." I squeezed her hand. "Can you be patient with me? I know it's a lot to ask."

"I can."

We sat without talking for a bit, listening to the rain. Among the pear trees at the back of her yard, birds started that joyful chorus of chirping that usually signified the end of a storm. I felt . . . unburdened. Even though I knew that later on, in the solitude of my dark room, I'd find plenty of reasons to doubt that telling Frankie had been a good decision—for right now, in this moment, I was at peace.

"How did your parents meet?"

I was surprised by Frankie's question. But it pleased me that she had asked it so casually. Maybe I hadn't scared her off with my confession about El Cadejo?

"Papa was an undergrad at Temple and participated in an immersion service trip to Guatemala during his senior year. This was not long after the horrible earthquake in 1976 that devastated the area around Guatemala City. Papa's group worked with a local relief organization to help rebuild the main hospital there. That's where he met Mamá.

She was a prodigy—one of the youngest premed students at Universidad Francisco Marroquín. He says the first time he saw her, she was barefoot and emptying a cistern into the large latrine they'd just dug to deal with medical waste. He said her raw, unspoiled beauty put a spell on him, and his life was forever changed. Of course Mamá says he's delusional and insists that he seduced her with Peanut M&Ms and his beautiful athlete's body. Whatever the truth was, they were married a year later, and Mamá finished her medical degree at Penn."

"That's a wonderful story. And very romantic." She smiled. "Your mother sounds like a force to be reckoned with."

"That's putting it mildly. She's ... *eccentric*."

"More eccentric than Lilah?" Frankie asked.

"Well. I guess the term 'eccentric' covers a lot of ground."

"You can say that again. I hope I get to meet her one day."

"Me, too." I thought about Mamá meeting Frankie. I waited for the prospect to make me feel anxious or like I was about to break out in hives.

It didn't happen.

The truth was, I thought Mamá would love Frankie.

I decided to try the words out. "I think she'd love you," I said. Frankie gave my fingers a gentle squeeze. "And that'll be especially true if you can find a way to keep us both out of jail."

"Then I'll have to make sure that happens." Frankie looked at me for clarification. "Or should I say *not* not make that happen?"

"Don't look at me. I suck at trying to decipher double negatives."

She laughed. "So, apropos of keeping you out of jail, what do you want to tell Eddie about the new job?"

"I'm ... on the fence about it."

"Okay."

"But the more I think about it, the more I wonder if there isn't a pretty easy way to pull it off. I mean, with some luck and a little bit of advance planning."

"It would have to be a *very* little bit of advance planning," Frankie cautioned. "Eddie said it had to be picked up before Friday."

"I know." I considered the timetable. "So, if we do this, we're going to need an outrageous idea that could only spring from the mind of someone who has no fear of the absurd. Someone who thinks on the scale of Cecil B. DeMille."

"Cecil B. DeMille? Like *The Ten Commandments,* Cecil B. DeMille?"

I nodded. "We need a credible, albeit sensational, reason to gain access to the Peninsula Club—a setting nearly as opulent and vulgar as any place frequented by Charlton Heston. As my appellate practice professor always said: 'A spoonful of strychnine makes the medicine irrelevant.' Ergo—and I cannot believe these words are even going to pass my lips—I think we should ask Sebastian for help."

Frankie all but gasped. "Are you serious?"

"I know it defies logic and all good sense. But, yes. I'm serious."

Frankie took a moment to let that idea sink in. "Wednesday is a professional development day for me, so no school. Think we could have everything in place by then?"

"I think so. The hardest part will be where to take the boat to get it out of the water and onto a trailer."

"Didn't Eddie say he would help with that part?"

"I believe he said he'd 'hook us up' with a truck and trailer. Have you ever pulled anything on a trailer?" I asked, hopefully.

"Not since college, when I moved back here with a U-Haul."

"Don't suppose it was greater than forty feet long, was it?"

"Not even close."

I drummed the fingers of my free hand on my knee. "We'll figure something out."

"Does this mean we're taking the job?"

"Not just yet. I think it means we tell Eddie we're thinking about taking it, and we'll give him a definitive answer tomorrow. That'll give us time to see what crazy scheme Sebastian comes up with and how many of my organs I'll have to digest to consider it."

Frankie laughed and leaned forward to kiss me on the cheek.

"I'll go call Eddie. You call Sebastian."

"Okay."

As Frankie got up to head into the house, a thought occurred to me.

"On your way back," I held up my empty sherry glass, "top me off? I think it's gonna be a long night."

Chapter Five

Ma, He's Making Eyes at Me

I'd love to report that I reached out to Sebastian only to discover that he'd suddenly decided to pull up stakes and move to South Dakota, thereby forcing us to abandon any hopes of jacking the Donzi. But no such luck. When I called him, he answered on the first ring. It took me the better part of five minutes to get him to suspend his rhapsodic expressions of delight about our success grabbing the Shelby—and his smug insistence that he knew I'd end up spending the night at Frankie's sooner or later.

"I am *not* spending the night over here, "I insisted. "And I'm calling because we need your help."

There was silence on the line.

"Would you mind repeating that last part?" he demanded.

I sighed. "You heard me."

"I did—and now I'm pissed that Doreen drank up the rest of our champagne. This is a red-letter day."

"You can lord it over me later, okay? We have another job offer from Eddie, and this one's a doozie. We need some . . . creative ideas about how best to pull it off."

"Not that I don't appreciate the offer, but does this have to happen tonight?"

"Yes, because there are multiple moving parts that have to be put into place and we need to make the grab no later than Friday. What's wrong with tonight?" I looked at my watch. It was barely seven-thirty. "Do you have other plans?"

"No. Just watching *Animal PD* on Nat Geo with Carol Jenkins. I was actually hoping *you* had other plans. Like maybe a spot of *under-cover* work, if you get my drift."

"In your dreams, puppet master."

"You say *my* dreams, I say *your* fantasies. It's six of one, half-dozen of the other."

"What-ever." My exasperation with him was mounting. I'd had to be crazy to even think about asking him to become involved in this ridiculous enterprise. "Can you come over here so we can strategize?"

"Of course. What do I need to bring? I've got some of that seven-layer dip left. Ask Frankie if she has any tortilla chips."

"Sebastian? We're planning a heist, not a late supper."

"That shows how much *you* know. The Stohlers are old-money Moravians. As a Yankee apostate, you're simply incapable of grasping the basic social contracts that define social gatherings in the South."

"I have no idea what you're talking about."

"Nick? It's common knowledge that there is only one thing a god-fearing Moravian needs to get into heaven: a covered dish."

"Yeah. Okay. Knock yourself out. I'll text you the address."

"Fine," he said. "But before you hang up, give me a quick rundown on the particulars."

"Sure. It's a boat—a *big* boat—owned by a man named Ransom Jackson. The kicker is that it's in the marina at the Peninsula Yacht Club on Lake Norman."

"*Interesting.*" Sebastian gave a low whistle. "This definitely calls for crudités."

I chose to ignore that. "See you in about twenty minutes?"

"I'll be there." He disconnected.

Frankie was in the kitchen refilling our glasses when I joined her. "How'd it go with Eddie?" I asked.

"He said he wasn't surprised to hear from me—then he asked if I'd really need until tomorrow to 'convince you' we should do it."

I was offended. "What the hell was that supposed to mean?"

Frankie handed me my glass. "I think it was his ham-fisted way of paying homage to my feminine wiles."

"More like your *outfit,*" I scoffed. "Perv."

"I thought you liked my outfit?" she teased.

"That's beside the point," I muttered.

"Not for me, it isn't."

I looked at her. We were standing in nearly the exact same spot we'd been in the other night when Lilah interrupted our . . . close encounter. My throat suddenly felt dry.

"Sebastian will be here in about twenty minutes," I croaked.

"Pity," she said.

I took a deep breath. "We're gonna need a plan for this, too."

"For this?" she asked. "For this . . . what?"

"*This.*" I waved a hand back and forth between us. "I can't be wanting to climb into your pants every ten seconds. It'll ruin everything."

"I'm not opposed to having plans, but exactly how could that ruin anything?"

"Because I won't be able to think clearly. And when I get distracted, I get stupid. And right now, neither of us can afford to get stupid."

"I guess that makes a bizarre kind of sense. I mean, as long as you can promise me one thing."

"What's that?" I asked warily.

She bent closer. "That this is a time-value plan with a date-certain expiration. You aren't the only one in this equation struggling with self-control."

Her admission made me smile. "I'm not?"

"*No.* Believe me."

I closed my eyes. "God, this is so damn frustrating. Why didn't we meet ten years ago? Why did it have to happen *now*, while we're both moonlighting as half-rate, muscle car Madoffs?"

"Because things happen the way they happen, Nick. There is no rhyme or reason. And ten years ago, you were still in law school and I was married—to a man. So, I'm not going to complain about the timetable. I'm going to fall on bended knee and thank the heavens that our paths finally crossed—whenever the hell they did."

"You're right," I said sheepishly. "Maybe we'll luck out and get adjoining cells at the Swannanoa Correctional Facility for Women?"

"One can only hope."

I smiled. A random thought occurred to me. "Your family—are you Moravians?"

"Where'd that come from?" Frankie sounded amused.

"Sebastian."

"Oh. *Of course*. Yes, we are."

"What is that, exactly? I mean, I've lived here long enough to know the basics, but I never really understood the faith . . . I mean, except for the cookies and those funky polyhedron Christmas stars."

Frankie thought about my question. "We're kind of a cross between Methodist and Lutheran."

That made sense. "I'm kind of a lapsed Catholic," I explained.

"I pretty much gathered that."

"Yeah?" Her statement didn't surprise me. "That ambient guilt is kind of hard to miss, isn't it?"

"I think you wear it well."

"I don't know about that. I think of it more as clawing your way through life while dragging an anchor."

Frankie laughed at my description. "Regrettably, my family's relationship with faith is a whole lot less intrusive. We pretty much attend candlelight Lovefeasts and eat lots of sugar cake."

"Damn. Must be nice not to grow up in the shadow of an angry God."

"If I had to guess, I'd say that God's umbrage is probably more nonsectarian."

"Really?" I was intrigued by that idea. "What do you think He'd have to say about our little cottage industry?"

"Repossessing cars?"

I nodded.

"Honestly, compared to the litany of other crimes against nature now commanding the headlines, I don't think our enterprise would even be a blip on His radar."

"You're probably right," I agreed. "If you've got a laptop or iPad, we can start doing some research."

"Of course I do. Follow me."

Frankie led the way to her living room.

I had just entered the search term *Peninsula Yacht Club* into her browser when car headlights flashed by her front window. Sebastian had arrived.

Frankie met him at the door. True to form, he was carrying a 1.5-liter bottle of Mascota Unanime and a large shopping bag. He kissed her on the cheek and handed both things off to her with a cheery, "Here you go, love chunks. I brought some goodies, in case we get the nibbles."

"How sweet." Frankie ushered him into the room. "Come in and sit down. We're just getting started."

She set the bottle of wine down on her coffee table and began pulling items from the bag.

"Interesting," I observed, as Frankie deposited an array of food products on the table. "A party-sized bag of Utz Ripples, I get. But three quarts of chowchow?"

Sebastian ignored me. "I just put these up last week," he explained to Frankie. "It's a particularly good batch, too. I found a new recipe at AsianFusion Girl that uses kimchi and gochujang. I've been using this on everything."

"Including corn flakes," I added.

Sebastian shot me a withering look before crossing the room and dropping into an oversized club chair. "Maybe you'll be happy to learn that I've got some tasty intel to share on our friend, Mr. Jackson?"

"*Already?*" I was dumbfounded. "I only told you his name half an hour ago."

"Hey." Sebastian held up a manicured index finger. "Time waits for no man. I happen to have some associates in the Lake Norman region. I made a few calls on the drive over here."

I sighed and closed Frankie's laptop. "Of course you did."

Frankie sat down beside me on the sofa, still holding one of the quarts of chowchow. "What'd you find out?" Her voice was tinged with excitement.

"Well," Sebastian crossed his legs. "Turns out that our lauded NASCAR racing team owner has been a *veeeerrrryyy* bad boy. He's in the throes of an epically nasty, regrettably public divorce, and the plaintiff, who we'll call Mrs. *Fluffy* Jackson, is suing our white-haired Don Juan's ass for half of *everything* he owns—right down to his pit box and impact wrenches. Oh, and she, by the way, is estranged wife number *three*—so half of everything ain't what it used to be." He pointed to the bottle of wine. "Do you want me to open that for you?"

"What?" Frankie looked down at the bottle. "Oh. Sure." She passed it back to Sebastian. "Let me get you an opener."

"Don't bother, love chunks. I travel with one." He flashed her the mini waiter's tool and crumb comb combo he always carried inside a jacket pocket. "But I wouldn't say nay to a glass."

Frankie started to get up, but I stopped her. "I'll go."

"You found all of that out on the ride over here?" I heard Frankie ask, as I headed for the kitchen.

"Honey, real estate is like one giant sorority," Sebastian explained. "You can always count on your sisters to know somebody who knows somebody who knows somebody else's not-so-secret bid'ness. There ain't no HIPAA rules when it comes to dishin' on whose lakefront condo is about to go up on the auction block. That information is fair game for every big-haired buyer's representative in the state."

I returned with three wineglasses. "You were born for this work."

"Don't I know it?" Sebastian poured us each a generous glass of the Unanime. "And it's about to pay big dividends for you."

"Let me guess," I said. "You already have a plan?"

"*Hello?* Does Ro-Ro pray every night to Saint Anthony to restore the lost youth of her old maid daughter? *Of course,* I have a plan."

I didn't really want any wine—not after our cocktails at dinner and the two glasses of Porto. But I took a big swallow, anyway. I knew that intoxication would be my best defense against the insanity I'd unleashed by asking Sebastian to become involved.

"Ooooh, tell us." Frankie's level of excitement wasn't making me feel any better about what was about to befall us.

"So," he began. "The Peninsula Yacht Club is a truly high-class establishment. One of the perks members get for their outrageous membership fees and slip rentals is concierge service: meaning any time you have an inkling, you can phone ahead and they'll pull up your water rocket, fill it with gas, and even stock it with hooch and a big damn party tray. All you have to do is show up, climb aboard, and hoist your Jolly Roger as you exit the marina." He retrieved the bag of chips and ripped it open. "Piece of cake."

"Yeah," I said. "Except for one tiny detail."

"What's that?" He withdrew a handful of ripple chips.

"Mr. Jackson isn't going to ask them to pull up his boat for us."

"Duh. Of course he isn't." Sebastian munched and swallowed. "*You* are."

"Me?" I pointed at my chest. "Are you crazy? Why would they do it for me?"

"Because you're going to impersonate one of the attorneys from the Charlotte firm that's representing him in his latest divorce."

I blinked. "I can't do that. It's totally illegal."

"Duh. So is stealing somebody's Donzi."

"We're not *stealing* it," I corrected him. "We're repossessing it."

"A rose by any other color . . ."

"Sebastian? I'm not kidding. I can't pull off pretending I represent Jackson. That's unethical on about twenty levels."

"Pish posh." He dismissed my concern. "Your ethics flew out the window the first time you jacked a car. Don't you have contacts at just about every firm in the state?"

"*No*. Just the big ones."

"Well, this happens to be a big one. It's Smith, Barnard, Bryan and Scales. I've seen your damn Rolodex. You have cards for *everyone*. Don't you know people there?"

It was painful for me to admit he was right. I actually did know a couple of attorneys at Smith Barnard.

"Maybe," I said tentatively.

"Aha! I knew it. How many?"

"Two. But one of them died about six months ago."

"How about the other one? Is he still above ground?"

I sighed. "As far as I know. But he's in mergers. He wouldn't do civil disputes."

"That's even more perfect." Sebastian clapped his hands together. "They won't know it's bogus. What's his name?"

"Chris Marx."

I heard Frankie stifle a laugh.

"*Chris?*" Sebastian's eyes widened. "Did you say *Chris?*"

I nodded.

"Hello, androgyny! Chris Marx it is. Now," Sebastian leaned forward, "do you have one of his calling cards?"

I thought about lying and saying "no." But I knew he'd see through me. I nodded reluctantly.

Frankie decided to intervene. "It's actually a good plan, Nick. And it keeps your name and reputation completely out of this in case they do any follow-up checking."

I took a deep breath. "I suppose that's true."

"Of course it's true," Sebastian asserted. "And if Jackson is the sleazebag he's rumored to be, the club won't have any reason to doubt his firm's involvement in protecting his cheating ass."

I was curious about one thing. "Exactly how did you find out Smith Barnard is representing him in this latest divorce action?"

He tsked. "That I cannot tell you." He raised three fingers in a salute. "Honor among brokers."

"Nick." Frankie grasped my arm. "This is genius. It could totally work."

I took another big swallow of my wine. Maybe seven or eight

glasses of this would make me more optimistic about Sebastian's scheme.

"We still have to concoct a convincing reason to persuade them to get the boat out for us." I was grasping at straws.

"Oh, I think we have one . . . and she's sitting right beside you on that couch."

I shot a panicked look at Frankie. *Oh, no fucking way . . . Not again.*

Before I could reject Sebastian's suggestion out of hand, Frankie spoke up.

"I'm game. Let's hear it."

"Are you insane?" I was nearly apoplectic.

"Let's at least hear what he has to say." Frankie passed me the bag of chips. "Here. Eat something."

I sat stupidly holding the bag while Sebastian shared the details of his plan.

"All you have to do," he said, "is identify yourself as one of Mr. Jackson's personal attorneys—namely *Chris*— and explain that you have a matter of some sensitivity that requires an accommodation from the concierge."

"Accommodation?" I asked.

"Don't interrupt," Sebastian chastised me. "As I was saying . . . you'll tell the concierge that Mr. Jackson plans to meet Miss Playmate Du Jour here," he gestured to Frankie, "at a private location on the lake. You'll explain that because of his delicate personal circumstances, he cannot risk being observed leaving the club with another woman, as you're sure the concierge can understand. Therefore, you'll explain that *you* will accompany the enticing Miss Du Jour on Mr. Jackson's boat, and deliver them both to the appointed rendezvous site. Oh, and you'll also assure the concierge that Mr. Jackson will reward his assurance of discretion *handsomely*."

"That's pure *genius*." Frankie was plainly impressed. She shot me an encouraging look. "Don't you think it's genius, Nick?"

I drained my wineglass.

"Don't worry about *her*," Sebastian waved me off dismissively. "We need to talk about your outfit."

"All right," Frankie agreed. "As long as it's not those damn cutoffs again, I'm fine with anything."

"Oh, honey, relax. We're not talking about the PBR crowd on this caper. We're kicking the dress code *way* uptown. Flashy chic all the way."

"Uptown?" I narrowed my eyes. I thought about all the high-priced female companions who occupied many of the pieds-à-terre in Charlotte and environs. "What *part* of uptown are we talking about here?"

"Well," he considered my question. "To give you a visual, think Padma Lakshmi meets slutty dolphin trainer."

"That's what I *thought* you meant," I said. "Forget it."

"Hold on, Nick. I want to hear his idea." Frankie refilled my glass. "Have some more wine."

"Okay," Sebastian continued. "I'm seeing a weekend-in-Kennebunkport sailorish kind of thing . . . ultra-short, sleeveless minidress. Maybe in navy with white piping? Zip front—unzipped low enough to show off your flotation devices. White stiletto sandals—knockoff Jimmy Choos if we can find them. Of course you'll need mirrored Aviators. And we'll have to tart up your hair."

Frankie nodded. "Think you can find everything quickly at local stores?"

"If I can't, your sister should put me in a box and bury me."

The two of them continued droning on about clothes, shoes, makeup and vague ramblings about somebody's BMW I could borrow for the drive down to Lake Norman. After my third glass of wine, I pretty much stopped listening to them. Exhaustion and inebriation overtook me. I kept sinking lower into the sofa cushions. My head rested against Frankie's shoulder, until gravity and advancing sleepiness lowered it squarely onto her lap. The last thing I remember before drifting off was the warmth of her skin, the soft vibration of her voice, and the sweet sensation of being wrapped up in a safe haven at last.

It was nearly 10 a.m. when I crawled out of bed on Sunday. I remembered nothing about how I got home, but since my car was MIA, I assumed Sebastian and Frankie must've poured me into his Audi.

Sebastian was nowhere to be found, but when I made my way to the kitchen, I discovered that he'd left me a thermos of coffee and a note taped to a grease-stained Bojangles bag. Big block letters ordered me to eat its contents. I took a cautious peek and discovered a monstrous, foil-wrapped country ham, egg and cheese biscuit.

It actually smelled pretty good.

Taking that as a hopeful sign, I carried the coffee and the biscuit out back to sit on our brick patio. It was a nice morning—mild temperature, low humidity, and not a cloud in the deep blue sky. It was a textbook Carolina spring day. The setting was so peaceful and unspoiled that I had a hard time squaring it with the insanity we'd been discussing last night.

As I ate my biscuit, I marveled that I wasn't hung over. *Don't know how I dodged that bullet.*

I wondered how Frankie had made out, and what she was up to.

And where the hell was Sebastian?

I'd also carried my iPad and cell phone outside with me. It seemed like a good time to start doing a little scouting related to our next heist. I spent some time looking at maps of Lake Norman waterways and trying to identify a remote public boat landing that might work as a site for us to take the Donzi out of the water without creating too much of a stir. I thought somewhere in Lincoln or Iredell counties might be good, since they both were far enough removed from the Peninsula Club to avoid having anyone recognize the boat, yet not too far from I-40, so we could make a straight shot back to K-Vegas once we had the thing trailered.

My cell phone rang. I picked it up, but didn't recognize the number.

"Hello?" I answered tentatively.

"Is this Vera?" A woman's husky-sounding voice asked.

"Um. Yes."

"This is Linda, from the NRB. Eddie asked me to give you a call and ask where you want the rig delivered?"

Rig? What rig?

"Um, hi there . . . *Linda.* I'm not sure I know what you mean . . . what kind of rig are you referencing?"

Linda cleared her throat. It sounded like she spat something out, too. There was a fair amount of wind noise on the line. "The quad cab and the trailer." Her voice sounded impatient. "Eddie said you needed them for a pickup. Where do you want me to drop them off? We're headed your way right now."

Oh, sweet mother of pearl . . .

"Um . . . I'm sorry Miss . . . er . . .Linda. I haven't really had time to think about where we need to keep the . . . rig. Does it have to be brought over today?"

"Eddie's orders were to hand it off to you today, and I'm already halfway to Winston." I could hear the blare of a car horn. "*Asshole!*"

"Excuse me?"

"*Not you.* Some douchebag just tried to cut me off. So what's it gonna be, Vera? I got another job this afternoon, so now is the only time I have to drop this rig off." The car horn blew a second time.

Geez Louise, lady. I tried to think of something. Frankie and I were both clueless about how to pull a forty-foot trailer—much less could we figure out how to back one down a boat ramp. We'd need a safe place to practice.

Think, Nick. Think . . . Okay, okay . . . I got an idea. Well. Half an idea.

"Do you know where Oak Hollow Mall is?" I asked Linda.

"In High Point?"

Bingo! The mall closed in 2017 and was now pretty much abandoned. Different civic groups rented spaces inside it for fundraisers, and High Point University now owned most of it. I'd just attended a benefit for a regional hospice organization over there, in the old Dillard's store.

"Yes," I told her. "That's the one. Any chance you could veer off and meet me there?"

"Yeah. I can cut over on Highway 311. Where do you want me to park it?"

"How about in the lot outside the entrance to Dillard's? I think it's on the Hartley Drive side."

"Sounds good to me. I'll be there in about fifteen minutes."

Shit. I wasn't even dressed yet. "I'll get there as fast as I can. It might take me closer to twenty-five or thirty minutes to meet you."

"No skin off my nose," Linda husked. "I'm on the clock." She hung up.

Great. Just great. What the hell were we going to do with a monster pickup and forty-foot boat trailer until Wednesday?

I checked the time on my cellphone. *Can't worry about that right now. I gotta haul ass.*

I got up and headed for my bedroom to get dressed. I was halfway out the door when it occurred to me that I didn't have a damn car.

"Tell me again why we're going to High Point?"

I had to hand it to Frankie; she had made record time getting to our house to pick me up.

"Linda," I explained again. "We're meeting Linda. She's dropping off the pickup truck and boat trailer."

We were already out of Winston-Salem, heading east on I-40. The turnoff for Highway 311 was about three miles away.

"I get that part," Frankie replied. "But why High Point?"

"It was the best place I could think of on the fly. In case you hadn't noticed, Sebastian and I live on a cul-de-sac. I had to think of someplace big enough and safe enough to park the damn thing until we could figure out what to do with it."

"Why didn't you ask her to bring it to my place?"

Okay, that was like a needle across a record.

"Truthfully, I never even thought of that. But even if I had suggested it, we'd still need a place to practice wrangling it."

"I suppose that's true," she agreed. "Good thinking."

"By the way, I don't know if you've ever talked with her, but Linda doesn't come across as the warm and fuzzy type."

"That seems pretty consistent with everything I've heard about her. It's probably not an accident that she's the only regular at the NRB who doesn't have a nickname. I don't think anyone is brave enough to suggest one."

"I don't doubt it."

"So we're meeting her at Oak Hollow Mall?"

"Yeah. Since it's mostly abandoned, I thought those big empty parking lots would give us plenty of space to practice. At least we won't have to worry about smashing into anything."

"Good thinking." Frankie laughed. "This sure isn't the way I thought I'd be spending my Sunday."

"Me, either."

"How are you feeling?"

"Pretty good, all things considered." I wondered if I needed to apologize for anything? I had a vague recollection that I'd fallen asleep on her lap, but didn't remember much after that. "Did I do anything stupid last night?"

Frankie shot me a sidelong glance. "Define stupid."

Oh, shit . . .

I must've looked as pathetic as I felt because Frankie took pity on me.

"You were *fine*," she assured me. "Stop worrying."

"Did you and Sebastian iron out all of your wardrobe details?"

"Pretty much. He said he wanted to hit some of the Tanger outlet stores this morning as soon as they opened. I didn't have the stamina for that kind of outing today, so I told him I trusted him if he found anything suitable."

"Have you taken leave of your senses?"

"Not in the slightest. Without Sebastian, I'd pretty much have to rely on Lilah for wardrobe advice." She turned and looked at me over the top of her sunglasses. "So, you decide: I can embrace being dressed like a slutty *demimondaine*—or I can show up looking like Morticia Addams."

"These are the only choices?" I asked.

"Well, I suppose I could also pull off a pretty convincing third-grade schoolmarm, but I don't think anyone would buy that our NASCAR magnate, Mr. Jackson, would risk his future financial security for a tryst with Caroline Ingalls."

"I don't know about that . . . she was pretty hot."

Frankie laughed. "You just like women who boss you around."

"Oh? Is that what I like?"

Frankie nodded. "Evidence would seem to suggest this."

"What evidence?"

"Let's start with the company you keep. There's Mamá, of course. And let's not forget Aunt Estela. Antigone goes without saying. And we need to include Sebastian—who has a more highly developed feminine side than either of us. He *definitely* counts. Then there's Carol Jenkins, who wins top honors as probably the bossiest of the bunch. And, finally, there's me."

I found it hard to disagree with Frankie's argument. "That's a pretty compelling list."

"I thought so," she replied smugly.

"But I have to take exception to one entry in your hall of fame: I don't really think *you* boss me around."

"Oh, *that*," Frankie dismissed my exception. "Don't worry. I'm saving up."

"Great. Just my luck."

We were nearing the exit for Eastchester Drive.

"Is this our turnoff for the mall?" she asked.

"Yep. Lemme text Linda and tell her we'll be there in five minutes."

Frankie turned on her blinker and moved over to exit the highway.

"I hope she's not pissed that we're so late."

We didn't have any problem spotting the truck and trailer rig as we made the circuit around Oak Hollow Mall. I sucked in a breath when I first saw it: the setup was massive. The whole conveyance had to be at least sixty feet long. Eddie hadn't been kidding when he said he'd hook us up. Linda had delivered a Ford Super Duty F450 Dually pickup hitched to a Heritage triple-axle boat trailer.

I was no boatswain, but even I was enough of a lesbian to recognize that this was some kind of sweet-ass rig. If Eddie had been willing to spring for a setup like this, I must've seriously underestimated the value of the Donzi we were making plans to recover.

I swallowed hard and pointed the spectacle out to Frankie. "There it is. Over there by Dillard's."

Frankie's jaw dropped. "Are you *kidding* me? How are we supposed to drive *that?* Even without a boat on it?"

"One nightmare at a time, okay? Let's just get this handoff over with."

Frankie drove us over and parked beside a second pickup that contained two cranky-looking women smoking cigarettes. They both had tanned, leathery skin and identical bleached-blonde hair helmets. They looked so much alike, I wondered if they were sisters. They made no effort to greet us.

We got out of the car and I nervously approached them.

"Are you Linda?" I asked. "I'm . . . Vera. This is Frankie Stohler. I'm sorry it took us so long to get over here. I didn't have a car and had to hitch a ride."

It was a shabby excuse. Apparently, Linda thought so, too. She blew out a slow plume of smoke and took her time sizing me up.

"You don't have a car?" she finally asked, with more than a trace of sarcasm. "Kind of in the wrong line of work then, aren't you?"

"You'd think so, wouldn't you? But I actually *do* have a car; it just wasn't at the house this morning when you called."

"Uh huh." She gave me a slow nod. "Denise and I been cooling our heels here for nearly an hour."

"We're both very sorry about that," Frankie offered. "Maybe you'd let us buy you some lunch for your trouble? I'm sure you both had better things to do today."

Linda's eyebrow twitched higher. "Don't worry about it, little sister. We're getting paid." I was encouraged that she'd used Weasel's nickname for Frankie. She shifted her gaze back to me. "Either of you ever piloted one of these rigs before?" She asked the question like she already knew the answer.

I was about to say "hell to the no" and throw myself on her mercy, when Frankie stepped in front of me.

"Vera's checked out on it," she assured Linda. "She's hauled boats before."

I looked at Frankie like she'd taken complete leave of her senses—but it was clear she'd already decided how this was going to go.

Linda shook her head. "Okay by me." She reached inside her shirt pocket and withdrew a set of keys that she promptly flipped to Frankie. "The tank's full. I left the drop-off address from Eddie on the passenger seat. Good luck." She started her truck. Before she pulled away, she leaned out the window and addressed us both again. "I don't know what the hell kind of game Eddie is playing by giving you two lightweights a job that takes a high-dollar setup like this, but that's none of my business. I did my part dropping this shit off. Whatever happens now happens. I got nothin' to do with it." She gave us a little parting salute. "Y'all keep it between the ditches."

We watched them drive off. Once their truck had rounded the mall and was out of sight, I turned and confronted Frankie.

"What in the holy hell was *that* about? Neither of us knows jack shit about how to drive this thing, and she *knew* it."

"Will you relax? I wasn't going to tell *her* that."

"Why the hell not? Maybe she would've helped us out."

"How, Nick? That was *Linda*—as in, I'd like nothing better than to eat the entrails of incompetents like you for lunch."

"Great. Just *great*." I sulked. "Now what do we do?"

Frankie took a look around the deserted parking lot. "Practice?"

"Practice?" I took a deep breath. *Why the hell not?* "Okay. You're the one with experience driving a bus. You go first."

I have to hand it to Frankie: the woman was fearless. She climbed into the cab of the big diesel pickup and fired it right up.

"Walk to the back and tell me if the brake lights and turn signals on the trailer all work."

I followed orders and waited while Frankie tested them each in turn. Everything checked out.

I noticed that the boat trailer had Ohio tags, meaning it probably was a rental. The truck was obviously from Eddie's fleet. It had the same type of gambling-themed license plate that all of his vehicles sported. This one proclaimed, "H82FLD."

Ironic, given our circumstances . . .

"Come on and get in," Frankie called out to me. I could see her retrieve the sheet of paper containing our drop-off instructions and tuck it behind her visor. "Maybe we'll just take turns doing some loops around the mall?"

"Yeah. Okay." I climbed into the passenger seat and snapped my seat belt into place. "Wagons Ho."

Frankie slid the truck into gear and we rolled forward slowly.

"Well, hell," she said with surprise as we picked up speed. "This is like nothing."

"Yeah, well don't get cocky. There are no other vehicles around, and there's no load on the trailer."

"True." Frankie reached the intersection with the loop road that made a wide circuit around the perimeter of the mall. "Well, here goes nothing."

I was impressed. She managed to navigate the turn pretty well. She knew enough to swing wide to allow the trailer plenty of clearance room. Of course, the ease of that was facilitated by the lack of oncoming cars.

"Are you sure you haven't done this before?" I asked.

"Not exactly. But my dad has a pontoon, and I've ridden with him a few times when he's taken it out to Belews Lake. That man takes caution to a new level. But believe me, his little getup is nowhere near as long or as unwieldy as this thing."

"That might be true, but you still seem pretty comfortable."

"Going in a straight line? Sure. When it comes to backing the thing up? *That* I don't see happening."

"Yeah," I agreed. "There's no getting around that little errand. We're going to have to figure something out."

Frankie completed our first loop. "Do you wanna give it a shot?"

"Hell no. You're doing great. Think you can drive this thing on the highway?"

"There's only one way to find out."

"I was afraid you'd say that."

Frankie smiled. "How about we make another couple of circuits, and maybe you can help me try to back it up?"

"I'm game if you are."

"One thing's for sure," Frankie insisted. "When we're on the highway, I'm getting into a lane and staying there. I don't care how long it takes us to get back from Charlotte."

"About that. I've been giving it some thought, and I think we ought to plan on taking the boat out of the water at someplace less trafficked. Maybe even a public boat landing, versus a marina? Someplace as far north of Charlotte as we can go."

"I like that idea," Frankie agreed. "The simpler, the better."

"There should be some smallish public boat landings farther north on the lake that might make it easier for us to get the Donzi onto the trailer. We'll have to scope those out and pick one that isn't too far from the Interstate. I had actually started looking around this morning before Linda called."

We'd made it back to the part of the lot behind the old Dillard's store.

Frankie put the truck in park and asked me to help her find something she could use to mark off a spot to try and back into. There was nothing inside the cab. I hopped out to look in the bed and was thrilled to find a couple of orange traffic cones strapped to a side rail with bungee cords.

I walked back to the front of the truck and showed them to her. "How about these?"

"Perfect," she said. "How wide is a boat ramp?"

"Beats the hell outta me. Maybe fifteen or twenty feet?"

"Sounds good. Maybe put them someplace over there?" She pointed to a distant spot ahead of the truck, perpendicular to where we were parked. "Then come back and help me adjust these mirrors."

After I positioned the cones, Frankie had me stand alternately at the rear corners of the trailer while she adjusted the big side mirrors. Once that was finished, she directed me to go stand near the cones so I could help her navigate by shouting "left" or "right," according to which way she needed to angle the trailer.

Frankie drove forward until she was well past the cones, then put the truck into reverse and commenced backing up.

The first couple of attempts were pretty terrifying and not even close. Once, I had to scream at her and jump out of the way before she ran me over. Another time, she nearly jackknifed the cab into the trailer. Three times, she knocked the cones over. Finally, she seemed to start getting the hang of it, and the trailer began moving the way she wanted it to. After her sixth or seventh attempt, the truck and trailer moved together in smooth syncopation. The boat trailer glided cleanly between the two cones.

Well I'll be damned . . .

"Try it again!" I yelled. "Just to be sure you can do it on demand."

She pulled away and repeated the maneuver. Once again, the trailer rolled cleanly between the cones.

"You're an Ace!" I bellowed. "You're a damn rock star!"

Frankie cut the engine. I jogged up to the truck and climbed up on the running board to plant a kiss squarely on her lips. "That has to be the sexiest thing I've ever experienced," I said when we parted.

"You're such a pushover," she gushed.

"It does make a girl wonder what else you can do with heavy

equipment if you really thought about it."

"Oh, yeah?" She gave me a sultry look. "In that case, climb on up into this cab and I'll show you my multi-axle license."

It was an intriguing prospect.

It was a Sunday morning in High Point, and all decent people were in church. Nobody was hanging around the parking lot of a deserted shopping mall.

I decided to follow orders.

After all, we'd already established that I was into bossy women . . .

It made the most sense to take the truck and trailer out to Frankie's place to store them until we were ready to set up for the Donzi heist on Wednesday.

We'd talked to each other on our cell phones throughout the entire drive back to Winston-Salem from High Point. I followed behind her like a flag car and had some anxious moments when we merged back onto I-40 near the airport and the highway expanded to six lanes. But Frankie told me to relax and assured me that one advantage of driving something so big was that most people did their best to avoid *you*. Even back in the city, she managed to negotiate turns onto narrower streets pretty well. I only saw the trailer go off the road once, and that was about as close as I ever cared to get to the near-demolition of a covered bus stop stand.

Frankie was an ace backing the thing into her driveway from Shattalon Drive. I followed behind her in her car, and stopped short of her driveway with the flashers on, effectively stopping traffic behind us so she could complete the maneuver cleanly. Fortunately, her place was far enough out from town that there weren't many cars on the road. She managed to park the rig mostly parallel to her driveway and did a credible job avoiding my Outback, which was still in her driveway from the night before. Part of me was sorry she didn't manage to crush it. I was still anxious to be rid of the car after the adventure we'd had driving Ice T. around town, strapped in the back.

After Frankie hopped out and locked the truck, we went inside her house to make a pot of coffee and continue our research for the Wednesday venture. I called Sebastian and told him where I was. He reported that his outing to the Tanger outlet stores had borne fruit, and he was about ten minutes out with a bag full of treasures for Miss Du Jour. When I shared his report with Frankie, she insisted that he come right over so she could see what he'd found.

I wasn't sure I shared her enthusiasm for the big reveal. In my experience, Sebastian was incapable of nuance. I was sure that whatever garments he'd procured for Frankie would be guaranteed to make her look like soft-porn clickbait.

Frankie must've been able to read my expression.

"Will you stop pouting," she demanded. "It's a job, not a fashion statement."

"I just don't trust him."

"*Oh, really?*"

"Okay," I admitted. "I don't trust *me*, either."

"That's what I thought." Frankie sat down beside me on the sofa. "What are you looking at?"

I showed her the screen of the iPad.

"This is a map of all the public boat landings on Lake Norman." I pointed at a site to the south, near the lower, bowl-shaped base of the lake. "Here is the Peninsula Yacht Club."

"Oh, crap. It's way the hell down there, isn't it?"

"Yeah. And that's the rub. We're gonna have to pilot the Donzi waaaaay back up through all these splintery little waterways to find some off-the-beaten-path boat ramp that's far enough away from the LPs to safely haul it outta the water."

Frankie gave me a quizzical look. "'LPs'?"

"Lake People."

"Of course." She dropped her head back and regarded the ceiling. "First. World. Problems."

"Exactly. I just wish I knew a safe way to get us where we need to go. This lake is like a rabbit warren."

"Isn't there such a thing as boat GPS?"

Was there? I'd never even thought of that.

"Let's find out," I suggested.

I Googled *GPS Navigation for Lake Norman*, and the browser displayed a link to *Make Wake*, an iPhone app for water navigation.

"Are you *kidding* me?" I clicked on it. "There's a damn GPS boat app for the iPhone. All we have to do is plug in our starting location, and the thing will navigate us to any destination we enter. There's even a category for public boat landings." I looked at Frankie with amazement. "We really might be able to pull this off."

She bumped my shoulder. "And they said it couldn't be done."

"Yeah? Well we *still* have to get inside the club and convince the concierge to let us take the damn thing out."

"Oh, we'll get in there all right. I think Sebastian's plan will work like a charm."

"Where would we be without your fantasies?"

"Hmmmm. Probably still staring longingly at each other over a bubbling stream of hydrogen peroxide."

I smiled at her and held up my bandaged fingers. "They don't hurt anymore."

"That's good. Our goal is to make sure nothing else hurts, either."

"I'd say you're on a roll with that one."

"You think?"

"I had my doubts before, but seeing you back up that boat trailer gave me concrete proof of your omnipotence."

"I don't know if Linda would agree with that assessment," Frankie mused. "Her pal, Denise, didn't seem too impressed by us, either."

"Yeah. What tipped you off? The disgusted way she flicked her cigarette butt about fifty feet from the truck? And you're right: Linda seemed pretty suspicious about why Eddie would trust us with such an apparent high-profile assignment."

"It *is* kind of strange," she agreed. "I mean, if you really stop and think about it."

"Please." I held up a hand. "Don't get me started on that. My stomach is already in knots."

"Poor baby." She patted the back of my hand.

"I mean it, Frankie. This stuff just keeps getting more and more impossible. It's like being locked in a room with Sebastian, and being forced to watch an endless loop of "Tammy the Uber Driver" videos on TikTok."

"What in the world are you talking about?"

"If you have to ask, you wouldn't understand. Just know that *this* is the man you're trusting your reputation to."

Frankie had just said the words, "Stop exaggerating," when we heard the unmistakable sound of a car pulling into her driveway.

I looked at her mournfully and closed the iPad. "Ready for Naughty Nellie's Show-n-Tell?"

"Be nice." Frankie got to her feet. "Let's go meet him."

When we got outside, Sebastian was walking around the truck and trailer rig, giving it a good going-over.

"Where'd you get this thing?" he asked. "The local Midnight Marine Supply?"

"Very funny," I replied. "Eddie had it delivered."

"Out here?" He looked at Frankie. "I'm impressed. You can't even get Papa John's to deliver this far out of town."

"Oh, Eddie didn't have it brought *here*," Frankie explained. "We had to go pick it up in High Point."

"Wait a minute . . . you two *drove* this thing out here?"

"She did." I pointed at Frankie. "I followed behind in her car."

Sebastian stepped forward and gave Frankie a resounding high five. "Get *down* with your bad self, Miss Stohler. You even parked it commando style. I knew those lesbyterian genes were bound to rear their tiny little mullet heads at some point."

"Oh, they're anything but dormant," Frankie assured him. "Or tiny."

"Do tell?" Sebastian looked back and forth between us. Then he stepped forward and swatted me on the arm. "You irrepressible lothario, you. I knew you weren't dead yet."

I did my best to avoid smiling, but didn't quite succeed.

I appealed to Frankie for help. "Why do I feel like I just got an *A* on the spelling bee?"

Sebastian answered for her. "*Libido*. Noun. *L-I-B-I-D-O*. An expression of the sex drive as an active component of human instinct. *Libido*."

I glared at him. "*Fuck*. Verb. As in, 'fuck you.'"

"You're welcome." He waved Frankie over to his car. "Help me carry this stuff in, girlfriend."

The two of them gushed and tittered all the way into the house. Once we all were settled in the living room, Sebastian displayed the fruits of his shopping trip.

"Check *this* out!" He withdrew a skimpy blue garment from a white bag with "TOMMY HILFIGER" stenciled across the front in thin, blocky letters. He held the item up. "*Voila*!"

"What is that?" I asked. "A beach hankie?"

"*No*. It's what any person with a functioning brain stem would recognize as a sleeveless, zip-front minidress." He tossed it to Frankie. "And it's just your size."

Frankie held it up against her body.

"Well, you got the word *mini* right," I observed. "How would you even sit down in that thing?"

"Honey, this dress ain't about sitting down—it's about advertising how all of your other parts stand up—just like God intended. Ain't that right, Frankie?"

Frankie was looking at the label. "I appreciate your optimism, Sebastian. But this is a size six. There's no way I'm getting into this—not without duct tape and Vaseline."

"Poppycock." He waved her off. "What size are you? An eight?"

"On a good day," she agreed.

"Then that's perfect. We want this to fit snugly."

"Snugly?" Frankie held it up again. "I'll be lucky if I can even get the damn thing zipped."

"And your problem with that would be?" He reached into another bag and withdrew a pair of white stiletto sandals. The heels had to be four inches high. "These aren't Jimmy Choos, but they only have to last a couple of hours." He handed them to Frankie.

"How am I going to walk in these?" she asked.

"Honey, once you're zipped into that dress, nobody's going to be paying attention to how well you walk. Besides, you only have to remain upright long enough to get from the car to the boat. Once you're safely aboard, you can deep-six the shoes—they only cost fifteen bucks. Oh! I almost forgot." He pulled out another small bag. "Here are your shades." He handed her an oversized pair of aviator sunglasses with mirrored lenses and a shiny chrome frame. "Go on, go on." He fluttered his hand at her. "Get changed. I wanna see the whole ensemble put together."

Frankie looked at me for permission.

I felt my facial tic firing up. "I need a drink," I said.

She winked at me and headed for her bedroom.

"Make sure you lose the bra!" Sebastian called after her.

I glowered at him. "Are you trying to kill me?"

"You know what, Vera?" He was meticulously folding tissue paper. "Everything is *not* about you. A shrink could really help you with this psychosis."

"I am so not going to survive this."

"Well, why don't we see if Frankie's got any bolt cutters and bust you out of that rusted chastity belt? I promise you'll feel much better once you finally breach the bulkhead of the curvaceous Miz Stohler."

"Not *that* this—*this* this."

He stopped folding. "I may need to run that statement through Google Translator . . ."

"*This*," I repeated. "This damn boat heist. I see the entire thing going horribly wrong and the two of us getting arrested—or worse."

"There's something worse than getting arrested? Like what? Having to eat off the buffet at that yacht club? Avoid their shrimp salad, by the way. I heard they had an outbreak of ciguatera at an overhyped poolside soirée last week."

"I'm seriously thinking about cutting you in your sleep . . ."

"Where's your sense of adventure? This job at the NRB has been *good* for you. It's brought you back to life. Which reminds me, Ro-Ro wants you to call her."

Mamá? I felt an instant surge of panic. "When did you talk with her?"

"About half an hour ago. She said she had some kind of water dream about you last night. Then she asked me if you'd lost your cell phone."

Sweet mother of pearl . . .

"Just what did you say to her?" I hurled the words at him like an accusation.

"Cool your neurotic jets. I told her you were working a lot of overtime and weren't around the house much."

"Thank god."

"But, dude?" he cautioned me. "You seriously *need* to call her. If you don't, she's going to get on a plane."

"I know, I know. Okay? I will. One trauma at a time."

"*Hoooooolllyyyy mama . . .*" Sebastian was looking over my shoulder with eyes like saucers.

I turned around to see Frankie entering the room. At least . . . I thought it was Frankie . . .

Sebastian was clapping. "Anchors Aweigh, baby!"

Frankie was looking down at her chest. At least I think that's what she was doing; it was hard to tell with those mirrored aviators.

"I think this thing is a bit too tight," she said. "I had to put on a plunge bodysuit just to get into it. And before you ask," she added, "it belongs to Lilah. I borrowed it for her annual Halloween party. It was a goth theme, and I went as Elvira."

"Tight?" Sebastian hurried across the room to stand in front of her. She now topped him by about three inches. "No, no, no. It just needs to be adjusted." He grabbed the tab on her zipper and yanked it down dangerously close to her . . . business parts. "Now it's *perfect*. Let those glorious girls *breathe*."

I was speechless.

"Turn around and let me see your tushie." Sebastian made a rapid spiral motion with his hand.

Frankie meekly complied.

I'd thought the Daisy Dukes were tight. *But this?* This existed in a new dimension of form-fitting.

"Surf butt!" Sebastian exclaimed. "Oh, doggies . . . it's high tide."

High tide? *Waitaminute* . . .

I jumped to my feet when I saw her. "You absolutely *cannot* wear that," I protested. "It's . . . too much."

"Too much?" Frankie looked at me over her shoulder. "Too much what? Does it look bad?"

Bad?

There was no known species where anything about how Frankie looked could ever be classified as "bad."

"Well . . . no," I stammered. "But . . . but . . . how will you drive the truck in that . . . that *outfit?*"

The only objection my frazzled brain could summon up was inane, and I knew it. Frankie knew it, too. She even lowered her sunglasses and gave me an ironic look that seemed to say, *Is that really the best excuse you can come up with?*

"Go take a cold shower." Sebastian waved me off. "We've got to play with Miss Du Jour's hair."

I sank down onto the sofa. "You're both going to kill me." I dropped my head into my hands.

"Oh, honey . . ." Frankie started to walk toward me, but Sebastian reached out and stopped her.

"Don't you *dare* go near her with those things exposed. She'll incinerate, and then what'll I do? We share a lease."

Frankie laughed at him. "How about I go change clothes? We can talk about my hair later."

Sebastian sighed dramatically. "If you must."

"I think it's for the best."

"But one last, important detail before you go." Sebastian held up a cautionary finger. "If *anything* goes awry when you get to the club, simply return your tits to their full upright and locked position. That will be enough of a distraction to get you two outta there."

"If you say so . . ." Frankie somehow managed to navigate well enough on those ridiculous shoes to execute a turn and head back toward her bedroom.

I spread my fingers and covertly peeked between them at her retreating backside.

Damn. That was some kind of moveable feast.

I paused in my reverie. *Did I really just think something that crude?*

On the other hand . . . maybe Sebastian had been on to something.

I wondered if Frankie had any bolt cutters . . .

The one detail we didn't have an answer for was how to retrieve the car from the Peninsula Club parking lot after we'd made our escape in the Donzi. For once, Sebastian didn't have a ready idea for that one. Solving this riddle was especially important since I was borrowing my former office buddy, Jason's ragtop Beemer for the errand. When I called to ask him if he'd mind lending it to me for a day, he didn't even hesitate.

"Why the hell not? Somebody might as well get some enjoyment out of it before we have to sell it off or the repo men come and grab it in the middle of the night."

I chose to ignore the last part of his prediction and said a silent prayer that Frankie and I wouldn't be the ones Antigone dispatched to pick up his ride if the NRB got the call.

"Come on, man—it's not that bad is it?"

"We're in the shitter out here, Nick. I'm up to my ass in past-due alligators. Nobody is hiring right now—at least not in Winston. Brittney refuses to move away from her family, so looking for work in Raleigh or Charlotte is off the table. I'm probably gonna end up moonlighting at LegalZoom and living out of a conversion van in the

Walmart parking lot."

"That's not gonna happen, Jason. You've got tons of contacts. Why not look for an in-house gig with one of the biotech firms downtown?"

"Have *you* done that?"

"Well. No . . ."

"Don't kid a kidder, okay? Neither of us wants to sit around on our asses all day, reviewing grant applications. Fuck that shit. It's not why we went to law school."

That much was true. "Remind me why we *did* go to law school?"

"To make as much money as we possibly can," he replied. "And by the way, how are you making out? Have you found anything yet?"

"Um . . ." I don't know why it never occurred to me that I might need to have an answer for that question all queued up. But truthfully, it wasn't really like Jason to spare much thought about how anyone else was doing. Most of the associates at TWAT had advanced cases of internalized myopia. "I'm doing a bit of freelance work. You know . . . just to make ends meet until I figure things out."

"I hear you." Kids started screaming in the background. "Jesus . . . I gotta go. When do you wanna pick up the car?"

"How about Tuesday evening? I'll have it back by the same time on Wednesday."

"That's fine. It's on fumes right now, so you'll have to gas it up."

"No sweat. I'll bring it back full, too."

"Yeah? Maybe you can borrow it once a week, then?" He gave a bitter-sounding laugh. The screaming on the line escalated to new decibel heights. "I gotta go. See you tomorrow." He hung up.

I lowered my phone and waited for my ear to stop ringing.

Kids. *I never understood why Mamá wanted a slew of them.*

My plan was to make a run down to Lake Norman to scope out the Yacht Club and see if there were any access points that didn't involve entering through the main club entrance. I figured there had to be some service entrances that were unattended. And I knew the club was bordered by a lot of privately owned lakefront McMansions. But I wanted to be sure about this detail. And I also needed to make a trip to the Stumpy Creek recreation area and take a look at the parameters of its public boat ramp.

I prayed that Frankie would be able to shoehorn our sixty-foot truck and trailer rig into position without creating any collateral damage. Our plan was to park the rig at Stumpy Creek on Wednesday morning, before making the drive down to the Yacht Club in Jason's BMW. That meant I'd need to follow Frankie from Winston-Salem to Stumpy Creek in the car.

Frankie was already grousing about having to drive the truck wearing the slutty dolphin trainer ensemble, but there was no real way around that . . . not unless she wanted to try and change clothes in a less-than-ideal, outdoor public restroom at Stumpy Creek.

She didn't see that happening.

"I'll just carry an extra pair of shoes," she resolved, "and make the best of it. But once the boat is loaded, I'm taking that ridiculous costume off—even if I have to change in the damn truck."

To be honest, I was totally okay with that scenario—mostly because I didn't think I'd be able to survive the ride back with her if she were sitting two feet away from me, gloriously stuffed into Lilah's bodysuit like a prime Kobe beef sausage.

I had my limits.

Frankie agreed to ride down with me on Tuesday evening. She wanted to scope out the scale of the parking area and boat ramp for herself. We agreed that we'd make a detour on the way back and stop at Bermuda Run to pick up Jason's car.

Monday after school let out, we had a date to head over to the Carolina Marina at Belews Lake to take her dad's pontoon out for a spin. That idea had been a late development, and wasn't one I felt all that comfortable with—but Frankie insisted that the practice would do me good. It didn't matter how many ways I tried to explain that there were zero similarities between a floating party barge and a six-figure water rocket. Her mind was made up.

"You can at least practice parking it," she insisted.

"You mean *docking* it?"

"Oh, please. Tying something up at a dock has to work the same way regardless of the horsepower of the watercraft."

"I guess that's true." I was still uncomfortable with the prospect. "What makes you think your dad will let us borrow it?"

"Because I didn't *ask* him—I asked Mom. And I told her I'd bring you with me when we stopped by to pick up the keys."

I hoped I hadn't heard her correctly. "You did what?"

"You heard me. So . . . are you ready to meet the parents?"

Sweet mother of pearl. Was I?

"Um. Your father isn't into gun collecting, is he?"

"Not the last time I checked, no."

"What, exactly, did you tell her about . . . us?"

"That's the beauty of it, Nick. I didn't have to tell her anything. I never bring *anyone* home—which is why Mom agreed so fast to lending us the boat."

"So, that means she thinks we're . . . *un articulo?*" I quoted Aunt Estela.

"If by that you mean 'a couple,' then yes, she does." When I didn't reply right away, Frankie asked, "Does that characterization bother you?"

Bother me? Far from it. I wanted to sit down on the floor and play with the new description like I'd just been handed a favorite toy at Christmas. I gave Frankie a shy smile.

"No. I'd say it's just about right."

The Stohlers lived in an imposing, early nineteenth-century house on Glade Street in Winston-Salem's West End historic district. It was a large, Colonial Revival-style home built by Frankie's great-grandfather, Jonas Stohler. The sprawling house with its terraced lawn and stone retaining walls sat high above the narrow, winding street below. It was two stories high and ringed with covered porches. The narrow, sloping lot was filled with flowering shrubs and ringed by a stately row of chalk maple trees.

There must be good money in the funeral business, I thought.

This place even dwarfed the monster house Aunt Estela and Uncle Rio bought in Radnor with their scratch-off card fortune.

I began to rethink my casual attire . . . but I could hardly have pulled off wearing a business suit to go boating on Belews Lake.

Frankie could sense my unease as we got out of the car and started ascending the flights of steps that led to the deep front porch.

"Relax." She took hold of my hand. "They're just nerdy lapsed Moravians. They won't bite you."

"You and Lilah grew up here?" I asked.

"Yep." She pointed at a bank of windows that wrapped around the side of the house on the second floor. "That was our room. I think it had originally been a sleeping porch."

"A what?"

"A sleeping porch. A lot of old houses in the South had those. Covered porches that were cooler places to sleep in the summer."

We'd no sooner set foot on the front porch when one of the double, oak front doors swung wide and Lilah, who was dressed like the black bird of Chernobyl, loomed inside the opening to greet us.

"Hey strangers," she drawled in that trademark Lorraine Bracco voice.

"What are *you* doing here, Li?" Frankie asked with suspicion.

"Mom told me you were bringing 'someone' home this afternoon. I guessed who it was and volunteered to pick up the champagne."

"Very funny. Why aren't you at work?"

Lilah shrugged. "It's slow today." She shifted her gaze to me. "People tend to cling to life longer in the springtime. It's a thing."

"I'll try to remember that," I said. "It's nice to see you again, Lilah."

"You, too, Nick." She clapped her pale hands together. "Come on in and let's start the interrogation."

"Li . . ." Frankie warned her sister.

"What? Am I wrong?" She stepped back so we could enter the house. "Just heed one useful tip when things get dicey, Nick. Anytime

Mom asks you a question you don't want to answer, just comment on what a lovely home she has. Works like a charm."

Lilah hadn't been kidding: the house was phenomenal. The living room looked like a spread from *Southern Living* magazine.

"Is that Frankie?" A woman's voice called from someplace at the rear of the house. I heard the echo of footsteps on the wide-planked floors, and an attractive, late middle-aged woman entered the room. She had stylish, short blond hair streaked with gray and was dressed in gardening clothes. She was energetically wiping her hands on a faded dish towel. "Hello sweetheart," she said to Frankie. She kissed her daughter on the cheek and faced me. She had bright blue eyes, just like Frankie's. "You must be Nick? I apologize for not shaking hands." She held up a dirt-stained palm. "I've been out back planting my herb garden."

"Don't apologize," I said. "It's very nice to meet you, Mrs. Stohler."

"Call me Beth. 'Mrs. Stohler' reminds me of Abel's mother, and I've been trying to drink less on weekdays."

"Except for special occasions," Lilah added, "like when Frankie brings a girlfriend home."

Beth glared at her eldest daughter. "As you can see, Nick, Lilah exists to provide comic relief."

"A unique quality in a mortician," Frankie added.

I smiled at Frankie's mother. In fact, it was hard not to. She had such a friendly and easygoing manner. It wasn't hard to imagine her running a successful hair salon.

"I envy Frankie having a sister," I said. "I'm an only child—so every day I walk the earth, I remind my very Catholic mother of how she was cursed by the fertility gods."

Beth laughed. "Lilah brought some munchies. Come on to the kitchen and sit beside me, Nick. I think we're going to get along just fine."

I stole a glance at Frankie. Her expression was downright smug. "Where's Dad?" she asked.

"He went out to the shed half an hour ago to get the boat keys,"

Beth explained. "But he's got a ratty old TV set hidden out there, and I'm positive he's watching the NFL draft. We might get to see him by nightfall."

"I'll go round him up," Lilah offered. "Frankie, you keep him away from the champagne." She looked at me. "Dad always likes the drama of shooting the cork out and ends up spraying half of it all over the kitchen."

Frankie looked surprised. "I thought you were kidding about the champagne?"

"I don't kid. About anything," Lilah replied, dryly. "You should know that by now."

She disappeared to find Frankie's father, and the rest of us made our way back to the Stohler's gargantuan kitchen. The room stretched across the entire back of the house and was surrounded by rows of windows on three sides. Although the space was equipped with what had to be a fortune in high-end, chef-grade appliances, it somehow managed to exude an understated, almost Shaker-like farmhouse appeal. The floor-to-ceiling cabinets were finished in pale green and sunlight reflected off the clear glass panes set into the upper doors. We sat down at a big rustic table surrounded by mismatched, painted chairs.

Double sets of atrium doors led outside to a series of terraced decks. The narrow but deep backyard was arrayed with clusters of potted plants and raised-bed gardens. I could see Lilah near the entrance to a tool shed, talking with someone—undoubtedly her father.

Beth passed me a platter containing cheese straws and cut-up veggies. It reminded me of Sebastian's comment about Moravians and crudités.

"So, tell me about your family, Nick," Beth asked. "Where are you from originally?"

"Philadelphia," I replied. "My father is an attorney and my mother is a doctor and part-time clairvoyant."

"That sounds like a useful combination of skills." Beth laughed at my description and poured me a glass of iced tea. "It's great to be able to multitask these days."

"Mamá says it's a useful way to keep me off the streets."

Frankie shot me a nervous look. Beth's next question proved that Frankie must've had a clairvoyant streak of her own.

"How did you two meet?"

Okay. There it was . . . the one explanation we hadn't thought to discuss ahead of time.

"Um . . ." I began.

Frankie piped up. "We met through mutual acquaintances . . . you know how that goes."

"That's right," I agreed. "My housemate, Sebastian, pretty much knows everyone in the county. I met him at Wake," I added. "While I was in law school."

"Oh. So you're an attorney, like your father?" Beth asked. "That's nice. Are you with one of the local firms?"

"I was," I explained. "But nearly seven years at Turner Witherspoon managed to convince me that corporate law is really not to my liking. Honestly, I'm not sure what my next move will be."

"I hope it's not away from Winston-Salem." Beth sounded like she meant it.

"That makes two of us," Frankie added.

I smiled at her. "It's not really a consideration now."

The back door opened and Lilah entered, followed by a smallish man with pale skin and wavy dark hair. It was clear that Lilah's natural color palette derived from her father's side of the family.

He came right over to me and extended his hand.

"Abel Stohler. Very nice to meet you, Nick."

We shook hands warmly. "You, too," I echoed.

He then crossed over to where Frankie sat and kissed her on the head. "Here's my baby girl."

Frankie hugged him. "Hi Daddy."

He pulled up a chair and sat down beside Frankie. "So. What are we drinking?"

"Tea, Abel." Beth passed him a tumbler. "Some of us think it's a bit too early for anything else."

He looked at Lilah. "You told me we had champagne? Was I brought in here under false pretenses?"

"I'll get it." Lilah tapped her mother on the shoulder as she headed for the refrigerator. "You were right. He was out there watching the draft."

Beth sighed.

"What? Can't a man be interested in football? It's not like I get to see many of the games during the season," he complained.

Lilah had returned from the fridge with a bottle of Veuve Clicquot.

"It's true. I don't know why they won't pass a law making it illegal to bury people on the Sabbath."

"It would seem like a reasonable extension of existing blue laws," I agreed.

Frankie's father stared at me for a moment before his eyes crinkled and he all but guffawed.

"Oh, hell," he roared. "You may have met your match, Li."

"Funeral humor." Lilah popped the cork on the Veuve. "It isn't just for breakfast anymore."

Beth retrieved a tray containing champagne flutes. Lilah filled them all and handed them out.

Abel raised his glass in a toast. "Here's to family: may there always be room for one more!"

Frankie and I smiled shyly at each other before clinking rims and drinking up.

We agreed that I'd fetch Frankie from South Fork Elementary School at three forty-five on Monday. By that time, she said, most of the kids would've been picked up by their parents or departed for home on buses, so I should have no trouble finding a parking space.

That *might've* been true if I'd remembered to actually park in the lot. Instead, when I approached the school, there was still a serpentine line of vehicles snaking around the campus along Country Club

Road. Most of the cars and SUVs contained cranky-looking women who looked like they'd rather be anywhere but there. I assumed there must've been some delay letting the kids out, so I dutifully took my place at the back of the long line.

About ten minutes later, I saw Frankie near the main entrance to the school. She and two kids were walking toward one of the parked cars. Her little companions wore brightly colored sneakers and carried fat backpacks. They held onto her hands as they walked, and I could see them both talking to her with great animation. When they stopped beside a Ford SUV, Frankie knelt down and hugged them each before helping them climb into the back seat and get buckled in. I could see the kids waving at her as they drove away from the school.

It was moving to witness this side of Frankie and see how much her kids genuinely adored her. That was a far cry from my own school experience at Immaculate Heart. At iMac, as we called it, the nuns operated more like angry members of God's secret police—all except Sister Anjelica, who seemed to have a soft spot for me. Watching Frankie's sweet camaraderie with her students reminded me of how special Sister Anjelica always made me feel.

But then, *Frankie* made me feel pretty special, too.

It took her about five minutes to notice my car, parked near the back of the line. She waved at me as she approached. I noticed she was carrying her inevitable quilted bag.

"Why are you parked way out here?" she asked, as she opened the passenger door and climbed in.

"I thought it was protocol."

"For *parents*. I'm lucky I saw you down here." She tossed her bag into the back seat. "I'm sorry you had to wait on me. I couldn't leave until all the kids got picked up."

"It was fine. I enjoyed watching you with them."

She smiled. "They're sweethearts."

"They seem pretty attached to you."

"It's mutual." She fastened her seat belt. "So. Are you ready to head to the lake and get wet?"

I had to bite my tongue to stifle ten or twenty irreverent responses to her innocent question.

Frankie must've read my mind because she swatted me.

"Get your mind out of the gutter and get this bolt bucket moving."

Forty minutes later, we were at the lake and Frankie had changed into shorts and a T-shirt.

It was amazing how quickly what I remembered about boating came back to me once we'd cast off and piloted the Stohler pontoon out onto the warm water of Belews Lake.

"Can we head up toward the power plant?" Frankie asked. "I always find that view to be so . . . romantic."

"I am *so* sure that's true. Nothing quite jump-starts the heart like a coal-burning steam plant hugging the horizon."

"It makes me hot," Frankie said. "Literally."

"I get why your father keeps his boat here, because of its easy accessibility from Winston-Salem. But warm water lakes like this have never been appealing to me for recreation—especially in the summer. Must be my Pennsylvania blood."

"I know. It's like being poached in second-hand bathwater."

"Nice image."

Frankie watched me steer for a minute. "I have to say, you look pretty comfortable driving this thing."

"Yeah? It's like you pulling that ridiculous trailer. This is the easy part. Bringing it in without taking out the pier will be the acid test."

"I don't know about that. I've seen Dad crash it into the dock numerous times. No one is immune."

"I'd rather not crash a Donzi that's worth more than our combined retirement savings into anything."

"You won't." Frankie stretched out on the padded bench seat that ran along one side of the bow. "I have faith in you. Anyone who can make Lilah crack a smile has my vote."

"That was a pretty good one, wasn't it?" I said smugly.

"Good? I think Dad was ready to adopt you on the spot."

I smiled at the recollection of his toast. "Do you think your mom bought our vague story about how we met?"

"No."

"Me either. I wonder why she didn't ask any follow-up questions?"

"Oh, she will . . . believe me."

"Do you think Lilah said anything to her?"

"About us? Of course. About the repo work?" She thought about the possibility. "I don't think so. If she'd ratted us out, Mom would've been all over it. And," she added for emphasis, "there definitely wouldn't have been champagne."

"I guess we should enjoy it while it lasts," I said morosely. "It probably won't remain a secret for long. Especially if this plan on Wednesday goes south in any one of the ten million ways it could."

"Why are you always so negative? Give our life of crime a rest and enjoy this gorgeous day."

Frankie was right. The day was perfect. There were quite a few other boaters on the lake. And even though it was still April, the water here was warm enough to lure several water-skiers out. I slowly picked up speed, and after a few minutes, I piloted the pontoon around a bend and saw our target dead ahead.

"Steam plant a-hoy," I called out.

Frankie sat up and scanned the horizon. "Isn't it *glorious?*" she gushed. "A monument to the wonders of coal ash. And here we are, floating above it all."

"'Consumed with that which it was nourished by,'" I quoted.

"Robert Frost?" Frankie asked.

"Nope. Shakespeare."

"Boy, was he ever prescient."

"Yeah. Who knew he had such foresight about creative ways to rape the environment?"

"I think he pretty much had foresight about creative ways to rape anything."

"Why did you become a teacher?" I asked. It was a random question, but was something I'd wondered about since meeting her. Frankie seemed too . . . *savvy* to be someone who spent her days teaching third graders multiplication tables.

But then, I didn't have the best memories of grade school, so my opinion of teachers probably wasn't all that informed.

Frankie was reasonably confused by my query. "That sure came out of nowhere. What makes you ask?"

"I don't know . . . maybe it's just the dichotomy between that and your work for the NRB? Or maybe it's because you're so not like any of the third grade teachers I remember."

"Interesting. And what were *they* like?"

I thought about my answer. "Angry spinsters who hated kids."

"Hmmmm. Well, I'm not really angry—and I definitely don't hate kids. But I think we'd both have to agree that I'm a full-fledged contender for spinsterhood."

"I wouldn't say that."

"Oh, come on, Nick." Frankie scoffed at my disagreement. "I'm nearly forty. I'm not married. I live alone. I don't date. I drive a ten-year-old car. And I don't even make enough money to afford to buy pencils for my students. Hence, the NRB and what you've rightly identified as the great dichotomy of my life."

I wanted to take exception to the "I don't date" part, but I was still too shy about our status to contradict her.

"So why become a public school teacher?" I asked instead.

"I don't know, to tell the truth. It's not like I can say that I was driven from a young age to devote my life to public education—although it is something I strongly believe in. In all honesty, I think that by the time I'd reached my junior year in college, I was so unmotivated by any career path that I just fell into this one by default. But, ironically, I discovered that I liked student teaching, and I was actually pretty good at it. And in a practical sense, anything that gave me a shot at guaranteed employment after graduation was also guaranteed to keep me safe from ending up in either of the family businesses. That was my primary objective. But after a couple of years, I decided that I liked being in the classroom. I especially liked having the chance to work with kids who weren't getting much other useful instruction—or attention, for that matter—away from school."

I was moved by Frankie's explanation. "That's really . . . *noble.* You know?"

"Oh, I don't know how 'noble' it is. My dad thinks I'm crazy. And that was especially true after my divorce, and I descended into his definition of reduced financial circumstances. Apparently, it's fine to be an underpaid public servant if you're married to a man who's the primary breadwinner. Since my divorce, he's offered me different jobs in his front office a zillion times."

"Ever thought about taking him up on one of them?"

"Not even once."

"So, you think you'll keep on doing this?"

"Teaching?" she asked.

I nodded.

"I honestly don't know. Before long, I'll have enough years in with the state to retire with a small pension. That might open up some new doors for me. Who knows?" She gave me a sly smile. "I might decide to go full-time with the NRB."

"Yeah, *that* I don't see happening."

"Never say never."

We'd motored to the edge of the traversable part of the steam plant section of the lake.

"Do you wanna hang around here for a bit? Or should we head back to the marina and try to dock this thing?"

"As much as I'd love to stay out here for the rest of the day, I suppose we should think about getting back. I still have lesson plans to finish for tomorrow."

"I guess we have been getting in the way of your schoolwork. I'm sorry about that."

"Don't be. I love spending time with you."

I felt irrationally pleased by that response. "You do?"

Frankie gave me a disbelieving look. "Do you really feel the need to ask me that?"

"I guess not," I said sheepishly.

I made a wide circle with the pontoon and began the trip back to face an uncertain tango with the dock. Frankie watched me navigate in silence.

After we'd passed Round Island and approached the cutback to Carolina Marina, I heard her sigh.

"I don't know what I'm going to do with you," she said.

"What do you mean?"

"I mean it's like we take one step forward, and two steps back."

"How is that my fault?" I whined. "You're the one who just said 'I'm not dating anyone.' How am I supposed to react to a statement like that?"

"I don't know, Nick. How do you want to react?"

I was out of my depth on this one—and not just because we were drifting along over fifty feet of water, either.

"Are we having an argument?" I asked with genuine confusion. "Because after yesterday afternoon at your parents' house, I thought we were on the same page with this."

"Define 'this.'"

"*This*," I said in frustration. "The whole relationship *this*."

Frankie seemed to relent a little. "I thought so, too. But every time you react with doubt or seem surprised by any expressions of attachment I make, it leads me to wonder if I'm assuming too much."

I threw back my head in frustration. An osprey was making lazy circles above us. I fully expected him to dive bomb our boat and proceed to defecate on my head.

"You're right," I said. "I'm . . . certifiable."

"Don't do that."

"Don't do what?"

"Don't beat yourself up. If you're not ready for anything more serious, well . . . just tell me. I'll be sad, but I'll live—and I'll certainly understand."

"It's not that."

"No?" she asked hopefully.

I shook my head.

"Then what is it?"

"It's . . . it's . . . *that.*" I turned and pointed at the wake behind our boat.

Frankie followed my gaze. "I don't . . ." She shifted her eyes back to me. "What am I supposed to see?"

"It's the *chain.*" I pointed again. "El Cadejo's fucking *chain.* That's what's following us . . . my damn curse. It's right out there inside that wake, hot on my trail and eager to fuck everything up—just like it always does." I amended my last statement. "Just like I always let it."

Frankie got up and crossed to the bridge to stand just beside me.

"So, don't let it." She leaned her head against my shoulder. "Not this time."

I wrapped my arm around her. "I don't want to."

"Then that's enough for now."

I wanted to believe her more than anything. "Are you sure?"

"I have to be." She leaned up to kiss me. "Besides, it's all a moot point. The cat's already out of the bag."

I looked down at her. "It is?"

"Uh huh. Haven't you heard?" She kissed me again. "We're now *un articulo.*"

Chapter Six

The Lake Song

Wednesday.

Sebastian insisted on dubbing it D-Day, for "Donzi Day."

I was meeting Frankie at her place at 10 a.m. for the drive down to the Peninsula Yacht Club in Jason's BMW.

Our plans had matured.

On our way home from Belews Lake, Frankie persuaded me that it made more sense to take the truck and boat trailer with us when we went down to scope out Stumpy Creek on Tuesday evening, and just leave them there overnight. That would free us up to scope out alternative access to the yacht club so Sebastian could sneak in and recover Jason's car after we made our escape in the Donzi. So I followed her down there in my car, and we lucked out when we pulled into the Stumpy Creek recreation area. The place had a fairly expansive, well-lighted parking area, and Frankie found a big enough space to pull the rig into as soon as we got there.

Check potential nightmare number one off the list.

Next, we made a site visit to the Peninsula Yacht Club. It took some driving around, but we did manage to discover an unattended entrance to the club's playground from Harbor Jib Road. If Feliz dropped him off near there, he could easily walk to the parking area where we'd leave Jason's BMW. Our plan was to park Jason's car near the access road that led to the club's boat ramp, located farther down Harbor Light Drive away from the main entrance. Feliz would be sure to have Sebastian there in plenty of time, so he could grab the car as soon as we were safely aboard the boat. We agreed that I would text him once that happened.

Check potential nightmare number two off the list.

Sebastian took the liberty of typing up a detailed script for me to use when I called the Yacht Club concierge to make my clandestine request to have Mr. Jackson's boat gassed up and ready to depart for a day of afternoon delights between Mr. Jackson and his anonymous companion. I'd identified myself simply as Chris Marx, one of Mr. Jackson's attorneys at Smith Barnard. Perversely, *that* errand ended up being the simplest of them all. The concierge never even bothered to ask me for any proof of my position or my relationship to the troubled Donzi owner. Although he *did* ask if I'd like to have the boat cooler stocked with wine and a cheese platter, like usual?

Like usual?

Apparently, Sebastian hadn't been exaggerating when he'd said that Mr. Jackson had been a *veeeerrrryyy* bad boy . . .

I cleared my throat and said that Mr. Jackson would appreciate the "usual" accommodations.

The concierge assured me they'd have the boat pulled up and ready for departure by 11 a.m., and that the attendant would be expecting Mr. Jackson's "guest" and me, and would show us to the vessel.

Could it *really* be this easy to make off with someone's $300,000 boat? It seemed so.

Check potential nightmare number three off the list.

When I woke up on Wednesday morning, I was actually disappointed that I'd mostly run out of nightmares.

That all changed when I got to Frankie's house to pick her up for the drive down to Lake Norman. I thought I'd seen it all when she'd modeled Sebastian's hand-picked hoochie-mama outfit on Sunday. I'd even popped a prophylactic Xanax this morning to help me mange my proximity to her . . . *charms* . . . for the duration of the afternoon. But it turned out my preview had only been just that: a hint of coming attractions.

There was something about seeing her fully made up and decked out in that ridiculous ensemble that just about blew every circuit in my personal fuse box. She'd done something to her hair to make it fall around her face like fluffy, textured beach waves. It looked wind-blown without being messy, and it was hot as hell. Her lipstick was doing things to make her mouth look full and slightly pouty, and the mirrored sunglasses added a perfect hint of bored indifference.

She was wearing the infamous four-inch stilettos, but swore she'd kick them off as soon as we got into the car.

I'd had the top down on Jason's blinding white BMW roadster when I got there to pick her up, but Frankie threatened to murder me if the wind messed up her hair.

"It took me *two hours* to look this cheap," she insisted. "We're not going to ruin it on the ride down there."

What I really wanted to know was how long it took for her to shimmy into that pushup bodysuit of Lilah's. Upon reflection, I decided I was better off not knowing. Frankie had already caught me staring at her cleavage—*twice*—and tugged the zipper up higher on the front of her dress.

"You need to keep your eyes on the road," she demanded. "I'm glad I left a change of clothes in the pickup."

"Yeah, that'll be a crime against nature."

"Suck it up, cupcake. As soon as that damn boat is loaded, this love goddess is going off the clock."

"You really know how to hurt a girl . . ."

"Hey." Frankie swiveled in her seat to face me. "I'm more than happy to have a division of labor on these escalating sex-kitten gigs. Next time, *you* can be the rent-a-girl and *I'll* drive the getaway car."

I laughed at her suggestion. "You think I'd look convincing in an outfit like that?"

Frankie lowered her sunglasses and looked me over.

"Oh, *hell* yeah."

"You're crazy."

"Nick? If you scowled less you could be a model."

"*What?* That's insane."

"Sebastian agrees with me. He says the greatest disappointment of his life, apart from the casting of Renée Zellweger to play Judy Garland, is his failure at getting you to dress like a girl."

I took umbrage at that remark. "I like my clothes."

"So do I. But we're having an academic discussion."

"I could never wear an outfit like that." I pointed at her ensemble. "I'd just look like I'm wearing bad drag—and I'd get a nosebleed on those shoes. Besides, my boobs are too small."

"That's a matter of opinion . . ." Frankie pulled off a credible imitation of Mae West.

"Who *are* you?"

Frankie laughed. "It must be the clothes."

"Yeah? If I didn't know better, I'd think you were flirting with me."

"You mean you're not sure?" she asked. "I must not be doing it right. Does this help?" She lowered her zipper about six inches.

I nearly ran Jason's car off the road.

"Hey!" Frankie quickly returned the zipper to its former, secure setting. "Bad idea. No more flirtage until this job is finished."

I had both hands on the wheel. "*Flirtage?*"

"I learned it from Sebastian."

"Of course you did."

"That man is a font of information."

"Yeah," I agreed. "He's a regular Renaissance man."

"How are you feeling about this job by now?" Frankie surveyed the landscape ahead. We were closing in on the intersection with I-77 and the straight shot south to Lake Norman. Depending on traffic, we were probably about thirty minutes—or three hours—out from the yacht club. "Confident? In control? Ready to get underway?"

"I probably wouldn't go quite that far. But I think, under the circumstances, I'm doing pretty well."

"Pretty well?" Frankie asked. "What does that mean, exactly?"

"It's hard to categorize." I thought about how best to describe my mood. "I'd say I've probably only digested about five of my organs so far—so that's definitely progress."

Frankie laid a hand on my arm. It was the first time I'd noticed her nail polish—cherry red. I stole a peek at her toes. Same color.

Wow. She really paid attention to detail . . .

"It's going to go *fine*, Nick." Frankie gave my arm a squeeze. "Everything's already set up. We'll be out of there in less than twenty minutes."

I wasn't ready to embrace her optimism. "Unless Jackson decides it's a great day to take his boat out..."

Frankie was unfazed by my hypothetical suggestion. "At 11 a.m. on a workday? I doubt it."

"I hope you're right."

"Did you remember to give Sebastian the extra key to this car?"

I nodded. "Jason looked at me a little strangely when I asked for a valet key. But I told him I was taking a date out to a special place."

"He bought that?"

"Oh, yeah. He looked outside and saw you sitting in my car."

"Really? What'd he say?"

"Um . . ." I equivocated. "A guy thing."

"Do I want to know what that means?"

I looked at her. "Probably not. But trust me, it was . . . complimentary. He went and got the key for me immediately."

"Maybe he was just happy to hear you were going out with someone?"

"Could be. I didn't have many opportunities to date when I was working at TWAT—as you know."

"I do know. I think maybe we need to change that."

I smiled at her. "I think we already have."

"Oh? In that case, where are you taking me?"

"If we manage to pull this off without ending up in jail or having to be rescued by the Lake Police, I promise to take you out to . . . what's your favorite restaurant?"

"In Winston-Salem?"

I nodded.

She smiled at me. "You already know the answer to that."

"I do." I agreed. "But I was thinking maybe someplace fancy—you know? With a fifty-page wine list."

"Hmmmm." Frankie considered my suggestion. "Can we take Fred along, too?"

I glanced over at her. Jason had been right. *Frankie was bangin' hot.* If he'd seen her in *this* outfit, his head would've exploded.

It was clear that I was overcomplicating this celebratory date idea. Why not go to the one place we both loved? "Sweet Potatoes it is," I proclaimed. "Maybe we can just get really gussied up?"

"I'd say that's the least I can do after showing up there dressed like a harlot the last time."

"You did make quite an impression." I made a point of looking her up and down. "As far as that goes, I'd say you're two for two."

Frankie puffed out her chest and dramatically crossed her perfect legs. "I've always been an overachiever."

I had to fight to keep the car under control while we merged onto I-77. *It was getting real now.* The dashboard clock read 10:40 a.m. With luck, we'd arrive right on time.

I pulled over about a block from the main entrance to the Peninsula Yacht Club on Harbor Light Boulevard, so I could lower the top on Jason's Beemer. Frankie grumbled at me, but I insisted that it was totally for effect.

"I want him to get a good look at you," I explained. "Try to look frosty."

"If you mess up my hair, I'm going to kill you." She unzipped the front of her dress to ensure that a tantalizing expanse of creamy décolletage was visible.

"I'll drive slow," I croaked.

After the top was down and stowed, we drove the remaining short distance to the club's ostentatious entrance. The parking lot was only about a third full, although I could see a number of pampered LPs carrying large drinks making their way from the club to the big patio area that overlooked the marina. There didn't appear to be many boats out on the water here—*yet*. I imagined that would all change later this afternoon, once the schools let out.

There was a steady breeze blowing in from the southwest. I hoped it wouldn't make the water too choppy for our run up to Stumpy Creek.

I'd only progressed about fifty feet onto the property when a tanned and handsome young man wearing a tight-fitting blue polo shirt with a yacht club logo stepped forward to greet us. He looked like a cross between Ryan Gosling and Troy Donahue.

I stopped the car and waited for him to approach us.

"Welcome to the Peninsula Club," he said. "May I help direct you?"

I showed him the calling card I'd found in my files. "Chris Marx with Smith Barnard," I explained, "representing Mr. Ransom Jackson. The concierge is expecting us."

"Oh." Ryan-Troy was having a hard time taking his eyes off Frankie. "Of, course. *Sure*. Yes. Just park . . . *wherever* . . . and I'll take you to the . . . um . . . *boat*, Miss . . . er . . .," he glanced at my card, "Marx. I think everything is ready for you."

"Thanks." I carefully pulled my card back from him and tucked it behind the sun visor. "I think we'll park over there," I pointed in the direction of the boat ramp, "in the shade. We'll be right back to meet you."

"Sure thing." He nodded stupidly and stepped back. "Take your time."

I drove off to find the remotest parking place possible.

"You'll really have to sell this," I said to Frankie as we waited on the car's top to close and lock into place. "With luck, we won't even have to meet the concierge."

I got out of the car and went around to the passenger side to open her door. I was nicely but casually dressed. Linen slacks with a striped short-sleeve shirt and Topsider shoes—perfect for boating. I'd also added an oversized pair of sunglasses, in a halfhearted attempt to disguise my features.

One thing was for sure: I looked nothing like the real Chris Marx. If memory served, he was an overweight redhead with thinning hair and an underbite.

Frankie managed to extract herself from the car without falling off her shoes.

"Just don't walk . . . too . . . *fast*," she warned me. "I can't concentrate on looking haughty *and* remaining upright on these fucking shoes."

"Buck up, hot stuff. We're nearly there."

I had to hand it to Frankie; she did an amazing job making her cautious peregrination look like an indifferent saunter. Ryan-Troy, who'd had the full benefit of watching her sashay across a parking lot that was half the length of a football field, was nearly salivating when we rejoined him.

"Right this way," he said, sweeping an arm toward the marina, located behind the sprawling clubhouse. "I texted the concierge and he said Mr. Jackson's boat is gassed up and ready for you."

We crossed a massive waterside patio dotted with small tables, umbrellas and chaise lounges. Most of the members in view were women: all blonde, all tanned, all emaciated, and all wearing variations of the same types of size zero, Lululemon creations. Several of the underfed women stared open-mouthed at Frankie—some with resentment; most with envy. When we'd reached the maze of interconnected wooden docks that led to scores of boat slips, Frankie reached out and took hold of Ryan-Troy's muscular arm.

"I'm sure you won't mind," she said with perfect indifference. "I'd hate to break a heel."

"Oh, no, ma'am," he replied with pride. It sounded to me like his voice had dropped an entire octave. "I'm happy to assist you."

I just bet you are, bucko . . .

I followed behind them and tried to keep my eyes off Frankie's ass. It wasn't easy.

Ryan-Troy was doing his best to chat her up.

Good luck with that, asshole. She don't play for your team anymore . . .

I wondered if all of the workers at this joint had to look like Ralph Lauren models?

Why doesn't he just offer to carry her ass to the damn boat?

We neared the end of our dock and I spotted Jackson's burgundy-hued stunner, bobbing near the fuel station. I did a surreptitious look around, but didn't see any signs of security cameras out here. That was very good luck. I surmised that most of the surveillance equipment would be focused on the slips, where the boats were stored. I attributed the absence of cameras out here to the safe assumption that anyone stealing a boat would certainly not bother to stop out here long enough to gas it up. And since a member of the club staff had pulled the Donzi up, we were pretty much in the clear, anyway.

Once we drew closer to our target, the sheer magnitude of our errand hit home.

Sweet mother of pearl.

Jackson's Donzi looked like a thoroughbred pawing the earth behind a starting gate. I was relieved to see the boat tied up at the end of an unoccupied dock. This kind of pole position would make our departure from the marina a whole lot easier. Thankfully, I didn't spot many other boats out cruising the main channel yet, so I didn't have to worry too much about dodging other watercraft on our way to open water.

Ryan-Troy stopped near the stern of the Donzi. He looked wounded when Frankie dropped his beefy arm.

"Well," he said. "Here she is. They have the starboard fridge all stocked for you, too, just like Mr. Jackson requested." He looked at me. "Will you need anything else, Miss . . . er . . ."

"Marx," I reiterated. "And, no," I assured him, "we're fine. Please tell the concierge to expect us back by seven."

"Sure thing," he agreed.

I carefully stepped down into the boat and held up a hand for

Frankie. Ryan-Troy quickly took hold of her other arm to assist her. Together, we more or less lifted her down into the Donzi. Once she had steadied herself and draped her glorious length along a port-side, upholstered settee, I maneuvered my way to the helm and nervously scanned the instruments.

Thank god I spent two hours watching damn videos about how to start one of these . . .

I took my seat in the cockpit and located the switches to start each of the boat's electric fuel pumps. When they'd completed the whir of their short cycles, I pushed the individual starter buttons in sequence to fire up both of the big boat's inboard motors.

The Donzi started to sing. Its full-throated rumble rolled out over the water.

I closed my eyes and said a silent prayer.

O God, our heavenly Father, whose glory fills the whole creation, and whose presence we find wherever we go: preserve those who travel; surround them with your loving care; protect them from every danger; and bring them in safety to their journey's end . . .

When I could trust myself to speak, I swiveled in my seat to face the spectacular vista of the club.

"Would you toss us those dock lines?" I asked Ryan-Troy. I was anxious to get out of there.

He complied and even magnanimously knelt to push the bow away from the dock.

"Have a great day on the water," he called out, with a parting wave.

I looked ahead over the bow of the boat. *Damn. This thing is the length of a city bus . . .*

I gingerly rested my hand on the throttles and slowly—*very slowly*—inched them forward. The big boat glided away from the dock. I had the sensation of sitting on a buckboard, trying to hold back a twenty-mule team. I was careful not to gain any speed until we had cleared the marina's no-wake zone, and I had a feel for the responsiveness of the engines.

Responsiveness? What a joke . . .

I don't know what the hell I'd been expecting. The staggered Mercury racing 860 engines were poised to run like gazelles if I so much as exhaled too sharply.

Once we'd rumbled clear of the marina and made our turn toward the lake's main channel, I gestured at Frankie to come join me at the helm.

She kicked off her shoes and made her way forward.

"Is that it?" she asked with excitement. "Did we do it?"

"You know?" I grinned at her. "I think we did."

"Well praise god, hallelujah." She flopped down into the wide bucket seat beside me. "Now what?"

"Now we take our sweet time getting this thing safely up to Stumpy Creek."

"How long will that take?"

"At the speed I intend to drive? About thirty minutes." I dug my cell phone out of the small bag I'd brought along and launched the *Make Wake* app.

Frankie pointed at a screen on the instrument panel. "Isn't that a GPS unit?"

"Probably. But I'm not messing with it. This thing is probably equipped with all kinds of tracking devices. I don't want to advertise where we are." I finished scrolling through various screens to begin the navigation process. The app worked like a charm. Once it loaded our coordinates and I chose our destination, it began displaying detailed on-screen instructions. I propped the phone up against the instrument console so I could hear the audible directions, and sat back to enjoy the ride.

"And, we're off like a herd of turtles." I smiled at Frankie, who was busy scanning the interior of the boat. "What are you looking for?"

"Didn't you hear that?" Frankie asked.

"Hear what?"

"There it is again." Frankie got to her feet. "It sounds like it's coming from down there." She pointed to the partially open access door that led below to the bow cabin. "Slow the engines."

"Frankie, we're barely moving as it is."

"Okay, then *stop*." She slid the door open all the way and bent over to look below. "*Oh, good lord!*"

"What is it?"

"There's a *cat* down there!"

"What?" I cut the engines entirely. "What do you mean, there's a cat down there?"

"You heard me. There's a cat . . . *a kitten*." She disappeared below and emerged a minute later carrying a fuzzy, gray- and black-striped bundle. It looked like it wasn't more than a couple of months old. Its mouth was going full-tilt boogie.

"What the *serious* fuck?" I couldn't believe what I was seeing. "How the hell did a cat get down there?"

"I don't know, but the poor thing is scared to death."

"Great. Just *great*. What are we supposed to do with a damn cat?"

Frankie cooed to the little beast and bounced it up and down in her arms. "I don't suppose we could take it back?"

"Frankie . . ." I began.

"Okay, okay. *We can't*." She kissed the little kitten on its head. "We'll just have to take it with us."

I thought about protesting, but what was the point? After all, we couldn't just tie the little thing to a life vest and set it adrift on the lake. And I knew Frankie would never agree to try and offload it near some obliging strangers at Stumpy Creek.

"Okay," I said with resignation. "We'll figure something out when we get back to Winston." A disturbing thought occurred to me. "Are you sure there aren't more of them down below?"

"I only saw this little one. She must've fallen in by accident. Is there a box or something we can put her in?"

"Beats the hell outta me. Maybe there's something inside one of those dry storage wells, beneath the seats."

"Good idea." Frankie handed me the cat and started looking beneath the seats. She was thrilled when she found a box containing a couple of folded foul weather ponchos and some towels. She removed the ponchos and arranged the towels to make a comfy nest. "Here you go, little one." She took the kitten and deposited it inside the box. It curled up into a ball and stopped hollering at once.

"I wonder if it has to go to the bathroom?" I asked, warily.

Frankie set the box down and discreetly closed the cabin access door. "It already did."

"Oh. *Nice.*" I thought about trying to clean it up, but changed my mind. "And *not* our problem."

Frankie scanned the boat interior again.

"What are you looking for now?"

"The fridge," she said. "Maybe there's something in there this kitten will eat. Besides, if this trip is gonna take half an hour, why not have some of that wine and cheese Mr. Jackson was kind enough to spring for?"

I shook my head and restarted the engines.

Why not, indeed?

We finally reached the narrow passage that led to the Stumpy Creek Recreation Area a little before noon. We were surprised that the lake was so much more heavily trafficked at the northern end. A couple dozen bass boats and Daysailers dotted the cove as we made our slow approach to the park and its public boat ramp.

"We're gonna have to tie up at one of those docks so you can hop out and get the trailer into position," I said to Frankie.

"Did you say 'hop out'? In *this* outfit?"

"It's either that or you go over the side and wade in . . . your call."

I'd all but stopped the Donzi, and we drifted about a hundred yards out from the small marina. Frankie took her time weighing her options.

"Well?" I asked. "What's it gonna be?" Already, curious bass fishermen were watching us as we drifted closer to shore. It occurred to me that not many boats of this type or stature probably frequented this public recreation area.

Frankie glowered at me. "I'm *thinking* about it, okay?"

"Okay." I decided for her. "We're docking. I'll get out first and give you—and our loud-mouthed stowaway—a hand up. Once you have the trailer in position, I'll move the boat over so we can load it."

"All right." She sighed. "Let's do it."

"Atta girl. Toss those bumpers out on my side. I'll tie it off as close as I can get to the ramp."

"Aye aye, captain."

Frankie complied and I began to motor the Donzi closer to the dock. I learned pretty quickly that with two motors, you could pretty much get a rig like this to do anything you wanted—even travel sideways. I was proud that I'd barely kissed the side of the dock when I cut the engines and jumped out to secure the mooring lines. Once I'd finished tying it up I extended a hand to Frankie.

"Okay, doll-face. It's showtime."

She tossed her shoes onto the dock before handing me the box containing our contraband, and stepped up onto a rear seat so I could help her scramble up out of the boat. It wasn't easy for her to avoid giving half a dozen admiring fishermen a dazzling display. A couple of them even gave her resounding wolf whistles. I was about to flip them off, but Frankie stopped me.

"Hang on . . . I think I have an idea."

I knew enough to be suspicious. "What *kind* of idea?"

"Watch and learn." She held onto my shoulder while she put her stilettos on. Then she fluffed out her hair, adjusted her mirrored shades, and held out her hand. "Give me the truck keys."

I pulled them from my bag and handed them to her nervously. "What are you going to do?"

"Desperate times call for desperate measures." She grabbed the zipper on the front of her dress and dramatically yanked it halfway to her navel.

"What the hell are you *doing?*" I hissed.

"Isn't it obvious? I'm calling in reinforcements." Frankie gave me a flamboyant head toss. "Watch the cat."

She turned on her four-inch heels and damn near strutted her way up the dock toward the cluster of small boats and her cache of admirers.

"Excuse me?" She gave the potbellied group of men a royal wave. "Would one of you kind gentlemen help me back our trailer down so we can get Daddy's boat out of the water? I'd be ever so grateful."

I recalled the Nat Geo documentary about salmon runs I'd watched with Sebastian and Carol Jenkins. That's about how fast those men fought their way to shore to help their damsel in distress. I watched, open-mouthed, as Frankie charmed them, first pointing out the Donzi and then showing them where our rig was parked. I feared a fight might break out as the men argued about which one of them could best jockey our trailer into position and successfully load the monster speedboat. Finally, one of them appeared to win out. Frankie handed him the keys and pointed me out. He looked my way, signaling that I should use the dock lines to walk the boat forward toward the ramp.

I was only too happy to comply.

Frankie accompanied her helpful volunteer to the pickup, where she retrieved the bag containing her change of clothing. I saw her thank him profusely before she headed for the public restroom to change.

Apparently, her desperation to be out of that costume overcame her disdain for the outdoor accommodations.

Once I'd tugged the Donzi along the dock into position, I waited while Frankie's burly savior retrieved our truck. Damn if he didn't back it up perfectly on the first try, and I watched with amazement as the trailer descended cleanly into the shallow water at the base of the boat ramp.

He set the brakes before climbing out and wading over to guide the bow of the Donzi cleanly onto the back of the boat trailer. Once he had the boat safely centered on the rear rockers of the trailer, he pulled it forward until he could attach the winch cable to the bow eye. He cranked the winch and the big boat rolled forward onto the transom notches and stopped when its bow rested snugly against the post roller at the front of the trailer. Frankie's helper then attached the emergency backup chains.

He examined his work before giving me a confident thumbs-up.

"Nice rig you got here." He gave the whole setup an approving nod. "That young lady's daddy is a lucky man."

"Yes, sir, he sure is," I agreed. "We can't thank you enough for helping us out."

"It ain't nothin'," he assured me. "Never could resist a couple of ladies in distress."

"Well, that's really generous. Would you let us pay you something to thank you for your help?"

"Nah. No call for that. It'd a been a crime for you two to have to wrestle this big thing out on your own. And I don't think your little friend woulda been much use tryin' to back this trailer up—not in them shoes." He adjusted his cap. "Well, let's get this thing up outta the water and get you good and secured before y'all head out."

I thanked him again before walking back to retrieve the box containing our newest plus one. After he'd pulled the trailer away from the boat ramp, he drove it to the parking area. Together, we connected the trailer lines to the truck harness, tested the brake lights and turn signals, and pulled the drain plugs to release any lake water from the boat. After securing the tie-downs and transom straps, he slapped a meaty hand against the hull of the Donzi and told me he guessed we were good to go.

"Where y'all headed?" he asked.

"Winston-Salem," Frankie answered from behind him.

He spun around in surprise to face her. It was almost painful to see the look of disappointment that crossed his face when he saw that her endowments were now safely under wraps.

"I simply cannot thank you enough," Frankie gushed. "I don't know how we would've managed without your help."

Apparently, her full-frontal charm offensive was still able to find its mark, even without her borrowed robes.

"You're welcome, little lady," he stammered. "I was more'n happy to help you out."

"My daddy would never forgive me if I didn't reward you properly for rescuing us," Frankie continued. "So please accept this small token of thanks—from him." She extended a hand containing a folded bill. "I insist."

"Well." He looked down at her hand. "I already told your friend it ain't necessary . . . but I guess if it makes you feel better, I'll take it."

Frankie beamed at him and pressed the bill into his hand. Then she leaned forward and kissed him on the cheek. "You're a prince."

He cleared his throat and nodded at her almost shyly.

"Come on, *Chris*," she said to me. "Get the cat and let's head for home."

I picked up the box and climbed into the passenger seat of the F450. Frankie tossed the bag containing her clothes into the back seat and got behind the wheel. As we pulled away from the marina, she blew the horn and waved good-bye to the newest member of her fan club.

I was pretty much in shock that we'd managed to pull the damn job off and said as much to Frankie.

"You need to have more faith in yourself," she replied. "It was a brilliant plan."

"Yeah, but I don't get any credit for that. It was all Sebastian."

"I disagree. You played your part perfectly. And you drove the boat out of there *and* helped get it out of the water."

"Your burly admirer did all of that. By the way, how much money did you give him?"

She shrugged. "A hundred bucks."

"Holy shit."

"It was the right thing to do. I'd have freaked out trying to back that thing up in front of all those people."

"I don't doubt it." I set the box containing the kitten down on the floorboard behind Frankie's seat. The striped ball of fur slept soundly, no doubt resting after the quarter pound of Iberico ham it had ingested on the boat.

"We need to find some cat food," Frankie pointed out. "Be on the lookout for a Sheetz."

"Yeah. I don't think so. We're *not* stopping. It can have some of Carol Jenkins' food when we get home."

"I suppose that's true."

We cruised up Highway 21, heading for the intersection with I-40.

"So, how's it handling now with the boat aboard?" I asked.

"Fine," she said. "Different. Maybe a little more sluggish?"

"I don't doubt it. That thing probably weighs about a thousand pounds."

Frankie's eyes grew wide.

"Don't worry," I assured her. "The trailer has brakes, too."

"I just want this *over* with."

"It will be soon enough." We rode along in silence for a bit. "You were a real rock star."

"Me? How so?"

"That whole ice princess thing at the club? Priceless. And then the way you worked that poor bass fisherman at the boat landing? He'd have pulled the damn thing out of the water with his teeth if you'd asked him to."

"He was very sweet."

"And horny."

"Oh, come on." Frankie looked at me. "He was just being nice."

"Frankie? He probably had a damn boner."

"He did not. You're exaggerating."

"Okay," I sulked. "Maybe a metaphorical one."

"You sound like you're jealous."

I tapped my foot against the floorboard.

"Nick?"

I looked at her.

"Are you jealous?"

"Of course not," I huffed. "That's ridiculous."

"All right," she said. "Good to know."

I tapped my foot some more.

"Okay," I finally fessed up. "Maybe I was a *little* jealous."

Frankie looked over at me. "Now it's *my* turn to say that's ridiculous. You, of all people, have nothing to be jealous about."

"I know. I can't help it."

"Maybe I can come up with a way to convince you."

That piqued my interest. "What did you have in mind?"

"Something that involves a creative reenactment, utilizing our stash in the back seat."

I was confused. "The cat?"

"Not *that* stash," Frankie said with impatience. "The *other* stash."

"Oh." Sometimes it took me a while to pick up the clue phone. "You mean . . . the *outfit?*"

I swore I could hear all kinds of minor key vibrations . . .

"Uh huh," Frankie drawled.

I took a deep breath—followed by a couple more, just for good measure.

"Yeah," I agreed. "That could maybe work."

Eddie's delivery instructions directed us to take the truck and boat to a rest stop on the outskirts of K-Vegas. He said he'd hook us up with a ride back to Winston after the handoff.

Everything about this setup made my scalp crawl. I said as much to Frankie as we neared our destination.

"Eddie's demand for secrecy about these jobs is practically giving me shingles. I keep trying to blow it off, but I can't."

"I know what you mean," Frankie agreed. "I never thought I'd say that having Antigone out of the loop on something would bother me so much. Linda's comments didn't make me feel any better, either."

"Do you think we should ask Antigone about this?"

"The boat?" she asked. "I don't know . . ."

I sighed. "I don't think we should agree to any more jobs that don't come through normal channels."

"You realize that probably means we won't get *any* jobs, then . . . right?"

That was true. Every assignment we'd had so far had come directly from Eddie. Well . . . except for the school bus. But even then, Antigone hadn't been keen on using us, and said the only reason we were getting it was because Eddie said so.

"Yeah. I guess." I thought about it from another angle. "Maybe we should try and follow up with Linda? See if she'll tell us why she was so amazed about us getting a job of this caliber?"

"I doubt she'll tell us anything."

There were scuffling noises coming from the back seat. I turned around and looked into the box on the floorboard behind Frankie. A pair of green eyes stared back at me. Then the little thing started belting out a monologue, like it was scolding me for something.

I turned back around. "Your friend is awake."

"Awwww," Frankie said with concern. "Pick her up and hold her. She's probably afraid."

"I'm *not* picking her up."

"Why not?"

"I don't want her to pee on me."

"Nick . . ."

"*Okay, okay.*" I reached behind her seat and retrieved the furry little ball with the great big mouth. It sat down and began kneading against my stomach. "Damn it!"

"What now?"

I detached the cat from my shirt and held it aloft. "This thing is like Edward Scissorhands. Its little razor toes are cutting the crap out of me."

"You are such a big baby."

I reached into the box and snagged one of the towels to fold against my abdomen before returning the cat to my lap. "What are you gonna do with this thing?"

"Me?" Frankie looked at me.

"Yeah. *You.* You're the one who wanted to bring it along."

"Well, we could hardly leave it in the boat."

"I don't see why not. It isn't like Antigone will be on hand to bust us for breaching the 'and contents' rule again."

"There's the rest stop sign." Frankie pointed it out. "Do you think Eddie will be there?"

"He should be. I texted him as soon as we got on I-40."

Frankie began to slow down so we could exit the highway.

"Trucks and trailers to the right," I read, as we drove along the ramp that led to the rest stop. "There's his Escalade. Back there by those picnic tables."

"I see it."

Frankie pulled into one of the long parking spaces and stopped. Eddie and another man had been seated at one of the tables smoking, but got up when they saw us pulling in.

I returned the protesting cat to its box.

"Who's that oddly proportioned man with Eddie?" Frankie asked.

"I have no idea." I took a closer look at him. "But something about him looks familiar."

When we got out of the truck, Eddie was all smiles.

"Look at that beautiful thing," he declared, as he extended his arms to encompass the Donzi. "Thirty-eight feet of pure gelt. Not a scratch on it. You two are such a mitzvah . . . it's *bashert*—my destiny!" He elbowed his companion. "Didn't I just tell you they'd pull it off? Good luck charms . . . the two of them. My little champions."

Eddie's strange companion didn't say anything, but was taking his time looking the boat over.

"Okay, girls." Eddie reached into his jacket pocket. "I ordered your Uber when you pulled in off the highway. It should be here in about ten minutes. Don't worry . . . it's paid for. And here's a little something to reward you tonight." He passed Frankie a fistful of bills. "Get something nice for dinner," he waved a hand, "on me."

Frankie stood holding the wad of money out away from her body like it was a garter snake some kid had just passed to her on a playground. She looked at me for help.

"That's not necessary, Eddie," I said. "We don't need any special reward."

"It's done." He held up his hands. "I insist." He looked at his friend. "We both do, right Clint?"

Clint looked like he couldn't care less about us or anything else. "Time to get moving." He consulted the shiny watch hanging from his bony wrist. "Tiny's waiting. We need to get this thing off the road."

"Yeah, yeah. You're all go and no show." Eddie faced me again. "You two got any shit in the truck you need to retrieve?"

"Yeah. A couple of things." I opened the back door on the pickup and pulled out Frankie's bag and the box containing our plus one. The cat started hollering like someone had thrown a switch.

"What the fuck is that?" Eddie asked.

"A stowaway," I explained. "By the time we discovered it, we were already out on the water, away from the club."

Frankie took her bag and the box from me and carried them over to the picnic table where Eddie and his colleague had been seated when we arrived.

Eddie chuckled and stepped closer to me. "Nice work, Vera," he whispered. "I knew you'd get some pussy outta this deal sooner or later."

I was horrified by his crude comment and shot a quick look at Frankie—but she was fussing with the kitten, and it was obvious she hadn't heard him.

I wanted to punch him in the face. I wanted that more than anything. I'm pretty sure he knew it, too. He actually took a step back from me.

What the hell were we thinking, going to work for this guy?

It was becoming impossible to square how someone like Antigone could stay in business with a man who would say what Eddie had just said to me. Global Gospel Radio wasn't a joke or some kind of elaborate prop to front for the NRB. Antigone Reece actually lived her faith . . . with a vengeance and out loud, with a couple thousand watts behind it. And Weasel? He was a decent guy who had a genuine fondness for Frankie. Even Hugh Don and Linda were pretty straight arrows with no-nonsense codes of ethics.

None of this felt right. Not anymore.

I wanted to go home and take a shower . . .

Clint was already climbing into the cab of the pickup. He was impatient to get rolling with his part of the handoff.

"We'll wait on our Uber at the picnic table," I told Eddie. "Thanks for the ride."

He nodded at me. I don't know if he regretted his comment or not. It was hard to tell what expression he wore behind those damn transition lenses.

"I'll be in touch," he said.

He walked off and got into his Escalade.

I waited while Clint started the truck and slowly pulled the Donzi out of the rest stop, with Eddie following along behind him. Once they had merged onto the highway, I joined Frankie and the cat at the table.

"What was that all about?" she asked me.

"You don't want to know."

"Lemme guess: Eddie said something inappropriate about me?"

"What makes you think that?" I tried to sound blasé.

"Call it women's intuition." She'd put the cat down on the grass at her feet, presumably so it could go potty if it needed to.

"Women's intuition?" I asked.

She nodded. "That, and the fact you looked like you wanted to knee him in the balls."

I tried hard not to laugh.

"I'm right, aren't I?" Frankie sounded amused.

"About me wanting to knee him in the . . . you know..."

"No. I have no doubt about that part. I'm right that he said something derogatory about me, aren't I?"

"Not derogatory—just . . . crude. And it was about me, and the cat."

"The cat? What could he possibly have said about the . . ." I saw enlightenment dawn in her eyes. "Oh, give me a *break!* That's the best he could come up with? What kind of stupid, sophomoric bullshit was that?"

"'The best he could come up with'?" I quoted.

"He's a pig."

"You'll get no argument from me on that."

The kitten had wandered off to a respectful distance before squatting and relieving itself.

"Look at that." Frankie nudged me. "She'll be housebroken in no time."

"Yeah, but whose house is she not going to be breaking?"

"Yours." Frankie said it like it was a *fait accompli.*

"Mine? I don't think so. Why not yours?"

"Allergies." Frankie pointed at her nose. "Remember?"

"Very convenient."

"Sebastian will take her," Frankie said with confidence. "Carol Jenkins needs a companion."

"You're nuts. Sebastian doesn't want another cat."

"Yes he does." Frankie held up her cell phone. "I already asked him." She bent over and tapped her fingers against her ankle. "Penny? Come on, little Penny. Come on, sweet girl. Let's get ready to go home."

Penny?

I was obviously missing something.

"What did you just call her?" I asked.

"Oh. Sebastian already named her." Frankie picked up my new roommate and handed her to me. "Meet Penny Morgan."

I sat there holding . . . *Penny* . . . who was busy chewing on my index finger.

"Sadly, I guess that bastard, Eddie, was right," I said with resignation.

"Not even close," Frankie corrected me. "But there's still a chance, if you play your cards right."

The Uber driver dropped us off at Frankie's house about forty-five minutes after we'd delivered the Donzi to Eddie and his pal, Clint. We both were surprised to see Jason's BMW parked in her driveway when we arrived. Sebastian got out of the car to greet us.

"Well, if this ain't convenient, I don't know what is."

He quickly engaged our Uber driver to take him back to our house.

"You don't have to do that," I protested. "You can ride home with me in Jason's car."

Sebastian ignored my protest. "Where's my precious baby?" he asked Frankie.

"Right here." Frankie passed him the box containing Penny Morgan. "She's a total snuggle bug."

"Oh, look at you," he gushed. "My little jewel of the sea."

I watched him coddle the kitten. "Aren't you the least bit worried that Carol Jenkins will eat this thing like a canapé?"

Sebastian recoiled from me in horror and covered Penny Morgan's ears with his hand.

"Don't you *dare* spread lies and misinformation around her; she's young and impressionable."

"Okay, *fine*," I said. "You're truly certifiable."

"Did you have any trouble getting the car?" Frankie asked him.

"Nope. Sailed right in and drove right out." He nodded toward the BMW. "As you can see, I removed that ridiculous charcoal face mask."

I was surprised. "How'd you get it off? I had to steam it the last time."

He gave me a withering look. "Noxzema. Of course."

"You travel with Noxzema?"

"Doesn't everyone?" He gave Frankie a kiss on the cheek and climbed into the back seat of his Uber. "See you tomorrow," he said to me.

Tomorrow? *Did he know something I didn't?*

I watched as the car slowly backed out of Frankie's driveway.

"That was . . . bizarre."

Frankie looked at me. "More bizarre than *anything* ever is with him?"

"Good point."

Frankie let out a tired-sounding breath. "Let's go inside. I want to get out of this damn bodysuit."

Okay, that got my attention. I hadn't realized she was still wearing it beneath her change of clothes.

"Pity," I said sadly. "But I guess all good things must come to an end."

"That depends," she said.

"On what?" I asked, warily.

"On whether I can extract myself from this thing without help. I think it might be permanently melded to my body."

I took a minute to indulge in the mental image that suggestion summoned up. It was a damn good one, worthy of focused and prolonged consideration.

Frankie watched me with amusement. "Finished yet?"

I looked at her guiltily. "Um . . . what?"

"You know what I mean." She squinted at me. "It's a paradox. If you were a guy, I'd be tempted to call you a sleazebag and storm off in a blazing fit of righteous indignation."

"But, I'm not a guy . . ."

"No." Frankie looked me over. "You sure aren't."

I felt a tingle begin in my toes. At least, I think it started in my toes. It was kind of hard to tell because in seconds, it had spread everyplace: my calves, my knees, my thighs, my belly, my chest, my hands, my arms—and, finally, my head.

Even in my agitated state, I marveled that my head was always last to get the news.

"So," I said in a voice that sounded nothing like my own, "where does that leave me?" As I asked, I said a silent prayer to all of Mamá's benevolent saints that, for once, I'd be left in one of the good places.

Frankie stepped closer to me. She took hold of my hands and

slowly brought them up until they came to rest firmly against her breasts.

"I think it leaves you right about here," she whispered.

I closed my eyes. I could feel myself starting to sway.

Sweet mother of pearl... don't let me faint. Not now. Not fucking now.

Frankie was kissing my neck. Nuzzling my ear. I could feel her hands twisting their way into my hair. I dropped my head back to breathe and opened my eyes. An explosion of colors—blue, white and green—filled up my tumbled world. They danced and parried, locked into an ageless rhythm of swirling together and coming apart. Never stopping. Always changing. Constantly withdrawing and returning, like the tides.

Or like my own human heart: weary of running, and daring to try again.

In that same timeless and unbridled way, we flowed into and around each other. It felt old and it felt new, all at the same time. We were like weary travelers after a long absence, returning at last to the comfort of a known place. I could feel Frankie's heart beating beneath my hands. I could hear her ragged breathing and taste her desire as it rose and mingled with my own.

We staggered toward her porch and somehow managed to navigate the steps without falling. Once inside, I tried to steer her to the couch, but she stopped me.

"Bedroom," she breathed against my mouth. "It's where grown-ups belong."

I didn't fight her. I couldn't. Together we were too strong for me. We were half undressed before we made it across the room. Her bodysuit was the last holdout when we finally fell together across her bed.

I stopped kissing her long enough to lamely express my escalating frustration.

"You really weren't kidding about this thing, were you?"

"Unfasten the gussets," she coaxed, before pulling my head back down for another kiss.

Gussets? I was losing focus again. "What gussets?"

"*Here.*" Frankie pushed my hand down between her legs.

I nearly passed out at the intimate contact. But sure enough, there they were: gussets. I fumbled around with them, and the rest of her surrounding real estate, for a couple of minutes. Pretty soon, I didn't much care about wrangling the gussets loose—or anything else. Nothing mattered anymore but the waves of heat and sensation that were emanating from our writhing bodies.

"Just. *Rip*. Them," Frankie finally ordered. "Now."

I did as she asked. I'd already learned it was in my best interest to do so.

In seconds, Frankie was freed from her prison—and everything she revealed made me a willing hostage to mine.

That was okay by me.

In love as in life, I was learning that things went better when the players agreed up-front on division of labor.

Chapter Seven

I Said My Pajamas (and Put on My Prayers)

Avena con leche is a homey, Guatemalan breakfast cereal Mamá used to make. It's pretty much a hot medley of oatmeal and milk with cinnamon and brown sugar, but Mamá always called it a "hug in a mug." On special days, when all three of us were at home, she'd sometimes add scrambled eggs with black beans and chopped tomatoes, and a side of crispy fried plantains. But I knew Frankie didn't have a lot of time to linger over her morning meal—or a ready supply of plantains—so I went with a stripped-down version of Mamá's classic fare.

I wanted to surprise her with coffee and breakfast in bed.

So when I woke up about an hour before her alarm was set to go off at six, I crept into her kitchen and found what I needed to make her a steaming hug in a mug. Frankie also had a bowl containing some Honeycrisp apples and a couple of bananas, so I sliced up one of each and added those to my humble breakfast tray.

Frankie was awake when I carried the goodies back into her bedroom. She was propped up on a couple of pillows with the covers pulled up beneath her arms. She'd turned on her small bedside light, but the room was still mostly dappled with shadows.

"I thought I heard something rustling around in my kitchen," she said sleepily. "For a minute, I thought it was Penny Morgan. Then I remembered that Sebastian took her home."

I carefully placed the tray on the ottoman that sat in front of her corner reading chair. A table beside the chair was covered with notebooks and highlighters.

"Remember anything else from last night?" I asked, somewhat smugly.

"Uh huh." She yawned. "I think there was something about gussets, followed by the birth of a new world order. Does that jibe with your recollection of the evening?"

I sat down on the bed beside her. "Pretty much."

Frankie leaned toward me and I met her halfway.

Yep. Yep. You betcha. That's a big 10-4. Everything I remembered from last night came roaring right back. Just as strong. Just as sweet. Just as hot.

"Why the hell did we wait so long?" I asked, when finally we drew apart.

"You're asking *me* this question? I all but threw myself at you."

"I *beg* your pardon. I think *I* was the one who ripped your gussets open . . . so to speak."

Frankie laughed. "Yeah, *that* line is destined to go down in the annals of foreplay."

"Foreplay? I don't know what part of the 'annals' you were stuck in at that point, but I had already moved way beyond foreplay. I think I was halfway to . . . aft-play."

"Aft-play? What the hell is that?"

"It inhabits the other side of foreplay," I explained. "It's a nautical term, which has mostly fallen out of use."

"I can see why." Frankie was trying to peek around me at the breakfast tray. "I'm sure I smell coffee. And . . . cinnamon?"

"That, you do." I retrieved the tray. "I made breakfast. Sort of." I passed her a large cup of coffee. "I hope this is okay. It's kind of strong."

"Good." Frankie took it from me gratefully. "I like it strong."

"Yeah," I made an exaggerated groan, "I noticed."

"Smart ass." Frankie took a careful sip of her coffee. "I don't recall hearing any complaints from you."

"You never will."

We smiled at each other.

"What else did you bring me?" Frankie asked.

"Ah." I retrieved some of the steaming *avena con leche*. "This is what my Mamá called a 'hug in a mug.' It's oatmeal with hot milk, cinnamon and brown sugar. A Guatemalan breakfast treat."

"Ohhhhh." Frankie deposited her coffee cup on the bedside table and reached out for it greedily. "Gimme."

"I also cut up some fruit." I placed the plate with the apple and banana slices on the bed between us. "Eat up. The bananas are turning brown."

"Brown food tastes good," she quipped in a husky voice.

I narrowed my eyes at her. "Is that some kind of double entendre?"

"Double entendre?" She looked confused. Then she got it. "Dear god . . . *no*. I was quoting Anne Burrell."

"Relax." I laughed at her. "I knew what you meant. I was teasing you."

"Asshole." Frankie returned to her oatmeal. "This is just so heavenly . . . it's like . . ."

"A hug in a mug?" I offered.

"Yes. Exactly."

"Well," I reached out and took hold of her free hand, "I wanted to send you off to work with something that would keep you warm inside."

"Oh, honey, believe me." Frankie leaned forward and kissed me. I could taste cinnamon on her tongue. "You already did."

Frankie left for school promptly at 7:15. But before she left, she enlisted my help with packing twelve bag lunches. We stood at her kitchen counter making and wrapping peanut butter and jelly sandwiches, and stuffed them into paper sacks along with tiny Ziploc bags of carrot sticks, plastic cups of applesauce, and an assortment of bananas and tangerines.

"Do you do this every day?" I asked.

"Mostly. The kids all get breakfast and hot lunches at school, but I have some who might not get meals at night. I want to be sure to send them home with something to eat."

"No supper?" That reality was an eye-opener for me. "That shouldn't happen."

"No. It shouldn't. But it does. And, sadly, more often than not."

I finished assembling the last few bags. "I'm embarrassed that I never took the time to think about this."

"Don't be. Most people don't *ever* think about it. But it's like Maya Angelou said: once you know better, do better."

"So I guess you weren't exaggerating when you said this is why you got the part-time job at the NRB?"

"Nope. I can teach them how to spell and how to think critically, but I can't prevent them from going to bed hungry—not without some additional income. And if they're hungry, acquiring the other skills isn't of much value."

"That beats the hell outta my reason for taking a job there."

"It's not a contest, Nick."

"I know. It just highlights my need to get off my butt and figure out my future. I don't want to tie myself to another dead-end job that prevents me from having a life and insulates me from caring about things that really matter."

"You won't."

"What makes you so sure?"

"Because it's not who you are." Frankie loaded the bagged meals into a canvas bag. "Once you know something, you can't unknow it."

"You think so?"

"I know so." She kissed me. "I hate to go, but if I don't leave now, I'll be late."

I followed her out and stashed the duffel bag full of lunches on the back seat of her car.

Frankie stepped into my arms and hugged me warmly.

"See you tonight?" she asked, hopefully.

"Count on it." I kissed the top of her head.

She got into her car and backed out. I waited until she drove out of sight before getting into Jason's Beemer and heading for home.

I'd already called Jason last night to apologize for not returning his car, as promised—but he was totally unconcerned about it, and said I could keep it for as long as I wanted. I figured I'd ask Sebastian if he could follow me out to Bermuda Run around lunchtime. I was pretty sure he'd agree.

Our house was quiet when I let myself in. There was no sign of Sebastian, so I assumed he must still be in bed. There were no signs of Carol Jenkins or Penny Morgan, either. I put on a pot of coffee and decided that this was the perfect time for me to try and catch Mamá. She didn't normally head into the clinic before nine, so I knew I'd have a good shot at catching her at home. When the coffee finished brewing, I poured myself a cup and carried it outside to our patio. I wanted to have a quiet—and private—place to make my call.

The phone was picked up on the first ring.

"Hello, sweet pea." It was Papa. "What are you doing home at this hour on a weekday?"

Shit. It was like him to recognize that I'd called from our house phone. I hadn't thought about that detail.

"I could ask you the same question, Papa."

"Guilty." He laughed. "I'm off to get a few holes of golf in with a client. What are you up to?"

"Pretty much the same," I lied. "I have a couple of errands to run this morning, so I thought I'd call and try to catch Mamá before she left for the clinic."

"Good plan. You're wise to put fences around those conversations. Especially when she's all queued up and ready for a first-class ass-ripping."

I closed my eyes. "What'd I do this time?"

"Hell if I know. She doesn't tend to explain her nuances of thought to me." When I didn't reply right away, he continued in a softer tone. "Is everything okay with you, sweet pea? Your Mamá and her crazy sister have the wind up about you. They're persuaded that you've fallen in with some bad crowd or are on the cusp of bad fortune. You know I think that woo-woo crap is nothing but a big load of bullshit, but that doesn't mean I don't worry when you go silent and we don't hear from you at all."

"I know, Papa. I'm okay. I promise."

"Just okay?" he repeated. "Just okay isn't good enough for my little girl."

I smiled. "I know. But I'm doing fine. I really am." I decided to haul out the big guns. "I met someone, Papa. Someone special."

"Well, hells bells," he roared. "Maybe your Mamá is right to believe in miracles."

"That's really why I called," I said, "to tell you both about her."

I could hear Mamá's voice in the background, chewing on Papa about something.

He'd lowered the phone to respond to her. "Yes, Maria. For the love of god . . . I'll pick it up. You've already asked me about this five times." He raised the handset back to his ear. "I've gotta run. I need to hit Hideaway Music on my way to the golf course and pick up a special order LP for your mother. If I don't get it, there'll be no peace in this valley tonight."

Mamá was listening to vinyl records?

"What is it?" I asked.

"Wagner. It's a replacement for one of mine that she ruined." I could hear Mamá's voice again—arguing with him about the record. "Hold on. I'm gonna let *her* explain it to you. I gotta scoot. Love you, baby. Call me later and tell me about your new girlfriend."

He handed the phone to Mamá.

"So, is that you, *doncella*? Or is El Cadejo playing tricks on me?"

"Hola, Mamá. It's good to hear your voice."

"If it is so wonderful, then why do you deprive yourself of it?"

"It's . . . I've been . . . really busy."

"So I hear. With this new girlfriend, undoubtedly?"

"Well," I stammered. "With that and . . . other things."

"Yes. I am eager to hear about these other things. And the new girlfriend."

I was desperate to find something less—confrontational—to open our conversation. "What's the Wagner album Papa is replacing?" I asked.

"Oh, *that*," she brushed it off. "It's an old one of his—from college. An opera. *Der fliegende Holländer.* He loves those German dirges."

"*The Flying Dutchman*?" I translated. "I remember that. The Philadelphia Orchestra performed it. Papa took us to see it on my twelfth birthday."

"You fell asleep," Mamá reminded me.

"It was sad," I defended myself. "And it was in German, so I didn't understand any of it."

"Yes," Mamá agreed with rare enthusiasm. "That is what I tell him. *It is too sad.* Too sad, and too slow. So I play it for him at a faster speed to make it sound better. Now he says it is ruined. Ridiculous."

"You played a vintage, vinyl LP recording at a faster speed?"

"Of course. It is amazing how a faster rpm takes the sadness out of German music. The world should know this."

I couldn't really dispute her claim. After all, adding a few well-placed rpms to my life had certainly dispatched my ambient despair.

"Karen told me you're seeing someone new." Mamá had shifted gears. "Is this the girlfriend you told Papa about?"

"Yes. I . . . want you both to meet her. I mean . . . sometime."

"Who is she?" Mamá didn't sound quite ready to toss out the welcome mat.

"Her name is Frankie . . . Frances. She's a schoolteacher. She's . . ."

How could I summarize Frankie in just a few words? Phrases like "hot as fuck" and "an expert at hot-wiring cars" weren't going to endear Mamá to my cause.

"She's not like anyone I've known before." I went with a simple truth.

"Ay no," Mamá replied. "I said that same thing when I met your Papa, and look where it got me?"

"Listening to Wagner at the wrong speed to take the sadness out of life?"

I heard her stifle a laugh. "I will be late for the clinic. We will talk more about this special Frances, *doncella*."

"Yes," I agreed. "We will. Bye, Mamá. I love you."

"*Te quiero, hija mía.*" She disconnected.

Well... I sat back with my coffee and admired the perfect morning. *That went well.*

Hugh Don was surprised to see me when I walked through the door at Old World Meats in Lexington.

He'd been wrapping up some chicken for a white-haired, rather rotund woman who was wearing a shiny tracksuit and Keds. She wore a lot of cologne, too. The air in the small shop was thick with the cloying scent of roses. She paid for her purchase and thanked Hugh Don profusely, saying she hoped she'd see him soon. He all but ignored her.

"I think she's sweet on you," I said, after she left the shop.

He scoffed at my observation.

"Old battle-ax comes in here about five times a week, sniffing around. Nobody eats that many chicken thighs. Her old man just died three months ago."

"So? Maybe she's really nice," I suggested.

"I don't need a woman yammering at my ass all night—not when I get it all day for free."

"You're just a crusty old geezer. You need to lighten up and let yourself live a little."

"Who the fuck sent you down here to blow sunshine up my ass?"

"Nobody. I just wanted to see you."

"Oh, yeah? What about?" When I didn't answer right away, he took a stab at a reason. "Things going okay at the NRB?" Hugh Don dragged an old metal stool up to the counter and sat down on it. "I gotta get off these legs. In the back, I have a chair on rollers, so I can move around better."

It was painful to me that someone as old and infirm as Hugh Don still had to work for a living. Everything about that felt wrong. The world needed a fleet of Antigones to make adjustments to this part of the natural order, too.

"Eddie not sending you any work?" I asked him.

"Nah. He don't ask me to do much anymore. Just special jobs now and then."

"Like the Maybach?"

"What are you gettin' at, Vera?" He coughed into the sleeve of his white coat. "You got something you wanna ask me about?"

I wasn't any good at subterfuge. I never had been. Hugh Don knew it, and so did I.

"Yeah. I guess I do."

"I figured you didn't ride all the way down here to stock up on ham hocks."

A big chalkboard behind him advertised that the smoked variety were on sale for $1.40 a pound.

"No. I wanted to ask you about a couple of . . . jobs. Things Eddie's asked Frankie and me to do."

"What about 'em?"

I shrugged. "Something about a couple of them seems off."

"Off can mean a lot of things."

"You aren't making this easy for me."

"Is that my job, Vera? To make things easy?"

I drummed my fingers on top of the display case. Maybe my impulse to come down here had been a bad idea.

Hugh Don watched me deliberate.

"Look," he said. "You got a good head on your shoulders. You think something don't smell right, you ask Antigone about it. That woman don't mess with jobs that ain't on the up and up."

"That's kind of the thing, Hugh Don. Most of the jobs we're

getting are coming straight from Eddie. And on this last one, he told us specifically not to talk about it with Antigone."

I could tell that last detail got his attention. But he still seemed reluctant to opine about Eddie's motivations.

"What makes you think there's something off about the jobs? In this kind of work, there ain't much that's what you'd call normal."

I deliberated about how many specifics to share with him. Eddie and Hugh Don had known each other a long time. I trusted Hugh Don, but I didn't want to alienate him by talking smack about Eddie, either.

"Well, a couple of weeks ago, we got a job to pick up a brand-new Cadillac hearse."

Hugh Don started laughing. "You in a cold-cut wagon? I'd a liked to see that."

"Yeah, it didn't work out so well. But that's another story. The thing is, after we'd done the job, Frankie's sister, Lilah, told us something that didn't make sense. Lilah's a funeral director in Winston," I explained. "Frankie's family runs the business."

"No shit?" Hugh Don shook his head. "That's fucked up."

"Yeah. Pretty much." I agreed.

"I guess the Caddy wadn't one of theirs?"

"No. And that's the thing. Lilah knew the place that defaulted on the hearse. But she said it had been *stolen*."

Hugh Don flashed a brown-stained palm. "That don't mean nothin'. People lie about that shit all the time. They don't want nobody to know they skipped out on payments."

"Yeah, but here's the thing: Lilah said she knew it had been stolen because the Stohlers had been in a bidding war with this place to buy it. She said the other place finally got it by paying cash on the barrel-head."

Hugh Don took a minute to digest Lilah's comment.

"You still got the work order for the Caddy?" he asked.

I nodded. "Frankie keeps all of that stuff."

"Then, shit, Vera—go look up the VIN and check out the title. It ain't damn rocket science."

I stood there in stunned silence. I was a damn *attorney,* and it never once occurred to me that I could do this simple thing to verify the lien-holder on the hearse, or on any of the other vehicles we'd recovered.

"I don't know why I didn't think of that," I admitted. "I feel like an idiot."

"Maybe you just been distracted? I seen that little Stohler gal . . . hard to blame you for that one."

I tried to suppress a smile, but didn't quite succeed.

"Anyway," Hugh Don continued, "this seems like an easy way to get answers. But, listen Vera—if you'n Frankie don't like the jobs Eddie is givin' you, then don't do 'em. And don't tell nobody I said this, but you can always ask Antigone about 'em, too. She'll set you straight."

I deliberated. "Has Eddie ever asked you to do anything you didn't feel right about?"

Hugh Don took his time answering. "Eddie's been a good friend to me. He took care of me when I . . . well. He helped me out at a time I needed it. I owe him a lot, so I ain't gonna tell tales outta school. You got concerns? You either quit the job or you tell Antigone. That's my advice."

"Okay. Thanks, man."

"You got one life to live, Vera. Just remember that when that big tow finally comes for you, you don't wanna go out with regrets. There ain't no do-overs." Hugh Don grunted as he got to his feet. "You drove all the way down here. Lemme hook you and that little gal up with something good for dinner."

I watched while he reached into the meat case and hauled out two of the biggest rib eye steaks I'd ever seen, and wrapped them up in butcher paper.

He passed the fat bundle across the counter to me. "These should grill up real good."

"These are beautiful, Hugh Don. What do I owe you for them?"

"Nothin'. Just cook 'em up right and have a nice evening with that little gal of yours."

I thought about asking Hugh Don what made him so sure Frankie was "my gal," but I figured anyone with a brain could see how hard I had to fight not to smile whenever her name came up.

"Thanks, man. This is really generous."

"Get on," he waved me toward the door. "I got work to do, and so do you."

"Okay." I gave him a little salute. "Thanks for dinner—and thanks for the good advice, too."

"You got good instincts, kid. Use 'em. Now I gotta head to the back and bring up some more red hots." He didn't bother to say goodbye. He turned around and grabbed hold of his walker before shuffling his way toward the prep area, leaving me standing alone in the small shop.

I hefted the fat package of steaks and hoped Frankie didn't have any plans for dinner.

As soon as I got back home, I made my way to my office to locate the folder containing copies of all of our NRB work orders. On my way down the hall, I passed by Carol Jenkins' room and stopped to take a peek inside. She and Penny Morgan were happily snuggled up together, sleeping in the rays of sun that poured in from the large corner windows.

Guess that worked out better than I thought . . .

As I stood in the doorway admiring the pair, Penny Morgan roused and saw me standing there. I expected her to recognize me and start mouthing off—but I was mistaken. I watched as all the hair stood up on her back before she started hissing at me.

Of course, that commotion woke Carol Jenkins up. Jabba the Catt glared at me with a hostile look that seemed to say, *"What did you expect, asshole?"*

I retreated from the doorway and continued on to the safety of my office, where I sat down and called a familiar number.

"Forsyth County Sheriff's Office," a female voice answered.

"Hey there, Possum. It's Nick."

For the record, Possum's real name was Irene. But the story went that her daddy nicknamed her Possum because she was a sneaky child who was always getting into things she shouldn't. Possum was the firm's go-to gal whenever we needed a modest accommodation from local law enforcement, or some quick public records research.

"Nick?" I heard a deep sigh. "Okay. Which one of the TWAT Tots got busted this time?"

"No, it's not any of them. I need a favor for myself."

"You get another speeding ticket?" Possum asked.

"No."

"Jury summons?"

"No."

"You late on your water bill or something?"

"No. It's none of that stuff. I need you to run a couple vehicle titles for me. I've got the VINs."

Possum didn't ask why I needed the information. That was the best part about working with her. As long as you weren't asking to do anything illegal, she'd usually help you out. She was good people.

"Okay. I'm ready to copy," she said. "Fire them off."

I read the three VINs to her. I decided only to check out our last couple of jobs—the ones that came directly from Eddie. I could hear Possum typing.

"Okay. That first one? Is it a 2019 Cadillac XTS Kensington?"

"That would be the one."

"Okay. I got it. It has a clean history. No flood damage or major repairs. It's not a reclaimed vehicle."

"Do you have the name of the lien-holder?"

"Let's see . . ." I could hear Possum clicking through screens. "Not seeing any liens. Looks like it's got a clean title history. Belongs to Blessed Slumber Mortuary on Ogburn Avenue in Winston-Salem."

I felt like the floor had just dropped away beneath my chair.

"Are you sure about that?" I asked.

"Yep. It's right here. Clear as day. Lemme look up this next one."

I waited while Possum did her search. I could feel my heart rate accelerating with every click of her keyboard.

"Okay," Possum said. "Is this next one a 1967 Mustang Shelby GT 500?"

"Yeah." I replied somberly. "That's it." I had a sinking feeling I knew what Possum was going to tell me.

"Okay. Clean vehicle report. No lien on this one either. The title is clear and registered to a Lawrence Cecil in Advance."

I rested my head against my hand. I was starting to feel sick.

I could hear Possum clicking away.

"This third one's not coming up with anything. It says invalid VIN. Reread me the number? Maybe I wrote it down wrong."

I started to give her the number again when something occurred to me. "Wait a minute. This one's not a car. It has a Hull Identification Number—not a VIN."

"It's a boat?" Possum asked.

"Yep. Can you search those, too?"

"Yeah. But I have to log into another database. Give me a minute."

"You are a goddess, Possum. I don't know what I'd do without you."

She laughed. "Hell. Someday I might need a favor from you."

"You mean like a quickie divorce?" I teased.

"It could happen. That man of mine's a worthless pile of cow dung."

I thought about Eddie. "Lots of that going around these days."

"Isn't that the truth?"

I listened to some more clicking and scrolling.

"Okay. Here it is." Possum gave a low whistle. "*Damn*. Nice ride."

"You found it?" I asked.

"Uh huh. A 2019 Donzi 38 ZRC?"

"That's the one."

"Okay." I heard her clicking away. "Let's see . . . yadda, yadda, no damage. No open recalls. Clean title. Belongs to a person named Ransom Jackson in Mooresville. Hey, doesn't he own that Roush Jackson Racing Team? I just heard him interviewed on Claire B. Lang's show."

"Yeah." I felt like I was going to throw up. "That's him."

"Must be nice. It says here that thing's insurance value is 320 grand." I heard a phone start ringing. "Crap, that's my other line," Possum said. "I gotta go. You need anything else?"

"No. That's it. Thanks, Possum. I owe you."

"No sweat. Call anytime."

She hung up.

I sat in my chair without moving for the better part of ten minutes while everything I'd just discovered began to trickle down and register with the parts of me that were still able to function. The longer I sat and stewed in the information, the more my anxiety increased.

I had no idea how I was going to tell Frankie about this.

I had no idea how I was going to keep from getting disbarred.

Shit . . . I had no idea how I was going to keep us both from going to jail.

The sick realization of what we'd been doing flowed over me like waves of molten lava.

Eddie hadn't been dispatching us to repossess vehicles from people who'd defaulted on their payments—quite the contrary.

He'd had us stealing them.

Frankie had said yes to my invitation to grill steaks together. I'd texted her with the idea as soon as I got into my car for the drive back from Lexington. She told me she'd be home by three-thirty, and said I should meet her at her house.

She also said she missed me—and that simple admission made my heart skip a few beats.

So the plan to meet her was still on, even though it now included one of the most difficult errands of my life.

I still had no idea how to give her the news about the work we'd been doing for the NRB.

Correction. It hadn't been for the NRB; it had been for Eddie.

It was a small clarification with a big damn difference.

I honestly had no idea how Frankie would react to the news. I guessed she'd go ballistic and insist that we confront him immediately. For my part, I wasn't so sure that was the best approach. It wasn't that I didn't want to string him up by his gonads for what he'd gotten us into. It was more that I wanted to understand what led him to involve us—a couple of true greenhorns—in such a dangerous scheme in the first place. The only reason I was even halfway willing to grant him that concession was because of what Hugh Don had said about how Eddie had helped him out at a time when he really needed it. There was also the paradox about why he'd picked Frankie and me to be his stooges.

I kept thinking about what Linda had said. What sense did it make for Eddie to pick two such inexperienced and clumsy novices to carry out heists that could easily have gone wrong and landed all three of us in legal jeopardy up to our eyebrows? At a minimum, we were talking at least three counts of Grand Theft Auto, and who knew what else. Why risk that kind of exposure by handing the jobs to us?

It was all too confusing.

The only thing I was really sure of was my certainty that, once her initial rage subsided, Frankie would have a clear head about what we needed to do. It was that whole German/Swiss/Moravian thing. One thing her people were good at—apart from making covered dishes and sugar cakes—was managing adversity.

At least, I prayed she'd be better at it than I was.

I arrived at her place right at three-thirty and was happy to see her Nissan already parked in the driveway. I grabbed my notes from the call with Possum, a bottle of wine, and the impossibly large package of meat.

Frankie must've heard me pull in because the front door opened magically as soon as I set foot on the porch. She looked fabulous.

But that wasn't unusual. I thought she always looked fabulous. She'd changed out of her school clothes and put on a pair of ratty cutoffs and a faded "Life Is Good" T-shirt.

I could've eaten her with a spoon . . .

Under other circumstances, that would've been my entire plan for how our evening would unfold. The realization made me even more pissed off about our circumstances.

"It took you long enough." Frankie pulled me in for a kiss. It was a good one, too. It went on for so long, I expected my ears to start spinning like airplane props.

"Here's the meat," I rasped, after she let me go. I passed her the package.

"Nice segue," she quipped. "Come on inside and let's make some dinner."

I followed her into the kitchen. I have to say that, even without the bodysuit, it was hard not to stare at her perfect . . . backyard.

"How was your day?" she asked, as she unwrapped the steaks.

"Oh, it was . . . eventful."

"Good god!" she exclaimed. "Where'd you get these things? Yucca Mountain?"

"Close. They're from Hugh Don. He insisted."

"You went to see Hugh Don?" Frankie transferred the massive rib eyes to a platter.

"Yeah. I wanted to ask him a few questions about Eddie and some of these jobs he's given us lately."

Frankie was lightly salting the meat. "Do you like black pepper?"

"Yeah. Lots."

"Me, too." Frankie picked up a grinder and cranked out a generous amount of pepper on each steak. "I already made a big salad. Given the size of these, I think that'll be enough food."

"Yeah. It'll probably take our systems six months to digest this much beef."

Frankie laughed. "Did Hugh Don have any insights that made sense?"

"Not really. But he did have some good advice."

"Oh?" Frankie looked at me. "What'd he say?"

"I brought a bottle of wine for us, too." I dodged her question and showed her the Invetro Super Tuscan I'd nabbed from our wine fridge at home. "Should I open it?"

"Oh, hell yes."

I took my time with the wine. I wanted to continue putting off telling her the bad news for as long as possible. I poured us each a generous amount.

"Do we need to let it breathe at all?" Frankie asked.

"It would probably be better if we did, but frankly, I don't give a damn."

"What's going on?"

"What do you mean?" I hedged.

"You don't seem like yourself."

"I don't?"

"No," she said. "You seem . . . tense. Is everything okay?"

I shrugged.

"Nick?"

I met her eyes. "Yes?"

"Is it . . . are you having second thoughts?"

Second thoughts? "About what?" I asked.

"Well. About us?" Her face was a perfect mixture of concern and bewilderment.

Sweet mother of pearl . . . now I'd fucking done it.

"Hell, no!" I blurted. "I have *no* second thoughts about us. I mean . . . none that aren't vaguely X-rated."

I could see her features relax. "That's a relief."

"Dear lord . . . I'm sorry I made you think that. Believe me, Frankie—I've never been happier in my life. I even called Mamá this morning and told her about you."

That revelation stopped her in her tracks. She seemed too stunned to reply.

"Okay," I said, nervously. "Don't tell me you're the one having second thoughts?"

"About you? Not gonna happen." She smiled. "Are you going to tell me what she said?"

"Mamá is a woman of few words—except for premonitions of disaster or insisting on acts of contrition."

"Well, I hope telling her about me wasn't an occasion for either of those."

"No. It wasn't. She sounded . . . interested."

"Is that good?"

"Oh, yeah," I explained. "It's very good."

"Then I'll try not to worry."

"Good. You don't need to."

"Let's go start the grill and get these things going. I thought we'd eat on the porch."

Frankie gave me the task of cooking the steaks while she ferried the salad, wine, plates and silverware to the small table on her porch. Something as ordinary as standing sentry over a hot gas grill began to lull me into believing that maybe our predicament wasn't as dire as I feared. After all, we hadn't done anything knowingly or with any kind of malice aforethought.

Who was I kidding? Our asses were grass . . .

I just wanted to pretend everything was okay so I could enjoy one last night of normalcy with Frankie.

We sat together on her porch and ate our fill of dry-aged beef and Frankie's monster salad of romaine hearts with sugar snap peas and pecan dressing. It was a warm evening, and we both commented on how great it was that the days were getting so much longer.

When we'd finished our meal and were relaxing with glasses of wine, Frankie followed up on my earlier comment about going to see Hugh Don.

"Are you going to tell me about your conversation with Hugh Don?"

"Yeah. I wanted to put if off until after we had dinner."

"Put it off? That sounds ominous."

"It might be."

"Okay," Frankie lowered her voice. "Now you're really starting to scare me."

"I don't mean to." I took a deep breath. "After I shared some of our concerns with Hugh Don, he suggested I do something obvious: run the titles on the vehicles. I felt like an idiot because that simple step had never occurred to me. I asked him if he'd ever been asked by Eddie to do any jobs that didn't feel right. He pretty much refused to answer. I gather that Hugh Don went through some bad times a while back, and Eddie helped him out. There's a lot of loyalty there."

"So did you?"

"Did I what?"

"Did you run the titles?"

I nodded. "I have a pal who works at the sheriff's department. I called her and she ran them for the hearse, the Shelby and the Donzi."

"I gather by the look on your face that the results weren't good news."

"No. All three of the vehicles were owned free and clear—no liens on any of them."

"*What?*" Frankie's eyes blazed. "How could they be behind on payments if they *owned* the damn things?"

"Precisely."

"So, that means . . ." Frankie didn't finish her declaration.

"Yeah," I said. "Pretty much."

"*We stole them?*" Frankie was aghast.

"So it seems."

"But . . . I . . . we . . . however are we going to . . ." Frankie gave up and rested her head in her hands. "We're fucked."

"Yeah. That about sums it up."

Frankie was near tears. "What are we going to do?"

"I honestly don't know, Frankie." I reached across the table and took hold of her hand. "If what I suspect is accurate, we're accessories to three counts, each, of Grand Theft Auto."

Frankie's jaw dropped. "But we didn't *know* that," she protested.

"We thought what we were doing was *legal.*"

"Believe me, I know. But we got paid for these jobs. We accepted Eddie's damn 'bonuses.' We're complicit, no matter how we try to defend it."

"Oh my god . . . could we go to jail?"

I didn't want to give her the likeliest answer to her question. "I honestly don't know. Maybe?"

Frankie got to her feet and started to stride around the porch. "We have to confront him. We have to find out if this is accurate." She stopped in her pacing and stared at me. "Maybe it's not what it seems? Maybe there's some reasonable explanation for the titles?"

Maybe hell would freeze over tonight, too . . .

"Maybe," I said. "I agree that we need to go talk with him."

"*Talk* with him? I want to do more than *talk* with him. I want to cut his nuts off and run them through a shredder."

I got up and crossed over to where she stood.

"Baby, you have to calm down." I gently took hold of her arms. "We won't get anything out of him if we go into it with guns—or machetes—blazing. We need to think clearly and have a plan."

"A plan for what, Nick? Emigrating to South America?"

"Hopefully it won't come to that. I think we need to tell Antigone about this first, and see what she advises."

"Are you nuts? You know exactly what she'll advise—I mean, after she rips us each about ten new assholes, kicks us off the property, and tells us to go beg Jesus for forgiveness because she's fresh out of caring."

"Frankie, please," I pleaded with her. "I need you to calm down and help me think clearly about all of this. We have to get some help. Antigone knows Eddie better than anyone. She'll have the best ideas about how to approach him to get the answers we need."

Frankie leaned her head against my chest. I wrapped my arms around her. "We'll figure something out. I promise." I did my best to sound hopeful, but inside, I knew it was a lost cause. I was sure to be disbarred, and we'd both be lucky to avoid jail time.

If only I knew someone who could tell us what to do to get out of this mess. Someone I could trust who would not judge us.

The realization hit me like a ton of bricks. I *did* know someone. I knew someone very well . . .

"Holy shit," I said.

Frankie lifted her head and met my eyes. "What is it?"

"I know who I can ask for legal advice."

"Someone at your firm?"

"Hell no." I shook my head. "I'm talking about someone we can trust. Someone who won't be compromised by knowing about this—and who will have our best interests at heart."

"Who?" Frankie asked hopefully.

I smiled broadly at her. "Papa."

Frankie cleared the table and drifted off to fix us each an after-dinner cognac while I called Papa.

I called his cell phone to be sure he answered and not Mamá. I could probably conceal the whole truth from Papa; with Mamá, that would be a lost cause.

"How am I lucky enough to get to talk with my daughter twice in the same day?"

"Hi, Papa. What are you doing?"

"Right now? I'm in my study going over some pretrial motions."

I could hear classical music playing in the background. I wondered if he'd picked up his new vinyl recording of *Fliegende Hollander.*

"Is Mamá around?" I tried to make the question sound casual.

"She's still at the hospital. She should be home in another hour or so. Do you need to talk with her?"

"Well. No. I really called to talk with you about . . . a friend in a legal jam."

"Okay." I could hear the squeak of his chair as he leaned back in it. "Shoot."

"It's complicated, but I'll give you the short version. A pal of mine took a temp job with a repo agency to make some extra money."

"Wait a minute," Papa interrupted me. "Did you say with a *repo* agency? As in, a place that repossesses cars?"

"Yes. That's right."

"Who the hell takes a temp job doing that?"

"More people than you might think. Apparently, the money is good. Anyway . . . um . . . he found out, by accident, that the owner was actually getting him to steal cars, not repossess them."

"What the hell? How stupid is this person?"

"Not stupid at all, really."

"So, this friend of yours had no idea the cars . . . were they cars?"

"Mostly. There was one boat. A Donzi."

"Oh, for Christ's sake. You might need to rethink your friends, Vera."

Okay. That was a bad sign. Papa only called me "Vera" *when I was in trouble.*

"Yeah," I replied. "But, he had no reason to suspect that the jobs weren't on the up and up."

"Was he paid for the work?"

"Well. Yeah. And he got a couple of . . . large bonuses."

"Hell's bells, Vera. Then he's complicit in the thefts. Ignorance is no defense."

"He's got no priors. Nothing in his past to suggest that he'd be involved in something nefarious."

Papa scoffed. "You know how many clients with no priors I have sitting in jail? Probably as many as your pal has lame-ass excuses for being so damn stupid."

I sighed. "I need to know what kind of advice I can give him, Papa. What can he do to minimize the consequences?"

"You mean besides change his name and hop a Greyhound headed for Zihuatanejo?"

I closed my eyes. "Yeah. Hopefully something other than that."

"Listen, sweet pea. Your friend has two options. He can hire good legal counsel, go to the cops and come clean with what he knows, and beg the court for leniency. With luck, he might get a reduced sentence. With a miracle, he might just get parole. But either way, he's gonna be disbarred. He'll never practice law again."

Fuck me. That's what I had feared. There had to be some way to save Frankie—even if my own career was ruined forever.

"You said there were two options? What's the second?"

"Walk away from it," Papa said, simply.

"What do you mean, walk away from it?" I wasn't sure I understood him.

"Your friend cleans up his act and prays none of the property is ever recovered. Or he prays that if it does turn up, he never gets linked to the thefts. He goes on like nothing ever happened. End of story."

I was shocked by his suggestion. "Does that ever work?" I asked.

"It can. As long as the stolen property never turns up."

Was that even a possibility? I had no idea what Eddie was even up to, much less what he'd had planned for disposition of the property after Frankie and I brought it in. What were the odds the things would never turn up again? And even if we decided to try and go forward in hopes we'd never get found out, how could we live with the constant fear of disclosure? It was an impossible scenario.

"Are you still there, Vera?"

I was so lost in thought, Papa must've wondered if we'd been disconnected.

"Yeah. Sorry, Papa. Just realizing there aren't any more hopeful outcomes for my friend."

"No," he agreed. "Not really. If he isn't willing to roll the dice and risk coming clean with the police, his best option is to keep his mouth shut and hope the stolen property never materializes again."

"Would that be your advice?"

"Are you asking me that as a defense attorney, or as an informed layperson?"

"I guess the latter." I already knew what Papa would tell a client.

"Is your friend religious at all?" he asked.

That question surprised me. "I think maybe . . . a little."

"I'd tell him to get his ass to church and start praying."

I closed my eyes and took a slow, deep breath. "Thanks, Papa. That's what I needed to know."

"You're a good person, Vera. Don't forget that."

"I'll try not to."

I could hear Papa's background music building to a slow but powerful crescendo. I recognized the leitmotif. *Wagner.* The Captain of the Flying Dutchman was bemoaning his fate: cursed to remain at sea forever because he'd committed the grave sin of blasphemy. Ultimately, the love of a faithful woman would redeem him—in the same way that Frankie's love was beginning to redeem me.

But was it too late for us?

"I hear the Wagner," I said to Papa. I wasn't ready to end our conversation on such a note of sadness. "I guess that means you got another copy of the opera?"

"Oh, hell yeah," he said. "And this one's going to be hidden from your Mamá so she can't destroy it."

"She just wants to save you from a life of sadness."

"I hope both of the women in my life share that goal."

"Me, too." I was fighting the impulse to cry and confess everything to him. I think he knew it, too.

"We both love you, Vera. Don't ever forget that."

"I won't. Thanks, Papa. I love you, too."

"Good luck with your friend. I know you'll give him good advice."

"I'll do my best. Bye, Papa."

"You keep in touch, sweet pea."

"I will. I promise."

After we'd disconnected, I sat quietly on Frankie's porch, thinking over our conversation. The two options Papa had outlined for our response to the situation dovetailed perfectly with what I'd already pieced together. We could come clean, rat Eddie out, and pray for clemency because neither of us had ever knowingly broken laws before. Or we could try to clean this mess up, divorce ourselves from any future involvement with Eddie, and pray that the stolen vehicles would never reappear.

There was no magic bullet that would get us out of this mess. It was ours, and we had to own it.

Papa had been right about something else, too. If we involved law enforcement, my legal career would be over.

I shot up straight in the chair as another realization hit me.

I never said my friend was an attorney.

So, why would Papa have volunteered that bit of information?

Sweet mother of pearl . . .

He knew.

I heard footsteps and looked up as Frankie joined me on the porch. She was carrying two large tumblers of amber liquid. She passed one to me and sat down on the swing.

"How did it go?" she asked.

"Before I answer, how much more cognac do you have?"

"Uh oh. That bad?"

"No." I tried my best to sound reassuring, but I knew I was failing badly. "He pretty much confirmed what I already knew."

Frankie narrowed her eyes. "Meaning we're fucked?"

"Yeah. Pretty much."

Frankie stared out across her backyard.

The sun was nearly down, and the pear trees at the back of her lot were casting fantastic, misshapen shadows. They looked like clusters of lanky ghouls, advancing toward the house with straggly outstretched arms.

She took a sip of her cognac and shifted on the swing to face me. "I have two questions."

"Okay."

"First, what the hell are we going to do? And second, why are you sitting so far away from me?"

That made me smile, which was quite a feat considering our circumstances. I got up and crossed over to the swing so I could sit down beside her. "Is this better?"

She leaned into me. "Much."

I kissed her hair. It smelled great—like rosemary and mint.

"First things first," I said. "We don't know what we don't know."

"Which means?" Frankie asked.

"Which means, we need to withhold making any decisions until we talk with Antigone—and Eddie."

"Okay. I'm good with that. Now, drink up and let's get this party started."

I laid a hand on her thigh. "Not tonight."

"What do you mean? Why not tonight? I don't want to waste any more time on this. We need answers."

"We do. But we've both been drinking, and we're not driving anyplace right now. Besides, I don't want to hit Antigone with this mess after hours."

Frankie exhaled. "I guess that makes sense."

"It does. And tomorrow is a school day for you. Let's wait until the weekend."

"If by 'the weekend,' you mean tomorrow night, I'm okay with that. I'm *not* okay with putting this off for any longer."

That was fair. "Okay," I agreed. "Tomorrow evening."

"Do you want me to call her and set it up?"

"No. I'm the one with the suspicions, so I'll do it."

"How do you think she'll want to approach Eddie?"

I thought about the possibilities. "I think her knee-jerk response will be to call up an airstrike on his likely coordinates."

Frankie actually laughed. "I'd sure miss those hot chips at the Sixty Six Grill."

"Me, too."

"So, how about *after* she has time to calm down?"

I gave her an ironic look. "You think she's capable of calming down?"

"When it concerns something this serious, I sure as hell hope so."

"I guess we'll find out." I sipped my cognac. It was doing the trick, and I felt my insides warming up nicely. On the other hand, sitting this close to Frankie wasn't hurting, either. I had a hard time reconciling my complete anxiety about our plight with the level of distraction our proximity was generating.

I decided to confess.

"I think I'm having impure thoughts."

"You are?" Frankie asked. Her tone was wistful. "And here, I thought there was something wrong with *me*."

"Oh, no . . . there's *nothing* wrong with you, I promise."

"How can you be so sure?"

"If you'll recall," I reminded her, "I made a pretty exhaustive examination last night."

"That is true," Frankie agreed.

"So, here we sit, in the shadow of all but certain ruination—yet I find myself having to fight to keep my hands off you. What the hell kind of person does that make me?"

Frankie thought about it. "A horny one?"

"I guess that kind of goes without saying," I admitted.

She moved closer to me. "Is there anything more we can do about this mess tonight?"

"I don't think so."

She kissed me. "Is there anything else you'd like to do tonight?"

"I can maybe think of one or two things."

She kissed me again, longer this time. "So what's stopping you?"

Good question. After all, our present circumstances proved that we'd long since abandoned rational adherence to decorum. What *was* stopping me?

I put down my tumbler and pulled her onto my lap.

"Not a damn thing," I answered.

I woke up at some point during the night and realized it was storming. Thunder rattled the windowpanes and rain was coming down in sheets. Random flashes of white light illuminated the room. Frankie was oblivious to it all. She was sound asleep and draped across my body like a second skin.

I didn't blame her for being oblivious to the storm raging outside. We'd stayed awake for quite a while after we'd made our stumbling trip to her bedroom from the porch. We came together fast and furious—an offshoot of the fear and stress we both were eager to shed. That initial frenzy soon relaxed into a gentler and more luxurious time of exploration. As night closed in around us, my mouth and hands learned to read the contours of Frankie's body in the same tactile way a sightless person discovers a new world through the language of braille.

I wasn't clear about many things, but I now understood that Frankie had become an addiction. *My* addiction. One I welcomed and was unwilling to surrender.

There had to be some way out of the hopeless maze we now found ourselves in. I refused to accept that these events would ruin us both, and possibly take us away from each other after we'd traveled so far to be together.

Papa said our best option would be to go forward as if none of this had ever happened. That, and pray the stolen property never resurfaced.

Could we trust that? Could we have faith in this part of Eddie's scheme? Could we hope that whatever arrangements he'd made for the cars and the Donzi were sophisticated enough that we'd never have to worry about discovery? And if we did decide to go blithely forward in newfound piety, what kind of people would that make us?

Good people, who got caught up in something unforeseen.

Was that really true? How many times had a voice inside me questioned the wisdom of what we were doing? How many times did I choose to ignore those warnings?

Every time.

The truth was that I *wanted* to succeed at this work. I wanted to prove I was smart and savvy enough to pull off the impossible—to do something that would astonish anyone who knew me as a person of caution and reserve. Even after that ridiculous Maybach caper with Hugh Don, I felt excited and energized by the fact that I'd *done* it. I'd actually stepped outside my comfort zone for the first time in my life—

with a vengeance—and pulled off one helluva fast one in the process.

Literally.

And I met Frankie in the process. How could everything that finally had gone so right, go so horribly wrong? And so fast?

Life is that way. Who can explain it? Mamá's voice came back to me. This was always her stock explanation for anything incomprehensible: thundersnow, canned flan, Kellyanne and George Conway's marriage, or Cousin Juana's 1980s glam-rock hairdo.

But Papa? Papa was a realist. Papa called things as he saw them. Papa knew how to cut through the bullshit, split logical hairs, and rank all of the likeliest outcomes from best to worst. And it turned out that Papa had a clairvoyant streak that rivaled Mamá's.

Papa knew I'd been talking about myself.

I was mortified.

As the storm continued to rage around us, I went back over everything Papa had said to me. Each one of his dire predictions echoed inside my head, locked in eerie syncopation with rumbling claps of thunder.

What had been his best advice?

"Your friend cleans up his act and prays none of the property is ever recovered. Or he prays that if it does turn up, he never gets linked to the thefts. He goes on like nothing ever happened. End of story."

In my viscera, I knew he was right. I understood how the oversized wheels of justice turned, and I knew the odds were that Frankie and I would get flattened by them if we came clean with what we'd been doing. We'd know a lot more after we confronted Eddie, and found out what kind of operation he was running. With luck, that would happen tomorrow.

Today, I corrected. It was nearly 3 a.m.

I felt Frankie stirring. "Why are you awake?" she muttered against my chest.

"There's a storm."

She squeezed me. "There sure was."

"Not *that* kind of storm." A flash of lightning lit up the room.

"*This* kind of storm."

"Oh." She raised her head and scanned the room. "How long has this been going on?"

"A while. You slept through most of it."

"Whose fault is that?"

"I'm not going to pretend I'm sorry about making you sleepy."

"Good." Frankie yawned. "Because you don't need to."

I wrapped my arms around her. "Are you ready to go back to sleep?"

"Nuh uh."

I didn't expect that answer. "You got something else in mind?"

Frankie crawled up my body so we were face to face. "Uh huh."

"You know it's still a school day today, right?" I reminded her, while I could still think rationally.

"Oh, I remember." Her hands were in motion. "I thought of a few new things I could teach you."

She was as good as her word, and our lesson continued for at least another hour—until the tandem storms finally blew themselves out.

Chapter Eight

Someone to Watch Over Me

Antigone wasn't happy when I called her the next morning to set up our meeting. She wasn't happy and she was demonstrably suspicious about our motivation.

"Not-Vera? Just what in thunder do you have to say to me that has to be said after 5 p.m. on a Friday?"

"Well," I explained, "it's a conversation we need to have privately and in person, without taking the chance that someone else will come into the office."

"Well, how in the hell likely do you think it is that people drop in here? For any damn thing?"

I could hear the exasperation in her voice, but I steeled my resolve.

"You're going to have to trust me, Antigone. This is important. We wouldn't ask if it weren't."

"You want *me* to trust *you*—a skinny damn ambulance chaser who isn't smart enough to make sure the hearse she's jacking isn't occupied?"

I was losing patience with this errand. "Look, if you don't care about hearing what I have to say, you can at least listen to Frankie."

That seemed to calm her down . . . a tad. Whatever she thought of Frankie, she respected her old family name.

"Make sure your asses are here at the crack of five. I ain't waitin' around on you."

"We'll be there. Thanks for doing this, Antigone." I hesitated. "We trust you, and we need your advice."

"Just don't ask me to loan you money." She harrumphed. "At least I don't need to worry you got that girl pregnant. The Lord works in mysterious ways, but thankfully, that ain't one of 'em. At least not yet."

I blinked. "Excuse me?"

"Something wrong with your hearing, Not-Vera?" The belt sander revved up again.

"Um . . . no ma'am . . ."

"Then don't be wastin' any more of my time. You can state your business later."

She hung up.

I held the phone away from my ear and stared at it.

This woman made Mamá look like a novice . . .

I spent the rest of the day at the public library, researching sentencing guidelines for first offenders convicted of Grand Theft Auto, and learning what I could about the nuances of off-loading stolen vehicles without a trace. I couldn't risk doing Internet searches like this on my home computer.

I'd already filled Sebastian in on what I'd discovered about the Donzi. I had to, since he was now implicated in the heist—thanks to me. He didn't seem the least bit bothered by the prospect of getting busted.

"Are you kidding me?" He waved it off. "What do you think real estate brokers do all day? Bust their humps looking for ways to be double sure they haven't inflated a buyer's credit score or 'accidentally' fat-fingered his annual income? I don't *think* so."

"This is hardly the same thing, Sebastian. We're talking three counts of Grand Theft Auto."

"*If* you get caught. *If.* And the only way you'll get caught is if the stuff turns up abandoned along some county road or sitting in the lot at Greensboro Auto Auctions. *And* then they have to have *evidence* that ties you to these jobs even if they do show up. So will you just learn how to *R-E-L-A-X?*"

"Don't start spelling shit, because I'm going to *P-A-N-I-C*. My head is already about to explode."

"Look, Nick. Anybody who fences a speedboat worth $300,000 isn't going to be stupid enough to off-load it domestically. Mark my words: that thing is already on its way to some oligarch's summer home on the Volga."

"How do you know so much about this?"

"Nat Geo. I told you . . . Carol Jenkins likes to watch *Locked Up Abroad*. They did a whole segment on this kind of thing two weeks ago. Lemme tell you, those prisons in Nigeria are NQOT."

"*NQOT?* What the hell does that mean?"

He rolled his eyes. "Not Quite Our Type. Do try to keep up."

I held up my hands in resignation. "Why did I think you'd be concerned about being drawn into this?"

"I don't know, maybe the sudden shock of too much sex has fried all of your circuit breakers?"

"Yeah." I got up. "I'm out of here. I've got some research to do before I meet Frankie to head to K-Vegas."

"What kind of research?" He batted his eyes at me. "Best Sapphic positions? Remedies for vaginal chafing?"

"Dwayne?" I held up three fingers on my right hand. "Read between the lines."

Antigone had been right about one thing: the NRB lot was deserted when we arrived at 4:49 on the dot. There weren't even any cars parked in front of the Weevil Vape Shoppe, which was a rarity because it had the most intact section of asphalt in the entire strip center.

Antigone buzzed us in as soon as we entered the office. She was seated at her desk, as usual, but her massive pocketbook was plopped on the center of her blotter alongside a fat set of car keys, indicating that she didn't intend for our conversation to last very long. Global Gospel Radio was broadcasting an up-tempo rendition of "Just As I

Am." The preponderance of electric guitar riffs made it clear this was not the Power Hour.

I wondered if she ever turned it off.

Probably not. God's word didn't sleep.

She didn't bother greeting us and chose to cut to the chase.

"Well, go ahead and state your business." She folded her arms across her ample bosom and glared at me like she was sizing me up through the sights on an AR-15.

"Do you mind if we sit down?" I asked. "This might take a while."

"If that's okay with you?" Frankie added quickly. "We know it's Friday night and you're probably anxious to be out of here."

"Little girl?" Antigone didn't seem moved by Frankie's obsequious approach. "*Anxious* doesn't come close to how I feel about gettin' out of this leaky rattrap on Friday nights. Now stop wastin' my time and state your damn business."

"Well," I cleared my throat. "We discovered some . . . *irregularities* associated with our last couple of jobs for Eddie."

That got her attention. "*What* jobs? I haven't given you any jobs since you botched that hearse pickup."

"That's kind of what I mean," I explained. "Eddie's given us a couple more that he didn't run through the office."

Antigone's eyes blazed. She dug inside her massive purse and pulled out a pack of smokes. She fired one up and nearly sucked the life out of it before she made any reply to my statement.

"You'd best be telling me what he asked you to do. And don't leave nothin' out—and don't even *think* about lying to make your part in this look better. I got *no* time for liars and less time for cheaters."

"Yes, ma'am." I glanced nervously at Frankie. Thankfully, she correctly interpreted my unspoken request and took up the narrative.

"So, Eddie first asked us to retrieve a car—a high-dollar muscle car—from a construction worker named Larry Cecil. He said the job was delicate because Mr. Cecil knew his creditors were after the vehicle, so he always kept it protected. He also told us Mr. Cecil carried a gun, so that made the recovery even trickier."

"*A gun?* He sent you two girl scouts after a car belonging to a man he knew was packing?"

We nodded in tandem.

Antigone grabbed her pack of cigarettes and tapped out the remainders. There were only two. She snagged the giant walkie-talkie from her credenza. "Lamar? Send Roger Coble up here with some more smokes. *Now.*" She slammed the thing back down and made rapid hurry-up gestures at Frankie. "C'mon, Debbie Reynolds. Gimme the rest of it."

Frankie swallowed. "We were able to recover the asset."

Antigone scoffed and shook her head. "What'd he do with the damn car?"

"Um," I replied, "we don't really know. He had us drop it off at the Sixty Six Grill. He had somebody else come pick it up." I could feel sweat beginning to run down my back. "But while we were there, he offered us another . . . assignment."

"*Sweet Jesus . . .*" I thought Antigone might reach across her desk and slap me. "Not-Vera? Do you fail to retain *any* of the sense you were born with?"

I really had no idea what response to make to that question. "I guess not?"

"Did he *pay* you for these damn jobs?"

"Well. Yes. And...," I hesitated. "He gave us bonuses, too. Big ones."

Antigone let out a long, slow breath. "What's the other one?" I must've looked confused because she snapped her long fingers in my face. "Hello? Earth to Not-Vera? What's the *other* damn job? The one you said he offered you after you turned over the car?"

"It was a . . . boat."

"Did you say a *boat?*" Antigone asked with disbelief.

I nodded.

"We don't do damn boats."

"Well, um . . . this one was special. It was a Donzi."

Antigone looked at Frankie for clarification.

"It's a speedboat," Frankie explained. "Very expensive. It was at a yacht club on Lake Norman."

Antigone flopped back against her desk chair, which screeched in protest. "You two morons are gonna send me off to an early grave. Is that part of your plan, missy?" She fired the accusation at Frankie. "Were you sent here to drum up business for your daddy's mortuary?"

"No, ma'am." Frankie made a valiant attempt at an act of contrition. I was impressed. I thought only Catholics were familiar with that practice. "You have to believe that we had no idea there was anything untoward about either of these assignments."

"*Untoward?*" Antigone fired up another cigarette. "If by 'untoward' you mean stupid, reckless and *illegal*, then you need to get your skinny ass out of the classroom. You ain't fit to teach them youngsters."

Frankie didn't reply. I thought she looked like she might cry.

The truth was that I wasn't far from it myself.

I stepped into the void.

"Yes. Hindsight is 20/20. And we should've known better. But we didn't. We believed the jobs were legitimate—probably because we wanted them to be that way. But we did them, and there's no getting out of that now. That's why we need your help."

"My help? Why the hell do you think you need *my* help, Not-Vera? You didn't seem to care much about 'my help' or opinions when you were going behind my back, makin' these secret deals with Eddie."

"It wasn't *like* that." I pleaded with her. "You have to believe us. We didn't know this was . . . unusual—or different from the way this place normally operates. Eddie told us he sometimes ran jobs this way because it was faster and cleaner. We didn't have any reason *not* to believe him."

Antigone narrowed her eyes. "If that's true, then why don't you believe him now? Why bring all this to me?"

She had a point . . . We'd reached the part of the conversation Papa always referred to as the *rat killing.*

"Because I went to see Hugh Don to ask him if Eddie had ever had him work this way."

"And what did Mr. Rockett tell you?" Antigone made it clear by the way she asked that she already knew the answer.

"He didn't tell me one way or the other. He told me I should come talk to you. And . . ." I hesitated.

"And what?"

"And he told me that if I had doubts I should just run the titles on the vehicles."

Antigone rolled her brown eyes. "I assume the fact that you two are sittin' here in front of me, lookin' for all the world like you're about to get fitted up for orange jumpsuits, means you did that?"

"Yes, ma'am. I did."

"And what did you find out?"

"You know what I found out. None of the vehicles had liens. All of them were owned free and clear." I sighed. "Which means, we didn't repossess them."

"No, you most certainly did *not*." Antigone energetically ground out her latest cigarette. I noticed for the first time that someone had emptied her Roadway ashtray. That alone had to be an indication that we'd entered The Last Times.

"We stole them, didn't we?" Frankie spoke the words so quietly, I barely heard her.

Antigone stared at her for a few seconds before yanking open a desk drawer and withdrawing a coin purse. She tossed it across the desk to Frankie. "Go get us one of them RC Colas from that vending machine in the lobby," she commanded. "I need a cold drink."

Frankie dutifully picked up the coin purse and headed for the lobby. Once she'd left the office, Antigone leaned toward me.

"Since you know the law, I'm gonna assume you know that you and that sweet gal are probably lookin' at some hard time if this all comes out?"

"Yeah," I said morosely. "I know that. I even called my father—he's a defense attorney in Philadelphia."

"What'd he tell you?"

"That we're pretty much toast—unless the vehicles never turn up again, or we're never linked to the thefts if they do."

"I wouldn't count on that." Antigone harrumphed. "Not if I know Eddie. That man's the only person I know who could lose money runnin' a damn yard sale."

"What are we gonna do? *Please?* I'm begging you, Antigone. We need your help to figure this out."

"Don't grovel at me, Not-Vera. It ain't becoming."

"Well I don't know what the hell else to do. We've got no place else to go."

"I don't know what misguided notion of yours makes you think I wanna get involved in *any* of this unholy mess."

"Well." It was time to haul out the big guns. "Maybe because that hearse was one of these jobs, too."

She didn't miss my inference.

"Say what?" she demanded.

"You heard me right. The hearse. They weren't in default on any loan, either. They *had* no loan. They owned the thing outright."

Antigone bolted up from her chair so fast the thing nearly toppled over. "*Where the hell is he?*"

Frankie picked that unfortunate moment to tap at the office door. Antigone slammed her hand down on the buzzer to let her back inside.

"Lamar dropped these off." Frankie held out two packs of Misty Menthol cigarettes—and the cold can of RC. "He said he didn't need to come in."

"Well, for once, he was right about *something*." Antigone snapped the cigarettes from Frankie's hand and tore open one of the packs.

Frankie looked at me with bewilderment. "Did I miss something?"

"I told her about the hearse," I said.

"Oh." Frankie sat down and nervously opened the can of cola. She gingerly pushed it across the desk. "It's nice and cold," she offered.

"Ain't this all just *fine and dandy*?" Antigone dropped her large frame back into her chair and stared at us menacingly. "You two have messed things up six ways from Sunday."

"Hey. You knew as much about that hearse as we did," I reminded her. "He tricked all of us."

"Girl, he didn't 'trick' us. He all but booked us first-class rooms at the damn Crowbar Hotel."

If it hadn't been so depressing, I'd have laughed at her characterization of prison. It was exactly the same as Lilah's.

"Maybe he's got some kind of reasonable explanation for the titles?" I suggested. "Maybe it's not as bad as we think?"

"Oh, yeah?" Antigone all but shotgunned the can of cola. "And maybe my damn schnauzer will stop lickin' his privates, too."

"Okay." Frankie held up a restraining palm. "Enough of the recriminations. We're all in this. Now we need to stop sniping at each other and figure out what we're going to do."

"Sure, Debbie Reynolds." Antigone folded her hands. "What do *you* suggest?"

"For starters, I think maybe we need to get Eddie over here to answer some questions."

Antigone stared at her for a moment. Then she reached for her phone.

"Who are you calling?" Frankie asked with alarm.

"Who the hell do you think?" Antigone punched in a series of numbers.

I saw her expression change when Eddie answered.

"I need you at the office," she demanded. "Right now."

Eddie must've started to argue with her, because Antigone proceeded to open a can of whoop-ass on him. "*Fool?* When have I *ever* told you I needed your sorry ass to come over here? You do it and you do it *now*. I ain't askin' you twice."

She slammed the phone down.

Frankie and I must've looked shell-shocked because Antigone blew out a plume of smoke and gave us a nod of satisfaction.

"He'll be here."

She was right. Ten minutes later, we heard the front door open and close. Antigone buzzed him through and stood up to meet him.

Eddie seemed surprised when he saw the two of us sitting there.

"What's going on?" he asked.

"Good question," Antigone shot back. "Why don't you tell us?"

"Tell you what?" His voice sounded suspicious. "You better have a good reason for dragging my ass over here on the Sabbath."

"A *good* reason?" Antigone turned to face the two of us. "I don't know, girls? What do you two think? Is three counts of Grand Theft Auto a good enough reason to get this slimy asswipe over here—on the damn 'Sabbath'—which I'm sure he *always* celebrates with pulled pork in that damn booth at the Sixty Six Grill? Please . . . you tell me, because I ain't really sure."

Eddie's jaw dropped. "What the fuck are you accusing me of?"

"Ain't nobody accusing you of anything—*yet.*" Antigone hauled over an extra metal chair that sat near her filing cabinets. "I think you should put your ass in this chair and tell me all about the last couple of jobs you had these girls do for you. You know . . . the hearse, and the *secret* ones you didn't see fit to run through this office. Ring any bells for you?"

"I'm not gonna stand here and let you accuse me of anything."

"You're right about that." Antigone grabbed Eddie by the arm and pushed him toward the chair. "Sit. Down," she commanded. The big woman bested him by at least six inches and more than a hundred pounds. He wisely decided to comply. "Now, let's talk."

"I got nothin' to say to you." Eddie's gaze swept past her and took us in, too. "You either."

"Stohler?" Antigone pointed at her desk. "Hand me my pocketbook."

Frankie reflexively complied. Antigone took hold of it and began withdrawing fat rolls of paper that were each bound together with rubber bands, and stacked them on a nearby table. There were so many of them, it became almost comical.

"What the hell is all of that?" Eddie asked.

"Receipts, you fool. I ain't stupid enough to work for a scumbag like you without making sure my ass is covered."

"So you carry all that shit around in your damn purse?" Eddie marveled. "What's wrong with the safe?"

"I don't trust no safe, and I sure as hell don't trust *you*. Okay. Here we go."

Antigone had obviously found what she was looking for. We were all shocked when she withdrew a shiny set of handcuffs. Before Eddie could register what she was doing and raise a protest, Antigone had him cuffed to the back of the metal chair.

"What the *fuck* do you think you're doing?" Eddie yanked furiously at the cuffs. "Let me outta these, you crazy bitch. This ain't funny."

"No, it ain't. And you're gonna tell me what kind of mess you got yourself—and these two girls—all wrapped up in. *And you're gonna do it right now*. So settle the hell down and make your peace with it. Nobody is going anyplace until you spill your guts. It's after six on Friday, and this shopping center is deader'n a Presbyterian church on Wednesday night. Nobody'll hear you holler for help. So unless you and that worn-out prostate wanna sit here and keep your legs crossed until Monday morning, I suggest you start talkin'."

Holy shit. Frankie and I exchanged glances. *No wonder Hugh Don told me to talk to Antigone . . .*

"Fuck . . ." Eddie blew out a frustrated breath. Then he sighed. "You might wanna sit down," he suggested. "It's gonna take a while."

Antigone nodded with satisfaction and reclaimed her seat behind the desk. She gestured at me. "Your witness, counselor."

"Eddie?" I asked as calmly as I could. "Did we steal those vehicles?"

"Which vehicles?" he asked.

It took an effort to remain composed as I listed them. "The Cadillac hearse. The Mustang Shelby. The Donzi. Did we steal them?"

"Define *steal*."

Antigone grumbled and started to get up again.

"Okay, okay!" Eddie said quickly. "Jesus. Stay calm." He must've noticed Antigone's nostrils flare the moment he took the Lord's name in vain. "Okay . . . *I'm sorry*. It was a slip of the tongue. *Relax*. Sheesh."

"I ran the titles on those three vehicles," I told him. "The owners had no liens. They owned them."

"That's right," he agreed. "They did."

"So why did you have us steal them?"

"That's just it: you didn't *steal* them. You . . . took them off their hands. It was a service, actually. We helped them out."

"A service?" I was dumbfounded. "Just what in the hell did we help them out with?"

"Insurance fraud," Frankie said.

I looked at her with surprise. "What did you say?"

"I'm right, aren't I?" Frankie asked Eddie. "They committed insurance fraud by reporting the vehicles stolen. That's what this is all about, isn't it?"

Eddie grinned at me. "I told you this gal was sharp."

"Wait a minute." I was still trying to process what was happening. "You mean we stole those vehicles because they *wanted* us to?"

"That's right," Eddie agreed.

"So . . . they don't *want* them back?"

"Hell fuck no."

There went my fantasy about returning the stolen property and walking away.

"Besides," Eddie added, "they're already on a boat, headed for Tin Can Island."

Tin Can Island?

I looked at Antigone for clarity.

She rolled her eyes. "It's in West Africa. A place where thieves offload hot, high-dollar rides."

"How do *you* know about that?" Eddie sounded impressed.

"I saw a program on Nat Geo about it, fool. Maybe a break from watchin' them porn channels all night might teach you something new, too?"

Antigone watched Nat Geo? I remembered when Frankie said I liked bossy women, and compared her to Carol Jenkins. *Frankie was on a roll . . .*

"Listen. None of this even matters." Eddie's tone exuded confidence. "Our noses are clean. Those vehicles are long gone and won't ever turn up again. By this time next week, they'll belong to some sheik in the Emirates. Nobody'll ever be the wiser." Eddie began to plead with Antigone. "I only need *one* more job. Just one more score, and I'll be out from under Tiny. Then everything can go back to the way it was. *I promise.*"

"*Tiny?* You got involved with Tiny again?" Antigone was furious. "How damn stupid are you?"

"I couldn't help it. It was just a couple of bets . . . harmless. They just came in wrong and I got behind. They added up. Tiny wanted his money and I didn't have it. *I had no choice.*"

"Fool. You always have a choice. You just never make the damn right one."

"He was gonna start . . . *doing shit*. You know? To me. My ex-wife. This place. I couldn't risk it. You *know* how he is . . . *I had no choice.*"

"How much do you owe him?" Antigone demanded.

Eddie shrugged.

"How *much*, fool?"

"Seventy large. Give or take."

"Wait a minute," I interjected. "You owe $70,000 to a loan shark?"

"It happens," he said.

I was flummoxed. "Then how were you paying us those huge bonuses?"

He shrugged again.

"*Kickbacks.*" It was Frankie again. "They were giving you kickbacks on the insurance payouts, weren't they?"

Eddie nodded.

Clearly, I needed to reassess my belief that Frankie was an untutored innocent . . .

"You mean to tell me your sorry ass was double-dipping?" Antigone barked. "As if all this wasn't bad enough, you had to add insult to damn injury?"

"Hey, I gotta be me, right?" Eddie looked at me. "Tell the truth, Vera. You liked those bonuses just fine, didn't you?"

I was too ashamed to answer him.

"Enough of this mess." Antigone pulled a notepad out of her desk and grabbed a pencil. "Tell me what the bets were."

"Why?"

"Just *do* it. I want a record so we can be straight with Tiny. And don't leave anything out."

"Does that mean you're gonna help me?" Eddie sounded hopeful.

"Right now, I don't know what I'm gonna do, fool. Just give me the damn list."

"*Okay, okay.* Keep your pantyhose on." Eddie sighed. "It started with Daytona. I lost 12K on Enos Spooner. What a schmuck."

"Stow the damn commentary," Antigone warned him. "Just give me the list."

"Yeah. All right. I lost 9K on the Food Lion 500 in Bristol. That pussy, Travis Wadd, spun out in the third lap. I put 5K on Koepka to finish first at the Masters."

Wait a minute . . . I remembered that one. "Did you make that bet with my firm's earnest money?" I asked.

Eddie shrugged and continued. "I lost 22K on a prop bid during the NFL draft. Then there was that bad bet on the Bog Snorkeling Championship in the UK. I lost big on that one . . . 14K. Let's see. Oh, yeah . . . I lost 3K at that damn Cheese Rolling Championship. I got scammed with a bad wheel of Double Gloucester. I think that shit had turned and the extra mold slowed it down. And then . . . okay—this was the last one. I lost a 6K bet on that worthless rat, Slump Buster . . ."

Antigone cut him off. "Do *not* even *tell* me you bet on that damn Ferret Bingo again?"

"So sue me," Eddie said. "But this one was *not* my fault. I was totally ripped off . . . there were rumors of tunnel tampering. You can check it out. You know how that shit goes down in Manila . . ."

"*Enough.*" Antigone threw down her pencil. "This totals $71,000." She looked at Eddie in disgust. "For that much money, I'd stew your saggy giblets myself. Now . . . how much did you make back fencing the property?"

"I *didn't* fence them. I turned them all over to Tiny. He took care of them. And in exchange, he marked down my debt."

"How much?" Antigone demanded.

"The first three jobs covered 30K. That Donzi was a big score." Eddie sounded proud. "He marked down 28 for that one alone. I only owe him thirteen large, now. One more good score, and I'm clear."

Something about Eddie's math bothered me. "Did you say the first *three* jobs *and* the boat covered most of your debt?"

"Yeah."

I'd only run titles on the two cars and the Donzi. That had to mean . . .

"*The school bus?*" I was nearly apoplectic. "We stole a school bus from a *church?*"

"I keep telling you, Vera. You didn't *steal* anything. Those holy rollers were up to their asses in alligators. They needed the cash they got for that bus to pay off some asshole choir director. He was extorting them by threatening to post X-rated pictures on Tumblr, from some bible retreat with the preacher's wife." He shook his head. "Kind of sad that nothing's sacred anymore."

"But they *chased* us." Frankie was indignant. "They shot at us. *With guns*. We barely got away."

"Yeah," Eddie explained. "That wasn't supposed to happen. Apparently, some men's group was meeting there to plan a pancake supper or some other kind of bullshit." He looked at Antigone. "I really don't understand your people's sacraments."

"Shut up, you fool." Antigone got up and grabbed her two packs of Mistys. "I need time to think."

She advanced toward Eddie, who watched her with wariness. Antigone stood silently in front of him and took her time finishing her cigarette.

"What are you gonna do?" he finally asked.

"Something I shoulda done years ago."

As Eddie began to protest, she picked up a wad of receipts and stuffed them into his open mouth. He kept fussing, but she shushed him. "You just be quiet and sit here until we get back. I need to get away from you right now, or I won't be responsible for my actions." She waved at Frankie and me. "Let's get outta here. We need to figure things out."

We got up from our chairs to join her.

"Wait a minute." Antigone walked back to her desk and cranked up the volume on her radio. She glared at Eddie. "Maybe spending some time listening to God's word will knock some sense into you."

She stormed across the room and all but yanked the door off its hinges on her way out.

It was like watching Rhett Butler leave Tara.

Eddie sat there, handcuffed to his chair with that big roll of receipts jammed into his mouth. He was no longer protesting. There was no point. He wasn't going anyplace, and neither were we.

Frankie and I exchanged nervous glances before meekly following Antigone out.

In the lobby, I heard Lamar's scratchy voice introduce the next musical selection.

"Jesus Paid It All."

We had no idea where Antigone intended to go, but once we got outside, she made a beeline for the trailer behind the building. Frankie and I followed her like lemmings. For all we knew, she could've been heading for the nearest cliff—but we stayed right on her worn-down heels.

Once we'd reached the single-wide trailer that housed Global Gospel Radio, I began to rebound from my stupor. Antigone led us inside and down a narrow, paneled hallway extending past the glass-enclosed broadcast booth. At the back end of the trailer, she waved us into a small conference room. The room was windowless and had an ugly, avocado green-colored shag carpet that had seen better days. The only light came from an overhead, box-like fluorescent fixture that started buzzing as soon as Antigone snapped it on. There was nothing on the walls except a faded portrait of Jesus at Gethsemane—appropriately mirroring the hopelessness of our situation.

There was a tinny-sounding speaker mounted high in one corner of the room, and we could hear the live radio broadcast. Mercifully, it was at a low volume.

Antigone pulled out one of several green-upholstered rolling chairs that surrounded a beat-up table and sat down.

Being the dutiful minions we'd become, we followed suit.

She deposited her pocketbook and the two packs of Misty Menthols on the table. I noticed for the first time that she'd also brought along the notepad containing Eddie's list of bad bets. I was curious to learn how she planned to deal with "Tiny," and discharge the rest of Eddie's debt. No matter how tough her talk was, I knew that Antigone would never toss Eddie to the wolves. The ways they interacted with each other were just too . . . filial. They were like *family*—maybe bizarre, estranged family that mostly wanted to kill each other—but family, nonetheless. And family stood by each other when times were tough.

Times were certainly tough right now.

Antigone looked at her watch with disgust. It was well after 7 p.m.

"Did you two get any dinner?" she asked.

After we both shook our heads, she hauled over the intercom that sat on the table and punched a button.

"Lamar? Tell Roger Coble to go out and get us some food."

"He's not here right now," Lamar answered.

"Well, where in thunder is he when I need him?"

"He had to run over to Radio Shack to pick us up a soldering iron."

"On a Friday night?" Antigone was unhappy with Lamar's explanation. "What the hell do we need that for, anyway?"

"We got a busted wire in the microphone. Electrical tape won't hold it no more."

She sighed. "Call him up and tell him to stop someplace and get us some supper."

"Okay," Lamar answered. "Do you all want drinks, too?"

"What the hell do you think, fool?" She pushed the intercom away and took up her pencil. "The first thing we gotta figure out is what we're gonna do with Eddie."

Frankie's jaw dropped. "You don't mean . . ."

Antigone stared at Frankie like she was a foreign life form. Then she sat back and laughed. I'd never heard her laugh before, and the experience was strange and fantastic—like listening to one of those You Tube recordings of a piranha bark.

"I'm not gonna *kill* him, little girl." Antigone was still chuckling. "Though I'd probably be doin' the world a favor if I did. We have to figure out how to get him free of that sleazy scumbag, Tiny. And we need someplace safe to stash his bony ass while we do it. I ain't gonna risk leaving him out on the loose so he can rack up more debt."

"Do you seriously think he would?" I asked. "I mean, after all of this?"

"Does day follow night? Do dogs return to their vomit? Of *course* he would. It's a damn addiction."

"That is true," I said to Frankie.

"Okay, so even if we *can* find some way to pay Tiny off and keep Eddie hidden, what are we going to do after that?" Frankie looked at Antigone. "We can't keep him locked up forever."

"I got an idea about that. *Boca.*"

"Boca?" I asked. "You mean, as in Florida?"

Antigone nodded. "His brother, Lou, runs a couple of Carvel Ice Cream shops down there. I think it's the perfect place to keep Eddie on ice."

"No pun intended," I quipped.

Frankie wasn't persuaded. "Why do you think he'll agree to go?"

"Because he don't get a vote. I'm gonna have his ass hand-delivered—*as freight.*"

I was confused. Did Antigone intend to hog-tie Eddie and ship him to Florida in a crate?

"What does 'as freight' mean?" I asked warily.

She jerked a thumb toward the front of the trailer. "I'll have Roger Coble drive him down there."

"Even if you can pull that off, what makes you believe he'll stay there?" Frankie didn't seem to buy Antigone's idea. "His business and all of his contacts are here in K-Vegas."

"Not for long. I got a plan for that, too."

"How can you possibly have worked all of this out in the time it took us to walk back here from the office?" I asked.

"Time waits for no man, Not-Vera." She seemed to rethink her statement. "It don't wait for laid-off woman lawyers, neither. But we got bigger fish to fry right now."

I had a feeling I knew where this was headed.

"The remaining $13,000 he still owes Tiny?" I suggested.

"Exactly. We all need to be clear of this maggot. And the only way to do that is to pay his slimy ass off. *Fast*. Before any more interest builds up. And I want to find out for myself if he really shipped that property off to Africa already. It ain't usual for hot cars to get disposed of this fast. They usually have to park 'em someplace safe first, so they can cool off. If those vehicles aren't on a boat but are still sitting around in some hospital parking garage, we got bigger problems."

I wasn't sure how we possibly could have bigger problems than we already had, but I could see her point.

"What makes you think this . . . *Tiny* . . . will tell you anything?"

"Because he knows he's got Eddie's giblets in a vise—but he doesn't know yet that we've got his in one, too. Information is power, Not-Vera. And we have good information about what Mr. Tiny and his associates have been up to after hours. Hustling bets as a two-bit bookie is one thing. Dabbling with four cases of hard insurance fraud *and* international trafficking of stolen cars is something else. Trust me—Tiny don't wanna go to jail any more'n we do. And we've got enough information to make sure he goes right along with us for the ride."

"Yeah, about that *ride?*" I said. "The last thing we need is to get tagged as accessories to whatever trafficking scam he's got going on. I'd rather not know *anything* about what happened to those vehicles. And I sure as hell don't want to add blackmail to my burgeoning list of crimes—and I don't think you do, either."

Antigone took a minute to think about everything I'd said, before picking up her open pack of Mistys.

"Pass me that ashtray, Stohler." Frankie did as she asked, and Antigone sat smoking for another full minute. Finally, she looked at me with something like admiration. "You got a good head on your shoulders, Not-Vera. I don't know why that place canned you."

"Me either," I agreed. "I think the only business we have with Tiny is getting the rest of Eddie's debt paid up. We're going to have to just pray the rest of it goes away."

"Yeah," Frankie interjected. "About that. I think wanting to help Eddie is admirable—but I don't really understand why we'd want to risk anything more to do it. He pretty much betrayed us all." She looked directly at Antigone. "You, especially."

"You think I ain't aware of that, Debbie Reynolds?" Antigone shot back. "I have my reasons."

Something occurred to me. It was like a camera flash going off.

"Hugh Don," I said.

Antigone glared at me. "What about him?"

"It's Hugh Don. And maybe Weasel and Linda, too? All of them. You and Eddie? You help these people out, don't you? Give them jobs. Give them chances to start over. That's why you still have loyalty to Eddie. He's not a bad man. He's just a flawed man. A flawed man in trouble."

You could've heard a pin drop in that threadbare conference room. Well—maybe a *big* pin, since an annoying mixture of static and strains of "Love Lifted Me" spewed from the wall-mounted speaker.

For a second, I actually thought I saw Antigone's eyes glisten—but it must've been an illusion.

She scowled and opened her mouth to reply just as someone knocked at the cheap conference room door. It opened slowly and Roger Coble cautiously peeked inside.

"I got your food." He said it like he was apologizing for some kind of transgression.

"Well bring it on in here," Antigone ordered. "We're starving."

Roger entered carrying an enormous bag and a caddy containing four large drink cups.

"What in thunder is this?" Antigone took the bag from him.

"It's . . . barbecue." Roger explained.

"I can *see* that, fool." Antigone started pulling boxes and oversized food containers out of a shopping bag with *Taste of the Carolinas* emblazoned across the side. "Five hundred restaurants in this county and *this* is what you picked? Clark's damn barbecue?"

Poor Roger looked like a deer in the headlights. "Um. Yes, ma'am."

"Well what the hell made you think we needed a 'Family Feast' for ten people*?* It looks like there's a gallon of pork here."

"Um. No, ma'am. It's . . . actually . . . two quarts—with some chicken, too . . . and four large sides. And I . . ." His voice trailed off.

"Well?" Antigone demanded. "You *what?*"

"I had a coupon . . ."

That seemed to take the wind out of Antigone's sails.

"Well," she said gruffly. "Make sure Lamar pays you back out of petty cash. And give yourself a five dollar tip."

"Yes, ma'am." Roger started to back toward the door.

"Hold up a minute." Antigone grabbed two of the plates that came with our family feast and began heaping them up with pork, chicken and large helpings of fried okra, coleslaw and French fries. She slapped a biscuit on top of each before she thrust the plates at Roger. "Here. You take these. And make sure you eat every bit of that okry on yours, too. I don't like your color lately . . . you look *pasty*. I think you need more iron."

Roger nodded at her and made his way to the door juggling the plates of food.

"Thank you, Roger," Frankie called after him. "This looks like a wonderful meal."

Antigone was busy fixing plates for all of us.

"I don't want any okra," I said, as she proceeded to pile them all high with servings of sides. "I don't really like it."

Antigone stopped mid-spoonful and stared at me. "Don't start with me, Not-Vera. This is *my* house. And in my house you eat what I put on your plate and you *like* it."

"But I . . ."

Frankie laid a restraining hand on my arm to stop me from arguing.

"I'll eat yours, too," she assured me. "I love it."

We divvied up the drinks. There were two strawberry Fantas and two sweet teas. Frankie and I opted for the Fantas. Neither of us wanted to be awake all night.

Well. Not because of caffeine, anyway . . .

While we ate, we talked about short-term strategies for keeping Eddie offline—and for finding legitimate repo jobs that offered high payouts. Antigone told us projects like those came across her desk from time to time, but that most of them were too specialized for the "talent" at the NRB.

"Besides," she explained, "we can't involve Linda or Weasel in this mess. Neither of them can risk getting sideways with the law. So that means anything we find has to be a job you two girl scouts can manage." She shook her head. "And them are words I never thought I'd say out loud, lemme tell you."

"I think it's a moot point, anyway," Frankie added. "Because we'll never find anything legitimate that pays a $13,000 recovery fee. It's impossible."

"It ain't impossible." Antigone held up a chicken leg like a pointer. "Not if we start off by takin' a big bite outta that thirteen grand."

"How do you propose we do that?" I asked. "Do you have that much cash on hand in any of the NRB accounts?"

"Don't talk nonsense, Not-Vera. There's no money in this business and you know it. You think I'd be emptying out them five-gallon paint cans every day if we had the damn money on hand to fix that leak?"

"Yeah. Where *is* that water coming from, anyway?" I knew it was irrelevant, but I couldn't resist asking.

"I don't question things that are above my pay grade, Not-Vera. And neither should you."

That actually made a strange kind of sense. I decided it was wise not to follow up.

"So, if the NRB has no cash on hand," I continued, "how do you propose we reduce the amount we have to come up with to pay Tiny off?"

"Easy." Antigone tossed a chicken bone into our discard box and licked her fingertips. "It's parked up in front of the Vape Shoppe."

I gaped at her. "Eddie's Escalade?"

"Uh huh. I think he's about to make a long-overdue charitable contribution to this ministry."

I sat back and marveled at the woman's genius. Even though it was several years old, Eddie's doped-out SUV had to be worth at least ten grand.

"That's brilliant."

"Wait a minute," Frankie said. "What makes either of you think he'll agree to sign it over?"

"He ain't gonna 'agree,' little girl—cause I ain't gonna ask. He's gonna *beg* me to take it—right after he spends the night as my guest down here in God's mobile Beulah Land, pondering his many transgressions."

"You mean you're going to . . ." I looked around the conference room. It had a door that accessed a small bathroom, indicating that this space had originally been the trailer's master bedroom. "You're going to lock him up . . . *in here?*"

Antigone actually smiled.

"That would be correct, Your Honor."

Frankie announced that we needed to stop by the mortuary on our way back to her place. She needed to return the pontoon keys to her father, since tomorrow was her parents' anniversary, and they were going to spend the day out at Belews Lake.

I think she could tell I was uncomfortable. Not so much because of the errand, but the venue.

"Will you relax?" she tried to assure me. "There won't be anything going on there at this hour."

That helped a little bit, but not much. Visiting another funeral home after hours didn't hold much appeal for me. And this time, we weren't simply doing a ring-n-run: we were going *inside*.

It was nearly 9 p.m. It had taken most of an hour to get Eddie's temporary quarters set up. We had to move the meeting table out and bring in a rollaway bed that Antigone kept on hand for extreme weather events to ensure that God's word could "keep broadcasting through the storms."

Lamar and Roger Coble were tasked with escorting Eddie back to the radio station from the NRB office. He was madder than a hornet, but relieved to get out of the handcuffs. He immediately made use of the small bathroom.

"I told you his prostate was a problem," Antigone remarked, while we all listened uncomfortably to the sound of Eddie relieving himself.

We didn't hang around to participate in the conversation Antigone had with Eddie once he was safely installed in the Lord's high-roller suite. She told us we were free to hit the road and said she'd be in touch with any news tomorrow.

The events of the evening had taken on an eerie, surreal quality.

But I was realizing that this pretty much constituted business as usual at the NRB.

"Do you think she'll find us anything?"

Frankie's question hovered in the dim space that separated us. It was so out of context, it took me a minute to figure out what she was asking.

"A job?" I suggested. I could see her nod. "If she manages to sell Eddie's Escalade, it should be possible. We won't have that much of a margin to make up."

"I think I've lost any interest or enthusiasm I had for this work."

"I know what you mean. I can't say I'm eager to take on any more assignments, either."

Frankie glanced at me before returning her eyes to the highway.

"What will you do, then?"

"Look for something else, I guess."

"Another law firm?"

"Probably."

We rode along in silence for a minute or so.

"Do you think you'll . . . look for something . . ." She didn't finish her question.

I answered for her. "Around here?" I waited until I saw the slow nod of her head. "Why would you think I'd look anyplace else?"

She looked at me. "Would you?"

I reached across the console and took hold of her hand. "Not a chance. Not now."

"Thank god." I heard her exhale. "I don't want to lose us, Nick. Not now, when we're just starting to discover that there's an 'us' to lose."

I squeezed her hand. "I don't either."

"Dear lord, I pray we can stay out of jail."

I laughed at the absurdity of her statement. "Bet you never thought you'd say *that* to a girlfriend, did you?"

"No, not really. But then, nothing about you has been typical."

"Ditto, Daisy Duke."

Frankie freed her hand and swatted me on the arm. "Very. Funny."

"Hey, cut me some slack. It was a great opportunity for snappy alliteration. But I do agree with you. We need to hope and pray that Eddie was right, and that property is already on its way to Nigeria."

"What do we do if we find out it isn't?"

"We sit back, stay quiet and trust Antigone."

Frankie exited the highway on Marshall Street, and headed for Old Salem.

"Gird your loins," she warned me, as we drew closer. "Because we're going in."

She turned into the large parking lot hidden behind the looming brick building that had housed Stohler's Funeral Home since its founding. There were very few cars. A row of shiny black hearses were neatly backed into spaces that lined up in front of a low, newer-looking brick structure that sat at the back of the lot, some distance from the graceful Georgian mansion that was home to the family business.

"What's that little building?" I asked.

Frankie turned her car off. "The crematory—or, as Lilah calls it, 'the Franklin Stove.'"

I felt my insides tense up.

"Oh, good lord." Frankie retrieved the pontoon keys from the center console and opened her door. "Will you relax? Nobody here is gonna bite you. Come on."

"Can't I just . . . wait out here?" I asked meekly.

"*No.* This is my heritage, Nick. Learn to live with it."

"Okay, already." I got out. "But no creepy stuff, okay? We drop the keys and go."

Frankie led us toward the back entrance to the building.

"What the hell do you think I have planned? A tour of the embalming suite?"

"Please . . ." I held up a hand. "Don't talk about that . . . *place*. The barbecue is already repeating on me."

'You're such a baby."

Frankie rang the buzzer.

While we waited for someone to let us inside, I looked around the grounds. The place was pretty pristine. I saw Beth Stohler's touch in the landscaping. I imagined there were a lot worse venues for a final send-off.

"At least this time, we're not making a deposit," I remarked.

Frankie nudged me in the ribs just as the outside lights came on, and we heard someone unlock the door. It swung open and Lilah stood there, resplendent in all of her Mistress of the Dark glory.

She looked surprised to see us.

"Did I miss something?" she said in that husky voice of hers. "The boys downstairs ordered some takeout from King's Crab Shack about ten minutes ago, but I told them it would never be here this early on a Friday night."

"No crab legs." Frankie held up the boat keys. "Just these. Dad wants to take it out tomorrow."

Lilah took the keys from her and stepped back so we could enter. "Come on in. He's already gone for the night. It's my turn to close up."

"Well, *damn*." Frankie said with exasperation. "Do you want me to run them by the house?"

"Don't bother. He'll be by in the morning." She looked at me. "We've got a double-truck," she explained. "Two viewings at the same damn time. It happens. So how're you doing, Nick?"

"I'm . . . fine."

Lilah laughed. "You don't look fine. You look like you're going to puke."

"No," I stammered. "I've just never made a social call on a . . ."

I didn't finish my statement.

"A 'Crepe Hanger'?" Lilah all but cackled. "Come on in, little girl, and I'll show you my parlor."

"Knock it off, Li," Frankie warned her sister. "We've had a long day."

"Yeah?" Lilah looked us both over. "Unless I miss my guess, you've had a couple of long nights, too. Do yourselves a favor, and take some breaks now and then—just to hydrate. Too much sex will kill you. On the other hand," she raised a long finger didactically, "since that just means I'll end up having to deal with you sooner—what the hell? Knock yourselves out."

"Li . . ." Frankie did her best to sound annoyed, but she didn't quite succeed. We smiled stupidly at each other.

"Good god." Lilah shook her dark head. "You two are so fucking adorable, it's sickening. If I didn't have a cold, dead heart, I'd be moved to tears."

"Yeah. Okay." It was clear Frankie wanted to move on. "Will you give the keys to Dad in the morning?"

"Of course."

"Great. Thanks. We're gonna take off."

"Hold on a second. I want to get you something." Lilah disappeared down a hallway illuminated by wall sconces that flickered like gaslights. When she returned, she carried two large bottles of Evian spring water. "Take these, please. And for god's sake, use them."

She handed one to each of us. Frankie gave her sister a dramatic eye roll, but hugged her warmly.

"You're a total head case, but I love you."

"I love you, too, Pippi Longstocking." Lilah patted Frankie's back and smiled at me. "You take care of my little sister. It won't go well for you if you hurt her." She pointed at the floor. "Remember: I work *downstairs*."

"I'll be good," I promised her.

We left and climbed inside Frankie's car for the drive to her place.

"That was . . . bizarre."

"You think?" Frankie asked. "Actually, that was pretty mellow for Lilah."

"She's an odd bird. Exotic, but alluring and kind of endearing."

"*Endearing?* I've heard Li called a lot of things, but never endearing."

"Do you think she really could tell that we're . . . you know?"

Frankie looked over at me. "Having mad monkey sex?"

"Well. Yeah. I mean . . . sort of."

"Of course she could tell. She's eccentric as hell, but not an idiot."

"No. She's definitely not an idiot." I thought about Lilah's observation. "Do you think she was right?"

"About what?" Frankie asked.

"Drinking water."

"I have no idea. Maybe?"

Better safe than sorry. I picked up one of the Evian bottles and cracked the seal.

"What are you doing?"

I grinned at her. "Hydrating."

Chapter Nine

Moonshine Lullaby

We sat on Frankie's porch swing in the morning sun, enjoying our second cups of coffee and watching woodpeckers jockey for position on the feeders in her backyard. When my cell phone rang, I was tempted to ignore it—until I read the caller ID.

"It's Antigone." I showed it to Frankie. "Do I want to answer it?"

"I don't know. Do you think she murdered Eddie overnight?"

"Fat chance. It's likelier he'd kill himself after being forced to listen to that music all night." I pushed the talk button. "Good morning, Antigone."

"No time for pleasantries, Not-Vera. I got you two a job."

"Already? It's barely been twelve hours."

"This one can't wait. It has to happen no later than tomorrow."

"Tomorrow?" I was flustered. "Why so soon?"

"I can't go into all that on the phone. You two get your butts over here and I'll give you the details."

"Wait a minute." I had a feeling she was about to sign off. "What about Eddie?"

"Don't you worry about Eddie. He had a talk with Tiny this morning, and everything's sorted out. I ain't sayin' more now. You'n Skipper meet me at the office in an hour."

She hung up before I could ask any more questions.

What the fuck? I dropped the phone to my lap.

"What'd she have to say?" Frankie asked.

"She said she has a job for us, and it has to happen no later than tomorrow."

"*Tomorrow?* Come on . . ."

"Hey. I got nothin'. She wants us to meet her at the NRB in an hour for details."

Frankie sighed. "Why do movies always depict a life of crime as glamorous?"

"Buck up, Bonnie Parker. This job is coming from the woman who runs Global Gospel Radio."

"Which means?"

"I doubt you'll have to wear any four-inch heels."

Frankie seemed pleased by that prospect. "I knew there was a benevolent God."

"You'll get no arguments from me on that one."

"Oh, I know." Frankie tossed her blonde hair. "I heard you call out to him multiple times last night."

I tossed my wadded-up napkin at her. "Harlot."

Frankie took a deep breath and let it out slowly. "Do we really have to go over there?"

"Afraid so." I put my arm around her. "But look at the bright side: if we pull this last one off, we're done. Eddie walks, and so do we."

"Unless one of the cars or that damn boat surfaces again."

"Now you sound like me."

"Fear of incarceration must be contagious." She rested her head on my shoulder. "I'm scared, Nick."

"I know." I kissed her hair. "I am, too."

"Just promise me it'll all be okay? Even if it's a lie."

"I promise. And it's not a lie. We'll get through this. And once we do, there'll be no more . . . freelancing. We'll find some other way to keep your kids in school supplies and suppers."

Frankie smiled. "You make me sound like Anne Sullivan."

I thought about the comparison.

"It kind of fits. I mean, I did just acquire a new appreciation for water . . ."

I noticed two things when we pulled into the lot at the NRB: the thrift store was having a sidewalk sale, and Eddie's Escalade was gone.

Antigone had obviously been waiting on us—impatiently—because the door buzzed the second we stepped inside the lobby.

"Why the hell did it take you two so long to get here?" she thundered when we reached her office. "I told you this damn job wouldn't wait."

"We got here as soon as we could," I said defensively. "There was some kind of craziness going on around Highway 52. The traffic was all backed up in both directions."

"Well if you'd bother to read a damn newspaper you'd know that stupid air show is goin' on out at Smith Reynolds—and you'd have enough sense to come a different way. Every year, all the geezers in the county roll out there to look at the same damn B-17s and P-51s that always show up. You know how many times I seen Glamorous *damn* Glen? Enough times to know he ain't glamorous. Now sit down." She gestured at the two chairs in front of her desk. "We got business to discuss."

We took our seats.

"How's Eddie?" Frankie asked.

"Right now, Eddie is probably having his third seven-and-seven, courtesy of Delta Airlines."

I was confused. "What do you mean?"

"His ass is on its way to damn Florida, where all used-up white people go."

"Already?" Frankie was incredulous. "How'd you pull that off so fast?"

"Little girl? By the time 5 a.m. rolled around this morning, that man woulda signed over his damn business to get outta that room at the station." She chuckled. "As a matter of fact, he *did* sign over his business—*and* his Caddy."

I couldn't believe what I was hearing. "Wait . . . Eddie signed the business over? *To you?*"

"No. Not to me. To the *ministry*."

"The radio station?" Frankie's jaw dropped. "Is that legal?"

Antigone shrugged her broad shoulders. "I don't see why not. It ain't like this place ever makes a profit, anyway. Besides, I'll just run it as a separate enterprise. No conflict of interest with the Lord's work that way."

That made a strange kind of sense. After all, it would be tough to truly love the sinner while you were jacking his ride . . .

My head was spinning. Eddie was gone and Antigone now owned the NRB?

Correction: Global Gospel Radio now owned the NRB.

"I'm—stunned." I looked at Antigone with wonder. "You weren't kidding when you said time waits for no man."

"You'll find that I don't kid about much, Not-Vera. Now . . ." she handed me a sheet of paper. "I made some calls last night, and these are the details of the job I got lined up. And if you two jokers can pull this off, its payout, plus the $10,250 I got for the Escalade, is enough to get Eddie out from under Tiny. Once that's tied off, his ass is on its own. We don't owe him nothin' else."

Frankie and I scanned the paper. I had to read the document three times before I trusted my eyes.

I looked at Frankie to see if she shared my concern, but she simply gave a small shrug and nodded.

"I think it's doable."

"Are you nuts?" I pointed at a paragraph on the paper. "*Cows?*" I looked up at Antigone. "Absolutely *not*. This is absurd."

"Your partner doesn't appear to agree with your views on this assignment, Not-Vera."

"I refuse to discuss this." I stood up. "How do you repossess fucking *cows?* That's not even possible."

"I have to differ with you on that, Not-Vera. Bein' delinquent on a loan is bein' delinquent on a loan. Don't matter if the asset in question sits on four tires or four damn hooves." Antigone handed Frankie a card. "This is the phone number of our client. He'll hook you up with a truck and trailer. I wanna be clear: them cows belong to him. This is a legitimate recovery job. The joker who's got 'em bought 'em to start up a dairy—and now he just won some highfalutin' cheese medal from some damn place where people care about mess like that. Now he's gettin' orders from every mail order joint in the country. But he *still* ain't paid up what he owes on them dotted Swiss cows . . . thinks he's some kind of Donald Trump and can just walk away from his obligations. *Our State Magazine* is doin' a big feature on this joker and his foreign-ass cows, and they're showing up on Monday—with a photographer. Our client wants them cows back on his own property no later'n Sunday night." She sat back in her chair and fired up a Misty Menthol. "That's the job."

Frankie had been listening intently. "Where are the cows right now?"

"Are you *crazy?*" I was starting to lose it. "Listen to yourself . . . *this is a herd of cows, Frankie.*" I referenced the paper. "Dutch Belted heifers."

"Technically, it ain't a herd." Antigone blew out a chestful of smoke. "It's only six."

"Oh. *Right.* My mistake. Because *six* dairy cows only weigh . . . what? Nine thousand pounds?"

"Nick, will you please calm down so we can discuss this?"

"What is there to discuss? Frankie?" I dropped back onto my chair. "I know *nothing* about cows. I grew up in southwest Philadelphia. The closest I ever got to a cow was when Mamá sent me out to the Reading Terminal Market to buy a wedge of beer-washed Bamboozle."

"I don't understand you people and your fascination with them fancy-ass cheeses," Antigone interjected. "What's wrong with plain ol' American cheese, like Velveeta?"

I was close to having a meltdown and I knew it.

Frankie could tell I needed some space to get my head around the particulars of this assignment.

"Do you mind if we take an hour or two to talk this over?" she asked Antigone. "We can let you know something no later than noon."

Antigone wasn't happy with that request. But she agreed to it anyway.

"Noon," she stated. "I ain't waitin' any longer. I gotta tell this man something so he can make other arrangements if we take a pass—and I'm hopin' we don't. I want this mess over with, and the sooner we pay Tiny off, the better."

"We both agree with you on that," Frankie assured her. She stood up. "Come on, Nick. Let's go someplace and talk this over."

"Hold up before you two take off." Antigone ground out her cigarette. "I had a talk with Tiny this morning. And I know you don't want to know nothin' about . . . things. So let's just say them chickens has flown the coop. They ain't gonna be on nobody's radar again. So you can relax about that part."

"We did not have this conversation," I clarified. "Not about chickens. Not about radar. Not about Tiny."

"I don't know what you're talkin' about, Not-Vera." Antigone fired up another smoke. "Who the hell is Tiny?"

"I'm happy to see we understand each other."

"You two get the hell outta here." Antigone waved us off. "I got work to do, settin' this dump up as a legitimate business."

We left her office, and Frankie drove us straight to the Sixty Six Grill, "For old time's sake."

We hadn't had time to get any breakfast that morning, so we decided to split an apple walnut chicken salad and BBQ brisket flatbread with hot chips. It was enough food for five people, but stress eating seemed appropriate for our circumstances.

"If we stay in this line of work much longer, I'm gonna gain nine thousand pounds."

"You mean, like the heifers?" Frankie asked.

I tossed a chip at her. "You're *not* helping. You know as well as I do that this is an insane assignment."

"I don't know any such thing. I don't think this job is any stranger or more complicated than getting that damn monster boat out of the most exclusive yacht club in the state. And unlike that one, this one doesn't require either of us to dress like a hooker. I'm fine with any job that doesn't involve squeezing my ass into that damn bodysuit again."

"Hmmm." I looked her over. "Not sure I'm on the same page with you on that one."

"That's because you're a pervert."

"You say potato . . ."

"Seriously, Nick. I think we can do this job. It's not going to be dangerous. I doubt there are any security cameras, or that the cows are kept under armed guard. All we have to do is locate them, and get them on the truck."

"Precisely. What's your method for persuading six 1,500-pound heifers that it would be fun to go joyriding after dark? Lure them onto the truck with vague promises of Dilly Bars?"

Frankie seemed to consider that idea. "I'm not sure dairy treats would have that much appeal. Maybe we could tempt them with whatever their favorite food is?"

"What? Like Twinkies or Nacho Cheese Doritos?"

"*No*. I was thinking things like apples, cabbage or root vegetable leaves. Treat foods. Something better than pasture grass."

"So we show up after dark with this basket of goodies and hope they all have the munchies?"

"Nick? They're *cows*. They always have the munchies."

I speared a slice of Granny Smith apple from our salad and ate it. It *was* pretty tasty—tart and fresh.

Maybe Frankie was on to something...

"I can't believe I'm even considering this. I think working for the NRB has finally sent me around the bend."

Frankie patted the back of my hand. "Well, look at the bright side. It's the last bend in this journey."

I gave her a half smile. "At least I'm ending up someplace nice."

"Prison?"

"Maybe a different kind of prison. One with better food and more fringe benefits."

Frankie squeezed my hand. "How about we finish up here, give Antigone a call, and then head up to the Yadkin Valley to scope out this cheese joint?"

"How are we gonna do that in broad daylight?"

"I Googled it while you were in the restroom washing your hands. It's part of a winery and they do tours on the weekends."

"Of course they do."

"Come on. It'll be fun."

I squinted at her. "Are you sure you weren't Ma Barker in a previous life?"

Frankie raised her glass of iced tea. "Drink up, cowboy. It's time to ride the range."

Grassy Knoll Winery and Farm was located in a rolling section of the Yadkin Valley that was dotted with wineries that were steadily gaining national recognition for producing award-winning varietals. The northern Piedmont's higher land elevations, loamy soil and moderate temperatures closely imitated growing conditions in the rarified wine growing regions of the Napa Valley. It was a happy discovery for North Carolina viticulturists that lands once used to grow tobacco were ideally suited to the cultivation of grapes. Some wineries continued to respect the heritage by interspersing tobacco plants with grape vines as a natural way to control soil pests. Grassy Knoll was no exception.

While Frankie drove, I did a bit more research on Grassy Knoll. It was an interesting story. Ironically, most of the information came from an earlier story in *Our State Magazine*.

The winery opened in 2003 to modest success. The transplanted vines were too young and the winemakers too inexperienced to yield anything remarkable. After the first decade and a half, the wines improved, but were not yet equal in quality to the classic varietals produced by the more mature French vinifera grapes cultivated at other wineries. So the winery struggled.

Its fortunes changed in 2015 when the owners decided to branch out and begin making cheese. Central to the success of this enterprise was their acquisition of six extremely rare Lakenvelder, or Dutch Belted, cows. The distinctively marked cows—black or red with wide, white belts—first made famous in America by P.T. Barnum, became known worldwide for their easy temperaments, long lives, and copious production of natural soft curd and easily digestible milk. Within a few years, Grassy Knoll was producing cheeses that began racking up national awards and gaining recognition in commercial markets. The fate and fortunes of Grassy Knoll Farm were cemented in 2019 when they took top honors at the World Cheese Awards in Bergamo, Italy, for their certified organic, washed rind cheese, *Clotilde*. Since that time, cheeses produced by the small creamery had become popular boutique additions to the stores of online retailers like Wolferman's, iGourmet, and Harry and David.

It turned out those lauded distinctions were of little benefit to Mr. Hollis Huggins Hardy, the neighboring Yadkin Valley dairy farmer who'd advanced the flailing winery the funds to construct their creamery—and acquire the enterprising herd of cows. Since making the loan in 2015, Mr. Hardy had been repaid less than 5 percent of the hefty balance owed, and had received nothing from Grassy Knoll since its elevation to the top ranks of premiere domestic cheese makers. His discovery that *Our State Magazine* was planning a major feature on Grassy Knoll and its prize coterie of milk cows was the proverbial last straw.

Mr. Hardy brought his plight straight to Antigone, telling her he was prepared to pay top dollar to put the kybosh on the creamery's up-coming fifteen seconds of fame. And he didn't much care about the cost to do it. The cows were rightfully his, he argued, and he was well within his rights to conscript them as incentive to force the cheese makers to pay up. He even offered use of a truck and cattle trailer to recover them. But the recovery had to happen fast, because the *Our State* reporter and photographer were showing up at Grassy Knoll Farm at daybreak on Monday morning—in time to witness the first milking of the six Dutch Belted heifers.

Frankie felt fairly confident about her ability to wrangle the cattle trailer. It was smaller by half than the triple-axle boat trailer we'd used to haul the Donzi to K-Vegas. The rig Mr. Hardy was offering up was only sixteen feet long and seven feet wide. He'd explained to Antigone that this size was acceptable for the job because we'd be transporting the cows less than ten miles to his farm, and the trailer was equipped with a gate that divided the space into two sections so the cows wouldn't fall or shift around in transit.

The tricky part—*and there was always a tricky part*—would be persuading the cows to *board* the trailer once we'd located them in the pasture where they grazed.

Frankie's plan for our tour of the winery and creamery was to scope out the farm grounds and try to ascertain where the cattle were kept overnight. Mr. Hardy had explained we'd be likelier to find the cows outside, grazing at will, since the nights had turned warmer and the moon was near full. That was the good news. The bad news was ascertaining where on the farm the cows might wander to, and what kind of road access we'd have to load and get them out.

Tours at Grassy Knoll were offered every two hours on Saturday. Reserve tours, which included wine and cheese tastings, took place only in the afternoon, at one-thirty and three-thirty. Frankie had signed us up for the three-thirty reserve tour and tasting. The Grassy Knoll website revealed that the dairy cows were milked twice at day: at 5:30 a.m. and again at 5:30 p.m.

"I'm thinking this three-thirty tour will give us a chance to get a good look at the cows," Frankie explained, as we made the drive up to the Yadkin Valley. "They should be visible in the pasture."

"Why do we *need* a good look at them?" I asked. "Are you afraid you wouldn't be able to pick them out of a police lineup?"

"Smart ass. They keep other kinds of cows there, too."

"Won't that make finding this group harder?"

"No," Frankie explained. "These cows are entirely grass fed, so they're allowed to wander out at night. The others aren't."

"How'd you find all that out?"

"I had to do something while you were in the restroom at the Sixty Six Grill. Why'd it take you so damn long to wash your hands?"

"There was a line," I complained. "Only one stall was working."

"That's regrettable."

"Yeah. I had to wait ten minutes on the lady in front of me. She was in there trying to teach her kid how to use the grown-up potty."

Frankie looked at me sorrowfully. "Poor baby."

We reached the sign for the turnoff to Grassy Knoll Farm and drove along a long, winding lane that ran between tidy rows of grapevines. It was a clear day and there were beautiful views of the Blue Ridge Mountains to the west and the sprawling Piedmont to the south. The winery, creamery, and scattered farm buildings were rustic in design, but pristine and meticulously cared for. Frankie parked in front of the winery entrance and we made our way inside to begin our tour.

We lucked out and there were only five other people in our group. The winery tour was first. We started outside, where the harvested grapes were delivered for destemming and crushing, and worked our way down through the various stages of fermenting, pressing, barreling and bottling. The tasting came last. We sampled eight varieties of supremely indifferent wines and had no difficulty imagining why the owners had turned their attention to cheese making.

The farm and creamery tour were the money shots of our research trip. We toured the dairy grounds in golf carts and got a firsthand look at the grassy pastures, paddocks and milking barns. It became clear in short order that the six Dutch Belted cows were the star attractions, since they were the talent behind the creamery's award-winning "Clotilde" cheese.

We even got a look at several framed photos of Clotilde, herself, the largest heifer in the group.

"There's always one gal in charge," our tour guide explained. "And Clotilde is the smartest one of the herd. Jenny, the head cheese maker here, says Clotilde is almost too smart—and it's hard sometimes to keep a step ahead of her. But she's a good leader, and the other gals in the herd fall right in line behind her."

Frankie and I exchanged glances.

"Where do you keep the cows at night?" Frankie asked. "My uncle had dairy cows, and they always brought them in before dark."

"That's right," he said. "And we do that for the other breeds. But these Dutch Belted cows only eat grass for food—we don't give them grain—so their milk stays 100 percent organic. That means they're free to roam and graze whenever they're not being milked."

"That's interesting," Frankie added. "Do they ever go very far from the barn?"

"Oh, yeah," he said. "Their favorite pasture is the long one that runs behind the grapevines on the south side of the property. You'll pass it on the way out. It dips down toward Swan Creek and has quite a few shade trees. You can usually get a good look at 'em from Pinnix Road. They like it down that way and always stay together in a group."

Score! I had to hand it to Frankie: she could get information out of a turnip.

Grassy Knoll made up for the indifference of its wine by the superlative quality of its cheeses. The creamery lobby sported a large showcase containing a couple dozen domestic medals and the lauded gold medal from the World Cheese Awards in Italy. We sampled six different cheeses and they were all excellent. But the Clotilde was exceptional. It was so good, we bought three six-ounce hunks of it to take home.

I wondered if we could expense it as part of our per diem.

Fat chance. The NRB was under new management now, and I doubted that Global Gospel Radio, LLC would offer liberal fringe benefit packages.

On the way out, we took our time surveying the long pasture the guide told us about. It was a little before 5 p.m., so the cows were probably off grazing someplace out of sight. We decided to detour and find Pinnix Road. We hadn't traveled very far along the two-lane road that followed the meandering Swan Creek when we saw them, standing in a group near a cluster of oak trees. Clotilde was easy to pick out. The guide hadn't been kidding: she was exponentially larger than the other five heifers.

Frankie pulled off the road, and we got out to stand near the fence and watch the cluster of bovines while they grazed.

I thought the experience was a lot like observing a crew of prison inmates working along a highway. In that scenario, Clotilde would've been the one holding the shotgun.

"They're big, Frankie."

"As cows go, I'd say they're actually on the small side."

"Yeah?" I looked at her. "As *freight* goes, they're pretty damn huge."

"Would you relax? If we get Clotilde on the truck, the others will follow her."

"It sounds like you expect to find them all queued-up—like they're waiting to get inside Walmart on Black Friday."

"I tend not to front-load things with negative expectations."

"So I've noticed."

"Come on." Frankie led the way back to her car. "Let's go meet up with Mr. Hardy and get the keys to his truck and trailer."

It goes without saying that I didn't share Frankie's optimism for how well this endeavor would unfold. But the sad truth was that we were in too deep, and we had a stake in getting Eddie free from Tiny's clutches. Once this was over? We could walk away from the NRB and not look back.

That was the hope, anyway.

The moon was nearly full on Sunday night, which proved to be both a blessing and a curse. A blessing because it was easier to see in the dark. A curse because it was easier to *be* seen in the dark.

We waited until late in the evening to make our trek to the Hardy farm to pick up the truck and cattle trailer. On the way, Frankie made a detour along Pinnix Road to see if we'd luck out and find Clotilde and the girls grazing in their favorite spot. Sure enough, they were there. The white belts around their broad middles glowed in the bluish moonlight like giant reflector strips. We didn't want to waste time and risk that the cows would mosey along to greener pastures, so we all but laid a patch along county back roads heading to the Hardy farm to retrieve the rig.

Frankie was right, and the thing was a lot easier to manipulate than the Donzi trailer. Mr. Hardy gave us a quick tutorial on how to operate the loading ramp and make use of the interior gate that bisected the space inside the trailer. He told us we'd fare best if we had three heifers in the forward compartment and three in the rear.

That was our plan.

Frankie had shopped earlier in the day for leafy root vegetables and had filled a big Ziploc bag with cut-up apples. "Incentive," she called it. I had my doubts. I'd had a good look at Clotilde the day before. She looked entirely too clued-in and . . . *crafty*. Those big brown eyes weren't vacant. There was something going on behind them—a *lot* of something. I had an uneasy feeling that, given the opportunity, Clotilde could be about as cooperative as Joan Crawford on the board at Pepsi-Cola.

I didn't trust her.

She was what Mamá called *La Siguanaba*, a shape-shifting demoness who drove her victims mad and left them to wander aimlessly in the wilderness.

I had a premonition about Clotilde: It wasn't going to end well for me.

When I had shared my suspicions with Frankie that morning, she told me I was nuts. I noted that this was becoming her stock response to everything.

She defended her blasé attitude about "the head gal."

"I have that thing with animals, remember?"

"What thing?"

"Hello?" she reminded me. "You? Carol Jenkins? Your bed? Does any of that ring any bells?"

"You think that skill is transferable between species?"

"There's only one way to find out."

So there we were—an hour before midnight—parked along a curve on Pinnix Road near the access gate to the creamery's long pasture, about to try our hand at rustling cattle.

Frankie rolled the side door of the trailer open, and we carefully extended the loading ramp.

"Ready?" she asked me.

I took a deep breath. "As I'll ever be."

Frankie grabbed the bag containing the leafy vegetables and handed me the Ziploc full of apple slices.

"Let's go make friends with them first."

We opened the gate and crept toward the cluster of heifers. They didn't pay much attention to us at first. They continued munching grass and switching their long, feathery tails. Frankie withdrew a large bundle of turnips from her bag and offered the leafy ends to the cow we'd identified as Clotilde.

"Here, baby . . . want some of these?" Frankie shook the bundle. Clotilde stopped chewing grass and eyed Frankie with suspicion before extending her neck and chomping off the ends of the turnips in one bite.

"Yeah," I said. "So *those* aren't gonna last long."

"That's okay." Frankie reached out a hand and patted Clotilde on her broad neck. "You're a beautiful girl, aren't you?" She dug into her bag and pulled out a bunch of celery. "Want some of this? It's organic."

Clotilde made short work of the celery tops.

Frankie took a step backward to see if Clotilde would follow her toward the truck.

She did.

"That's my smart, beautiful girl," Frankie cooed. "Let's see what else we have in here for you." She took another step backward. "Try these golden beets. They're fresh."

Frankie and Clotilde continued their slow *pas de deux* toward the gate and the loading ramp.

"Nick?" she all but whispered. "Go around behind the rest of them and see if you can walk them along behind us."

"How?"

"Spread your arms and just try to herd them."

"Oh, yeah, *sure*," I protested. "It may surprise you to learn that I flunked out of border collie school."

"*Please?*" Frankie continued backing up with Clotilde in tow." I'm running out of bait."

I had a premonition that this wasn't going to go well. There was nothing unusual about that. Expecting the worst, most extreme outcomes was kind of my stock-in-trade. Still . . . trying to coax five Buick-sized heifers to leave the bucolic serenity of a grassy, moonlit pasture and board a dusty sixteen-foot cattle trailer was destined to become a new high in my lexicon of failed endeavors.

I nervously took my place behind the cow bringing up the rear.

Okay, I thought. *Not the best anatomical reference.*

I took care to watch where I stepped. It was clear these "gals" didn't adhere to the best bathroom etiquette.

I spread my arms wide and slowly advanced toward the group.

"Come on, gals. Let's all move along . . . nothing to see here." They didn't budge, but continued to stand in place, munching grass and switching their tails. "We've got good deli and cold beer on the truck." No dice. I waved my arms and took another step closer. "The first five of you who board will get fruit cup." Bupkis. I tried gently nudging the rear heifer. "C'mon, big Bertha, let's go get some nosh." Nothing. "Sooey . . . sooey . . ."

"Nick? What the hell are you doing?"

"I'm trying to get these fat broads to move their asses. What do you *think* I'm doing?"

"Using a hog call is probably not going to accomplish that."

"So sue me. Who knew poor language skills would be deemed

offensive to cows?"

Frankie opened her mouth to respond, but stopped suddenly and whipped her head to the side.

"What was that?"

"What?"

"*That*. Don't you hear that?"

"I can't hear anything but my pulse hammering in advance of a coronary."

"Shhhhh. Shut up and listen. There it is again . . ."

This time, I heard it, too. It was a low, stuttering noise. Almost like a purr. And it was getting closer.

"What the fuck *is* that?" I hissed.

"I don't know. It sounds . . . mechanical."

Frankie was right. It sounded just like . . . *oh, sweet mother of pearl.*

"*It's a chain saw*," I cried. "Somebody is starting up a fucking *chain saw*. We need to get out of here. *Now*."

I lunged to the right to get around big Bertha when something slammed into my back. It nearly knocked me down. I stumbled and started to run. The rumbling noise was right on my heels. I felt something sharp rap me between the shoulder blades.

What the hell was happening? I ran as fast as I could, tripping and stumbling over the uneven ground, but the thing stayed right on my heels. I heard a loud squawk, followed by another sharp rap—on my butt this time.

I whirled around and was suddenly face to face with the biggest, ugliest bird-like creature I'd ever seen. Its skin glowed blue in the moonlight, but its eyes were menacing and black as pitch.

"What the fuck *are* you?"

The demon creature was at least five feet tall and built like a linebacker. It took advantage of my stupor and lunged at me. I reflexively threw out my hands and pushed back against its feathered chest, barely avoiding a machete-tipped beak in the face.

I could hear Frankie screaming.

"Run! Nick, run! Head for the truck! Head for the truck!"

I made a wide circuit of the heifers, who, by the way, kept placidly munching away on tufts of grass like it was any ol' Sunday night. Only Clotilde seemed to be watching the show with any kind of interest. I tried to cut back toward the open gate and the truck but the psychotic Big Bird stayed right behind me. I tried every maneuver I could think of—switchbacks, fast cuts, side lunges—nothing worked. I couldn't shake the damn thing. Its intent was plainly murderous and it ran like the wind. I lost count of how many butts and pecks I got in our mad scramble around the pasture. My lungs burned and I knew I couldn't keep running for much longer. I heard another loud squawk followed by that rumbling motor noise again and realized that Frankie had entered the fray. She was now taunting the demon bird with a long, leafy branch and trying to draw it away from me.

"The truck," she hollered. "Run to the truck!"

It took every ounce of remaining strength I possessed to make a last, mad dash toward the pasture gate. Unfortunately for me, hell's chicken didn't take Frankie's bait and stayed fast on my heels. I reached the gate and literally jumped the final three feet to land squarely on the metal loading ramp, staggering my way up into the cattle car.

Did the crazed nuclear yardbird give up and peel off?

Oh, hell no. It followed me right up the fucking ramp, like any damn assassin would.

It only took half a second for me to realize this had not been the brightest move . . .

"Not the trailer!" Frankie screamed. "The *truck!* Get inside the damn *truck!*"

Now I'd done it. I had nowhere to hide. We bounced and careened off the sides of the cattle car like racquetballs. In desperation, I lunged behind the open gate that divided the space and slammed it shut. My feathered assailant was really pissed off after that maneuver. It squawked and yammered and repeatedly slammed its fat, angry bulk against the metal barrier, craning its neck and trying to reach me through the bars.

I was done for and I knew it. I heard the rusty latch give way, and saw my life flash before my eyes as the gate started to swing open.

Freddy Krueger was inside the house, and I was about to become an oversized hunk of Swiss cheese.

I backed into a corner, folded my arms in front of my face, and prepared to meet my fate.

The floor of the trailer began to rock and shift. A sound like thunder filled my ears.

I lowered my arms and looked at Satan's velociraptor, who also seemed alarmed. He briefly glared at me before pivoting toward the ramp.

There was Clotilde, lumbering her way up into the trailer. I noticed that she still had remnants of . . . *crudités* . . . sticking out of her mouth.

Incredibly, the other five heifers were lined up and following right along behind her.

What the fuck? That cheese dude hadn't been kidding when he'd said there was always a head gal . . .

Clotilde marched right toward the front of the trailer where I cowered in my corner behind . . . whatever in the hell that damn feathered thing was.

Frankie was outside the trailer door.

"Come on, come on," she urged me. "Get out of there while it's distracted."

Distracted? I didn't bother to argue with her. I slid along the side wall of the trailer and somehow managed to climb over the gate. I pretty much fell to the floor on the other side. Every muscle in my body ached. My arms and shoulders throbbed from the punctures and cuts I knew I had sustained. I all but crawled toward the ramp.

"Help me get the rest of them secured." Frankie stood on the end of the ramp, gently shooing the last two heifers up into the trailer.

I managed to herd two more of the cows into the front compartment, where Clotilde and the assassin seemed to be having some kind of reunion. Once their fat asses cleared the gate I slammed it closed and secured the latch. By that time, the remaining three heifers had crammed into the remaining space.

Frankie stood by the open door, extending her hand to me.

"Come on, baby. Come on out of there. *It's over*. You did it. You fucking *did* it."

I essentially fell down the ramp into her waiting arms. Frankie hugged me so tightly I thought I might faint from the pain. But I didn't care. In that moment, all I wanted was to hang on to her and never let go.

"Oh, my god," she muttered. "I love you, I love you. I thought that thing was gonna kill you."

"Me, too," I murmured into her hair. "I don't know why it backed off."

"It was Clotilde. I think it was protecting Clotilde." She kissed the side of my face. "Can you stand up on your own? We need to close this door before that thing changes its mind."

I raised my head. "We're taking it *with* us?"

"I think we have to, Nick."

"Won't it go after the cows?" I looked nervously up inside the trailer.

"I don't think so." Frankie gently released me and walked to the end of the ramp. "Can you help me lift this thing and slide it back beneath the trailer?"

I did my best to help her, but each movement was like a new threshold of agony. All I wanted was a hot, soaking bath and a liter of D'Ussé cognac.

Frankie rolled the access door closed and latched it into place.

"Come on, baby. Let's get you out of here."

She helped me get settled inside the truck before retreating to secure the pasture gate. Two minutes later, we pulled out and were headed for the Hardy farm bearing the last load of cargo needed to settle Eddie's debt to Tiny and, hopefully, keep our asses out of jail.

Frankie kept talking to me in a low voice—trying to reassure me.

"It's over, Nick. *It's over*. We did it. *We're through*."

I felt like I was trapped inside a dense haze. I gazed at her through a tumbled mixture of pain and euphoria that hovered dangerously near the border of hysteria.

Moonlight suffused her features with soft blue and white light. She looked unreal . . . almost *beatified*—like Mamá's tiny icon of Pedro de San José Betancur, the first Guatemalan saint. I stopped breathing for a moment, not sure what I was actually seeing. Not sure about anything that was happening. Where I was. What we'd done. How we got to this place.

Frankie looked back at me and in an instant, what had been a panicked moment of illusion was replaced by one of comfort and recognition. I knew her again. And I knew myself, too.

"What you said to me," I began, "when I got out of the trailer. Did you mean it?"

She didn't ask me to clarify which part. She knew what I meant.

"Yeah." She slowly nodded. "Is that okay?"

"It's . . . better than okay."

"Good." She sounded relieved.

We'd reached the intersection of Pinnix Road and Mineral Springs Road. From there, it was a straight shot to the Hardy farm, located just south of the Yadkin River.

Maybe our nightmare *had* ended? *Was that too much to hope for?*

I watched Frankie navigate the turn onto Mineral Springs Road. Behind us, our passengers were blessedly quiet and didn't seem to be moving around much. Even that mutant Big Bird seemed to have settled down.

In a few minutes, we'd be at the Hardy farm, and this entire chapter of my life would be over.

Well. Not all of it. There was one part I was determined to hang on to.

I reached out and took hold of her hand.

"I love you, too," I said.

I could see Frankie's shy smile. She squeezed my fingers, but didn't say anything. She didn't need to.

We made the rest of the trip in relaxed and happy silence.

Mr. Hardy and a couple of other men were waiting on us when we pulled in with our load of bovine contraband. That was expected.

What we didn't expect to see was the other person waiting with him.

Antigone.

"Is that who I think it is?" I pointed to where they stood together, near the entrance to a paddock.

"Dear god. I think so. What is she doing up here at this hour?"

"Beats the hell outta me. But it can't be good news."

Frankie brought our rig to a halt and jumped out to meet them. It took me a few moments longer to get my legs moving. I'd been sitting long enough to begin stiffening up. I joined Frankie.

"What in tarnation happened to your face?" Antigone demanded. "And don't tell me you didn't get them damn cows."

"Thanks for your concern," I replied. "We got 'em, all right. They're in the back."

Mr. Hardy gestured toward the farmhands, who proceeded to set up some portable fencing to create a walled chute leading to the open paddock. While they worked, Frankie attempted to explain the drama that had ensued when we attempted to herd the cows onto the truck. She didn't get very far into her story before the chain saw inside the trailer fired up.

Antigone's eyes blazed. "What on God's green earth is *that?*"

"A complication?" Frankie offered.

"Stohler? You'd best know better about bringin' that mess to me. We already discussed these damn complications."

"Yes, ma'am, we did," Frankie explained. "But this one found *us*—not the reverse."

The chain saw was running full out, and Mr. Hardy's farm hands exchanged nervous looks when something began slamming into the interior wall of the trailer.

"Oh, law." It was Mr. Hardy. He looked at us apologetically. "That un's on me. I plum forgot to tell you gals about Clovis."

Clovis?

"Who the hell is Clovis?" I asked.

"That emu." Hardy nodded his head toward the trailer. "Him and Clotilde are pretty much a bonded pair. She don't go no place without him."

"An *emu?*" I looked at Frankie. "That's what that feathered fiend is? *An emu?*"

"Yep." Hardy nodded. "I had to sell him right along with all them cows. Wouldn't a been no way Clotilde woulda gone over there without Clovis. And if she don't go, the rest of 'em don't go, neither."

The farmhands extended the ramp and cautiously rolled back the trailer door.

In short order, and with an appalling lack of drama, they off-loaded the three heifers in the back compartment, who dutifully followed the makeshift path that led into the paddock. One of the brave men then climbed into the truck and opened the gate to retrieve the three remaining cows. Clotilde was last to disembark—followed by Clovis. He stuck his ugly head out and took in his surroundings. I reflexively stepped behind Antigone to hide, just in case he saw me and decided to renew acquaintance with my derriere. He fluffed up his feathers and puffed out his chest before dutifully following Clotilde down the ramp and into the paddock.

Antigone watched the entire display with silent annoyance. Once the cattle—and the emu—were safely pastured, she whirled to face me.

"Get out from behind me, you fool."

I meekly obeyed her, noticing for the first time that she was dressed entirely in black. I supposed she was wearing her "night ops" uniform.

She faced me with an angry glare.

"I would just like to understand what it is with you two and the damn plus ones?"

"With all due respect, Miss Antigone," Hardy interjected, "that emu wadn't their fault. You can see he gave this young lady here what for . . . she's got feathers all up in her hair."

My hands shot up to my head. *Feathers? Again?*

Antigone reached out and yanked one from behind my shirt collar.

"You're a mess, Not-Vera. I thought a woman with your education would stay put together better."

"Well, I'm *sorry* to disappoint you. I was too busy running for my life to pay attention to my presentation."

"Don't get your panties all in a wad, Not-Vera. You two did the job and that's what matters here." Antigone faced Mr. Hardy. "Are you satisfied with the service rendered this night by the National Recovery Bureau?"

"Yes, ma'am, I am. These two gals done real good. I guarantee that come 5 a.m., them folks at Grassy Knoll are gonna be creamin' somethin' else besides milk, if you catch my drift."

Antigone nodded. "Then it would appear that our business here is concluded."

"I got a check all made out for you." Hardy withdrew an envelope from his pocket and handed it to her. He faced us. "And here's a bonus for you gals, too. I know'd this was a last-minute job on a Sunday night, and you two done real good."

Frankie took the folded bills from him, and I saw her eyes grow wide.

"Mr. Hardy, this is too much . . ."

He cut her off. "Naw. You take it. It's like I told your boss here: this wadn't about the money—it was about the principle. Those folks didn't do right by me. I was more'n willin' to let 'em slide a bit when they wadn't breakin' even—but when they started makin' lots of money on them cheeses and gettin' all that media hoopla, they still didn't see fit to honor their obligations."

"It's the way of the world these days," Antigone commiserated. "I despair for the sad fate of humanity."

"Yes, ma'am," Hardy agreed. "Most days, I do, too. But thankfully, there's good folks like you who can help a feller out when he needs a hand-up from a friend."

"We were happy to have been of service to you." Antigone extended a hand and Mr. Hardy shook it warmly. "You call on us anytime. And please tell other troubled business owners about your positive experience with the all-new NRB."

"You know I will."

Antigone faced Frankie and me. "Now you two get on home. And you get them cuts cleaned up, Not-Vera. You were out there dancin' around in a damn pasture. You don't wanna risk them things goin' septic. I ain't gonna be responsible for no damn ER bills."

Frankie took hold of my arm. "Come on, Nick. Let's get out of here."

She didn't have to ask me twice.

Since Frankie had picked me up at my house earlier, before our nighttime trek to the Hardy farm, she drove me back there when we returned to Winston-Salem. Although I was still in a fair amount of discomfort after going twelve rounds with Clovis, I was more than a little disappointed that she didn't head straight to her place, as had been our custom lately.

"I guess you need to get home and try to get some sleep?" I asked. "I keep forgetting that tomorrow is a school day."

"It is," she agreed. "But not for me. I called in earlier to tell them I wouldn't be in tomorrow."

I wasn't expecting that response. "You did?"

"Uh huh. I figured it would be a lost cause to try and pull myself together well enough to manage it. Normally, I'd tough it out. But I haven't so much as taken a sick day in more than three years, so they assured me right away that it wasn't a problem."

"I had no idea you'd done that."

"I know. I didn't tell you on purpose."

"Why not?"

"Because I didn't want you to worry—and I knew you would."

I'd been nursing a cut on one of my fingers. Clovis had dinged me good on my right hand during one of my defensive maneuvers, and it was throbbing. I thought about Antigone's comment about sepsis. I held up my hand so Frankie could see it in the half-light inside the car.

"Do you think this will get infected?"

"I hope not. We're going to douse it with peroxide as soon as we get you home."

"I'm not sure if we have any."

"No worries. I brought some with me. It's in my bag."

"You did?" I was surprised. "What made you think to do that?"

Frankie looked over at me. "You're kidding, right? Given our track record, I think it'll be wise to travel with it going forward."

Something about that explanation made me happy. Not the part about my seeming penchant for being attacked by psychotic poultry—the part about her assumption that we'd always be together.

I recalled that we'd both used the L-word earlier. In truth, it was hard to recall much of anything else.

"Why *are* we going to my house?" I asked.

"I thought it would be nice for a change. And you probably miss sleeping in your own bed."

I thought about her observation. Did I miss it? *Nope. Not a bit.*

"Will you stay over with me?" I asked hopefully.

"That was kind of my plan. Assuming it's okay with Sebastian?"

"He'd be fine with it. Too fine, actually. He'd probably have made popcorn and sat across the room to watch us make goo-goo eyes at each other—with real-time commentary."

"What do you mean by 'would have' made popcorn?"

"He's not at home. It's Ricky's birthday, so he's spending the night up at Doreen's."

"Oh. Did they have a party or something?"

"Yeah." I laughed. "Sebastian was cooking."

"Oh, dear . . ."

"No kidding. There'll probably be a pandemic of listeria sweeping across Forsyth County by morning."

"Hopefully, Doreen has enough unopened bourbon on hand to fight off contagion."

"I'd say that's likely."

We'd reached my neighborhood. Most of the houses were completely dark, which was hardly surprising since it was after 1 a.m. Frankie pulled into our driveway and stopped, but didn't turn off the car.

"Are you sure you're okay with me coming in?" she asked. "I don't have to. It's been a long day for both of us. I wouldn't blame you at all if you just want to pop a couple of ibuprofen and get right into bed."

"I'm all about the ibuprofen and bed—but I'd rather not do the latter alone."

"In that case," Frankie turned the car off, "what are we waiting for?"

I gave her a half smile. "Maybe for my brain to start communicating with my legs so I can manage to stand up?"

"Poor baby." Frankie leaned across the seat and kissed me softly. "I promise to take good care of you."

I knew she probably meant the words anecdotally, and as a response to the events of the evening. But that didn't stop me from wanting to ask her to write her promise down on paper, sign it, and have it notarized. The truth was I *did* want Frankie to take care of me . . . and I wanted to take care of *her*—in all of those sappy, smarmy, over-romanticized ways described by bad poems in greeting cards. But I was too damned embarrassed to confess it.

"I'd like that," I said instead. I cursed myself for my cowardice.

Frankie held my face between her warm hands. "I mean it, Nick. I want to take good care of you, and I want to be good *for* you, too. I've never wanted anything this much."

Frankie's honest and straightforward admission stopped me dead in my tracks.

"You're a lot braver than me," I confessed. "I was too chicken to admit the same thing to you."

"Well," she smiled at me, "I do teach eight-year-olds for a living, so I've had a lot more practice at simplifying the hard stuff."

I had to smile at that characterization. It was true: Frankie was a superlative teacher. First, last and always. It took me a while to comprehend that this was one of the best things about her. This and the fact that she always managed to make me laugh—at myself, and at the absurdity of the situations we'd managed to find ourselves in.

It was a great division of labor. Or it *would* be, just as soon as I figured out what my part of the equation was . . .

We kissed again.

"Wanna go inside?" I whispered. "I can show you my etchings."

"Is that what you call your birthmark?"

"What birthmark?" I drew away and tried, in vain, to look at my own back.

"Oh, good god." Frankie opened her door. "I'm *kidding*. Let's go inside."

I followed her to the house, still wondering about the phantom birthmark comment. To be fair, I'd never actually *seen* my own back, so I wasn't quite ready to believe she'd been kidding.

Once we were inside, Frankie asked if I wanted to take a hot bath to ease my muscle aches. As great as that sounded, what I wanted more was to sit down with her and have a drink to relax. Okay. Maybe a *lot* of drinks. I hadn't thought we'd have the luxury to do this since it was so late on a Sunday night and I'd been certain she'd have to teach school tomorrow.

Frankie was dubious about my suggestion at first.

"If you drink, you probably shouldn't take any pain relievers," she said. "So be sure that's what you really want."

I didn't have to think about it. "All I want right now is for us to collapse someplace and celebrate that this job is over, Eddie is out from under that loan shark, and we don't have to worry about any of those damn rides we jacked turning up again and sending us to prison."

"You're right. Screw Motrin. Which cabinet houses the hooch?"

"Thataway." I pointed toward the kitchen. "It's in the tall cabinet beside the fridge."

Frankie was perusing bottles when I joined her.

"What's this?" She pulled out a bottle of red-orange liqueur.

"It's Aperol. One of Sebastian's must-haves. It tastes like orange and rhubarb."

Frankie looked it over. "Must-have for what?"

"Some candy-ass spritz thing he likes to make with Prosecco and club soda."

"Interesting." Frankie replaced the bottle. "How about we stick with the classics?"

"Way ahead of you." I reached for our bottle of D'Ussé and snagged two glasses. "C'mon. Let's go pull up some couch."

"Hold on a minute. We aren't going anywhere until we dress some of those wounds."

"Frankieeeee . . ."

"Forget about whining. I listened to you moan all the way home. We're not doing anything until we get these cleaned up."

I gave up and allowed her to inspect, clean and disinfect all of my cuts and scrapes with peroxide and triple antibiotic ointment. Mercifully, none of them but the cut on my finger required bandaging. When she finished, we took our drinks into the living room and sat down together on the sofa. I turned on some music. Lately, I'd been listening a lot to the Yo Yo Ma channel on Pandora. The musical selections were a perfect mix of light classical and contemporary orchestral compositions. Sebastian said it was like listening to bad hold music when you called your accountant, but allowed the accommodation because it "calmed my ass down."

"This is lovely," Frankie observed, "but doleful. What is it?"

"I think it's the main theme from *Schindler's List*."

"Oh. *Very* uplifting. Should I be worried that you know this?"

"It's Carol Jenkins' favorite," I explained.

"Of course it is."

"To be fair, it sometimes fits my more somber moods, too."

"Not tonight. Tonight, you need to be celebrating."

"I *am* celebrating." I slouched lower on the sofa. "Once I can wrap my head around the fact that we managed to pull off that cow heist, I'll be ecstatic."

"We *did* pull it off, didn't we?" Frankie sounded downright proud.

"Yeah. We got lucky."

"I hate to disagree with you, but the only 'lucky' part was Clovis following you into the trailer."

I looked at her with disbelief. "You call *that* lucky? My backside sure as hell doesn't agree with your definition of luck."

"Well, you have to admit that without Clovis, Clotilde would never have boarded that trailer. And the other cows would've stayed right alongside her in the pasture."

"Do you even *hear* what we're talking about? *Clovis and Clotilde?* It's like we're talking about damn Abelard and Heloise."

"Mr. Hardy did say it was a love affair for the ages."

"Yeah? So were Ahab and Jezebel. But nobody celebrates *that* fabled union."

"Don't be such a curmudgeon. Drink your cognac."

During the short lull between musical selections, I became aware of a muffled sound that steadily gained in intensity. It sounded vaguely like . . . stomping. Correction: like *two* somethings stomping.

Carol Jenkins and Penny Morgan pounded into the room from the kitchen. They detoured long enough to take turns rubbing against Frankie's legs before continuing on toward the hallway leading to their room. We watched them saunter off in single file.

"I cannot believe how much that kitten has grown," Frankie said.

"Yeah. Eating dry-aged beef will do that."

"Oh, stop it. You don't feed her that."

"You're right. I don't. Sebastian does."

Carol Jenkins stopped abruptly at the entrance to the hallway. She turned around and glared at me before arching her back and hissing. Penny Morgan quickly followed suit, and the pair continued on their way.

I thrust a hand toward the departing felines. "See what I deal with?"

"Why does she dislike you so much?"

"Sebastian thinks it's because I screwed up setting her TiVo once."

"*Her* TiVo?" Frankie looked doubtful. "The cat has TiVo?"

"Hell yes. I was supposed to record back-to-back episodes of *Science of Stupid* and mistakenly got a marathon rebroadcast of the best of *Petticoat Junction*. It didn't work out well for me."

"I really wonder about you two sometimes."

"Us two?"

"You and Carol Jenkins."

"Hey, don't blame me. She's *his* damn cat."

She didn't reply. We sat drinking our cognac and listening to Yo Yo Ma play one of Bach's *Suites for Unaccompanied Cello*. Frankie finished her drink and set the glass down on the table beside the sofa. That's when she noticed the framed photo atop a tower of Sebastian's oversized books about creating form and function in interior spaces. She picked it up and examined it more closely.

"Who is this woman? She's very striking."

"That's Mamá."

"This is your *mother?*" Frankie asked with awe. "She's gorgeous."

I sighed. "Yeah. I know. Papa always said she made a mistake going into pediatrics because she could've made a fortune as a cosmetic surgeon."

"No kidding. She could be one of the models in those ads for body contouring you always see in airline magazines."

"Don't remind me, okay? It was hard enough growing up with that as a role model. It might've been more bearable if all that beauty hadn't come packaged with her devotion to vengeful deities and an unforgiving God."

"No wonder your father was smitten." Frankie returned the photo to its place atop Sebastian's altar to the home design gods.

"You say smitten, he says bewitched. With them, it's always a moving target."

"I think they sound like a match made in heaven."

"It was a match made someplace . . . not sure about the precise geography, though."

I kept thinking about her "love affair for the ages" comment about Clotilde and that damn emu.

"What about us?" I asked, before I could stop myself. "Do you think we'll be a match that stands the test of time?"

To give credit where it was due, Frankie didn't look at me like I'd lost my mind. She seemed to roll with my question and correctly connect the dots.

"Let's see . . ." She gave me a contemplative look. "We successfully waged a crime spree across the Tar Heel State. We committed at least six felonies and innumerable other offenses—any of which could've landed us in jail. We've survived crazed Baptists with guns, dead bodies, drooling construction workers hurling salacious compliments in two languages, philandering race car owners, and marauding pasture birds. Oh . . . *and* my sister, Lilah. So, I don't know, Nick." She shifted on the couch to face me. "You tell me: Do *you* think we have what it takes to go the distance?"

I gave her a crooked smile. "Listening to that list, I thought it was pretty much even money—until you got to Lilah."

"Yeah. I figured she'd be a pretty good closer."

"No pun intended."

Frankie socked me on the arm.

"Hey!" I feigned umbrage. "Don't hit me on the *one* part of my body that doesn't already ache."

"Oh, poor baby." Frankie leaned over and slowly kissed the spot. "Does that make it better?"

Actually, it made just about everything feel better—and more alert.

"Maybe . . ." I got an idea. "Think it would work on other parts, too?"

"Which parts?" Frankie raised an eyebrow.

"Take your pick. They pretty much all hurt."

Frankie smiled and bent toward me. "Like here?" She kissed the side of my neck.

I swallowed hard, but managed to nod.

"How about here?" She kissed my ear.

Okay. Enough torture.

I pulled her over onto my lap.

After a few minutes of focused and exhaustive attention to most of my sore spots, Frankie suggested we continue our therapy session in my room. Since her ministrations had all but reduced me to a pile of gelatin, I didn't have the wherewithal or the least inclination to disagree with her.

We made our slow and deliberate way to bed, where we spent the rest of the short night wrapped around each other like sweet vines of kudzu. As I drifted off to sleep, I thanked a merciful God that we weren't adrift on a boat, stumbling around a dark cow pasture, or crammed inside a hopped-up muscle car.

We were at home. Safe, warm and together.

Right where we belonged.

Epilogue

Together, Wherever We Go

On Friday night, we decided to celebrate our good luck and enjoy our sweet release from the nightmare events surrounding our work for Fast Eddie and the NRB. I met Frankie at her place after school let out, and we hired an Uber to drive us downtown to Sweet Potatoes. As usual, Fred saw us as the driver let us out in front of the restaurant, and our cocktails arrived immediately after we took our seats at the bar.

The place was jammed. The hostess told us it would probably be twenty-thirty minutes before they had a free table—but we were fine with that. Fred said he'd hook us up with an appetizer while we waited.

"Is this a holiday weekend or something?" I asked Frankie. There were at least ten other people having drinks at the bar while they waited for tables to become available.

"Not quite," she replied. "But Memorial Day is only a week off. Summer is coming, and people are ready to party."

"Well, I second that idea."

"Me, too. Only six more weeks of school until I'm a free woman."

I smirked at her.

"What?" Frankie demanded.

"It's stupid."

"Okay. So, it's stupid. Tell me."

"I was gonna say you're cheap, but you ain't free."

"Wonderful." Frankie rolled her eyes. "I'm on a date with Groucho Marx."

I laughed.

The music was great. Dinah Washington was busy filling us in on a man who was always late.

Frankie looked fabulous. But that wasn't out of the ordinary. Frankie always looked fabulous.

"You're so damn beautiful." I said.

"You're nuts. I look haggard."

Haggard? I looked her over. "Nope. Seeing all kinds of great terrain displayed on that stool. Not seeing anything even remotely haggard."

I could tell Frankie was trying hard not to smile. "Did you dip into Carol Jenkins' Xanax, or something?"

"Honey, I don't need Xanax to be this happy. I just need you."

Frankie gave up pretending to be embarrassed. She reached over and took hold of my hand.

"Well it's a good thing you have me, then."

"I'll say. It's the first time in my life I haven't felt like half of something."

"What do you mean by that?"

"It's just a thing." I shrugged. "All my life, I've felt . . . incomplete. Like I didn't quite fit. Not quite Black. Not quite Latina. *Not at all white*. But not really anything in between, either. And those dichotomies—real or imagined—followed me everywhere. College. Law School. Work. My relationships. I've always felt like an outsider." I squeezed her hand. "But now, I feel like I've found a place where all the parts of me seem to fit. With a person who makes me feel like I'm all of something. With you."

"I love you." Frankie's simple declaration was all the confirmation I needed.

"I love you, too." I bent forward and kissed her gently. "But I'm still not eating any okra."

"Well ain't that a damn shame?" A voice like a belt sander rang out from just behind us. "You need to be eatin' them vegetables, Not-Vera. Your color ain't good."

Frankie and I lurched apart. *Antigone?*

"What are *you* doing here?" we blurted in unison.

"Close your damn mouths. There ain't no flies in here."

"Um. I'm . . . we're . . . Why are you in Winston?" I asked.

"I'm known to venture out to visit with family from time to time." She looked past me and waved at someone across the room. "Hey, ViVi," she called out, before fixing an incriminating stare squarely back on me. "It just so happens the chef here is my daddy's fifth cousin, twice removed."

God moves in mysterious ways, His wonders to perform.

It appeared Mamá had been right about that one . . .

"Are you here for dinner?" Frankie asked. "Would you like to join us?"

I looked at Frankie like she'd lost her last marble.

Antigone shook her head.

"I don't tend to mix business with pleasure, which I think you might have noticed by now." She withdrew a fat envelope from her ubiquitous handbag and slapped it down on the bar between us. "I got a job offer for you two, and I figured I might find you here."

"What made you think that?" I asked.

"Because I'm good at my damn job, Not-Vera. We've been over this before."

"Okay." I held up a hand. "But we're not interested in any more jobs, Antigone. We told you that. Our time with the NRB is over."

"This ain't a job for the *old* NRB. This is a legitimate, aboveboard and decent job for the *new* NRB—now an official subsidiary of Global Gospel Radio, LLC. And much as it pains me to confess it, you two appear to possess an uncommon ability to persevere and triumph over what we in the industry call 'unique recovery assignments.'"

I narrowed my eyes. "Are you speaking in some kind of code?"

"I'm fixin' to lose patience with this errand, Not-Vera." Antigone consulted her watch. "And my damn takeout order is probably congealing in its box next door at Miss Ora's. Now," she reached between us and tapped the envelope, "you take a look at this offer. These high-payin' recovery jobs been coming in hand over fist since you two delivered them damn Photoshopped dotted Swiss cows to Hollis Hardy. People talk and word gets spread around. That's how this business thrives. So now, the born-again NRB has the potential to tap into a rare, niche market—one that was unavailable to us before. But to succeed, it needs the commitment of full-time employees, with all the benefits accruing thereto. I'm talking about agents of recovery who don't know enough to be scared, or have the sense to back off when something advertises that it's damn impossible. And that, God help me, is the two of you."

Frankie and I looked at each other.

"You're offering us *jobs?*" I asked Antigone. "Real jobs? With real benefits?"

"Was I just speaking in some foreign language to you, Not-Vera?"

"No, ma'am."

"Then I got nothin' else to say. You look that offer over and get back to me no later'n tomorrow morning. I ain't waitin' around on you two clowns."

She harrumphed and turned on her heel to sweep toward the crowd clustered near the door, which parted before her like the waters of the Red Sea beneath the staff of Moses.

Frankie looked completely shell-shocked. I wasn't far behind her.

"What are we going to do?" she asked with wonder.

"What do you mean, 'what are we going to do'? We're going to do nothing."

"You aren't even the tiniest bit curious about her offer?"

"Frankie? That's like asking me if I've ever thought about taking strychnine, just for the hell of it."

"Okay, okay." She pushed the envelope away. "I suppose you're right."

I nursed my Manhattan and tried to ignore the fat envelope. It sat on the bar between us and all but hummed.

"Will you get rid of that thing?" I asked Frankie. "It's totally giving me the yips."

Frankie picked it up and stuck it into the outside pocket of her bag.

To be fair, we both did a fairly credible job of ignoring it—and Antigone's sudden appearance—throughout our dinner. It was only after we'd finished eating and were nursing large tumblers of Hennessy that I found my gaze continually straying to the envelope, peeking out of Frankie's purse.

"Nick? If you're going to spend the rest of the evening staring at it, just go ahead and open the damn thing."

I looked at Frankie guiltily. "I was *not* staring at it."

"You weren't?"

"*No.* I don't need a job offer from her. It's an absurd idea. I've already got great feelers out with three top-tier firms, right here in Winston-Salem."

"Sure you do. And any one of them would afford you the privilege of doing the fulfilling work you're so passionate about—as we've discussed numerous times."

"Frankie? Not helping."

I sat tapping my foot in agitation and stole another glance at Antigone's envelope.

A full-time job jacking cars—and god knew what else? The entire prospect was insane. How would I ever defend such a move to my parents?

My parents . . . good god. I was nearly forty years old. *I was accountable to no one.* And I finally had the only thing in life I really cared about.

I looked over at Frankie, who continued to regard me with a look of amusement.

"Okay, wise guy," I said. "You think you know me better than I know myself, don't you?"

"Uh huh." She folded her arms. "Pretty much."

Sonofabitch. I gave up and grabbed the envelope out of her purse and tore it open.

Frankie watched me intently while I scanned the document. After I'd finished reading it—twice—I carefully refolded it and returned it to the envelope. I picked up my tumbler of cognac and drained it.

"Well?" Frankie demanded. "Are you going to tell me what it says?"

"Oh, yeah." I said, showing her my empty glass. "But before I do, we're gonna need a shit ton more of these . . ."

It was worth noting that Frankie didn't look the least bit surprised.

Acknowledgments

Some could argue (convincingly) that *The Big Tow* is a product of my on-again, off-again love affair with the South. I moved to North Carolina more than forty years ago—an untutored and inexperienced Yankee who had rarely dipped a toe below the Mason-Dixon Line. After college, I decided to remain here to pursue a career and make a life. I like to think that as the decades passed, I've learned to practice what the great writer Doris Betts taught: I paid attention. I listened—and I kept notes. *Mental* notes. Notes about quirky anecdotes, bits of overheard conversation, creative family names, folklore, cooking, family secrets, time-honored traditions, idioms, platitudes, euphemisms—and stories about Jesus. *Lots* of stories about Jesus.

Much of that unceremoniously tumbled out when I sat down to write this book: my homage to the place and the people I love. If any of my depictions or the liberties I've taken with people, events, and personalities seem to strain credibility, well . . . all I can offer is a very sincere, "bless your heart."

I owe huge debts of gratitude to a group of extraordinary women who were generous (and brave) enough to read early and later drafts of this book. Cheryl Head, Penny Mickelbury, Abigail Padgett, Leona Beasley and, especially, Michelle Brooks (who actually *is* the prototype for Not-Vera—or would've been if that character had managed to cobble together some better fashion sense. It's impossible for me to overstate the value Michelle added to the process of accurately creating Nick's unique voice. And just so you know, the story about Mamá and the Wagner LP is one hundred percent true. Thank you, Michelle, for letting me borrow so many wonderful stories drawn from your own childhood. I hope I did you proud.

My dear friend, Marilyn Whicker was brave enough to read every page of this book as I hammered it out (in forced isolation at our dining room table), and supplied me with endless riches and a veritable index to the town of K-Vegas (yes, it's real). Thank you, Midway. I loved sharing this process with you.

If reading *The Big Tow* made you hungry, I can tell you exactly who to blame. Stephanie Tyson and Vivián Joyner operate, what to my mind, is the best little restaurant in this or *any*, town: Sweet Potatoes. If ever you have the great good fortune to find yourself in Winston-Salem, make sure you save time to visit them on Trade Street, and savor the extraordinary fare they're serving up at this little slice of God's culinary acre. I am indebted to these extraordinary women for allowing me to feature their restaurant (and menu) in this book. And I wasn't kidding about the cocktails served up by their handsome bartender, Fred, either.

I offer a special (albeit curious) homage to the legendary Miss Ethel Merman for unwittingly lending me a slew of her unforgettable song titles to use as chapter headings. Don't ask—I'm not even sure I understand it.

My amazing attorney (and self-appointed literary agent), Kirk Sanders was a godsend when it came to parsing the nuances of car repossessions and insurance fraud, not necessarily in that order. Kirk has some brilliant ideas, too, for a second book—should Nick and Frankie ever decide to take Antigone up on her generous offer of employment. We'll have to see how that cookie crumbles . . .

Sandy Lowe? Thanks for the pears . . . and everything that led to such a special gift.

Hayden Sharpe endures as my stalwart go-to when I need sage advice on things like how to dress a slutty dolphin trainer. Hey . . . I'm not really a girl—so thanks, Biz, for always bailing me out in style. We'll see if any other readers catch all the *Spy* movie references.

It could be said that when you have Fay Jacobs as your editor, the world is your oyster. The world was certainly *my* oyster when Fay applied her keen eye and perfect flair for comedic timing to this farcical run-on sentence. The book is better, smarter and a helluva lot funnier because of Fay. I thank Bywater Books for sharing her great talent with me. Fay? For this author, writing *anything* that could make *you* laugh stands as a signature life accomplishment. And thanks for lending me that cheese ball anecdote . . .

Stefani Deoul is simply . . . essential. I am so grateful that fate brought us together. Thanks, Stef, for the encouragement when I needed it—and thanks for coming up with the perfect title for this book.

Nancy Squires and Elizabeth Andersen make everything they touch better. I am deeply indebted to both of these women for their careful and thoughtful reads of this book—and not just because they make me sound a lot smarter than I am.

How would any of us navigate this vast literary wasteland without the guidance and selfless beneficence of Cherie Moran? I am humbled every time I hear the story of how Cherie gave up her meteoric rise on the Formula One circuit on that fateful day during the Italian Grand Prix. Cherie, hugely pregnant, realized her water had broken while she navigated her Bugatti through an especially tricky circuit of turns at Monza, just north of Milan. Cherie's ensuing epic labor outlasted the championship race by more than sixteen hours. Cherie named her baby girl, Sandro "Sandy" Botticelli Moran, in honor of the experience—and she predicted that one day, the world would celebrate that little Sandro came their way. We are all living proof of how that prophesy came true. Thank you Cherie!

Special thanks to Susie Bright at Audible for always being brave enough to take a chance on me. And to my extraordinary narrator, Christine Williams for bringing these books to life in sound.

My entire Bywater Books and Amble Press family mean the world to me. How lucky am I to have found a home with such an extraordinary group of authors? Just being around you all makes me feel . . . taller. And better looking. I will always be indebted to Kelly Smith for bringing me home.

Listen up, y'all: Marianne K. Martin, Salem West and Michael Nava are out to change the world. You know what? I think they *might* just pull it off. And I'm grateful to go along for the ride.

Last but never least—Buddha, you are and always will be my best friend, confidant, soulmate and creative partner. Thank you for sharing the best of everything with me. Thanks, especially, for being the non-hysterical co-parent that Dave and Ella so desperately need. I love my life with you. But I *still* want to move to Vermont . . .

–Ann McMan
Winston-Salem, NC

About the Author

Ann McMan is the author of ten novels and two collections of short stories. She is a two-time Lambda Literary Award winner, a nine-time winner of Golden Crown Literary Society Awards, a three-time IPPY medalist, and a recipient of the Alice B. Medal for her body of work. She resides in Winston-Salem, NC with her wife, Salem West, two precocious dogs, and an exhaustive supply of vacuum cleaner bags.

Bywater
BOOKS